*"You are so lovely, so perfect!"*

Sir Robert's voice was low and deep. His eyes looked down into hers and suddenly Mademoiselle Fantôme felt herself begin to tremble. She did not know why, for she was not afraid. The most wonderful feeling she had ever known was creeping over her, burning through her like a flame.

He drew her closer and she could feel his heart beating quickly and strongly. She knew then with a happiness she had not believed possible that he loved her even as she loved him.

"Until tomorrow, my beloved," she said softly, and suddenly he was gone.

But when the morrow came, the mystery of her past rose up to haunt them. Would their love be strong enough to survive that strange secret?

# A
# GHOST
# IN
# MONTE
# CARLO

*Barbara Cartland*

**PYRAMID BOOKS**  **NEW YORK**

**A GHOST IN MONTE CARLO**

A PYRAMID BOOK

Pyramid edition published May 1793

Copyright 1951 by Barbara Cartland

All Rights Reserved

ISBN 0-515-03019-8

Printed in the United States of America

Pyramid Books are published by Pyramid Communications, Inc. Its trademarks, consisting of the word "Pyramid" and the portrayal of a pyramid, are registered in the United States Patent Office.

Pyramid Communications, Inc., 919 Third Avenue, New York, New York 10022

# 1

There was the sound of footsteps crossing the landing; the rattle of a laden breakfast tray being set down on a table; a little rasping cough and lastly a light knock on the bedroom door.

Without waiting for a reply Jeanne entered and crossed the room to draw back the curtains.

Watching her figure, bulky and indistinct in the shrouded light, Emilie wondered how many years it was since she had first been wakened by those familiar sounds.

It was never the opening of the door which roused her, but the preliminaries to it—Jeanne's footsteps on the landing, the rattle of the breakfast tray and her cough.

Was it eighteen years that Jeanne had been in her employment? No, nineteen; and they had known each other since childhood.

The curtains slid back to reveal a wintry day, the roofs of Paris grey and damp beneath a dull sky through which a pale sun was striving ineffectually to shine.

Emilie sat up in bed with a sharp movement.

She had been awake for a long time; indeed it was doubtful if she had slept more than an hour or two the whole night; and glancing at her reflection in the dressing-table mirror which faced the bed, she was well aware that the sleepless hours had taken their toll.

She looked old this morning, old and unattractive,

although perhaps the colour of her hair had something to do with that. But Emilie had no time to think of herself. There were other and more important things which required her attention.

Slipping her arms into a dressing-jacket of thick wool, Emilie patted her pillows behind her and waited until Jeanne had set down her breakfast.

She seemed to take an unconscionable time in doing so and then she began to rearrange the tray with care, moving first the coffee-pot a trifle to the left, then the cup and saucer a little to the right, and now it appeared that a spoon required her attention.

Emilie was not deceived. She knew well that Jeanne was waiting for her to speak. Sharply, because it always annoyed her when Jeanne forestalled her decisions, she said:

"Shut the door, Jeanne."

"*Oui,* Madame, I was just about to do so."

"Then hurry, and sit down while I talk, for you must listen attentively. There is much for us to do."

Jeanne crossed the room, walking as if her legs were stiff and her feet hurt a little.

She had the large bones and slow movements of a peasant from one of the Northern Departments. Her hair was grey, but her face was curiously unlined and her eyes were as bright as a child's. At sixty she had no difficulty in doing the finest and most delicate embroidery.

Jeanne closed the door and returned to the bedside, settling herself on a hard chair, her work-roughened hands clasped together in her lap.

Emilie, glancing at her over the rim of her coffee-cup, thought she looked like a schoolgirl waiting for her teacher to speak, and felt annoyed by the impression.

Jeanne was both her friend and her confidante, and

2

yet at times she deliberately assumed the humility and servile disinterestedness of an ordinary servant.

This usually meant that she was hurt or annoyed; and with what was for her an unusually clear perception Emilie realized that at the moment Jeanne was both these things.

So she knew then! All the trouble they had taken last night to move quietly so as not to waken her had been unnecessary. Jeanne had been awake and now was resentful that she had not been called downstairs.

Emilie set down her coffee-cup with a clatter in the saucer.

"Jeanne, something occurred last night," she said. "A visitor arrived."

"Indeed, Madame!"

Jeanne's reply was without surprise. Quite unexpectedly Emilie laughed.

"Stop looking injured, Jeanne! You know as well as I do that someone came here unexpectedly; I repeat unexpectedly.

"I had no idea she was coming, not for three weeks at any rate, and long before that I meant to tell you all about it. The child informs me that she wrote four days ago, but the post is so abominable that her letter has never been received.

"Think of it, Jeanne, the poor girl arriving alone at the station with no-one to meet her, no-one to welcome her. She had barely enough money for a conveyance."

"It is Mademoiselle who has arrived then," Jeanne said sourly.

Emilie was still smiling good-humouredly.

"You know very well that it is Mademoiselle, for if you have not already inspected her luggage in the hall, you have peeped into the guest bedroom to look at her. She is still asleep, I suppose?"

Jeanne forgot her pride.

"*Oui, oui,* Madame, she is sleeping like an angel! When I saw her, my heart almost stopped beating. 'A veritable angel', I said, 'from Heaven itself'."

"The child is pretty," Emilie agreed. "I had always believed that she would be so, but this last year has made all the difference. She is eighteen! Can you believe, Jeanne, that eighteen years have passed since Alice died?"

Emilie's voice was suddenly raw with pain; her lips tightened and her eyes seemed to narrow a little.

Then with a gesture she thrust her breakfast tray aside and went on, her voice rising:

"Attention, Jeanne, for there is a great deal to be done this very instant."

"I am listening, Madame."

Jeanne's voice was calm, but her eyes never left Emilie's face. She noticed every change of expression, every flicker of the dark eyes, every twitch of the thin, hard lips.

At times Emilie Bleuet looked compellingly handsome, but this morning was not one of them. The clear light was piteously revealing and every wrinkle, every line on her thin face seemed to be magnified.

It contrived, too, to illuminate the discoloured skin of her neck, the sagging jawline, the deep frown between her eyebrows and the long lines etching themselves from her nostrils to the thin curves of her mouth.

But there was nothing unusual in this. Jeanne was familiar with the best and worst of Emilie's looks, and it was no secret between the two women that, although their birth date was the same, Emilie was the younger by only twelve months. Jeanne had been born on the 7th January, 1814; Emilie the following year.

Emilie was therefore fifty-nine, and at that age no

4

woman could expect the hand of time to lie anything but heavily upon her.

But what was strange was the excitement in Emilie's expression. Jeanne had never known her so excited, with a kind of inner tension which made her eyes glitter and affected her speech.

Only in moments of stress and of complete self-forgetfulness did Emilie relapse into her native accent. Usually her French was Parisian, careful, formal and spoken in a voice of frigid impassivity.

But this morning her voice was the echo of Jeanne's, and anyone listening to them would have known that they both hailed from the shores of Brittany.

Emilie drew a deep breath and then she began:

"I planned to tell you all this, Jeanne, in a few days' time. I was expecting my niece to arrive at the end of this month. I was indeed astonished to see her when she came here last night.

"She tells me that the Reverend Mother of the Convent died and the Nuns decided to send the pupils home three weeks earlier than had been intended.

"Mademoiselle wrote to me; but, as I have already said, the letter has not arrived."

Emilie paused for a moment, her fingers twisting together; then she looked at Jeanne and her voice sank to little more than a whisper:

"Today, Jeanne," she said, "we start a new life, you and I. The past is finished."

"A new life, Madame!" Jeanne echoed. "But what can you mean by that?"

"What I say," Emilie snapped, and her voice was normal again. "This is no figure of speech, Jeanne, but a sober fact. The day before yesterday I sold the business."

"Madame!"

There was no mistaking the astonishment in Jeanne's voice now.

"Yes, I sold it, and sold it well. No one, I venture to think, could have done better. But from today, Jeanne, *Numéro cinq Rue de Roi* has ceased to exist as far as we are concerned; in fact it never has existed. And Madame Bleuet is dead too."

"Is that why you have changed your hair, Madame?" Jeanne asked.

"Exactly!" Emilie said, looking again at her reflection in the mirror. "My hair is grey, as God intended it to be! It ages me, Jeanne, but there is no reason now for me to look young or attractive. Indeed, I have other plans, quite different plans.

"I am going to be a Countess, Jeanne—*Madame la Comtesse*. It sounds well, doesn't it? That is what I intend to be from today and you must not forget it."

*"Mon Dieu!* But Madame, how can you? I mean——"

"Listen, Jeanne, and do not interrupt. We have very little time. In a short while Mademoiselle will be awake and our story must be clear. I am *Madame la Comtesse*. I have married and been widowed.

"You must remember, Jeanne, that Mademoiselle did not know of Monsieur Bleuet. I never told her about him. When I visited the Convent, I went there as Mademoiselle Riguad.

"I communicated both with the Nuns and with Mademoiselle in the same manner. It was safer from every point of view and now I am thankful I was so cautious.

"Now for your part—a few days ago as I was passing down the *Rue de Madeleine* I saw some baggage for sale in a shop window. It was a poor shop which sells shop-soiled or second-hand articles.

"There was quite a quantity of luggage, Jeanne, of good solid leather and stamped with a coronet. You

6

will go this morning and buy it for me. It will lend support to my story."

"Baggage, Madame? Then you intend to go away?"

"Yes, Jeanne, I am leaving here and you are coming with us—with Mademoiselle and myself. I told you the past was dead, the future begins."

"But where are we going, Madame? And why this pretence?"

"I shall not tell you all my secrets, Jeanne. I have never done that, have I? I prefer to work alone, for it is wiser that way. I have only myself to blame if things go wrong; but this time they will not go wrong, they will succeed!

"For eighteen years I have planned for this moment and worked for it. Yes, worked hard! All I have done has been for this."

Emilie's voice seemed almost to hiss the words. Her eyes were mere slits in her bloodless face. Then with a sudden change of expression she threw out her hands.

"Do not look so bewildered, Jeanne. You have but to trust me. Hurry and buy the luggage, for we shall need it. Then there are my clothes to be seen to; most of the gowns are useless."

"Useless?"

Jeanne's tone as she echoed the word was more bewildered than ever.

"But of course! Quite useless! I am an aristocrat, Jeanne, a lady! Open the door of the wardrobe and tell me how many of the dresses hanging there will be suitable for me now."

Obediently and half as if she were hypnotized Jeanne crossed the room to the huge mahogany wardrobe which occupied the whole of one wall of the bedroom. With a gesture she threw open the double doors.

The wardrobe was tightly packed with gowns of all descriptions. They seemed, as they hung there, blended

7

into all the colours of the rainbow, to come alive, for the frills, ribbons and laces with which they were trimmed fluttered in the draught caused by the opening of the doors.

"You can sell them for me," Emilie said from the bed. "They will not fetch much, but Widow Wyatt in the Market—cheat though she is—will give you a better price than anyone else. Tell her what they cost and drive the best bargain you can.

"There is the green velveteen new but these three months, and the cyclamen *satin de laine* which was only delivered a week before Christmas."

"But Madame, you have only worn the cyclamen three times!"

As she spoke, Jeanne took the gown almost lovingly from its hanger. Of satin with wide crepeline frills, it was ornamented with bows of velvet ribbon, the corsage and narrow sleeves besprinkled with diamanté.

It was obvious that the dress was expensive, but in the morning light it looked garish.

There was something common and also suggestive about it as it hung from Jeanne's hands, its boned bodice billowing out as if it still concealed some ghostly figure within it.

"Take it away, Jeanne," Emilie commanded sharply. "I realize now what I must have looked like in it."

Obediently Jeanne put the dress back on the hanger and shut the wardrobe door.

"And if these are disposed of—what will Madame wear?" she enquired.

"New clothes—both day and evening gowns which must be made for me at once; and Mademoiselle's need will be the same as mine. You will go immediately and ask Madame Guibout to call on us. Tell her it is of the utmost importance and an order of some magnitude."

"Madame Guibout! She will be expensive!"

8

"I am well aware of that, Jeanne. This is a moment when we do not spare money. As I have told you, a new life begins."

Even as Emilie spoke, the tone of her voice seeming almost a trumpet call which echoed round the room, there came a knock on the door. For a second the eyes of mistress and maid met and neither spoke.

Then almost as if it were an effort Emilie said:

*"Entrez!"*

The door opened and Mistral came in.

She was still in her nightgown, a long white cambric robe which the Nuns made for their pupils, and round her shoulders for warmth she wore a white cashmere shawl.

She came slowly into the room, her eyes alight, her lips smiling; and as she crossed to the foot of her Aunt's bed the sunshine touched her head and turned it into a torch of living gold so that it seemed to illuminate the room with its very brilliance.

Her hair, parted in the centre to frame her small face, fell over her breasts in two thick heavy plaits which reached below her knees.

It was the colour of corn which is just ripening, of the sun when it first rises from the horizon. It was also, she was to learn later, the colour and softness of budding mimosa.

It was hair which is only found on Anglo-Saxons, the fair flaxen hair which goes with the blue eyes and pale complexions of the English.

But astonishingly Mistral's eyes were not blue. They were dark, almost purple in their depths, and fringed with dark eyelashes which gave her a strange and unexpected look of mystery.

Watching her, Emilie wondered for a fleeting moment why she had ever thought that Mistral resembled her

Mother; and then, even as she wondered, the resemblance was there again.

A turn of the head, a spontaneous smile, and it was Alice, not Mistral, who stood at the foot of the bed, her eyes looking at her with an expression of unsuppressed joy and happiness.

Yet Alice's eyes had been blue and she could never have been mistaken for anything but what she was—an Englishwoman and an aristocrat.

But, Emilie acknowledged grudgingly, Mistral's beauty was even more striking.

That strange combination of golden hair and dark eyes was fascinatingly lovely; her lips, perfectly curved, were naturally red against the fairness of her skin.

But there was just something faintly un-English about her, something which made one wonder what secrets those dark eyes held.

Nevertheless there was no possibility of being mistaken about one thing—Mistral was a lady, as her Mother had been.

From the crown of her head, held proudly with an indescribable grace, to the soles of her small feet with their high-arched insteps she was an aristocrat.

There was something in the manner in which she moved, in the long thin fingers and her tiny straight nose which proclaimed her blue blood as clearly as if she carried her pedigree in her hand.

Emilie gave a little sigh and held out her hand. Mistral flew to her side.

"*Bonjour,* Aunt Emilie. Do forgive me for having slept so late, but I was so tired last night that I remembered nothing until I awoke but a few moments ago and wondered where I was."

Mistral's French was pure and perfect.

"I wanted you to sleep late, dear," Emilie replied.

"And now Jeanne will bring you your breakfast. Do you remember Jeanne?"

As swift as a swallow's flight Mistral had crossed the room and was holding out both her hands to Jeanne.

"Of course I remember you," she cried. "I remember the bonbons you used to give me when you brushed my hair. When I first went to the Convent, I missed both your bon-bons and you more than I can say. I had to brush my own hair then and how I hated it for being long and getting into tangles! I used to long to cut it off."

"*Hélas,* Mademoiselle, it would have been a crime!" Jeanne exclaimed, beaming all over her face. "And to think you should remember me after twelve years! *Tiens,* but you were always the sweetest little girl in all Brittany."

"I missed Brittany too," Mistral said softly.

Then turning towards her Aunt, she added:

"But oh, Aunt Emilie, it is so exciting to be here, and this house is charming. Why have you never let me visit you before?"

"It is a long story, Mistral," Emilie replied. "And there are several other and more important things I want to talk to you about at this moment. Jeanne will fetch your breakfast here and we can talk as you eat."

"Oh, that will be lovely!" Mistral exclaimed as Jeanne hurried from the room. "I am glad we can talk. There are such a lot of things I want to know. I am not complaining, you must not think that; I was happy at the Convent, but sometimes I felt lonely.

"All the other girls seemed to have families and lots of relations. I only had you. You have always been kind to me, but I saw so little of you and not having a home to come to in the holidays made me feel different."

11

"I can understand that," Emilie replied, "but there were reasons why I could not have you. There is no need to go into them, for things have changed and now we can be together."

"That is wonderful, Aunt Emilie. If you only knew how happy that makes me. I was sometimes afraid, terribly afraid, that you would never take me away and that I should have to stay at the Convent for ever and become a Nun."

"You would not have liked that?" Emilie asked curiously.

Mistral shook her head.

"I knew in my heart of hearts that I had no vocation.

"I loved the Nuns. No one could help but love and admire them. They were saints most of them and always I used to pray that I would become as good as they were, but all the time something inside me seemed to say that I was not to stay.

"I wanted to know more about the world outside, I wanted to live a different life. Oh, perhaps I am being silly and you will laugh at me, but I sometimes felt as if voices were calling to me to live more fully, to enjoy the world before I dedicated myself unreservedly to the Service of Heaven."

Mistral's voice was soft and almost mystical as she spoke.

Emilie, watching her, taking in the sense of what she said, was yet acutely aware of many other things—the almost magnetic quality of the girl's voice, the soft seduction of her parted lips, the pure unawakened loveliness of her widened eyes, and the emotions which seemed to radiate from her as she spoke.

"You were right in what you thought," Emilie said after a moment. "You are young, Mistral, and it would be a pity to shut up anyone who is both young and pretty behind the high walls of a Convent."

12

"Pretty? Do you mean me?" Mistral asked. "Oh, Aunt Emilie, do you really think so? I hoped I was, but I was never sure. I looked so different from the other girls."

"Didn't they tell you you were pretty?" Emilie enquired.

Two dimples appeared in Mistral's cheeks.

"Sometimes! But at other times they teased me because my hair was so fair. I was the only English girl in the Convent and the only one who was not a brunette."

"The only English girl!" Emilie repeated. "Yes, Mistral, you are English, for your Mother was English."

"And my Father?"

Mistral asked the question quickly, and even as the words left her lips, she saw a shadow cross Emilie's face and her expression change.

The benevolent smiling Aunt who had been talking to her seemed to vanish, and instead there was a woman whose whole face seemed to be contorted.

Mistral had never seen hatred before, but she recognized it now, recognized it in the clenched lips, the narrowed eyes, the lines which seemed to accentuate everywhere until Emilie's face was as hideous as a gargoyle.

But even as Mistral gasped, even as she felt fear like a dark cloud rise within her, Emilie's expression changed again.

"We will not speak of your Father," she said. "Not now. One day I will tell you about him, but for the moment there are other and more important things for us to do.

"You have come to live with me, Mistral, and I am glad to have you; but there is one thing that I must make clear—very clear—from the beginning. I expect obedience.

13

"You will obey me whether you understand the reason for my commands or whether you do not. You will obey me implicitly and without question from now onwards. Is that understood?"

Emilie's voice was hard and once again Mistral felt a sensation of fear, but resolutely she put it from her.

"Of course I will, Aunt Emilie. I have no wish to do anything else."

"That is good! Then I will tell you what we are about to do. Today we will order your clothes. I have sent for Madame Guibout, one of the best couturières in Paris.

"She is expensive, but rightly so, for she was trained by Monsieur Worth who is patronized by the Empress Eugénie. She will make you all the clothes you need.

"Yes, your gowns will be expensive, but they will be flattering and, when you wear them, you will feel confident and assured of your power to attract attention."

"Oh, thank you, thank you, Aunt Emilie," Mistral breathed. "If you only knew how I have longed——"

"Let me continue," Emilie interrupted. "I have other things to tell you."

"Yes, Aunt Emilie."

"We have only seen each other, you and I, at short intervals since you went to the Convent twelve years ago. I do not know how much you know or remember about your childhood and your family history.

"Your grandfather was the Hon. John Wytham, youngest son of Lord Wytham, an English nobleman. I was his eldest child, but he never married my Mother who was French.

"Your real grandmother was an Englishwoman belonging to a distinguished family. She died when your Mother was five years old, leaving her to be brought up by her parents, Sir Hereward and Lady Burghfield. Your Mother was neglected and treated harshly by her

14

relatives, and your grandfather, when he discovered this, brought her to Brittany and left her in the charge of my Mother . . . and myself.

"Your grandfather was not a rich man, and he was a very extravagent one. I have supported you—I alone! For those past twelve years during which you have been educated I have paid all your fees; I have bought your clothes; I arranged for you to have special instruction. I paid extra for your music and for your lessons in English, French and German.

"The classes you attended for elocution, dancing and deportment were all supplementary. I paid for them— I personally."

"I did not know of this," Mistral said. "Thank you, Aunt Emilie!"

"I have no desire to be thanked," Emilie said quickly. "I am only telling you this so that you shall understand your own position.

"Your relatives in England made no attempt to find your Mother when she left them, and as your grandfather had little communication with England during the last years of his life, I doubt if they were ever informed of your existence.

"I am therefore your only relative, your Aunt—your entire family."

"Yes, Aunt Emilie."

Mistral was perturbed. There was something truculent, almost aggressive, in her Aunt's way of speaking.

"Sufficient then that we understand one another," Emilie went on. "Now I have something else to tell you—I am married. I married a Comte. He is dead, and there is no need for us to speak of him, but I am in fact *Madame la Comtesse*. Where we are going I shall not use my title. I shall use another name and remain incognito for reasons of my own."

15

"We are going away!" Mistral exclaimed. "Where to?"

"I am coming to that in due course," Emilie replied. "We are going a long journey and one which I have planned for many years."

"You planned to go . . . with me?" Mistral enquired.

"Yes, I planned to go with you," Emilie replied. "We will talk no more of it until we are ready, but you will remember one thing. You will not discuss my affairs or your own with anyone. It does not matter how many people ask or enquire about us, you will tell them nothing."

"But if people ask who I am?" Mistral asked. "What am I to reply? Am I, too, to have another name?"

"Most certainly," Emilie replied. "You are to tell no-one that your name is Wytham. Is that clear? The word Wytham must never pass your lips. I shall be . . . Madame . . . yes, Madame Secret! It is an appropriate nomination.

"People will be curious—I want them to be curious; people will ask questions—I want them to ask questions; people will talk—I want them to talk."

"But, Aunt Emilie, I do not understand."

"Does it matter if you do or not? I have already told you, Mistral, you must obey me. I must also add that you must trust me. I know what is best for you, as I know what is best for myself. Is that clear?"

"Yes, Aunt Emilie."

"Then we are agreed. We will journey together, you and I, and my reason for the journey will for the moment remain—my secret."

Mistral would have said something, but at that moment there came a knock on the door and Jeanne came into the room.

"Madame Guibout is here, Madame."

"Good," Emilie said. "Ask her to come in. Mistral,

16

you go at once and put on your clothes with the exception of your gown. Madame will wish to fit you in your petticoats."

"But first Mademoiselle must have her breakfast," Jeanne exclaimed. "I put it in her room nearly twenty minutes ago, as I thought you desired me to do."

"How stupid you are, Jeanne! I wished Mademoiselle to have it here; but never mind! Eat it in your room while you dress, Mistral, but do not be too long."

"Very well, Aunt Emilie," Mistral said obediently and followed Jeanne from the room.

Emilie watched her go. As she reached the door, Mistral glanced back over her shoulder, giving her Aunt a shy smile. She made a little gesture of farewell, and for a moment Emilie thought it was Alice who smiled.

Alice who made the little gesture with her head. Emilie almost cried out at the resemblance, then the door closed behind Mistral and she was alone.

"Alice!"

She whispered the name to herself. It seemed only yesterday that she had seen her smile so sweetly. How lovely she had been and how lovable! How much those soft clinging arms had meant round her neck.

She could see Alice now as she was when John Wytham brought her from England at the age of ten, a thin, frightened little girl, with eyes which seemed too big for her face—tear-drenched blue eyes, and lips which were ready to tremble at a harsh word.

Emilie had been feeding the chickens on the farm when her Father arrived. She could see him now driving up the lane, the black horses rearing and prancing as if they were just fresh from the stable.

He drew up with a flourish, threw the reins to a groom, jumped down and held out his arms to a small child who had been seated beside him on the driving seat.

17

He walked through the garden gate and up the cinder path, carrying Alice in his arms. She clung to him, hiding her face against his neck so that nothing could be seen of her except her long golden hair hanging down the back of her blue velvet jacket.

John Wytham's greeting of Emilie, his eldest daughter, had been robust and characteristic.

"Well, Emilie—got yourself a husband yet?"

Emilie might have replied to him in many different ways. She might have said that being the illegitimate result of a union between an English painter and the daughter of a French farmer was not exactly an asset when it came to marriage.

She might have told him that the only men she met in this obscure if beautiful part of Brittany were peasants and farmers, none of whom interested her because her English blood made her unduly fastidious.

She might have replied that, if he could only be unselfish enough to remember that a French girl needs a dowry, she might find a husband; but that with what money he had given her Mother these past ten years they could not have kept an animal alive.

But Emilie, tongue-tied as she always was in her Father's presence, could only answer his question with a stammered:

"N . . . no . . . F . . . Father!"

John Wytham pinched her cheek, and surrendering to his charm she smiled at him.

"And you are over thirty! It's time you hurried up and got a lover or you will be too late. Where's your mother?"

"Inside!"

Without another word he passed her and went into the house. Emilie followed him into the big, oakbeamed kitchen. Her mother had been cooking supper,

18

and there was a savoury smell coming from the pots and pans on the hearth.

Marie Riguad's face was flushed from the fire and her hair, now beginning to turn grey, was untidy; but her figure was slim as a girl's and when she saw who stood there her voice rang out joyously, eager and excited as a young child's.

"John!"

"Yes, John! Are you surprised to see me after all these years?"

"It is only four years since you last visited us, and I knew you would come again."

"You did, did you? And you were right. I have brought someone with me."

Very gently he set Alice down on the table. She gave an inarticulate murmur and continued to hide her face against him.

"This is Alice," he said briefly to Marie.

"I guessed that," she answered. "You spoke of her the last time you were here. You said your wife's parents were looking after her."

"But I didn't tell you how those damned in-laws of mine were treating her, did I?

"My stuck-up father-in-law, always too good for me, and his lady wife with her nose in the air and a patronising way of giving you two fingers, as if you might steal the rest of her hand if she parted with more.

"It's not surprising that the child's been unhappy with them; but I didn't realise how unhappy until I went to see her a few days ago. It was not what she told me, for they had got her too cowed for her to say much, but I forced her Nurse to tell me the truth.

"She told me Alice was bullied and punished, told continually that she was not wanted and that her Father was a bad man.

"I let them see how bad I was. I told them to go to the devil, and I took the child away with me. She is sick, and miserable, so I brought her to you, Marie.

"I'm finished with responsibility, I'm finished with England. I'm going off to paint, but I can't lug an ailing brat around with me. Will you take her?"

Emilie had hardly listened to her Mother's reply, for she knew what it would be even before it came swiftly from her parted lips:

"You know I will, John."

Like Marie Riguad she had eyes and ears only for John Wytham. The great strength of him seemed to fill the room. He was tall and handsome, and inexperienced though she was about men, Emilie knew that he was wild.

There was something untamed, uncivilized about his very gaiety, about his sensual mouth, about the way his eyes seemed magnetically to hold the attention of anyone who watched him.

"That is settled then," he said. "Here is some money. I will send you some more when I have it."

He threw a bundle of bank-notes on the table and it seemed to Emilie that there was an enormous amount of them. She was to learn that there were not to be many more.

"You will stay, John? At least you will stay to supper?" Marie Riguad gasped piteously as he turned towards the door.

"No, my dear, I have other commitments. Thank you for taking Alice."

He disengaged the clinging fingers of the child and gave her a kiss on the top of her head, then turned towards the woman he had loved when he was twenty, and who had loved him for over thirty years.

He put his fingers under her chin and tilted back her

20

head. She looked up into his eyes, her face soft and transfigured.

"So you still love me!" he said after a moment. "Well, well, I was always a lucky man."

He kissed her on the lips, then walked from the kitchen, and Marie made no further attempt to stop him. She only stood staring after him, her hand to her breasts which were pounding tumultuously beneath the cheap flannel of her blouse.

It was Emilie who watched him go.

Emilie who saw him turn the black horses in the narrow lane with competent skill, who heard the last murmur of his voice, who saw him raise his hat and wave it to her with a flamboyant gesture as the horses set off at a tremendous speed, the chaise rocking behind them in the cart tracks.

Then another sound attracted her attention. It was the cry of a child.

"Papa! Papa! Do not leave me!"

It was a piteous cry, a cry of utter desolation as a small figure came running from the kitchen into the garden.

It was then that Emilie caught Alice up in her arms, holding her tight, feeling her body trembling, quivering in her arms, the warm salt of her tears falling on her cheeks.

*"Pauvre petite!"* she murmured. "It is all right, it is all right! I will look after you."

She did not know then how prophetic her words were. Now she could see the rising spiral of the tasks which then lay ahead of her—Alice being coaxed to eat, Alice afraid of the dark, Alice fleeing from the cows, Alice wanting to be taken for a walk, Alice crying because the village children had teased her, Alice requiring teachers, doctors, medicines, books, dresses, shoes, amusements. Alice waiting for her long hair to be brushed while it covered her white shoulders like a golden veil.

Emilie sighed.

There was a sound outside the door and she realised that her memories had taken but a few seconds, although it seemed to her that they passed in a pageant as slow as the years in which they had taken place.

"Madame Guibout, Madame."

Jeanne ushered in the couturière. She was a small vivacious woman, her complexion sallow from the long hours in stifling rooms, her eyes strained and bloodshot from too close a concentration on the garments she created so skilfully.

"*Bonjour, Madame.*"

It took but a few seconds to exchange greetings and then as one business woman to another Emilie and Madame Guibout dispensed with civility.

"Travelling gowns, morning costumes, Ball dresses, robes de style, manteaux, dolmans, paletots and casaques! Mademoiselle will want everything," Emilie said.

"And for yourself, Madame?"

"An entire trousseau."

"And how soon?"

"I desire the impossible! Three days—a week at the outside!"

"It will be expensive."

"I am aware of that," Emilie said, "but I shall look to you not to cheat me."

"I shall want extra assistants. They are not cheap."

"That is understood!"

"It will mean an exhausting number of fittings for both yourself and Mademoiselle."

"We shall be here when you require us."

"Then it will be done, Madame."

"Thank you."

Madame Guibout crossed the room and opened the door. Outside two assistants were standing, their arms almost breaking under the strain of the materials they carried.

There were satins, velvets, cashmeres, failles, muslins, foulards, alpacas, poplins, rolls and patterns in every texture and colour.

Madame Guibout beckoned them in. She took a roll of azure blue velvet and threw it over the end of the bed.

"From Lyons," she said briefly.

Emilie thought of it against Mistral's hair. Once Alice had worn the same colour in the spring.

The door was still open and Mistral came running in.

"I am nearly dressed, as you told me, Aunt Emilie," she said. "Oh, what lovely, lovely colours!"

She put out her hand to touch the blue velvet and as she did so Madame Guibout covered it with a bale of grey gauze. It was as soft as the mist which lies over a lake in the morning before the sun has risen, the hue of a wood pigeon's breast, of the fine ashes which fall from a smouldering fire.

"For yourself, Madame," Madame Guibout said.

Emilie stared at the gauze and then at Mistral.

"No, for Mademoiselle," she said quietly.

"For me?" Mistral said in surprise.

"Yes, for you," Emilie repeated, "for everything you wear, every gown, every cloak, will be in just that colour—fantôme grey."

"But, Aunt Emilie, I shall look like a ghost!" Mistral exclaimed.

"Exactly!" Emilie said. "You will look like a ghost— a ghost in Monte Carlo."

23

# 2

Sir Robert Stanford shut the door of the Villa quietly behind him and stood for a moment looking out towards the sea.

It had been a brilliant night, but now the moon was but an echo of herself and already there was the first faint glow in the east which foretold that the dawn was not far away.

The sea breeze was rising, too, and Sir Robert, feeling it on his face, drew a sudden deep breath as if its sharp astringency revived and invigorated him.

He was in fact experiencing that acute sensibility which comes to a man in the very early hours of the morning when, having satiated his physical desires and exhausted his body, his spiritual needs stand revealed clearly and by an intuitive sixth sense.

Behind him in the quietness of the Villa des Roses was a warm scented darkness, exotic, clinging, enveloping; but out here the air, while sweet with the fragrance of mimosa and orange-blossom, was curiously stimulating.

Sir Robert threw back his head and looked up at the sky, then again he looked at the garden before him, at the steps leading down from the villa amid a profusion of plants and shrubs, their colours, dimmed by the night, awaiting only the rising sun to reveal them in their almost oriental splendour.

Yet strangely enough, as he looked, Sir Robert saw not the loveliness of the Mediterranean landscape but the parkland and the smooth green lawns of his home in Northamptonshire.

He could see it very clearly at this moment—the grey house set like a jewel in the midst of its terraces, its roofs and chimneys silhouetted against a clear sky, its architectural perfection reflected on one side by a lake over which one had to pass to reach the pillared portico.

It was a magnificent house, a home of which any man might be proud; but why the dawn breeze blowing across the Mediterranean should remind him of Cheveron he did not know.

Yet it was as if it stood there in front of him, silently accusing him, wordlessly demanding from him an explanation; and as all men do in a moment of weakness, Sir Robert began to excuse himself.

Why, he argued, should he be tied to a house, to a name, a heritage, however noble, however fine? He would live his life his own way. Why not? He was old enough to know his own mind!

And as he argued, Sir Robert remembered that a letter lay waiting for him in his suite at the Hotel.

It had arrived earlier in the evening, and having glanced at the handwriting he left it lying on the table unopened.

It was yet another letter from his Mother; and now it seemed to him that it was lying in wait for his return, somehow infinitely menacing in its very inefficacy.

Insistently the memory of his last interview with his Mother came flooding back to him.

He could remember every word, every inclination, every movement—the way the firelight had flickered on her pale face, the silent solemnity of the snow lying outside the windows of Cheveron, masking the familiar outlines of the landscape, but making it almost unbelievably beautiful.

"So you are going to Monte Carlo?" his Mother had

25

said, and he knew by the tone of her voice that she did not approve.

"Yes, to Monte Carlo," he repeated. "It will be lovely at this time of the year. I wonder you never decide to go south, Mother. It is extremely good for one's health."

"I have no doubt of it," Lady Stanford replied, "but I have many duties and responsibilities which keep me here, Robert."

There was no mistaking the inference in her voice, and her son smiled not too pleasantly in reply.

"Then I hope you will also discharge mine for me, dear Mother."

"If I could do so, I would," Lady Stanford replied, "but unfortunately I am only a woman. You are the owner of this estate, Robert; you have inherited the proud position which your Father held before you. You are the head of the family and the Stanfords have always been true to their traditions."

Sir Robert had crossed the room to stand looking out on to the snow-covered lawns.

Behind him there was silence for several minutes and then at last his Mother, in a voice which seemed almost strangled in her throat, asked:

"That . . . that woman . . . does she go with you?"

Sir Robert turned to face her.

"I believe Lady Violet Featherstone . . . if that is to whom you refer . . . will be at her Villa in Monte Carlo."

"Oh, Robert, how can you go there with her? Can you not understand that she is ruining you, utterly ruining you?"

Sir Robert sauntered back to the fireplace.

"In what way?" he asked. "Financially, intellectually, physically? No! I am of course well aware of the correct answer. Socially—that is what you mean, isn't it, Mother?"

26

In answer Lady Stanford held a black-edged handkerchief to her eyes. There was something in her tears, in her very helplessness which enraged her son so that he desired to hurt her still further.

"Pray do not distress yourself, Mother," he said. "As you have just reminded me, I am the owner of a great estate and the happy possessor of a vast fortune. People will be ready to forgive my wife anything, yes, anything, rather than that the doors of Cheveron should be closed against them."

If he had meant to wound his Mother, he had succeeded.

"Robert!"

Her enunciation of his name was a cry both of surprise and of horror.

"Robert, you cannot mean . . . that you would . . . marry . . . this woman . . . and bring her here?"

"And why not?" Sir Robert enquired suavely. "Have you forgotten, Mother, that Lady Violet is the daughter of a Duke?"

"I have not forgotten that," Lady Stanford said, "but good breeding only makes her behaviour the more inexcusable. Besides, if you are to marry Lady Violet, she will have to obtain a divorce from her husband. Have you thought of that? A divorce, Robert!"

"I have thought of it," Sir Robert replied.

Lady Stanford rose to her feet.

Once she had been a beautiful woman. She still had remnants of that beauty and a grace which had grown rather than diminished with age. She looked very dignified now, although her face was ashen and there were traces of tears on her cheeks.

"Very well, Robert," she said quietly. "You are old enough to be your own master. If you choose to marry this woman, no-one can stop you. She has a bad reputation and is ten years older than you are, but I

27

know that nothing I or anyone else can say will alter your decision once you have made up your mind.

"However, on this I am determined. If you marry Violet Featherstone, I will not accept her. That is all I have to say."

"I understand."

Lady Stanford turned towards the door. Sir Robert opened it for her, an angry ironical smile twisting his lips as he waited for his Mother to leave the room.

She looked at him for a moment, hoping perhaps for some softening in his expression; but when his eyes met hers, hostile, suspicious and resentful, she turned her head without another word and went from the room.

He had been cruel! Sir Robert knew that now; and yet at the time he had been angry with that bitter, burning anger which invariably rose within him when he could not get his own way and things could not be twisted and turned exactly as he wished them.

Why, he had asked himself then, as he had asked so often before, had he not met Violet when they were both younger?

He ignored the fact that when she married he had been only a boy at Eton, and he remembered only that she was a lovely woman and that he desired her.

How different she was from any of those tongue-tied girls whom his Mother considered would make him an eligible wife!

How different from the other women with whom he had flirted or to whom he had made love, but who had invariably become boring with their importunate demands upon him, with their protestations of love, which grew all the more fervent as his diminished!

He was never quite sure of Violet. One moment she would be pliable, gentle, and he would believe that she was ready to surrender herself utterly to him, her body and her love his for the taking.

Then even as he held her in his arms, she would elude him. She would mock his very ardency, laugh at his passion, and he would feel and know her elusiveness even before she spoke.

She did not belong to him but to herself. She was a will-o'-the-wisp, dancing over a quagmire of emotion.

There was something in her very recklessness and defiance which drew him. Violet cared nothing about what the world said of her.

She was well aware of how they talked; she knew that her relations and the majority of her friends sided openly with her husband, whom she had left a few months ago after eighteen years of marriage, because, she said, she knew all his stories and they had begun to bore her.

The gossips who had been talking about Lady Violet Featherstone for years with bated breath were not surprised; but what did surprise them was that Violet had not run away with anyone in particular.

She had merely set up a separate establishment of her own and had continued to dance her way into the hearts of almost every young man she met.

It was then that Sir Robert had met her, and from the first moment of their meeting he thought and dreamt of no-one else.

He was not a boy to take the most serious step in his life without thought, without consideration. He was well aware that if he did propose marriage to Violet Featherstone, it would mean grave changes in the plans he had already made for his future.

He might appear defiant to his Mother, he might outwardly pretend it was a simple thing to take Violet to

Cheveron as his wife, but he knew in his heart of hearts that it would be both complicated and difficult.

And yet when Violet smiled at him, when she looked up at him from under her eyelashes, when she teased him in that delicious, intimate manner which was one of her most engaging tricks, he felt that nothing in the world mattered beside the eventual conquest of this fascinating, unaccountable woman.

But now, as at other times when he was free of her, the beauty of Cheveron confronted him.

He could hear his Mother's voice and he knew she did not plead alone. There were the tenants, the question of his entering the House of Commons, the position he held in the County, the part the Stanfords had always played in Court circles.

How trivial they all appeared in themselves, yet they mounted one by one into a formidable opposition, a veritable mountain when one compared them with the tiny frailty of Violet herself—lovely, fascinating and alluring, and at times maddeningly elusive.

Robert was suddenly aware that he had stood a long time outside the Villa des Roses and that he felt cold. The breeze had been stronger than he thought.

He began to walk down the garden. The path twisted, there were steps every few yards and he descended lower and lower until an iron gate, beautifully wrought, let him out on to a narrow road.

He did not turn down the road, but instead walked across it and entered by a gate on the other side into the public gardens, laid out but a few years previously by the industrious François Blanc when he built the new town of Monte Carlo.

They were not yet complete, but already they gave promise of great beauty. The path through them twisted and turned beneath olive and palm trees, beside hedges of choisya and banks of rosemary. There was the heavy fragrance of eucalyptus and the exotic sweetness of jasmine and myrtle.

In the daytime, a passer-by would be entranced by the cascades of scarlet geranium, the beds of purple violets and garlands of blue heliotrope. But in the stillness of the night and in the shadow of the trees even the flowers seemed asleep.

Sir Robert was not concerned with the beauty around him. He was still thinking of Cheveron.

He was remembering the mornings when he had risen before breakfast to find the grass drenched with dew, a golden radiance in the sky and the air filled with the songs of birds; he was remembering long days of partridge shooting over the roots and stubbles of corn-fields, a covey winging their way over the ploughed land, his spaniel coming back triumphantly with a fallen bird in its mouth.

He was recalling the long ride home after a day's hunting when the lights of Cheveron had blazed a welcome through the wintry darkness.

Cheveron, always Cheveron! When he should be thinking only of Violet, of her lips against his, of her arms entwined round his neck.

He had reached the end of a flight of steps and rounded a grey rock overhung with wistaria when he felt someone bump into him and a voice gave a startled cry.

He put out his hands to save whoever it was from falling, and was aware that he held a woman in his arms.

"Look out! Be careful!" he said.

Because he was taken by surprise and his thoughts were far away at Cheveron, instinctively he spoke in English.

The woman gave a little gasp.

*"Pardon, Monsieur,"* she said, and then, after he had

31

spoken, she added in English: "Oh, but you are English."

"Yes, I am English," Sir Robert replied. "Is anything the matter?"

It was difficult to see her clearly for they were in the shadow of an aloe tree, but he was aware that her breath was coming quickly as if she had been running, and also that she was frightened.

"No, no, it is all right now that you are here," the woman answered. "It was just that . . . that a man spoke to me. I think, perhaps, he had taken too much . . . to drink. For a moment I did not understand what he said . . . and stupidly I stopped to listen. Then when I realized what . . . what he was saying, I . . . I ran away."

"I will go and deal with him," Sir Robert said grimly, but even as he said the words, it occurred to him that this might be a trap of some sort.

Nice women who minded being accosted by strange men did not walk alone in the gardens of Monte Carlo at dawn. He hesitated; and as if instinctively she sensed both the change in his attitude and what he was thinking, the woman drew away from him.

"It is all right now . . . thank you," she said. "It . . . it was my fault, of course, for coming out . . . alone. It was wrong of me, I know . . . but I was awake and I did so want to see the sunrise over the sea."

There was something so childlike both in her explanation and in her voice, that instantly Sir Robert's suspicions vanished.

This was not a trap, and the woman . . . or girl, for he guessed her to be very young . . . was genuine, he was certain of that.

"You will not have long to wait," he said. "I think you will see best from here."

He pointed a little to the left where the path widened

to the edge of a deep defile and was bounded only by an iron railing.

"Oh, thank you."

The woman walked away from him out of the shadow of the trees, and now at last Sir Robert could see that she was really no more than a girl.

She was wearing a grey cloak of some soft material which fell from her shoulders to the ground, the hood shadowed her hair, and in the pale light he could just see the outline of her face—delicate features, wide eyes, dark lashes, and beautifully moulded lips which were parted excitedly as she looked out to sea.

"It was here that Ste. Dévote landed," she said softly.

Hardly conscious that he had done so, Sir Robert had followed her and now he asked:

"What did you say?"

She looked up at him.

"I was really speaking to myself. I . . . I must not keep you, Sir."

"I think I should stay by you a few minutes in case the man who frightened you reappears."

She glanced over her shoulder a little apprehensively. From where they stood she could see the path leading down through the gardens towards the town. It was empty.

"He has gone," she said.

"Then you can enjoy the sunrise in peace! But I would still like you to repeat what you said just now."

"I said, 'This was where Ste. Dévote landed.'"

"I thought that is what you said, and yet I had the idea that I must have been mistaken. There are not many Saints in Monte Carlo."

She laughed at that, a little soft musical laugh.

"Not now, perhaps, but Ste. Dévote came here in A.D. 300."

"Indeed! And became the Patron Saint of the Rock."

"Yes, she did, but I thought you did not know about her."

"I don't—I guessed. Tell me more."

"Ste. Dévote lived in Corsica and was assassinated after she became a Christian. The Priest who had converted her planned to take her body to Africa, but the ship was blown off its course. In a dream the Priest saw a white dove fly from the breast of the dead girl and settle in a narrow ravine.

"When he awoke, behold, the ship had landed on the beach of Monaco and before them, perched in a narrow ravine, was a white dove."

The girl's voice was low, sweet and mystical as she recounted the legend.

"Who told you all this?" Sir Robert asked.

"A Nun at the Convent. She came from Monaco and always she talked about her home and the loveliness of the orange groves, of Mont Angel, of villages in the mountains and of Ste. Dévote who had inspired her to take her vows."

"And so it was because of this Nun that you wanted to see the sunrise over Monte Carlo?"

"Not over Monte Carlo, but over the Bay of Hercules and over Monaco; and look, down there is where I am sure the Chapel of Ste. Dévote lies."

She pointed. But Sir Robert looked not in the direction her fingers indicated but at the fingers themselves. They were long and thin, exquisitely graceful in their gesture.

"Oh, look!"

The words seemed to come with a kind of ecstasy from between her lips.

The first rays of the golden sun were creeping up the sky and swiftly, as the dawn comes in the south, a sudden transformation took place.

One moment all was grey and colourless, the next

34

there was the blue of the sea, the glory of the sky, the majesty of the snow-capped mountains, while around them lay a riot of purple and crimson, violet and heliotrope.

The dawn! The wonder of that moment when day meets night, the first song of the birds serenading the sun!

"Lovely! Lovely!" the girl cried; and now at last Sir Robert could see her face clearly, and he almost echoed her words aloud.

She was lovely, yes, lovely. He had never seen a more strange, more arresting face. And how young she was!

She was as young as the day just beginning before their very eyes, as young as the buds on the mimosa trees, as the spring shoots of pale green amongst the olives, as the blossom in the orange groves.

"I feel your name ought to be Dawn," he said.

As if with an effort she took her eyes from the landscape and looked up at him.

"Dawn!" she repeated. "Oh no, it is Mistral."

"Mistral!" he repeated. "What a strange name for a girl! It is the name of a very unpleasant wind in this part of the world."

"Yes, I know that," Mistral replied.

There was something in her tone which told him it would not be wise to question her further on this subject. Instead he asked:

"And what is your other name?"

She was on the point of telling him, for her lips moved to frame the word, but then quickly, as if she suddenly remembered something, a shadow appeared to pass over her face.

"I . . . I had best not tell you that," she replied. "As you know, I have no right to be here. My Aunt would be very angry with me. It was wrong, very wrong of me to come without permission, but I was awake and

35

Sister Heloise told me so often how beautiful the dawn was. And she was right—absolutely right."

"I think you, too, were right to come and see for yourself," Sir Robert said. "I have found in my life that it is always wiser to do what one wants and ask permission afterwards."

Mistral smiled.

"The Nuns would say that was a prevarication of right and wrong."

"And do you always do what the Nuns taught you?"

"Always up to now. I have never had the opportunity of doing anything else. You see, I only left the Convent a little over a week ago."

"You have been there a long time?"

"Since I was six."

"Six!" Sir Robert repeated. "But your home? You live in France?"

"Please, you must not ask me so many questions," Mistral replied.

"I am sorry." Sir Robert spoke seriously. "You must think me extremely gauche and ill-bred, but it is just that you are so very different from anyone I have ever met before, and there is something very intriguing at having encountered each other at dawn, neither of us knowing who we are or when we may meet again. Will you permit me, Mademoiselle, to introduce myself?"

"As there is no-one else to do it, I suppose you must," Mistral replied.

She smiled again and Sir Robert thought that it was like the sun touching the blue of the sea.

"My name is Stanford," he said. "Sir Robert Stanford."

He watched her face as he spoke and knew that she had never heard of him. Suddenly he had an insane desire to add: "I am a very rich, important and influential Englishman."

It was ridiculous, of course, but he wanted to shine in this strange child's eyes. Why, he could not explain even to himself.

"How do you do, Sir Robert?"

Mistral swept him a little curtsey, and now she had turned once again towards the sea.

"Look at the colour of it," she said. "I never believed that it could be so blue. I thought it was one of those stories that people tell you. But, it is blue—blue as the Madonna's robes in the Lady Chapel."

She had forgotten him and Sir Robert felt curiously piqued that the Mediterranean should have more appeal than he. Somewhere afar off a clock struck. It struck six times. Mistral counted the strokes.

"Six o'clock!" she said. "I must go back. My Aunt wakens early and I know she would be very angry if she knew where I had been."

"And would the Nuns approve of your deceiving your Aunt?" Sir Robert asked teasingly.

Her little face was serious as she shook her head.

"No, they would say it was very wrong," she replied, "and I, too, think it is wrong and I shall do penance for it. But just for once I wanted to do something by myself. I wanted to forget all the rules and regulations that I have always obeyed. There is always someone giving them to me."

She glanced to where she had told him the Chapel of Ste. Dévote stood and he felt she was praying. It was easy to watch her face when she was unaware of his scrutiny.

He thought he had never seen such amazing eyes. They were not English, yet the girl spoke English like an Englishwoman, while many of her gestures appeared to be French.

It was strange how she appeared anxious to be secretive, but it should not be hard to find out who she was.

37

It would be difficult, even in Monte Carlo, for such beauty to remain hidden for long.

"And now I must go."

Mistral turned. There was something in her expression which made him certain that she had been praying. She put out her hand.

"Thank you, Sir Robert, for your kindness. I am very grateful."

He took her hand in his.

"We will meet again, little Mistral?" he asked.

"I do not expect so," she replied.

"But why not? May I not call upon your Aunt?"

"No, please!" There was a touch of panic in her voice. "My Aunt would be very angry if she thought I had spoken to a stranger. She has given me strict instructions about what I am to do and what not to do. She would also be horrified and shocked if she thought I had come here alone. Please, Sir Robert, do not let anyone know that we have met. Promise me?"

"I will promise on one condition," Sir Robert replied.

"A condition?"

Her voice was troubled, and she tried to draw her hand from his grasp, but he would not let it go.

"Yes, a condition," he said firmly. "It is this, that if you are in any trouble, if you find yourself upset or perturbed by anything that happens in Monte Carlo, you will tell me. I am staying at the *Hotel Hermitage*. You have but to send a note or a message and I will come to you at once. If we cannot meet where you live, then we can meet here. Is it a promise?"

The anxiety on Mistral's face cleared away.

"Yes, I will promise that. It is kind of you."

"In return I promise to tell no-one that we have met and, if we meet again in public, to pretend that we are strangers. But I shall not forget this morning."

"And I shall not forget it either," Mistral replied. "The dawn was just as Sister Héloise described it, lovely—lovely beyond words."

"Yes, lovely beyond words," Sir Robert repeated slowly and insistently, looking down into her face.

For a moment her eyes were held by his; then as if he frightened her, she turned from him and went running down the path between the brilliant flowers with her grey cloak flying out a little behind her.

She moved swiftly and with a grace which reminded him of some woodland nymph, until a turn in the gardens took her from his sight.

He did not attempt to follow her. Instead he put his elbows on the railings and stared out to sea.

"Lovely—lovely beyond words," was how she had described it. And it was true. Slowly the sun rose and everything was intensified in brilliance.

Now the last shadows of the night had disappeared from the sky, the sea was blindingly blue, and far away in the distance the island of Corsica was dimly discernible like a lilac cloud.

"Lovely beyond words!" Sir Robert repeated; then slowly, so slowly that it took him quite a time, he walked back to his hotel.

There was no need for the night porter to let him in. Already the chambermaids were astir, the marble doorsteps were being scrubbed.

Sir Robert took his key from the desk and went up to his suite. It was empty and shrouded in darkness, for he had told his valet not to wait up for him.

The air in the big sitting-room seemed stale and stifling until he had pulled back the curtains and flung open the windows. Then as the light streamed into the room, he saw his Mother's letter waiting for him, lying in the centre of the big writing-table.

He stood looking at it for a long time until without touching it he walked across the room to where on the mantelpiece stood a photograph of Violet.

She had placed it there herself the day before, giving it to him as a present, already enclosed in a wide silver frame.

"I would hate you to forget me when I am not with you," she had said in one of her moments of tenderness.

"As if I could do that," Sir Robert protested.

"I find it very easy to forget people," Violet smiled.

He had felt a wave of jealousy sweep over him.

"Will you forget me easily?" he asked, and he caught her in his arms and kissed her savagely until she cried out for mercy.

But he would not let her go.

"Will you forget this? . . . and this? . . . and this?" he asked, kissing her again and again.

Yet even as he did so, even as he was incensed by jealousy sweeping over him in a red flood-tide, he had been aware that she had roused him deliberately; and some logical part of his brain had chid him for being a fool, at allowing himself to play the part which was expected of him.

Now Sir Robert looked at Violet's photograph.

She was attractive, there was no denying that. The dark chestnut hair drawn back from her low forehead, the faint smile in her eyes, the enticing twist of her lips.

She was not a beauty by classical standards and yet when she entered a room no-one could ignore her presence. His Mother thought she was a bad woman; and yet was Violet really bad?

Sir Robert was surprised at the question. How had it ever come into his mind? He had never asked it before.

"I suppose it must be the effect of that funny little girl I met in the gardens," he thought.

40

She had said that she was going to do penance for having done something of which her Aunt would not approve. Penance for watching the dawn! He wondered what sort of penance she would do if she did something really wrong.

One day he would ask her; and then he wondered if she could answer such a question. Her knowledge of what was wrong would be very limited. She would obviously be lamentably ignorant of the world, having been brought up by Nuns from the age of six.

Poor little thing! He wondered what life held for her in the future. It was unlikely that she would remain so innocent for long with a face like that. Well, at any rate it had nothing to do with him.

He wondered now why he had asked her to come to him if she was in any trouble. If she took him at his word, it might be a difficult situation to explain to Violet. And yet even Violet had no right to question his actions yet.

He had not asked her to marry him, but he had no doubt she would accept him if he did so.

Still his Mother's letter waited for him. Well, he was not going to open it now. He would pretend to himself that it had only arrived the following morning and he would read it at breakfast.

Almost as if she were in the room he heard a quiet voice say, "The Nuns would call that a prevarication."

Quite suddenly Sir Robert felt annoyed.

Damn the girl with her conscience and her prayers, and damn the letter lying there, white and accusing. Why couldn't his Mother leave him alone? If he wished to go to the devil, he would go his own way without so much weeping and wailing about it.

He was tired, he would go to bed.

It was too late at night or too early in the morning, whichever way one liked to put it, for a man to be

41

confronted with the ethics of good and evil, right and wrong.

Sir Robert crossed the room, walked into his bedroom and slammed the door behind him. The wind coming in from the open windows stirred the papers on the writing-desk.

The letter from Lady Stanford did not move. It lay in the centre of the desk, the sunshine enveloping it with a golden warmth.

# 3

Emilie glanced around the sitting-room with an air of satisfaction. The breakfast laid on a spotless white cloth in the window was appetizing and elegantly served.

So far things had gone exactly as she had planned them and she felt the thrill that a General might feel when his troops have been successful in some carefully prepared manoeuvre.

She and Mistral had arrived at the *Hôtel de Paris* the night before. They had travelled in what appeared to Emilie to be astonishing comfort on the Railway which now connected Monaco with Nice.

Inevitably she must compare every step of the journey with the one she had taken nineteen years earlier with Alice.

Then they had travelled slowly and in much discomfort; and when finally they reached Nice, they had been confronted with the choice of an uncomfortable antediluvian vehicle, which carried eleven passengers daily between Nice and Monaco, or an extremely un-safe-looking steamer which put out to sea erratically and was known at times to lie in harbour for a week on end without attempting the journey.

They had chosen on that occasion to go by land and had been bumped for what seemed like four months rather than four hours over a half-finished road, being regaled as they went with tales of robbers and bandits who often found it well worth while to hold up the few carriages which dared the journey.

From the windows of the sitting-room Emilie could look across the gardens of the Casino directly on to the sea.

To the west she could see the harbour and beyond it the great rock of Monaco, its ancient Palace and Fortress still standing grimly sentinal as they had done for over 500 years.

But Emilie was more interested in the view which she knew lay behind the hotel—a view of a town which had sprung up like a gaudily tinted mushroom; a brilliant, vivid place, rising roof upon roof up the hillside, white and glittering and seeming in its opulence and magnificence to be the result of some magical power from a wizard's wand.

Surely that was just what François Blanc had been to Monte Carlo—a wizard, for he had created from a barren poverty-stricken rock a veritable wonderland of wealth and luxury, gaiety and pleasure.

Emilie had not believed all that the newspapers had told her these past years. But now that her eyes had seen the revelation for herself, she was astonished.

The hotel, too, exceeded anything she had expected; and when, with Mistral beside her and Jeanne following humbly behind, she had swept into the foyer and crossed the big hall, feeling her feet sink into the pile of the luxurious carpet, taking in with one quick glance the marble pillars, the glittering mirrors, the profusion of palms and flowers, she had for one moment felt half afraid of her own courage at daring to enter such a world.

Then something stronger than herself, some force within her drove her forward so that when she reached the reception-desk she was able to act convincingly the little play she had already rehearsed in her mind.

"A suite has been engaged for me," she said, "by my man of affairs, Monsieur Anjou."

The clerk bowed.

"It has indeed, Madame, and we have been expecting you. May I welcome you to the *Hôtel de Paris* and to Monte Carlo?"

The inclination of Emilie's head was a model of condescension.

"Everything is prepared, Madame," the clerk said. "If you will be good enough to sign the register, I will have you escorted upstairs."

Emilie picked up the big quill pen and turned towards the open, leather-bound book which lay on the desk; then she hesitated, making sure that the clerk saw her hesitation.

She glanced back at Jeanne who stood a little distance away holding in her hands a leather jewel case on which a coronet was prominently embossed.

"It is a little . . . difficult," Emilie said at length. "My niece and I are here for a holiday. We wish to have a quiet time and would remain . . . incognito."

"I am sure your wishes will be respected, Madame," the clerk said, but there was the light of curiosity in his eyes.

"Yes, incognito," Emilie repeated. "That is the right word."

She dipped the pen in the ink and in a strong, bold hand wrote:

*"Madame . . ."*

44

Then again she hesitated until finally with a little laugh she added a name.

"I am *Madame Secret*," she said, "at least for my stay here in this charming holiday resort."

"It is as Madame wishes," the clerk said; but Emilie noticed that once again he glanced towards the jewel case with its embossed coronet in Jeanne's hands.

But Emilie still hesitated.

"My niece . . ." she said at last and wrote another name.

Mistral glanced at what her Aunt had written. The bold, large handwriting was easily decipherable. Emilie had written *Mademoiselle Fantôme*.

The suite into which they were shown was delightful.

It consisted of a large room for Emilie, a smaller one for Mistral, a sitting-room with a balcony connecting the two.

Emilie had instructed a lawyer in Paris to write for the best apartments that the hotel could command; and while he had obeyed her, giving no name but saying only that a client of his would be arriving in Monte Carlo on the 28th February, Emilie had not anticipated anything so comfortable from what she remembered as an untended, straggling orange grove.

It was late in the evening when they arrived and despite the disappointment in Mistral's face she had insisted on dining upstairs.

"I do not wish you to be seen until our trunks are unpacked," she said. "When we appear, we must be dressed in our best so that people will notice us."

"But, Aunt Emilie, I thought you said that you wished to be incognito?" Mistral asked bewildered.

Emilie looked at her in a strange way, and then said abruptly:

"Do not ask so many questions, Mistral. I am tired. Tomorrow I will explain things to you—at least those which it is important for you to know; but tonight I shall retire early. I wish to be alone."

"But of course, Aunt Emilie, I understand," Mistral said. "You must be very tired after such a long journey. Indeed I am tired myself, but more with excitement than anything else. I cannot tell you how I long to see Monte Carlo and the Mediterranean. I wish it was not so dark."

She went to the open, uncurtained window, staring out into the deep purple twilight. Emilie called her back almost irritably.

"Go and help Jeanne with the unpacking, child, and do not show yourself at the window."

"Yes, Aunt Emilie."

But alone in the sitting-room, Emilie herself crossed to the window and did just what she had forbidden Mistral to do. She stared out into the twilight trying to see what lay outside.

She too was impatient that the night must pass before she could see more.

When their evening meal was finished, Emilie retired to her room; and when Jeanne came to her to help her to undress, asking her solicitously if she would like a glass of milk or a hot brick in her bed, she sent her away saying she wanted only to be left alone.

And when at last this wish was realized, Emilie laid on a chair a heavy despatch box. It was a big casket covered in purple leather and without the big gilt coronet which adorned her other luggage.

Nevertheless it was a distinguished piece of luggage and almost without realizing it Emilie's hand caressed the leather before she drew a key from her purse and turned it in the lock.

The box was filled not with state papers for which it had been originally intended, but strangely enough with scrapbooks, made of brown paper such as were sold for children to stick transfers in and young ladies their valentines.

Slowly, with what appeared to be almost a tenderness, Emilie drew the books from the leather box. She chose one and opened it.

It was filled with newspaper cuttings. There were six scrapbooks equally filled with cuttings dating back for eighteen years and all referring to one place and one person.

The authorities of Monte Carlo would have been interested if they could have seen Emilie's scrap-books, for they constituted in themselves an almost unique history of the rise of the town.

At the beginning of the book the cuttings referred to events occurring at irregular intervals, sometimes two or three months elapsing between each one, and then they referred only to the Grand Duke Ivan of Russia.

As the years passed, the cuttings grew more numerous. François Blanc, the genius of Homburg, had been invited to set up a Casino in Monaco and a new name was to be chosen. The natives called it *"Les Spelugues"*, but this was not considered suitable as it had an improper meaning, and finally it was decided that the Casino and the new town which was being built around it should be called Monte Carlo.

Now there was hardly a day when a fresh cutting had not been added to the book—cuttings describing the beauties and the importance of the new buildings, cuttings mentioning the amusements, galas, balls, fêtes, concerts and the games such as whist, écarté, piquet, faro, boston and reverse, as well as roulette and *trente-et-quarante*, which were being played in the Casino.

There were columns of print, paeans of praise from enthusiastic correspondents, and nearly everyone of them mentioned the distinguished visitors who were to be found in this new and exciting playground of wealthy society.

Princes—Montenegrin, Russian, Serbian, Bulgarian —Rajahs, Maharajahs, Grand Dukes, Arch-Dukes and swarms of lesser nobility, all received their comment; and there was a veritable fanfare of exaltation when two years earlier, in 1872, England's Prince and Princess of Wales had visited the Principality.

Although the whole list of names were included in Emilie's book, there was only one name she sought amongst them, and each time he was mentioned she had underlined the printed word with a blue pencil.

It was easy to see at a glance from the blue pencil marks, which stood out clearly, how often this name occurred among those present at the Casino, among those attending the opening of the Opera Season, among those taking part in the pigeon shooting.

Always the same name, always underlined in blue —"His Imperial Highness, the Grand Duke Ivan of Russia."

In later years and especially in the last two or three years another name was invariably added to the first— "His Imperial Highness, the Grand Duke Ivan of Russia and his son, His Serene Highness, Prince Nikolai."

Slowly Emilie's fingers turned the pages of the scrapbooks. Some of the earlier books were already well worn and a little ragged from the many times they had been read and handled.

And yet to Emilie sitting alone in her bedroom at the *Hôtel de Paris* it was as if she read her cuttings for the first time. For eighteen years she had waited for this moment.

It was after midnight when she raised her head and put the scrap-books back in their leather-covered casket.

But she did not feel tired, as any ordinary woman of nearly sixty might have felt tired at the end of such a long journey. Instead she felt as if she had an inexhaustible strength.

Nothing and nobody could prevent her now from doing what she had set out to do.

As she thought of what lay ahead, her eyes narrowed and a smile twisted her lips. She looked evil at that moment; but after a while, as her thoughts wandered back into the past, her eyes softened, as invariably they did when she thought of Alice—Alice who had been the one thing she had loved in her life.

How different her rest would be tonight in the big comfortable bed awaiting her from what it had been when she had come here last with Alice!

Then they had arrived battered and bruised from their journey from Nice, but they had been greeted with cries of excitement and a loving welcome from the Aunt and cousins with whom they had come to stay.

Emilie had never met them before, those nephews and nieces of her Mother's and her own first cousins, and she had not expected such a warm greeting or such a sincere one when she had written to ask if she and Alice might visit them for a month or so.

She had almost expected a refusal in reply to her letter despite the fact that Marie had spoken of Louise as being her favourite sister.

Aunt Louise had indeed taken them to her ample bosom, and her family of six boys and four girls had been none the less generous in their efforts at hospitality.

Emilie had always been inclined to be superior and stand-offish with her French relatives, for she liked to remember that her Father was an Englishman.

She had also when she was quite young been aware of her own illegitimacy and felt aggressively self-conscious that this stood as a barrier between her and her Mother's family. But in actual fact she need not have worried herself on this score.

The Riguad family accepted the result of Marie's courtship with the young Englishman as philosophically as they accepted a bad lambing season or a storm which did damage to the crops.

It was a pity, but there was nothing to be done about it, they would aver with a shrug of their shoulders; and they were far more awkward with Emilie because she had a sharp tongue and they felt that her English blood made her despise them than because they had any inclination to cast aspersions upon her parentage.

Just as her grandfather, old Louis Riguad, had accepted philosophically and without reproach the irregularities of Marie's love affair and eventually Emilie's own arrival at the farm, so the rest of the family had looked upon it as part of the inscrutable ways of Providence.

If anything, they were rather proud of Emilie's connection with a distinguished English family, especially after John Wytham brought Alice to Brittany. Alice was a true aristocrat, the Riguads told themselves.

They all learned of her arrival at the farm in the extraordinary way that news travels among families without the aid of the written word, and they knew too that she was the result of John Wytham's marriage with a lady of his own class.

That the child of such a union should be brought to Marie Riguad's home to be brought up by her was a compliment to the whole Riguad family. If Emilie had feared that she and Alice might prove unwelcome at Monaco, her mind was set at rest within a few minutes of her arrival.

Talking excitedly, gesticulating and striving to point out all the possible objects of interest at the same time as they asked questions about the journey, the Riguad family bore Emilie and Alice off down the hill to their home.

It was a noisy, triumphant procession and Alice, white-faced and fair, walking in the midst of the dark-haired and dark-skinned Riguads, looked like a creature from another world.

The Riguad's home was only an old-fashioned shack, almost on the shore itself; but as their aunt and uncle explained, they were lucky to have that, although it meant a long way for the boys to walk to where they could graze the goats.

The peasants' houses in Monaco were few and in very bad repair. How could they be anything else when the whole Principality was impoverished and there seemed to be no possible way of improving conditions?

The Princess Caroline, wife of Florestan I, it was true, had tried to introduce lace-making and the manufacture of perfumes among the industries of the Peninsula.

There was also flower-growing and the distillation of alcohol, but none of these seemed to be very successful and as communication with the outside world was so difficult it was easier in most cases to remain poor and hungry, but happy and lazy in the sunshine.

Certainly Emilie and Alice had been happy in the Riguad's ramshackle house by the sea. Alice's cough, the reason for which the whole journey had been undertaken, began to get better.

It appeared regularly every winter when the raw winds swept across the flat plains of Brittany and the damp mists lay over the ground in the early morning.

Her face, too, lost that white pinched look and her laugh rang out more frequently. In Emilie's eyes at any rate she seemed to assume a new beauty.

Yes, they had been happy in those spring days

51

nineteen years ago until something happened, something which even now Emilie could not remember without clenching her hands, without feeling the slow dull anger rise within her, virulent and malignant. She could see it all happening so clearly.

Alice in her blue frock, which matched the blue of her eyes, had taken the youngest Riguad child, a baby of two, up to the top of the rock to look at the Palace. Alice had been attracted by the Palace.

She had never known much about Princes and Kings, for in the past eight years in Brittany people had seldom mentioned such exalted personages. Now the Palace and its encircling walls and the high battlements appeared to fascinate her. It was her favourite walk.

She would climb from the shore to the top of the rock to sit there and look at the Palace, watching the soldiers go in and out and occasionally seeing Prince Florestan come driving past, his carriage drawn by a pair of magnificent white horses.

Occasionally, too, she would look at the only other great building on the Peninsula.

It was called a Chateau, but to Alice it, too, appeared to be a Palace. It reminded her somewhat strangely of her grandfather's house in England. It was of grey stone with one great tower in the centre of it, and there were wrought-iron gates surmounted by crowns opening on to the road.

Although the garden was filled with flowers and fountains it had a grandeur which in itself held for Alice an inexplicable attraction.

It was here, they told her, that the Grand Duke Ivan of Russia lived. A friend of the reigning Prince, he had built the Chateau about six years earlier. He had meant it to serve him as an occasional holiday residence when he visited his friend, the Prince of Monaco.

But when it was completed, he found the climate and the house itself so much to his liking that he stayed on almost indefinitely, returning to Russia at very infrequent intervals and every year adding to the size of his Chateau until it looked as if it would eventually be larger and more impressive than the Palace itself.

"What is he like, the Grand Duke?" Alice had asked.

"He is tall and very handsome," someone replied, "but now he is sad, for his wife, a lovely Russian lady, has died. The cold in Russia was too intense for her. They went back, it is said, because the Czar wished them to be present at a Court Ball; but it was cold, very cold, and the Grand Duchess caught a chill. She grew worse and worse, and not all the Doctors in Russia could save her."

"Oh, poor thing!" Alice exclaimed. "So now the Grand Duke is alone?"

"Not entirely," she was told. "The Grand Duchess left behind her little baby, Prince Nikolai. He is two years old, a dear little boy, and always he lives here because if he goes to Russia the Grand Duke is afraid that the cold will kill him too—poor little motherless babe."

Emilie could remember how interested Alice had become in the widowed Grand Duke and his little son. Day after day she used to go up to the top of the rock to look at the Chateau d'Horizon where the Duke lived. And then it happened.

The Duke's carriage, coming swiftly and unexpectedly along the dusty track which served the Peninsula as a road, nearly ran down the Riguad baby, little Thérèse.

Just in time Alice was able to snatch her from under the horses' hoofs, but she stood there white and shaken while the baby screamed in terror.

The carriage was drawn to a standstill and the Grand

Duke himself descended to speak to Alice and to reassure the frightened baby.

No-one else was present and no-one ever knew exactly what he said or what Alice replied; but she must have told him of her interest in his house and perhaps how it reminded her of her grandfather's mansion in England, for the next day the Duke's carriage called at the Riguad's shack to take Alice to the Chateau.

It was only when the carriage arrived that Alice related what had happened the day before; and before Emilie, dumbfounded and astonished, could make any protestation, she had driven off alone.

If Emilie was speechless then, she was certainly not speechless when Alice returned. She took her out on to the shore, for there was little privacy to be found in the Riguad household, and she extracted from her the whole story of her meeting with the Grand Duke. Word by word she learned all that had taken place that afternoon at the Chateau.

"He is very kind," Alice kept saying, "and his little son is so sweet."

"That is not the point," Emilie insisted. "Why did he ask you?"

"He wanted to show me his Chateau."

"And why should he want to show you his house? He has friends of his own class."

Alice merely looked at her.

"I think I am his friend," she said quietly.

It was then that Emilie had raved at her, speaking brutally as she had never spoken in all the eight years that they had lived together.

She told Alice what she knew already, that her Father had never married Marie Riguad. She told her how her grandfather had come and fetched him away back to England, promising a sum of money for the unborn child which Marie expected, but forgetting either deliberately or inadvertently to send it.

"It was to have been my dowry," Emilie said, "but do you think it would have been any help to me, born between two worlds, half of noble blood and half of peasant stock? The men who wanted me were like dirt, and the ones I might have liked considered that I was beneath them."

"Poor Emilie!" Alice said simply, but Emilie had known that she had not understood.

Driven by her own fear she added:

"That is what will happen to you, and to the child you may have if you persist in making friends with men like the Grand Duke. He will never be anything to you. He knows where you are staying and that we, the Riguads, are your relations.

"Can you imagine that someone like that will offer you marriage? No, he is interested in you because you are pretty, because you are young.

"There are thousands of women of his own world only too ready to marry him should he but say the word. A man like that is not concerned with marriage. You are not to see him again, do you hear me?"

Emilie had spoken passionately and somehow it was infinitely frightening that Alice did not answer her. Instead she sat staring out to sea, her eyes almost as blue as the water on which they rested.

"Do you hear me?" Emilie repeated.

Alice had turned her face towards her then.

"Yes, I hear you."

"And you will obey me?" Emilie insisted. "It is understood, Alice, that you are not to see him again, you are not to accept any other invitations to the Chateau d'Horizon."

But still Alice did not answer. Emilie was certain, though, that she would not disobey. She had never had any trouble with Alice, who had always been very obedient.

Then Fate had taken a hand, or so it seemed later to Emilie. The very next day brought a letter from the farm. Marie Riguad was ill. She had fallen down and broken her leg and Emilie must return at once.

For a moment she contemplated taking Alice with her, and then she thought that such a precaution was ridiculous. They had only just arrived, the change and warm sunshine had already done Alice good.

It would be cruel to take her back, to drag her away to the north, to subject her to the bitter March winds and storms of Brittany which invariably left her weak and listless.

Emilie decided to go alone, but before she went she spoke to Alice once again about the Grand Duke.

"He has doubtless forgotten about you by now," she said; "but in case an invitation comes, you are to refuse it. Do you understand? You are not to show yourself near his house either, but stay here on the shore. As soon as Mother is better, I will return for you."

Emilie had left. She could remember driving away over the rough road, leaning out of the window waving, waving until Alice was lost to sight.

It had been that last picture which was to haunt Emilie now on her first night in the *Hôtel de Paris*. Alice with the sun on her face, her head thrown back, her fair hair glinting like a halo round her head, the wheels of the coach drawing them further and further apart.

She must have dreamt of Alice too lying in the big room on the warm, comfortable mattress, for when she awoke she heard her own voice whispering: "Alice, Alice!"

It seemed to start the day all wrong, and Mistral found her very cross at breakfast.

"Oh, Aunt Emilie," Mistral cried. "This is the loveliest place in the whole world. I had no idea the sea could be so blue."

"Come and eat your breakfast, Mistral," Emilie said sharply, "and stop running in and out of the balcony. I spoke to you about it last night."

"But, Aunt Emilie, surely you don't mind today? We are going out, aren't we?"

Emilie made up her mind.

"No, Mistral, we are not. You are staying here and in these rooms until dinner time, then you shall make an appearance."

"But, Aunt Emilie . . ."

There was no reproach, just utter consternation in the young voice.

"Now, Mistral, do not argue. I have told you that you must obey me, that I have my reasons for whatever decisions I make."

"But not to go out, our first day in Monte Carlo!"

Emilie's lips tightened.

"We are staying here for some time. Tomorrow we will inspect the place, not that I imagine there is a great deal to see. Today we shall not appear until the hour for dinner."

Mistral knew what that inflexible quality of determination in Emilie's voice meant. She sighed. She knew it was no use asking her to change her mind.

"Aunt Emilie," she said after a long pause, "there is something I want to ask you."

"What is it?"

"Why was I christened Mistral? I have often wondered and have often meant to ask you."

"Your Mother chose the name. She chose it because she hated the wind that blows here along the shore."

"Because she hated it?" Mistral echoed. "Then my Mother came here? She knew Monte Carlo?"

"Yes, your Mother came here," Emilie said grimly; "but she did not know Monte Carlo. It was not built nineteen years ago."

"Nineteen years ago," Mistral repeated. "Then she was here just before I was born. Oh, Aunt Emilie, how exciting! Did she love it? Perhaps that is why it seems so beautiful and wonderful to me, because my Mother liked it when she was here."

"I have not said your Mother liked it," Emilie replied. "When she told me what your name was to be, she said, "It will be a girl and I want her to be called Mistral. That terrible wind, I can hear it still. Yes, call her Mistral'."

"Why did she say that?" Mistral asked; "and if she said it before I was born, how was she certain that I would be a girl? I might have been a boy."

"She seemed very sure that you would be a girl," Emilie said briefly.

Even as she spoke, she could see Alice's haunted eyes. They had worn the same look when she had chosen the name Mistral as when she had said to Emilie:

"You are not to tell him! Swear on the Bible that you will never tell him that I am to have a child."

She could hear Alice's voice almost hysterical with fear. She could see her face, white and haunted, and she had promised because at that moment there was nothing she would not have done to soothe her distress.

But afterwards how bitterly she had regretted, not once but many times, that promise which had been given on the Bible.

Even towards the very end, when Alice's life was fading away and the Doctor had given her up, for there was nothing more that he could do, Alice had whispered:

"Promise you will not tell him about Mistral?"

Emilie had knelt sobbing at the side of the bed. She

had promised, but later, when Alice had gone and they had carried her slender, wasted body away to the Churchyard, Emilie would have given everything she had in the world to retract that promise.

She had wanted to leave there and then for Monaco, to confront the Grand Duke with his crime, to call him a murderer, to show him the motherless Mistral, to know the satisfaction of denouncing him as a seducer and a betrayer.

But she had kept her promise, partly because of her religious convictions, partly because of her love for Alice, and partly because she was innately superstitious.

Emilie knew she could never break that vow given on three separate occasions; but she had vowed vengeance, vowed it by all that she held sacred, and by the very memory of Alice herself.

One day, somehow, she would make the Grand Duke suffer as he had made Alice suffer and indirectly herself as well.

During the long nights when she had fought for the life of Mistral, when she had walked the screaming child up and down the kitchen almost from dusk until dawn, Emilie had found time to think; and gradually, as she thought, a plan formed within her mind, a plan which would take long years to put into operation, which would require endless scheming and plotting. But as her hatred and her desire for vengeance grew, as it intensified, day by day, week by week, year by year, until its tentacles were so firmly fixed within her that she could no longer escape from them or indeed live without them, so was she certain that one day all that she dreamt of would be fulfilled and her vengeance assured.

And now at last, after eighteen years, the curtain was rising on the first Act, the Prelude in which Mistral had grown to womanhood was finished. Looking at her,

Emilie was satisfied. She was lovely—lovely enough for the part she had to play in this drama.

And then, as she looked at Mistral, the girl's eyes, clear and unclouded, were raised to hers, and for a moment she bore such a look of Alice that Emilie felt something contract within her heart.

It was Alice who looked at her, Alice who was worried and whose lips trembled a little.

"Please, Aunt Emilie, please, please explain things a little bit to me. It is all rather frightening, this secrecy."

But even as Mistral pleaded, she knew it was hopeless. Her Aunt's eyes seemed to soften and then abruptly Emilie turned her head away and walked across the room to the fireplace.

Mistral did not know that it was her very simplicity which had defeated her. Emilie had known at that moment that she could not possibly put into words what she had in mind.

"You must trust me," Emilie said, and her voice was hard. "Besides, for the moment there is nothing to explain. Tonight we dine downstairs. You will wear grey chiffon with the pleated frills.

"I have learned from the Manager that there is to be a Gala dinner tonight. The whole of Monte Carlo will be here. You will see all the celebrities and afterwards we will go across to the Concert Room at the Casino."

Mistral clasped her hands together.

"Shall we see people gambling, Aunt Emilie?"

"We will watch the tables," Emilie said. "It is an interesting sight if only for the satisfaction of watching other people make fools of themselves."

"Is it wrong to gamble?" Mistral asked.

"Wrong?" Emilie repeated the word with an inflection of interrogation. "I see nothing wrong in doing what interests or amuses one. People who tell you that gambling is wrong are usually characterless and so weak that they cannot prevent themselves from pouring away at the tables money they can ill-afford. No, why should you think it wrong?"

"I only wondered," Mistral answered. "A Nun at the Convent told me that, although gambling had brought great prosperity to Monaco and the poor of the Principality had benefited by it, she felt that it was wrong as it encouraged the lust for money."

"A narrow creed from a narrow woman walled up in seclusion," Emilie sneered. "You will be wise not to take your sense of values from Nuns, Mistral."

"I have had little opportunity of doing anything else until now," Mistral replied quietly.

Her reply was not impertinent, it was just a statement of fact, but for the moment Emilie looked startled.

"You are right," she said. "I had forgotten how long you have been there. It is true that you know nothing of the world, I must not forget that."

"Why did you never let me come back to the farm?" Mistral asked.

"Because I had left the farm myself," Emilie replied. "I wanted you to be brought up a lady like your Mother. The farm was rough and, when my grandfather died, there was not enough money to keep it together unless I had slaved there day after day, year after year, until it killed me.

"I wanted to pay for your education, Mistral, I wanted a proper life for myself, and so, when you went to the Convent, I went to Paris."

"To Paris!" Mistral ejaculated. "And you were happy, Aunt Emilie?"

"I worked very hard, Mistral, and I suppose in my own way I was content. I had an objective in view and at least I was getting nearer to it."

Mistral rose from the table and walked across the room to her Aunt. Emilie was taller than she was. She raised her lovely oval face to the older woman's and said in a very low voice:

"Aunt Emilie, you do like having me with you now, don't you?"

It was the cry of a child for comfort, it was the yearning for love of someone who has never known love; but Emilie, who would have understood the same appeal eighteen years earlier in Alice's voice, was deaf to it in Mistral's.

"Of course, Mistral," she said frigidly. "I am very glad to have you and I am sure we shall enjoy ourselves together. Now call Jeanne, for I have some instructions to give her."

She did not notice the disappointment in the girl's face, did not see the sudden pain in those dark violet eyes and the soft droop of her lips.

Obediently Mistral went from the room to call Jeanne.

# 4

"I think everyone in Monte Carlo is here tonight," Lady Violet Featherstone remarked.

She looked around the big dining-room of the *Hôtel de Paris* where the tables were filling up so quickly that the appearance of each newcomer in the doorway seemed to provide another dilemma for the *Maître d'Hôtel*.

"Alfonse was telling me that this is the best season they have ever known," Lord Drayton remarked from the other side of the table. "As the gross profits last year were six million francs—that is no *façon de parler*. We should have bought some shares five or six years ago."

Sir Robert smiled.

"It is too late now!"

"For you, Robert, that is not a tragedy," Lord Drayton remarked. "What would you do with any more money?"

"I can answer that question," Lady Violet said. "He would spend it on me, of course."

"And what better excuse for being extravagant?" Lord Drayton replied with somewhat ponderous gallantry.

Sir Robert took the menu from an attentive waiter.

"Well, what are we going to eat? Violet, will you start with caviare or oysters?"

"You order the dinner, Robert," she answered. "I want to watch the people, they always amuse me."

It was not surprising that Lady Violet, used as she was to the glittering society at Monte Carlo, should feel interested in what she saw around her tonight.

The Gala dinner at the *Hôtel de Paris* had been arranged as a compliment to a celebrated Italian opera singer who was to appear for the first time in the Concert Room at the Casino.

But any excuse served for a Gala evening; and because this was indeed the most brilliant and successful winter season the Principality had ever known, there seemed to be packed into those few acres of land all the wealth, beauty and aristocracy of Europe.

There were German Barons and their wives, eager to forget their country's recent war with France, their lineage dating back into antiquity, their pockets bulging with gold.

There were Grand Dukes from Russia, handsome, aristocratic and incredibly wealthy, who by their very appearance seemed to give an air of distinction to the gambling-rooms and the cafés.

There were also visitors from England, men and women bearing ancient and honourable names, who stared curiously at the cosmopolitan crowd which thronged around them and who managed in some subtle way of their own to remain reserved and aloof however gay and congenial the atmosphere.

There were Rajahs from India, Sultans from Turkey, Señors from Spain, Beys from Algeria, the most elegant and *distingué* of the French *beau monde*, and a sprinkling of Americans—big, badly dressed men with their elegant, over-dressed wives, who seemed a little ill at ease, but whose fortunes were fabulous.

Besides these were artists, professional gamblers, crooks, parasites and the hangers-on who appear wherever there is a game of chance, and likely pickings.

And last, but not least, there were women, women of all nationalities, creeds, classes and types of beauty —every one of them outstanding, every one of them worth a second, third or fourth glance, and every one of them adding something to the gaiety and beauty of the place by their very presence.

Lady Violet, looking round the dining-room, thought she had never seen a more splendid array of jewellery.

There were diamond tiaras which glittered and shone as if they were royal crowns, there were necklaces of emeralds and rubies and sapphires, ropes of pearls, pendants of aquamarines and amethysts, bracelets of turquoises and opals, brooches, ear-rings, lockets, diadems—all resplendent with precious gems, each a silent witness to a woman's beauty.

Lady Violet gave a little sigh.

"I thought my emeralds were quite an adequate decoration until I came here this evening."

Lord Drayton glanced at the necklace around her

throat and at the long emerald ear-rings which dangled from her small ears.

"Yours are very fine stones," he said.

"But insignificant beside those the Princess is wearing."

He glanced across the room. A Polish Princess was literally blazing with emeralds; they crowned her head, encircled her neck, glittered on her wrists and fingers and almost covered the bodice of her low-cut gown.

"It is certainly difficult to compete with the Ossinpof collection," Sir Robert said, "but I daresay Her Highness would give them all to you if you could exchange ages at the same time."

It was palpably true. The Princess was over fifty and doing her best to pretend that she was a mere twenty-five.

She was rouged, dyed and corsetted until she could hardly breathe, and the emeralds must have been little consolation for a youth which slipped away from her year by year.

Lady Violet in contrast at thirty-six was in the full bloom of her good looks. She had never been a great beauty, but she had something of more value—charm and an attraction which drew men to her and made them lose both their heads and their hearts if she so much as smiled at them.

She had always been fêted and courted from the moment she had made her début into Society, and it was entirely due to a disinterested and self-centered Mother that she had been allowed to marry one of the first men who proposed to her, because she wished to escape the confining boredom of her home life.

As a child Lady Violet had longed to live fully. Life for her in later years meant one continuous whirl of thrills, excitements and sensations.

Brought up in the wilds of Lincolnshire, for the

Duke and Duchess believed in keeping their family in the country while they enjoyed themselves in London, Violet rebelled against the monotony of dull governesses and even duller lessons and against the selfishness of her parents, who thought that children were fortunate if they had three good meals a day and a bed to sleep in and were entitled to no other consideration.

But being a rebel was disconcertingly ineffective until at eighteen Violet was taken to London for her first Season and was presented at Court.

Up till that date she had met few men, and in welcome contrast to the local Parson, who was nearly eighty, and the local M.F.H., who was married with six children, Eric Featherstone seemed a veritable Don Juan.

Realizing, too, that when her short season in London was ended she would be sent back to Lincolnshire and forgotten until the following year, Violet had accepted Eric, believing herself quite genuinely to be in love with him.

How mistaken she was she learned shortly after her marriage; but as a young married woman with a quite considerable fortune at her disposal she took the social world by storm. She was so gay and amusing that she managed to make herself charming and acceptable to the women as well as captivating to the men.

It was only after some years of social triumphs that Violet began to wish for new things to do, for fresh amusements and other fields to conquer.

Unfortunately there were no children to draw her and her husband closer together, and she quickly found that he was pleasant and good-natured but very dull, and that he had few interests in life other than fishing, shooting and hunting, which he did conventionally year after year with the same friends and in the same places.

Eric Featherstone hated change of any sort; to Violet it became the breath of life.

She wanted something new to stimulate her, something fresh about which she could be enthusiastic, eager and excited, something novel over which she could argue and take sides.

Anything that was ordinary and commonplace began to bore her, and it was not long before people came into the same category.

She did not understand that her restlessness was in part due to the fact that she had an active and capable brain which was seldom exercised amongst the friends and acquaintances of her own particular world.

In Society no woman was required to be clever, and even wit in a lady was slightly suspect; and though Violet managed by sheer personality to become a law unto herself, she could not create companions of her own sex with whom she could share her intelligence.

Gradually her life began to be spent more and more amongst men. She found in love affairs the thrill she needed, the excitement she craved. It gave her a sense of power to know that a man was her abject slave, that men would follow wherever she might lead them.

Clever and intelligent in other walks of life, they would become, when they were with her, as shy and awkward as schoolboys.

She became more and more masterful, more and more autocratic. She made almost insatiable demands on those who loved her, merely to see if her wishes would be obeyed.

But she found that even love could become wearisome, even lovers could be as boring as ordinary men; so still she craved new and fresh people, new and fresh sensations.

A hundred times she thought herself in love, a hundred times she knew she had been mistaken. Then she met Robert Stanford.

The attraction between them was magnetic and instantaneous, and even as Violet was aware that this tall, broad-shouldered man was to mean something in her life, she was also aware that she had met her master.

Here was a man who was not going to be so easy to lead or to drive, here was a man who was not to be conquered but would be a conqueror.

So because for the first time Violet had met someone whom she could admire and look up to, she fell completely and abjectly in love.

She was clever enough not to let Sir Robert know it. She realized that in some ways he was not unlike herself. He had had too much, things had fallen into his lap too easily.

If he wanted anything, he had just to put out his hand and take it; and so she remained elusive and only she knew how hard at times it was to be that where Robert was concerned.

He was ridiculously good-looking, she thought, looking at him now from under her eyelashes when, having ordered the dinner and turned over the pages of the big wine list, he chose the wines with care.

There was to be a special Spanish sherry with the soup, a light German wine with the fish, claret from Bordeaux with the game and champagne to follow.

The cellar at the *Hôtel de Paris* was as famous as was its cuisine. François Blanc had not forgotten that a man who has dined and wined well makes a better gambler from the Casino's viewpoint than one who is frugal and therefore inclined to be cautious.

"And now," Sir Robert said, turning to his guests, "tell me all the local gossip. I drove over to Nice today and therefore I am out of touch with the latest excitements."

"I don't believe there are any," Lady Violet replied. "Have you heard anything, Arthur?"

Lord Drayton shook his head.

"I have entered myself for the pigeon shooting contest tomorrow afternoon, and find to my chagrin that they are offering 10 to 1 against my chances. It is very humiliating for a man who believed himself to be a good shot."

Lady Violet laughed.

"Oh, poor Arthur! But I should feel furious, not humiliated, and should make up my mind to win just to spite all the popular favourites."

"It is those Austrian sportsmen," he grumbled. "They are too good for most of us."

"Do you mean to say that nothing has happened while I have been away?" Sir Robert enquired. "No new arrival to cause a sensation, no . . . ?"

He stopped in the middle of the sentence. His eyes were turned towards the far end of the room. Because of the expression on his face both Lady Violet and Lord Drayton looked in the same direction. Other people were doing the same thing.

Two women had come in and were at that moment being led by Alfonse across the room to a table in the far corner. Sir Robert had noticed that it was about the only table left empty in the whole dining-room.

It was a table for two by the window, the heavy satin curtains forming a background for the simple white flowers with which the table was decorated.

It was the furthest table from the door and to reach it the two women must cross the full length of the room and endure the stares of everyone present.

It was almost impossible not to stare, however well-bred, however disinterested in strangers one might be, for the two women were a very arresting sight. The elder, obviously the chaperone of the one that followed, was tall and distinguished in appearance.

She held herself superbly and moved as if she were alone in her own drawing-room and no-one else were present. In a dress of deep purple velvet with an almost regal appearance, she wore a cap of velvet ribbon and real lace over her grey hair.

But no-one wasted a second glance on the older woman, it was the younger at whom everyone looked and continued to look until she had reached her table.

Thin, slender and very young, there was something extraordinarily arresting in her exquisite oval face and huge dark eyes. But perhaps it was not her face which first attracted attention.

Her golden hair seemed to catch the light from the gas-lit chandeliers and hold it in the smooth waves which, falling from a centre parting, hid her ears and was swept up into a great golden chignon at the back of her head. It almost appeared as if the golden brilliance of her head was too heavy for her graceful neck.

There was something lovely, young and untouched about her as she walked through the centre of the room, her face very pale, indeed almost as white as the ivory of her shoulders which rose from her low-cut dress.

And her dress was surprising too, for it was all grey —grey gauze sweeping out over vast petticoats of frilled satin, the flounces and frills caught back into the slightest suspicions of a bustle, as was the latest fashion.

All in grey, she seemed to move like a ghost across the room; and as she drew level with Sir Robert's table, he could see that, wreathing her hair, where other women would have worn flowers, were the softest grey velvet leaves almost like shadows among the dancing gold.

She looked neither to right nor left, until she reached

the table, where the older woman seated herself and waiters hurried to draw in their chairs.

Lady Violet gave a little sigh.

"Her pearls, Robert! Did you see her pearls?"

Sir Robert felt as if Lady Violet's voice brought him back from a great distance.

He had been looking at Mistral's face, remembering how, very early that morning, he had seen that same exquisite little nose silhouetted against the sunlight. He was remembering the expression in those dark eyes when he had sensed that she was praying.

He knew the way her lips curved when she smiled, he knew the exquisite grace with which she lifted her chin and the way her eyelashes would suddenly appear long and dark against her cheeks. But he had not known that her hair was golden.

Somehow he had thought it would be dark in keeping perhaps with the shadows of the grey hood which had hidden it from him when they talked together as the night slipped away.

But it was golden—golden as the sun itself which had seemed to come at her bidding from behind the mountains to awaken the sea. And now, as he looked at her, he thought that she made every other woman in the room seem tarnished.

There was something in her very simplicity, in the sombre colour of her dress, in the purity of her white shoulders which dimmed even the sparkle of jewels and the gilded splendour of the room itself.

"Did you see them, Robert?" Lady Violet insisted, and he realized that he had not answered her and she was waiting for his reply.

With an effort he took his eyes from Mistral to look at the woman at his side. He had never realized before, he thought, how old Violet sometimes looked.

He always thought of her as being so young—younger

than himself—but now at this moment he could see that middle-age was not far away.

She was waiting for him to answer.

"Her pearls," he replied. "No, was she wearing any?"

"Oh, Robert, how like a man! Of course she was wearing pearls, and such pearls! I have never seen anything like them. They were grey."

"Nonsense!" Sir Robert said. "It must have been the reflection of her dress."

He looked across towards the end of the room, but though he could see Mistral's golden hair, it was too far away for him to see either the details of her jewellery or the expression on her face.

"But they were, I tell you," Lady Violet insisted. "You saw them, Arthur, I am sure."

"She is a beauty if ever there was one," Lord Drayton replied. "We will find out who she is. Here, waiter."

He beckoned a waiter to his side. "Tell Alfonse I wish to speak to him."

*"Oui, Monsieur."*

The waiter hurried towards the *Maître d'Hôtel;* but it seemed as if other people had the same idea, for Alfonse, who knew everything and everybody, was very much in demand at other tables. It was some time before he was able to obey Lord Drayton's request.

"You wish to speak to me, m'lord?" he said when at length he reached their table.

"Who is she, Alfonse?"

"The young lady in grey?"

Alfonse queried with the air of one who is not mistaken in what he assumes.

"Of course! Is there any other woman of consequence in the room tonight?"

"She is registered, m'lord, as *Mademoiselle Fantôme;* but I understand that her Aunt, the lady who accompanies her, is travelling incognito."

72

"Incognito indeed! Then who is she? You know everyone, Alfonse," Lord Drayton said.

"I regret, m'lord, that for once I am at a loss. I have never seen either lady before in the whole of my life, I am certain of that."

"Then they cannot have been to many places," Lady Violet said, "for Alfonse has been everywhere and seen everyone, haven't you, Alfonse?"

Alfonse bowed, delighted. It was the kind of flattery he most enjoyed.

"You are very kind, m'lady. It is with the deepest regret that I cannot gratify your curiosity and, if I may say so, that of the majority of my patrons here this evening. The young lady has caused a sensation."

"She has indeed," Lady Violet said. "That was just what you were asking for, Robert, wasn't it? What a good thing you were here tonight, for if we had told you about it you would not have believed us! It is not often one can cause a sensation in Monte Carlo, isn't that true, Alfonse?"

"It is indeed true, m'lady. We have, if I may be permitted to say so, a profusion of beautiful women."

He bowed and would have made his apologies when another waiter appeared and whispered in his ear.

"Go and tell them as little as you have told us," Lord Drayton said. "I am disappointed in you, Alfonse. I thought you were infallible."

"I am desolated to lose my reputation," Alfonse said.

He glided away towards the occupants of the other table who had requested his presence.

"Her pearls are grey, I tell you," Lady Violet said when he had gone.

Lord Drayton put his eyeglass into his eye, looked towards Mistral, then let it drop.

"I don't believe there are such things."

"Will you bet on it?" Lady Violet enquired.

73

He shook his head.

"Where jewellery is concerned, you are betting on a certainty. I shan't give you the satisfaction of winning any money. Besides, the Casino has first call on it. I did rather well last night and it's only fair they should get a chance to take it off me tonight."

"Are you going to the Concert?" Violet asked.

Lord Drayton shook his head.

"I hate music."

"Well, Robert and I will go for a short while," Lady Violet said, "and then, if it proves boring, we will join you in the gambling-rooms. I doubt if we shall stay long, sopranos invariably give me a headache, they are so noisy."

"I find *trente-et-quarante* much more soothing," Lord Drayton replied.

If they were blasé about the Italian singer, to Mistral it was a moment of entrancement when her voice soared out high and clear under the painted ceiling of the Concert Room, and even the fashionable audience seemed to hold their breath as they listened.

It was like being transported to a new world, she thought, a world of colour and sound, a world she had never known existed, although she had loved to listen to the Nuns singing in the Chapel at the Convent.

But how different this was!

The distinguished company glittering and sparkling with jewels, the uncurtained windows opening out into the scented darkness, the large orchestra playing as Mistral had never heard music played before, and then the magic of a voice rising and falling, seeming in its very loveliness to draw the hearts of those who listened.

When the concert ended, Mistral sat for a moment in silence as the applause broke out around her, and the face she turned to Emilie was alive with emotion.

"It was so lovely, Aunt Emilie," she said, "I feel

74

as if I could cry and laugh both at the same time. I never knew that music could make one feel like this."

Emilie glanced at her sharply. She had not expected that Mistral would be so temperamental. There was no doubt from her shining eyes and parted lips that the music had excited her.

She had thought that Mistral would be subdued and passionless after the long years in the Convent, but it seemed that her feelings were easily aroused. In that way lay danger. Deliberately Emilie stifled a yawn.

"Concerts are usually somewhat fatiguing," she said, "as you will doubtless find out in time. You have a lot to learn, dear child."

Her tone was crushing, and a little of the ecstasy died from Mistral's face.

The audience were leaving their seats. Emilie rose, but deliberately took a long time to arrange her lace scarf around her shoulders so that she and Mistral were almost the last to leave the Concert Hall.

"I think we will look in at the gaming-rooms," she said as they came out into the wide corridor.

"Oh, Aunt Emilie, I did hope you would suggest it. For a moment I was terribly afraid that we were going back to the Hotel."

"We will not stay long," Emilie said crushingly.

She led the way to where an attendant in uniform was admitting people through a glass door. Almost on tiptoe with excitement Mistral followed her and then at last they were in the gambling-rooms.

She had a first impression of hundreds of lighted chandeliers, of massive pillars with capitals of gold, of paintings which upon a golden background depicted enormous groups of Goddesses and Cupids, of mosaics and carvings, statues and palms.

It was all so overwhelming that she was dazzled and bewildered.

There was little noise—only the low murmur of voices, the clink of gold and silver, the click-clack of a small ball whizzing round a huge wheel of polished brass.

There were seven gaming-tables, Mistral saw, covered in green cloth; those for roulette were quite flat, their edges protected with leather. At these the Croupiers with their long rakes spoke in level, unemotional tones:

*"Messieurs et Mesdames, faites vos jeux!"*

*"Rien ne va plus!"*

Each table had attracted a little crowd, the majority of the players watching the play with immobile faces so that it was difficult to tell whether they were winning or losing, or whether indeed they were playing at all.

Emilie passed by several tables and came at last to one at the far end of the room. She watched the play for some minutes and then suddenly a woman who had been seated rose and, gathering up what remained of a pile of gold louis, left the table.

The Croupier glanced at Emilie who was standing just behind the empty chair. For a moment she hesitated, but almost as if she were hypnotized against her will she sat down at the table.

She passed a bank-note, for what seemed to Mistral a large sum, towards the Croupier and changed it for gold. With fascinated eyes Mistral watched her Aunt place several louis on *impair*. Emilie lost her first stake and the second; the third time she won.

Mistral wanted to give a little cry of joy, but she was too frightened of being snubbed and could only stand silent with wide, excited eyes behind her Aunt's chair. A woman on the other side of Emilie rose.

She was small and very old and she seemed to stumble a little so that instinctively Mistral put out a hand to help her.

"Thank you, my dear, you are very kind," she said,

76

speaking French with a foreign accent. "Let me take your arm . . . I would be grateful if you will help me to the door. It is difficult for me to see."

Mistral offered her arm and, as she did so, she was aware that the little woman was almost blinded by the tears in her eyes.

"Oh, you are unhappy!" Mistral exclaimed.

"Yes, I am unhappy," the woman answered, "because I have lost! I have lost all my money! Always it is the same, I lose, yes, lose everything."

"But that is terrible," Mistral said. "What will you do?"

"I will go home, my dear. You are kind to help me."

The tone of the old lady's voice was piteous and Mistral felt her heart contract at so much suffering.

Slowly, with the blue-veined, withered hand trembling on Mistral's arm, they reached the outside door. By now the tears were running down the wrinkled cheeks, though the old lady made no attempt to wipe them away.

"But I cannot let you go like this, Madame," Mistral said. "It is so terrible for you to lose everything. What will you do?"

But before she was answered, a liveried footman who was waiting outside the open door of the Casino came forward.

"The carriage is here, Madame," he said.

"There is someone to take you home then?" Mistral said in relief.

She had half expected that, having no money, the poor old lady would have to walk destitute in the street.

"Yes, but I have to go home," the old lady said. "I have lost everything! How unhappy I am!"

"Please do not cry!" Mistral pleaded, wondering if she dared wipe the tears from the old woman's face.

But before she could do so, there was the sound of

horses' hoofs outside, a carriage drew up at the door, a footman hurried forward to offer the old lady his arm.

"Thank you, my dear, thank you," she said to Mistral. "You have been very kind."

She let the footman help her down the steps, the tears still filling her eyes; and then, as she watched her go, Mistral was startled by a voice from behind her.

"Surely you are not leaving?" someone asked.

Mistral turned swiftly to find Sir Robert at her side.

"No, I am not leaving; but that poor old woman, she has lost everything. What can one do to help her?"

Sir Robert smiled.

"You need not distress yourself unduly. That is Countess Kisselev. She is an habitué here. She comes regularly for the winter months. She gambles so unrestrainedly that her grandsons allow her only so many louis a day and when she has lost them she has to go home."

"But she was crying," Mistral said in astonishment.

"She always cries when she loses," Sir Robert said. "I assure you she is a very wealthy woman, but she cannot resist the lure of the Casino."

Mistral laughed.

"She deceived me completely. She looked so miserable that if I had any money I would have given it to her. It is lucky that I am penniless."

"Have you lost it already?" Sir Robert asked.

As he spoke, a carriage drove up at the doorway. He put his hand on Mistral's arm.

"Come this way quickly," he said insistently.

She let him lead her a little way down a passage into a small reading-room which was deserted.

"Why have you brought me here?" she asked.

"I was afraid someone might come and interrupt us," he said. "I want to talk to you."

"But I must not stay," Mistral said quickly. "I must

go back to my Aunt. She is playing at one of the tables."

"Then she won't miss you for a moment or two."

"If she saw us talking together, she might ask how we met," Mistral said anxiously.

"She won't see us," Sir Robert said reassuringly. "I will keep you but a moment. Tell me how you are enjoying yourself."

"I saw you at dinner," Mistral replied. "You had friends with you. Everyone in the dining-room seemed to be with friends. It made me feel a little lonely."

"I don't think you need have felt envious of anyone tonight," Sir Robert said, "for everyone was envying you."

"Envying me?" Mistral asked in astonishment. "But why?"

"For your youth and beauty," Sir Robert answered, "and the women were of course all envying you your necklace."

Mistral's fingers went up to the pearls round her neck. They were grey, Sir Robert noticed, a strange filmy grey like the inside of an oyster shell. He had never seen pearls like them, they were astounding.

"They were my Mother's," Mistral said quietly. "Aunt Emilie gave them to me tonight and said I might wear them. I have never had anything of my Mother's before, but . . . I wish they weren't grey."

"They are unique, magnificent," Sir Robert said. "I should not think there is another necklace like it in the whole world. Your Mother must have been a very wealthy woman to possess such wonderful jewels."

"No, she was . . ." Mistral began impulsively, then stopped, seeming to bite back the very words from her lips. "You must not ask me questions. Aunt Emilie would be very angry! And now . . . I must go."

"Don't go," Sir Robert said. "I have told you that

79

the women were envying you tonight, but wouldn't you like to know what the men were thinking?"

"About me?" Mistral enquired innocently.

"But of course! Everyone was talking about you, and they were both thinking and saying that you were the most beautiful person they had ever seen in the whole of their lives."

Mistral's long lashes veiled her eyes and swept her cheeks, then she turned away.

"But you are not going," Sir Robert said desperately when he saw that was her intention. "Have I said something to offend you?"

"I think you are laughing at me," Mistral said in a very small voice.

"I promise I was doing nothing of the sort," Sir Robert answered. "I was speaking the truth. Don't you realize, you ridiculous child, how lovely you are?"

She looked up at him then and he saw the colour rise in her cheeks.

"Nobody has ever told me so," she said after a moment.

"But they must have done," Sir Robert protested. "You must have met men sometimes—even in your Convent."

Mistral smiled, and there was a hint of mischief in her eyes.

"Yes, indeed, I have met men before, but they were either the Priests, who came to perform the services at the Convent, or the parents of the other pupils, who visited us once a year on prize-giving day."

"And they did not tell you you were beautiful?" Sir Robert enquired.

"They did not, and therefore I think you must be mistaken."

"On the contrary, I am merely in a better position

to judge than they. Shall I tell you how beautiful you are?"

His voice was low and unexpectedly deep. Mistral's eyes dropped before his and once again she turned towards the door.

"I must go," she said. "Please, please do not keep me."

There was no mistaking her determination this time to escape him, but he reached out and caught her hand, drawing her flying feet to a standstill and holding her fingers in his.

"Promise me one thing before you go—that I may see you again?"

"I can promise nothing," Mistral replied. "You do not understand. Aunt Emilie would be very angry indeed if she found out that I had spoken to anyone."

"Don't let her bully you," Sir Robert said.

"But I must do what she wants," Mistral protested. "She is my Aunt, besides I am . . . a little frightened of her, I think."

"If you want me, you know where to find me," Sir Robert said.

He bent his head and kissed her hand. The skin was soft and cool.

Then he had a quick impression of surprise in her eyes, of the colour rising once again in her cheeks, before with a sudden flurry and rustle of the flounces of her gown she was gone. Sir Robert made no attempt to follow her.

Instead, for several moments he walked up and down the little reading-room.

When he looked up, it was to see Lord Drayton standing in the doorway.

"What on earth are you doing here, Robert?" he asked. "I have been looking for you everywhere. Come and have a drink. I have lost a packet. I shall try my luck again later."

"A drink is what I need," Sir Robert answered.

"Has Violet gone home?" Lord Drayton enquired.

Sir Robert nodded.

"She would listen to that damned opera singer and music always gives her a headache."

"It would be cheaper to have a headache than to lose what I have lost in the meantime," Lord Drayton remarked.

He led the way across the gambling-room to the bar. Mistral, standing beside Emilie's chair, saw them go.

She thought how tall Sir Robert looked, how he stood out amongst the other men in the Casino; then with a feeling of guilt she turned her attention to the pile of louis growing steadily bigger in front of Emilie.

A man strolled up to the other side of the table. He stood watching the play.

He was young, dark and exceedingly handsome, with eyes which seemed to be permanently amused at what they saw. After a moment he placed a pile of louis on number twenty-one.

'Rien ne va plus!" the Croupier intoned.

The ball spun round and round. There was no other sound.

"Vingt-et-un, rouge et impair!"

The young man laughed as his very considerable winnings were pushed towards him, then he flung down five louis for the Croupier.

"Merci, Monsieur. Vous avez de la chance!"

"J'ai toujours de la bonne fortune."

There was something irresistibly gay both in his bearing and in his voice. He strolled away and Mistral suddenly realized that she was not the only person who had been watching the lucky stranger. Emilie's eyes were on him, too.

Suddenly she pushed back her chair a little and called an attendant.

"Who is the gentleman who won just now?" she asked.

"That is His Serene Highness Prince Nikolai, Madame."

"Prince Nikolai!" Emilie repeated softly.

*"Oui, Madame."*

Emilie pushed the pile of louis she had won into her reticule and got to her feet.

"Come along, Mistral," she said impatiently, and Mistral, wondering at her Aunt's air of determination and hurry, followed her.

# 5

A covered passageway had been added this year from the Villa Shalimar to the Villa Mimosa. Shalimar had been built three years previously and sold, as soon as it was finished, to the Rajah of Jehangar.

It was an enormous, pretentious building, dazzling white, which commanded from its position high up on the hill above Monte Carlo a magnificent view of the town below and the sea beyond.

Large though it was, the Rajah had found himself the previous year cramped for space when he had accommodated not only his official staff with its crowd of Aides-de-Camp, Secretaries, Major-domos and their personal attendants, but also the lady of his choice, who invariably accompanied him on his annual visits to Monte Carlo.

And so at great expense the Rajah purchased the Villa Mimosa and with some architectural ingenuity, for the Villas were on different levels, had it joined to the Villa Shalimar.

The Villa Mimosa this year housed Miss Stella Style. She was large, blonde, and extremely decorative.

The Rajah had seen her in the chorus of one of the big London theatres and had lost his heart from the moment she swept on to the stage with her fair hair hanging loose over her naked shoulders.

The Rajah had pursued his usual and invariably successful method of wooing.

He sent Stella a basket of orchids which required two attendants to carry it into the already over-crowded dressing-room she shared with a dozen other girls, and when she had recovered sufficiently from her astonishment to examine the basket more closely, she found a diamond bracelet concealed among the blooms and a note from the Rajah asking her out to supper.

As Crissie pointed out, the Rajah's invitation could not have come at a better time. Stella agreed with her, of course, for she invariably agreed with Crissie, but she did think it was unnecessary to have too much emphasis laid on the fact that her admirers were getting fewer and that she was finding it increasingly difficult to keep them interested.

This, as Crissie also told her not for the first time, was due entirely to her own laziness. Stella at twenty-seven was as pretty as she had been at seventeen.

Her looks had never been anything but of the pink and white china doll variety, which in London was too commonplace to cause much comment, but which abroad proved almost sensational. Her figure was perfect, although slightly on the large side, which fortunately appeared at the moment to be on the verge of becoming fashionable.

And her hair, although it owed much of the brilliance of its colour to a skillful coiffeur in Wardour Street, was nevertheless long and luxuriant enough to ensure its being one of the assets which kept her on the pay-roll of the more popular West-end theatres.

Stella was lazy; and if Crissie bewailed the fact once, she bewailed it over a dozen times a day.

Sometimes she felt as if she could strike Stella for her good-humoured stupidity, for the smile which was her invariable response to the most acid criticism, for the carefree, unworried manner in which she invariably received the information that yet another admirer had departed or been filched away from her by a more assiduous rival.

A conversation between the sisters a week before the Rajah appeared so providentially was typical of a hundred others.

"You haven't had a flower of any sort for over a fortnight," Crissie had said. "Not even a dead daisy has turned up with your name on it. What's happened to young Lord Ripon? Is he out of town?"

"I don't think so," Stella replied. "Dilly said she was supping with him last night after the show."

"So Dilly's got him, has she?" Crissie said, her voice hard and bitter. "Why did you let her take him? She set her cap at him from the moment he set foot inside the Stage Door."

"She can have him," Stella answered, yawning a little. "He was a bore anyway, always talking about racing. I never did care for horses."

"But you could pretend, couldn't you?" Crissie asked. Stella laughed.

"I did try, but I got their anatomy all muddled up. Funny things, horses, they have different names from us for what appears to me to be a very similar part of the body. . . ."

"Oh, damn the horses!" Crissie stamped her foot. "It's his lordship I'm thinking about. He's rich, Stella, rich and generous. But what have you got out of it I'd like to know! A brooch that won't fetch more than ten pounds, gloves that you didn't want and half a dozen boxes of chocolates. Chocolates, I ask you!"

"They're good ones at any rate," Stella remarked good-humouredly. "Why don't you have one?"

But Crissie had stamped her foot and nagged at Stella until the latter fell asleep still with a smile on her lips. Nothing seemed to perturb Stella's good humour and she had learned long ago not to listen to Crissie when she was annoyed.

Sometimes after one of these scenes Crissie would look at herself in the mirror and wonder why Providence in the creating of herself and Stella had been so cruel.

For cruel it was to give Crissie a shrewd, quick brain with a deformed hunch-backed body and to dole out to Stella a beautiful body and no brain whatsoever.

"If only I could look like Stella," Crissie would think. "I could get anywhere . . . anywhere."

Instead the role she had to play was to propel, push and nag the lazy, unambitious Stella into taking advantage of her very obvious attractions.

But time and time again Crissie's plans came to nothing simply through Stella's natural inertia. If Crissie had been born rapacious, Stella had been born happy. Whatever happened, however much they were up against it, Stella remained the same.

She simply did not know the meaning of the word "envy" and she had never been jealous of anyone in her life. She had no ambitions whatsoever, and when she was out of a job it was doubtful if she could have ever had the sense to find another had it not been for Crissie.

It was Crissie who made her work, Crissie who made her take trouble over her appearance, who reminded her to speak with a refined accent, who made her accept invitations.

It was even Crissie who forced Stella into keeping appointments with her various admirers who, having viewed her through their opera glasses from the front of the house, came hurrying round to the Stage Door when the performance was ended. It was Crissie who answered their notes, who wrote and thanked them for their flowers; and when there were a number of them, it was Crissie who remembered which was which.

Not that Stella did not like having admirers; she did. She liked everybody!

She liked the smart, well-turned out gentlemen with their private hansoms who waited for her at the Stage Door, but she liked equally well the men who moved the scenery, the boys who carried up the bouquets of flowers, the members of the orchestra and even the disagreeable, wizened old door-keeper for whom nobody else had a good word.

It was not only men who found a place in her affections. She liked the girls with whom she acted, the wardrobe mistress, the dressers, the chars who cleaned out the theatre, and the smart, fluffy little programme sellers who would sometimes bring messages back-stage.

Stella liked them all; in fact, as Crissie used to say with exasperation, she would like the Devil himself if he turned up at the theatre.

Long ago Crissie had really learned that it was useless to lecture Stella, but she really could not help doing it continually and unceasingly.

From the moment the sisters got up in the morning to the moment they went to bed at night Crissie's high, sharp, bitter voice would be nattering at Stella like the yapping of a toy terrier. But nothing she said seemed to have the slightest effect.

Stella would give away her week's wages without a second thought as to how she and Crissie would manage the following week.

Stella would lend her best evening gown, her slippers, her gloves or her mantle to any chorus girl who told her a hard-luck story about an invitation from a Duke and nothing to wear if she accepted it.

Stella found it impossible to pass a beggar in the street or a child looking into a sweet shop without opening her purse.

And so Crissie had to be ceaselessly protecting not only Stella's interests but her own, for they rose and fell together.

Few people believed they were sisters; indeed, whenever Stella had a gentleman friend with a proprietary interest in her affairs, Crissie was invariably introduced as "my dresser", a pretence which never lasted long because Stella was too lazy to keep it up and inevitably gave the game away.

Crissie was well aware that in appearance she was no asset to Stella. Men were inclined to look slightly disgusted or uncomfortable when they learned that this small, wizened creature was Stella's sister, and it made them even more embarrassed when they learned that there were only two years difference in age between the girls.

"You're not to tell him who I am," Crissie would say to Stella time and time again.

"Why not?" Stella would reply. "I'm not ashamed of you, Crissie. You're worth fifty of me."

In her heart of hearts Crissie agreed with her; but men were not interested in brains, not the type of men they met anyway; and so they went on year after year, Crissie making plans for Stella and Stella destroying them or making them unworkable from the very beginning by her sheer good-humoured laziness.

The appearance of the Rajah of Jehangar was an unprecedented piece of good fortune.

Bad luck had seemed to haunt Stella for months. A show at the Gaiety Theatre, in which she had had a real chance to show her physical attractions, closed down after a month.

There had been some delay before she was re-engaged at Daly's; and then, three weeks after they had opened, she went down with such a bad cold and a high temperature that Crissie was forced to keep her at home.

This was a double tragedy, for just before Stella fell ill she had attracted the attention of a South African millionaire who was visiting London. His affections were not seriously engaged, and when she failed to appear at a supper party he was giving for her, he speedily transferred his attention to one of the other girls in her act.

There were Doctors' bills, medicines and special food to be paid for, and the rent was overdue by several weeks before Stella went back to the theatre again.

The only good effect of her illness was that it seemed to make her prettier than she had been before. At times she was almost too buxom. As Crissie said when she was angry, she looked and behaved like "a fat cow".

With her face a little thinner and her waist several inches smaller from enforced starvation Stella appeared more than usually dazzling.

The Rajah thought so, anyway. To Crissie it was a miracle that, from having been in dirty, smoky London, hard-up and in debt six weeks ago, they should now find themselves in the sunshine at Monte Carlo, living in luxurious surroundings which even exceeded her wildest dreams.

Many people would have found the Villa Mimosa rather vulgar, but to Crissie it was a veritable fairyland. The softness of the beds, the curtains of silk and brocade, the thick pile of the carpets, the ornate, gaudy decorations were to Crissie all objects of unparalleled beauty.

Stella liked them too, but then Crissie had known her like their lodgings in a back room in Manchester or a dingy attic overlooking the docks at Liverpool. She had long ago ceased to pay much attention to Stella's opinion about anything.

"He's crazy about you, that's certain sure," she said now.

She was standing in the window of their sitting-room at the Villa Mimosa, her hunched back sharply silhouetted against the blue sky outside.

Stella, lying on the sofa, reading a yellow-backed novel and with a huge box of chocolates at her side, did not answer. Crissie waited for a moment, then turned towards her.

"Did you hear what I said?" she asked.

Stella looked up from her novel reluctantly. As she did so, she reached out her hand for another chocolate —a large one, ornamented with a crystallized violet on the top.

She was extremely pretty as she lay there, dressed in a pink satin gown which the Rajah had brought her in Paris. It threw a delicate flush over her white skin and brought into prominence the blue of her eyes.

It also accentuated very noticeably the curves of her figure, which seemed to Crissie to have grown even more pronounced during the last few days at the Villa.

"Stop eating chocolates and listen to me, Stella.

You'll be getting as fat as a porker if you go on like that. The food here is too rich."

"It's jolly good," Stella replied, "and I like François."

"He talks too much," Crissie snapped more from habit than conviction.

Like Stella she had discovered that François, who was Chef at the Villa, was an unfailing source of information about everything and everybody at Monte Carlo.

"He's promised to buy me some truffles when he goes into the town today," Stella remarked dreamily. "I adore truffles."

"Instead of thinking about food, listen to me," Crissie said. "The Rajah is crazy about you."

"You said that before."

"You didn't reply."

"It didn't seem to need a reply," Stella smiled. "We shouldn't be here if he wasn't fond of me."

"I know that," Crissie said. "People get crazy about you, Stella, but they don't stay crazy. If you lose the Rajah, I think I'll murder you with my own hands."

Stella laughed.

"Then you'd better start eating more and getting your strength up," she said. "Do you know how many women have stayed in this Villa before us?"

"I don't know and I don't care," Crissie answered.

"Well, François will tell you," Stella said. "He says the Rajah gets bored with women quicker than anyone he's ever met, and he's worked for several Rajahs and Maharajahs. He was telling me what they have to eat. Goodness, Crissie, you wouldn't believe that people could eat so much and yet be able to walk about on two legs."

"Stella, will you pay attention to what I'm saying to you?" Crissie asked, her voice almost ominously quiet.

"Go ahead, I'm all ears," Stella replied.

She selected another chocolate with care, this time one decorated with crystallized rose-leaves.

"This is our one chance," Crissie said, "and maybe our last—who knows?"

"Chance of what?" Stella asked, her mouth full.

"Of security, of being unafraid in the future, of knowing that whatever happens we shan't starve," Crissie said. "The Rajah is generous, Stella, there's never been a man like him, not in your life at any rate. Do you know how much that diamond necklace is worth, the one he bought you in Paris?"

"I've no idea."

Stella's voice was quite indifferent.

"Nearly a thousand pounds," Crissie said. "Think of it, Stella! A thousand pounds! Then there's the bracelet he sent you the first night and that brooch he gave you last week. I haven't had them valued yet, but the cash I've got safe. There's the bit left over from the dress-maker's bill, the discount I got at the hat shop and what you've brought back from the Casino—altogether four thousand and twenty francs."

"That reminds me," Stella remarked, "I want some money this afternoon. I've got to buy myself some perfume."

"Buy yourself!" Crissie ejaculated. "Are you mad? Ask the Rajah for what you want. He'll give it to you. If you think you're going to touch one penny of the money I've got safe, you've got another think coming. Ask him for your perfume and for a lot more things besides."

"He may say no!"

"Oh, do be sensible, Stella, for once. He likes you to ask for things. You're so stupid when a man's mad about you. He'd give you the moon if it was in his power to do so. And what do you do? You just sit there saying nothing, a silly smile on your face, when if you frowned he might bring you rubies or emeralds to make you look happy again."

"It seems so awful to take so much," Stella said simply.

Crissie gripped her chair until the knuckles showed white.

"So much!" she exclaimed. "When he's got millions! When in his Palace in India he has vaults filled with diamonds and pearls, gold and ivory! You're a fool, Stella! So much from a man like that! Why, if he draped you in diamonds from head to foot, he wouldn't notice the difference in his bank balance. Lord, but you make me sick!"

"All right, Crissie, I'll do my best," Stella said soothingly, but her voice was not very convincing.

Tense with emotion, Crissie got up from the chair and walked across to the window again. Suddenly she gave an exclamation.

"Listen, Stella, I've thought of something."

But Stella had already returned to her novel, and with an exclamation of anger Crissie walked across the room and snatched the book from her hands.

"Listen, I said!"

"Oh, Crissie, don't be so cross! I've said I will do my best, haven't I?"

"Your best is not good enough," Crissie replied angrily. "I tell you I've thought of something! You know that girl they're all talking about, the girl in grey with the wonderful pearls?"

"Do you mean 'the Ghost'?"

"Yes, that's the one! François told me that all Monte Carlo is gossiping about her."

"I'm not surprised," Stella said. "She's awfully pretty and she looks sort of different from other women. Of course, wearing grey like that makes her stand out,

93

but it isn't only that; there's something in her face . . .
I can't explain."

"And are her pearls as wonderful as François says?"

"I wouldn't know," Stella replied. "They're sort of
grey and dull compared with diamonds, but the Rajah
says he's never seen anything like them. I told him I
thought his were much finer."

"You would," Crissie remarked scornfully.

"Now what's wrong with that?" Stella enquired. "He
was as pleased as Punch that I admired something of
his."

"Those he wears are his State ones," Crissie said.
"You know as well as I do that he can't give them
away. But why shouldn't he buy some for you, why
shouldn't he buy those belonging to the ghost girl?"

"Buy her pearls for me?" Stella asked. "But I don't
like pearls. Besides, I don't expect she wants to sell
them."

"Stella! Stella! Do you want to drive me insane?"
Crissie cried, the expression on her face so wild that
Stella stared at her half alarmed. "Don't you understand? If you ask the Rajah for something really
valuable and he gives it to you, we're safe. François
says those pearls are worth a king's ransom."

"François knows everything!"

"Ask the Rajah to give the pearls to you as a present.
It doesn't matter, you poor numskull, if you like pearls
or you don't like them. You won't wear them, not after
we leave here at any rate; but when they're sold we
will be rich, both of us for ever."

"But supposing he says no?" Stella suggested.

"Is he likely to?" Crissie asked scornfully. "He's in
love with you and he'll want to show off. Put him on
his mettle, bet him that he won't have enough money
to buy them, and if he has, that he won't be able to get

94

them. That's the way to make him interested. Once you have got them, it won't matter to you how quickly he finds someone else."

Stella gave a little sigh.

"I see what you mean, Crissie," she said, "but it's awfully difficult . . . I mean, asking for something as expensive as that. You couldn't do it for me, could you? Tell him it's for my birthday or something?"

"And I suppose, looking into my lovely blue eyes, that he would promise me them at once!" Crissie retorted sarcastically. "Don't be a half-wit, Stella, you know you've got to choose the right moment for a thing like that. Use your brains for once, though Heaven knows you haven't got any and pick the right moment. It means everything to us. Promise me you will do your best."

"I'll try, Crissie," Stella said meekly. "What else did François say about that girl?"

"He said everyone was talking about her and trying to find out who she was. But the other woman who calls herself her Aunt was too clever, and so far they have no idea who they are or where they have come from. Even Alfonse of the *Hôtel de Paris* knows nothing—and that, François says, has never happened before."

"She looks nice," Stella said.

Crissie glanced at her quickly.

"Now don't you start thinking she's too nice for you to want anything that she has," she said. "I know the way your mind works. Before we know where we are, we will all feel sorry for her and say that she must keep her pearl necklace because it is the only one she has."

Stella laughed.

"You've got a poor opinion of me, Crissie."

"That's about the only sensible thing you have said for some time," Crissie replied; and marching out of the room, she slammed the door behind her.

Stella stretched her arms above her head and wished Crissie would not get so worked up about things.

She had always been the same. Perhaps it was because she had had an unhappy childhood. Stella could remember how unkind her Father and Mother had been to their elder daughter.

They had been acrobats, well spoken of in their profession and both good looking in their own way.

Crissie had been born after her Mother had had a fall. She said the rope was faulty, but her Father always said that it was her timing which was wrong, owing, perhaps, to her own unnatural heaviness.

But whatever it was, Crissie had been born three months early, weakly and malformed, and it was only the appearance of Stella two years later which had healed the wound to their parents' self-esteem at having produced anything so abnormal as their first child.

Stella had been a large, good-tempered baby. She smiled and chuckled her way through babyhood and from the moment she could toddle had been spoilt by everyone in the theatre.

It seemed inevitable that Crissie should be jealous of her young sister, but instead she had taken up a proprietory attitude. Stella was hers, to bully and protect, to tease and defend. If Stella did anything wrong, it was Crissie who took the blame. If Stella was scolded, Crissie would defend her pugnaciously.

Stella accepted Crissie's championship, as she accepted other tributes, with smiling good humour and an equanimity which made no complaint one way or another.

Stella, having finished stretching herself, was just about to start another Chapter of her novel when the door opened. Thinking it was Crissie returning, she turned her head and saw that instead of her sister it was the Rajah.

"Hullo!"

Both her voice and her smile were pleasant and flattering, and he crossed the room quickly to the sofa, taking her hand in his and covering it with kisses.

"I have been riding," he said, "or I should have come to see you earlier."

"You look very smart dressed like that," Stella said, and the Rajah's dark eyes lightened at the compliment.

He was a short, thin little man, and when they stood close to each other, his head barely reached to Stella's shoulder. Yet he was strong and wiry despite his over-luxurious way of living and the dissipations in which he indulged.

But no-one could live such a life for long, and in a few years he would be taking to drink and drugs to flog a depreciated vitality and a fading virility.

At the moment, however, the Rajah was young enough to gratify his sensual hedonism without thought of the future. There was a glint in his eyes as he looked down at Stella.

"Would you like to come and watch the pigeon-shooting this afternoon?" he asked.

"If you like," Stella replied. "Though I am not all that keen on guns; they make my head ache."

"Then we can go for a drive or—we can stay here."

There was a sudden fire in the Rajah's tone as he made the last suggestion.

"I don't mind what we do," Stella replied lazily.

"But I want you to mind," he answered quickly. "I want to do what pleases you. For my own part I am content when we are together. You look very beautiful today."

"That's because of the dress you gave me," Stella

97

said. "It came from Paris this morning. Do you like it? I'd better get up so that you can see it properly."

She made a movement as if to rise, but the Rajah stopped her, his hand against her shoulder.

"No, lie there," he said softly. "You look entrancing, a goddess reclining on a cloud."

"I'm so glad the cloud is a pretty substantial one," Stella laughed.

"No, no, do not laugh," the Rajah interrupted. "You are very beautiful. I am very much in love with you! More in love than I have been for a very long time . . . perhaps ever before."

Stella smiled sleepily at him, glad that she should be able to give so much pleasure. Then she remembered Crissie. With difficulty she found the right words.

"If you love me so much," she said at length, "would you like to prove it?"

For a moment the warmth seemed to vanish from the Rajah's eyes; then as he looked down into her eyes and at the fullness of her red lips, he seemed to surrender himself to a sudden impulse.

"I will prove my love any way you wish," he answered.

"It is something so difficult I don't believe you could do it," Stella said, remembering Crissie's instructions to put him on his mettle.

"There are few things I cannot do," the Rajah boasted vainly, and it seemed to Stella little foolishly.

"I am wondering if you could buy me the pearls belonging to that girl . . . the one they call 'the Ghost'."

Even as Stella said the words she wondered at her own audacity.

It was one thing to accept presents from people anxious to give them, and another thing to ask for something of tremendous value. Stella had never bothered about standards or having any rules to regulate her behaviour.

No-one had ever told her that she ought to have any, but while she thought it was kind and nice of people to give her things, yet she felt that to ask for something which hadn't been offered was greedy and rather indecent.

She felt hot and uncomfortable now at having to ask this kind little man for yet another present; and because she was embarrassed, because, as she phrased it in her own mind, it was a bit too much of a good thing when he had given her so much already, her conscience galvanized her into being unexpectedly demonstrative.

For perhaps the first time since she had known him Stella held out her arms spontaneously and as the Rajah bent towards her, she put them round his neck.

"If it's too much trouble, don't you bother about it," she whispered, half afraid that Crissie would overhear her.

The Rajah's arms closed round her almost fiercely.

"You shall have anything you want," she heard him say, "anything! You are beautiful, one of the most beautiful women I have ever seen. I will get those pearls for you whatever they cost. . . ."

It was when he was dressing for dinner that evening in the Villa Shalimar that the Rajah remembered his promise to Stella. He sent a valet for his Aide-de-Camp. The gentleman came hurriedly at the summons. He was in evening dress and carried a silk-lined opera cape over his arm.

"Are you going out?" the Rajah enquired.

"Your Highness informed me that you would not require my services this evening."

"No, of course not. I shall see you at the Casino, I presume?"

"I am not so certain," the Aide-de-Camp replied. "I am dining with a very charming lady."

The two men's eyes met and the Rajah gave a short laugh.

"Good hunting!" he said.

The Aide-de-Camp bowed.

"Your Highness is most kind."

"All the same, I did not send for you to enquire your plans for the evening. I wanted to ask you what you know about this girl who is causing such a stir."

*"Mademoiselle Fantôme?"* the Aide-de-Camp enquired.

"Exactly!"

"Very little, Your Highness. It appears that nothing is known about her."

"Everyone says the same," the Rajah remarked. "Strangely enough, I keep thinking that I have seen her chaperone somewhere before, the one they call *Madame Secret.* As you know, I have no memory for names but I seldom forget a face. I have met her or seen her somewhere, I am absolutely certain of that; and yet the exact moment eludes me. It is not often my memory is at fault."

"Indeed not! Your Highness's memory is astonishing."

"Doubtless it will come back to me," the Rajah said; "but you might make a few inquiries, discreetly, of course, and find out if they are in such prosperous circumstances as they appear. The Manager of the *Hôtel de Paris* is an old friend of mine. Tell him that I want all the information he can give me."

"Your Highness can rest assured that I will do my best. If the Manager fails," the Aide-de-Camp said reflectively, "I know someone who might help—a man called Dulton. He can ferret out most things—for a consideration, of course."

"I am not particularly concerned as to what it costs."

"I understand, Your Highness."

The Aide-de-Camp bowed himself from the room.

The Rajah took a last glance in the mirror. Tonight he was wearing an enormous ruby in the front of his turban. It was surrounded by diamonds and the jewels shone and glittered and were in strange contrast to the immaculate severity of his evening clothes cut by an English tailor.

The big leather jewel-case in which all his jewels were contained lay open on the dressing-table, and standing in the corner of the room, were the two "Keepers of the Jewels", men who guarded them day and night and who were ready to die in defence of what they guarded.

The Rajah glanced down at the velvet-lined cases. He took out a ruby ring and slipped it on to the little finger of his left hand.

Beside it was a sapphire of great beauty, not particularly dark in colour, but as it caught the light of the candelabra on the dressing-table, it reminded the Rajah for the moment of Stella's eyes. He took it out of its velvet case, turned it over in his fingers, stared at it and seemed about to put it in his pocket, then changed his mind.

He set it back in its case. It should be the pearls or nothing, he decided. It was a challenge he could not resist.

They would be expensive, but that did not concern him one way or another. It was a question of pride, of being able to obtain what might prove almost unobtainable.

After another glance in the mirror he was ready and, ignoring the low obeisance of his servants, he went from his bedroom and down the broad staircase which led to the hall.

Outside the carriage was waiting. Servants in red and white uniform flung open the door and assisted the Rajah into the cushioned comfort within the vehicle.

Then the footman sprang up on to the box and with the brake hard on the wheels the horses started off down the steep drive and along the few hundred yards of road which led to the entrance of the Villa Mimosa.

Stella was waiting for him. She was looking particularly attractive tonight in another Paris gown of green crêpe trimmed with lace and draperies of pale rose satin. Her hair fell from the back of her head in a dozen long curls and was garlanded with a wreath of roses sprinkled with tiny gems.

The perfume the Rajah had bought for her late that afternoon was pungent and intoxicating as she entered the coach beside him, and as the door closed, he lifted her hand to his mouth, his lips seeking out each finger.

"Where are we going for dinner?" Stella asked. "I'm very hungry."

The Rajah's teeth were for a moment hard against the ball of her thumb.

"I, too, am hungry for you!" he replied, then added in answer to her question: "I ordered a table at the *Hôtel de Paris*."

"I'm glad about that," Stella answered. "We had the most wonderful dinner there the night before last."

"Yes, we can eat well, and I thought at the same time that we might see the lady with the pearls."

" 'The Ghost'!" Stella exclaimed. "Everyone calls her 'the Ghost'."

"Who has told you that everyone does?" the Rajah asked.

"François," Stella answered simply.

"François?" the Rajah repeated and it was a question.

"Your Chef!"

The Rajah laughed.

"So my Chef is a gossip and he gossips with you!"

"He comes to see me in the morning," Stella explained, "to enquire what I should like to eat during the day. He says he is a great artiste and artistes always desire to please their patrons. When he is not talking about food, he talks about people."

"So it was François who made you desire the pearls belonging to 'the Ghost'?" the Rajah asked.

"No, it was . . ." Stella began, then stopped.

She realized suddenly that it would be unwise to tell the Rajah who had put the idea into her head. He did not like Crissie, she knew that. He thought that her deformity was ugly and that a hunchback in the house brought bad luck upon it.

No, it would be unwise to mention Crissie, especially when the Rajah was in such good humour and had promised that he would buy her the pearls belonging to "the Ghost".

To cover up the slip she had nearly made Stella put her hand on the Rajah's knee and bent her head down towards his shoulder.

"Why are you so kind to me?" she asked in a soft voice.

"Do you really want me to answer that question?" the Rajah enquired.

She saw the gleam in his eyes as they passed a gas lamp.

# 6

Mistral knelt in the little Chapel of Ste. Dévote.

It was over-shadowed by the deep ravine at the foot of which it was built, so that little light penetrated through the stained-glass windows, and inside the Church it was dim and dark save for the candles flickering in front of the Lady Chapel and the Sanctuary light hanging before the Altar.

There were but half a dozen people present for Benediction although it was the Feast of St. Joseph, and Mistral, saying the prayers that the Nuns had taught her, suddenly remembered Sir Robert's words, "There are few Saints in Monte Carlo."

She could hear quite clearly the humorous note in his voice, see the hint of laughter in his grey eyes as he looked down at her. How handsome he was!

It was funny, Mistral thought, but ever since that morning when they had met in the gardens she found him indissolubly linked in her mind with Ste. Dévote.

She had only to think of Ste. Dévote being carried across the sea from Corsica and instantly Sir Robert came to her mind too.

She had only to ask her Aunt if she could attend Early Mass, or walk down the steps which led to the great gorge which separated the sober town of Monaco from the frivolous town of Monte Carlo, for Sir Robert to be insistently in her thoughts.

She saw him practically every night in the distance; but as they had arranged at their first meeting, when they were in public they behaved as if they were complete strangers to one another.

Always he seemed to be with the same lady, the one whom people spoke of as Lady Violet and who had very beautiful chestnut hair. She was attractive, Mistral thought, though she must be nearly middle-aged.

But she could not be sure of this, for many people seemed old to Mistral at eighteen and she often chid herself for thinking people were older than they were.

But somehow she felt she was not mistaken about Lady Violet. Although the Englishwoman was smartly dressed and had undoubted attractions which made the men around her laugh at everything she said, there was something in the way she held herself, in the lines of her neck, in the sharpness of her jaw, or perhaps an occasional tiredness in her eyes which proclaimed the truth.

Mistral found herself watching for Sir Robert and Lady Violet.

When she entered the dining-room at the *Hôtel de Paris,* she would glance quickly at the table they nearly always occupied whenever they dined there. When she went on to the Casino with her Aunt, she knew that, while she stood watching the gamblers, there was only one person she really wanted to see.

She felt that, if she had been blindfolded, she would have known instantly when Sir Robert entered the rooms.

He had so much personality that he was outstanding even amongst the big cosmopolitan crowd thronging, moving about the tables.

There were men of every nationality—handsome, distinguished, aristocratic; and yet Mistral thought their faces seemed to have so little in them, to be so devoid of character. Sir Robert was different.

There was something noble in his face, something

resolute and strong which appeared to her to be lacking in other men. When he laughed, which was often when he was with Lady Violet, he looked young, yet at other times, when his face was in repose, he looked older and grave.

Mistral wondered if he were happy. She had the idea that something troubled him, but when she had those thoughts she rebuked herself for being imaginative.

Besides, Aunt Emilie would be annoyed if she knew how often she thought about Sir Robert.

Her prayers finished, Mistral rose and walked down the aisle. Jeanne was sitting waiting for her in a back pew.

She found it hard to kneel, for her rheumatism had been troubling her these past few days, and so, when they went to the Chapel together, she waited for Mistral at the back where she could sit unobserved.

Jeanne rose and joined Mistral and after crossing themselves with Holy Water they went through the porch into the bright sunshine.

For a moment Mistral's eyes were dazzled and she could only blink in the hot afternoon sunshine; then she was aware that someone was coming up the steps towards her and that waiting in the roadway was an open carriage. Before she had time to be sure to whom it belonged, Prince Nikolai stood beside her and had raised her hand to his lips.

"Your Aunt told me I should find you here, Mademoiselle," he said. "Will you permit me to take you for a drive before you return to the Hotel?"

"It is very kind of Your Serene Highness," Mistral said quietly.

There was a troubled note in her voice. She looked up at the Prince, at the smile on his lips, the excitement in his dark eyes which seemed to be scrutinizing her face—feature by feature; then she looked away.

The horses drawing the open carriage were magnificent. Jet black, they were prancing a little with impatience and tossing their long manes.

"Please come with me, Mademoiselle."

The Prince's words were humble, yet his voice was authoritative. Instinctively Mistral knew that he never for one moment anticipated that she would refuse him, and she wished she could do that very thing.

She would have liked to walk back alone with Jeanne, to enjoy the sunshine with that sense of well-being and peace which was always hers after she had been to Church.

But instead a very different programme awaited her and she was half afraid.

It was not that she did not like the Prince; she did, although his very impetuosity was at times rather frightening. But it was not really the Prince of whom she was scared, but of her Aunt's attitude towards him.

He was a part of some plan of Aunt Emilie's, Mistral was sure of that, and recently she had begun to be suspicious of and terrified by this plan, whatever it might be, which made her Aunt give her strange orders and which prevented her from behaving normally and ordinarily as might any other girl of her age.

Why, for instance, had Aunt Emilie said that she was to speak to no other man in Monte Carlo except the Prince? Why had she said that she must be particularly nice to His Serene Highness? Mistral shrank from the implications in that word 'nice'. She had indeed questioned her Aunt about it.

"What do you mean by 'nice'. Aunt Emilie?" she had asked in all seriousness.

"I mean you are to encourage him,' Emilie snapped.

"Encourage him to do what?" Mistral enquired.

Emilie opened her mouth to reply; then she looked

at Mistral and, seeing the enquiring innocence of her eyes, she was at a loss for words.

"Be pleasant to the Prince," she said hastily. "Make him feel that he is welcome in our company and that you like him."

"I do like him," Mistral said. "But why may I not be nice to anyone else, Aunt Emilie? There are other men who might like us to welcome them too."

As she spoke, she thought of Sir Robert; and she had not been prepared for the anger in her Aunt's raised voice or the darkness of her expression.

"There are no other men we want to welcome," Emilie said furiously. "Have I not made that clear already? It is Prince Nikolai with whom we are concerned. You will be nice to him and to no-one else. If you disobey me, I shall punish you! But I think you would be wise not to disobey my orders."

There was something so menacing in Emilie's expression that instinctively Mistral shrank away from her.

"I will do as you say, Aunt Emilie," she said and somehow managed to escape from the room and into the sanctuary of her own bedroom.

What did it all mean? And why was Prince Nikolai so especially favoured by Aunt Emilie?

It had begun on the very first night they had visited the Casino. Emilie had risen from the roulette table when Prince Nikolai walked away from it and had followed him.

Mistral was sure of that now, although at the time she thought she was mistaken and her Aunt was just promenading through the rooms aimlessly as other people did.

Then, as the Prince had paused, obviously undecided as to which table he would visit next, Aunt Emilie had fallen against him.

108

She said that her foot had caught in the carpet; but Mistral could see no reason why it should have done so at just that particular spot.

Aunt Emilie had stumbled and in doing so had caught at the Prince's arm as if for support, and the gold pieces that he held in his hand had been scattered over the floor.

People sprang forward from all sides to pick them up while Aunt Emilie apologized.

"You must forgive me, sir," she said. "I cannot apologize sufficiently for my clumsiness. My foot caught in the carpet and it was only by clinging on to you that I saved myself from falling. I am afaraid I am too old to fall easily."

"Pray do not mention it again, Madame," the Prince said courteously. "I am glad to have been of service."

A lackey held out a handful of louis.

"These are all I have managed to save, Your Serene Highness," he said. "I'm afraid some have been taken for luck."

The Prince laughed.

"Keep the rest yourself and I hope they bring you luck too."

The man was overcome.

"That is more than gracious of Your Serene Highness . . . I thank Your Serene Highness a thousand times."

Aunt Emilie's eyebrows were raised.

"Your Serene Highness!" she repeated. "But, of course, I can see the likeness now. You must be Prince Nikolai! I knew your Father many years ago. You are very like him."

"I thank you for the compliment," the Prince said. "I am one of my Father's most devoted admirers."

He glanced at Mistral standing a little behind her

Aunt, a silent spectator of all that was happening. Emilie had not hesitated.

"Will Your Serene Highness permit me to present my niece?" she enquired, and added to Mistral: "This is the son of the Grand Duke Ivan of Russia, dear. When I came here many years ago, the Grand Duke was the only distinguished visitor to the Principality— a very handsome man and his son takes after him."

Mistral curtsied. The Prince kissed her hand, and having looked once into her dark eyes, he looked again. Eagerly he turned to Emilie.

"Will you permit me to offer you, Madame, and your niece, a little supper? My Father would wish me to be courteous to an old friend of his."

That was how it had all begun, Mistral thought, and now day after day it seemed to her as if she became more involved in this strange web which Emilie was weaving around the Prince and herself.

There was nothing she could say, nothing she could do except obey her Aunt; and now standing at the top of the Chapel steps, she was sure that this tête-à-tête with the Prince, unchaperoned, had been planned by Emilie.

It was by no means a spontaneous invitation on the Prince's part to invite her to drive with him—whether he knew it or not—and somehow it took all the pleasures from everything to know that it was all planned, all part of some strange puzzle to which only her Aunt held the key.

Once again she longed to obey an inner impulse and refuse the Prince's invitation and say that she would walk home with Jeanne; but she knew, even as she thought of it, that it was impossible.

Even when she was not there, Aunt Emilie's presence could be felt; even though they were not spoken aloud, her orders were clear and unchallengeable.

"I will walk home, Mademoiselle," Jeanne said quietly, and Mistral was sure that she, too, had had her instructions.

"Very well, Jeanne," she said, and without looking at the Prince she walked down the steps of the Chapel.

A footman in gorgeous livery assisted her into the carriage. He had a strange face, Mistral thought, with almond-shaped eyes and high cheek-bones.

As he shut the door behind the Prince and climbed up on the box, Mistral said:

"What nationality is your footman? He looks like a Chinese."

"Actually he is a Russian," the Prince replied, "but he was born on the borders of Siberia and Tibet. He has been my personal servant since I was a babe. I call him my Keeper, for he guards me both day and night. In the daytime he is always in attendance on me, and at night he sleeps on the threshold of my room. No harm can come to me when Potoc is about."

"How romantic it all sounds!" Mistral exclaimed.

The Prince laughed.

"But like romance it can sometimes be terribly tiresome! You will agree with me because you, too, have a keeper!"

"I?"

Mistral looked towards him in surprise.

"Yes, you," the Prince replied. "Your Aunt is a dragon. She frightens me most terribly."

"I too, am frightened of Aunt Emilie," Mistral confessed, "but I cannot see why you should be frightened of her. She is always very nice to you."

"I think that is what frightens me," the Prince said, but he smiled and there was obviously no truth in his assertion. "But tell me about yourself, little Mademoiselle; why do you always wear grey?"

He touched Mistral's skirt as he spoke, for the wide

folds of grey foulard were spread wide over the carriage seat; and then he looked at the soft fichu of grey muslin crossed over her breast and at the tiny bonnet trimmed with grey feathers which did little to conceal the shining beauty of her hair.

"I cannot answer that question," Mistral faltered.

"Why not? Is it a secret—like your real identity and that of your Aunt?"

"Yes . . . I suppose so!"

"Clever—very clever."

The Prince seemed to be speaking to himself. Then he added:

"But must we have secrets from one another—you and I? Now that we are alone, an unexpected privilege, let us talk about you, most adorable little grey fantôme, and forget the rest of the world for a little while—including your Aunt."

Mistral pressed her fingers together in her lap. There was something in the Prince's tone, in the caressing, almost possessive note in his voice, which made her want to run away. They were driving along the shore.

She wanted to look at the sea, at the lemon groves on the other side of the road, at the hillside beyond them on which the sheep were grazing; but instead she dared not let her attention wander from the man at her side.

She liked the Prince because he always laughed and joked. He was very young and very gay; and yet, whenever the opportunity arose, he said things to her which made her shiver inside, and feel the blood rise in her cheeks.

It was not so much what he said as the way in which he said it and the feeling that she had that he was playing with her all the time, that his compliments, elegant though they were, were not sincere but part of a game which she did not understand.

"I have no wish to talk about myself," Mistral said hastily. "It is a dull subject; and besides, there is very little I can tell you. Tell me instead about the country-side and who live in all these magnificent Villas."

"Why should I know or think of such dull, prosaic things," the Prince said, as he leant forward to look into her face, his eyes resting on her lips, "when at the moment all that is of interest to me is here in this carriage—within reach of my arms?"

"But you must know," Mistral insisted, speaking quickly because she was uncomfortable beneath his scrutiny and felt herself blushing at the implication in his words. "Where do you live, for instance? With your Father?"

The Prince's attention was diverted for an instant by this question.

"So you are a little curious about me?" he exclaimed. "No, I no longer live with my Father. When I was twenty-one two months ago, he gave me a Villa of my own. My Father is old-fashioned and his Chateau is near the Palace in the old and quiet part of Monaco.

"My Villa is very smart and very new. It is high up above the new town, on the road to Monte Agel. There I am on my own to do as I like, behave as I wish! It is magnificent—that feeling of independence."

"How lucky you are!"

Mistral spoke with a sudden heartfelt sincerity. She wished at that moment that she, too, could live her own life and do as she liked.

"One day I would like to show you my Villa," the Prince said, his eyes on Mistral's face once again. "Will you come and visit me? I would like that, but I sup-pose we shall have to ask your Aunt. There are many other things I would like to show you, too, such as the Corniche Road by moonlight—if we could be alone."

"My Aunt would never allow that," Mistral said quickly.

"I wonder if I could persuade her," the Prince said reflectively.

"No, please do not try."

Mistral's voice was almost panic-stricken, but now the Prince put out his hand and took hers from her lap. It trembled beneath his fingers like the fluttering of a captured bird.

"I believe you are really frightened of me," he exclaimed. "Why, you silly little thing, there is nothing to frighten you. I would never hurt you."

His tone was unexpectedly kind and gentle, and suddenly Mistral felt her eyes filling with tears.

"It is not . . . that . . . I am . . . really frightened," she stammered. "It is just . . . that I do not . . . understand."

"What don't you understand?" the Prince asked, "and please don't cry. You are so sweet that I wouldn't do anything to distress you."

"I am sorry to be so stupid," Mistral said, freeing her hand to grope for a handkerchief.

The Prince supplied one from his own pocket. It was of soft linen and smelt of orange blossom. Mistral wiped her eyes and offered it back to him.

"I . . . am ashamed . . . of myself," she whispered.

The Prince's face was suddenly serious. He took the handkerchief and put it away in his breast pocket.

"Now let us speak frankly," he said in quite a different tone. "Why are you upset and why are you frightened of me? Tell me the truth and I will try to help you if I can."

Mistral looked up into his face. There was something new in his expression which reassured her, and she answered slowly:

"It is so . . . difficult to put what I feel into words

. . . but when you talk to me . . . like you did . . . just now you seem to be laughing at me and . . . at the same time . . . compelling me to do something that I do not want to do . . . even though I do not know what it is!

"There is something underneath what you say . . . a different meaning from the words you use . . . oh, dear, I cannot explain. . . . How stupid I . . . must sound to you . . . you will not understand. . . ."

"I think I do understand," the Prince said quietly. "You are very young and you have only just come from a Convent. Your Aunt told me that. It is true, isn't it?"

Mistral nodded.

"You have never been made love to, and yet you are so beautiful that every man who sees you will want to make love to you. What is frightening you is love. Does that make it seem any better?"

"I do not think so," Mistral answered truthfully. "I did not think somehow that . . . love would be like that. I have thought about it, of course, and the girls at the Convent often spoke about men and love, but . . . I thought it would be more . . . sacred . . . something holy."

There was a little pause and then the Prince said quietly:

"You are right! Real love is like that, but—there are many kinds of love."

"Oh, I see!" Mistral said. "And what one ordinarily meets is the . . . other kind?"

"Exactly! In fact that is what one meets almost invariably in a place like Monte Carlo."

Mistral puckered her forehead.

"It is not serious then . . . just something to laugh about?"

"Where most people are concerned."

115

"It . . . it doesn't make me want to laugh somehow, but . . . but I will try."

The Prince made a movement.

"No," he said quickly. "Just be yourself; do not pretend, do not act a part you do not feel."

Mistral raised large troubled eyes to his face.

"Then what can I do?" she asked.

The Prince looked out to sea.

"You are too young to be here," he said.

"Here?" Mistral asked. "With you?"

"Yes," the Prince answered, "but I didn't mean that a moment ago. Now that I think of it, you should not be driving with me unchaperoned any more than you should be wandering about Monte Carlo with your Aunt, being talked about and gossiped about by every wagging tongue in the place."

"But why should people talk about me?" Mistral asked.

The Prince glanced at her sharply as if he suspected the very innocence of her question, and then, when he saw that she had asked it in all simplicity, he laughed gently.

Taking one of her hands he slipped it through his arm and patted it reassuringly as a brother might comfort a favourite sister.

"Don't worry your head about such things now," he said, "just try and enjoy our drive together. It is a lovely day and there is nothing to frighten either of us."

There was an extraordinary change in him which Mistral sensed but could not explain. She smiled up at him without embarrassment and the colour came back into her cheeks.

"I am going to tell you all the things that you want to know as we drive along," the Prince went on; and soon he was holding her entranced with his stories of the Principality.

116

Sister Héloise at the Convent had talked to her of Ste. Dévote and of the beauty of Monaco, but she had only been a simple woman and it was from the Prince that Mistral learned a little of the history of the famous rock.

He told her how in the Stone Age the first inhabitants of Monaco lived in caves overlooking the sea. How later the place was occupied by the Phoenicians during their voyages of discovery round the Mediterranean, and how they erected a temple to Melkart, the God of the Sun and all living things.

The legend Mistral liked best was how the Greeks identified the Phoenician God with Hercules and how it was at Monaco that Hercules had performed one of his twelve labours and carried off the golden apples from the dragon-defended garden of the Hesperides.

"Of course everyone in Monaco today maintains that those golden apples were our own succulent golden oranges!" the Prince laughed.

"Tell me more," Mistral begged.

So he showed her where Caesar embarked for his campaign against Pompey and where in the year 7 B.C. the gigantic statue of Augustus was erected on the heights of La Tuibie to commemorate his final victory over the Gauls.

It was easy for Mistral to visualize all the Prince told her, for high above the white houses and russet-red roofs of Monte Carlo she could dimly discern the rock villages which hung like birds' nests on the mountain crags.

There, reached by old, old mule paths, were twisted trees planted by Ligurians or Romans and ancient archways between leaning peasant houses.

There, too, the Prince told her, were men and women with dark Saracenic eyes, who sang the age-old songs of the wandering troubadours from Provence or the strange lilting music of Moorish chants.

"I would love to hear them," Mistral cried.

"One day I will take you there," the Prince promised.

She no longer shrank from the idea of being with him and answered confidently.

"I would like that. Please tell me more. How much there is to know about Monte Carlo besides the fact that it has a Casino!"

"There is an old proverb," the Prince replied, "which says, 'The shine of gold makes me blind'."

"So they are blind to all this," Mistral sighed, looking to where a shepherd boy, wearing a mantle of goat skin and playing a flute like those played a thousand years earlier by his Grecian forbears, was tending a flock of fleecy sheep in a field of scented clover.

In more modern times the history of Monaco grew sad and stormy and the Prince related how the powerful patrician families of Guelf and Ghibelline turned the place into a battlefield, how the brilliance and prosperity begun during the reign of Prince Honoré II was swept away by the French Revolution.

Prince Honoré had been intelligent and a lover of beauty; he had brought to the Palace a splendid collection of works of art and founded a picture gallery which contained paintings by the greatest artists of the Renaissance.

The revolutionaries deposed Honoré III—then the reigning Prince—confiscated his possessions and pillaged the Palace. The art collections were stolen or auctioned at ridiculous prices. The Palace was used first as a Hospital, then as a Workhouse, its glories disappeared, it sank into a dismal neglect.

"It is heartbreaking," Mistral cried. "What happened then?"

"By chance," the Prince replied, "Gabriel Honoré,

118

afterwards Honoré V, met Napoleon on the 1st March, 1815, on his return from Elba. Both sovereigns informed each other that they were about to return to their own States. It was not thought of as an important meeting at the time, but chance encounters in life often have far-reaching and strange results. A chance encounter can alter one's whole future."

Mistral's thoughts turned towards Sir Robert. Theirs had been a chance encounter that night when they met in the darkness of the garden. But would there be far-reaching or strange results from it?

When Sir Robert left Monte Carlo, she might never see him again. Her heart contracted at the thought. She did not know why, but that chance encounter had left its mark upon her and she could not forget it.

She was aware that the Prince was silent, his eyes on her face.

"Of what are you thinking?" he asked.

"Of chance encounters!" she answered truthfully.

"Our meeting was one in point," the Prince replied.

"So it was!" Mistral agreed in surprise, then remembered that so far as Aunt Emilie was concerned the element of chance was slender.

"Perhaps it will have far-reaching results," the Prince smiled. "Who knows?"

"Who indeed?" Mistral answered.

But it seemed to her for a moment that the sun was less brilliant and the wind was cold.

They drove on and on, while the Prince talked; and when at length the horses were turned and they started homewards, the shadows were lengthening and the sky was crimson behind the great Rock. As they neared the Hotel, Mistral said:

"I have been very happy this afternoon. Thank you for being so kind."

As she looked up into the Prince's face, it seemed to

her that there was an expression of pity in his eyes, although she thought that she must have been mistaken.

"I have enjoyed it, too," he said, "and if ever I can be of service to you, you have but to ask my help."

"Thank you," Mistral said simply.

His words brought back the memory of Sir Robert that very first morning when he told her, if ever she was in trouble, to send him a message or a note.

How kind people were, Mistral thought happily; and then as the carriage drew up at the door of the *Hôtel de Paris* and the Prince helped her out, she said:

"I hope we shall see you again soon?"

She was not certain why she asked the question save that suddenly the thought of Aunt Emilie waiting for her in the Hotel had brought with it the uncomfortable feeling that, though she had been so happy and content in the Prince's company this afternoon, she had somehow failed in what was expected of her.

She could not explain the feeling even to herself, nevertheless it was there and she was only reassured when the Prince said:

"I promise that you will see me very often. You are not frightened of me any more, are you?"

Mistral shook her head.

"Indeed not, but you will not tell Aunt Emilie how stupid I was, will you?"

"Of course not!" The Prince's tone was reassuring. "You do not really think I would sneak on you, do you?"

His eyes were laughing at her and she knew he was teasing her, but now she was not afraid and could laugh with him.

Gaiety and laughter were things that could never frighten her, and now that he had lost that strange possessive attitude she wondered if her fear had only been a figment of her imagination.

She was feeling very happy as she went up to the suite. To her surprise Aunt Emilie was out and Jeanne was there alone, mending a torn handkerchief by the light from the open window.

"Where is Aunt Emilie?" Mistral asked.

"She has gone to the Casino," Jeanne answered. "She left a message for me to say that she would be back soon. But those that start gambling lose all sense of time."

"I should not have thought somehow that Aunt Emilie would like gambling," Mistral said. "She always seems to me to be rather careful of money."

"She is!" Jeanne answered. "She hates losing it, but she likes winning it."

"I suppose everyone is like that," Mistral said with a laugh. "But I do not think I want to gamble even if I won. I watch the people's faces when they are playing. They look tense, greedy and cross. You seldom see anyone look happy and really amused by it, except perhaps the Prince, but he is always laughing."

"Did you enjoy your drive?" Jeanne asked.

Mistral nodded her head.

"It was lovely. The Prince told me all sorts of legends about Monaco. It has a wonderful history, Jeanne."

"What else did he say to you?"

"Nothing much else," Mistral answered. "What did you expect him to say?"

She thought that Jeanne looked at her queerly, then the old woman started to fold up her work.

"I didn't expect anything," she said.

Mistral sat down suddenly on a stool at Jeanne's feet and looked out of the window.

"Why do you think Aunt Emilie lets me go out alone with the Prince, Jeanne?" she asked after a moment. "She is perfectly furious if I even think of speaking to anyone else; and when a nice old man tried to talk to me at the Casino last night and offered me a cup of coffee, she almost annihilated him, she was so angry."

"A kind old man!" Jeanne repeated. "I expect he was no better than he ought to be. Old men should stay at home looking after their grand-children instead of talking to young and pretty girls."

Mistral laughed.

"Jeanne, you are as bad as Aunt Emilie! But why does she get cross with me? I do try to do what she wants."

There was something pathetic in the young voice, and Jeanne instinctively put out her hand and laid it on Mistral's head.

"Now don't you go worrying too much about your Aunt," she said. "She has had a hard life one way and another, and it has made her a bit queer and not herself at times. Monsieur Bleuet was not an easy man to live with either, though he could be kindness itself when it suited him.

"But your Aunt found him difficult, and it's hard for a woman when her husband is not naturally congenial to her."

"Husband? Monsieur Bleuet?" Mistral asked in tones of surprise. "I thought Aunt Emilie had married a Comte?"

There was no disguising the consternation in Jeanne's face. Her hands flew up to her cheeks as the blood rose slowly and painfully into them.

"There now, what have I said?" she exclaimed.

"It is of no consequence," Mistral said quickly. "Do not perturb yourself, Jeanne. If I was not meant to know, I will forget what you said."

"You best do that then," Jeanne said, "or your Aunt will half murder me. Listen, child, she has her own reasons for not telling you things; and now, stupid old fool that I am, I have let the cat out of the bag. But

122

keep it to yourself, please, or you will get me into bad trouble."

"Of course, I will not say a word," Mistral answered, "but it is true then, that Aunt Emilie's husband was called Monsieur Bleuet and that she is not really *Madame la Comtesse?*"

"That's the truth, God help me!" Jeanne said, glancing over her shoulder as if she half expected to see Emilie listening to them in the shadows.

"And is he dead?" Mistral enquired.

"Yes, he's dead," Jeanne said. "He died seven years ago next Christmas, and to tell the truth I know no more than you do why your Aunt should pretend to be the widow of a Comte."

Mistral sighed.

"I hate mysteries," she said. "I cannot understand why people want to have secrets. They are nasty, spooky things, in which a person gets all involved and before you know where you are, you are telling lies."

"That's true enough, my dear, so don't you have any secrets," Jeanne said approvingly.

"I will not," Mistral said, and then remembered Sir Robert.

That was a secret, and one of her very own. So perhaps after all everyone had them!

Who was she to criticize Aunt Emilie, Mistral thought humbly; and because she felt that Jeanne was still perturbed at what she had unwittingly revealed, she got to her feet and put her arms round the old woman's shoulder.

"Pray do not worry," she said. "The secret is safe enough—yours and mine."

"God bless you, *ma chère,*" Jeanne said suddenly, "and God help you too, whatever lies ahead."

Her words came from the heart and Mistral suddenly felt apprehensive as if something unknown was lying in wait for her just around the corner. It was then that they heard the door of the sitting-room and instinctively they turned towards it, drawing apart.

The door opened and Emilie came in. She was dressed in a smart costume of green ottoman silk trimmed with plaid, and there were feathers in her green hat.

"Ah, here you are, Mistral," she said. "Did you enjoy your drive?"

"Yes, Aunt Emilie. The Prince came to the Church and told me that you had said he might take me out in his carriage."

"Yes, I gave him permission," Emilie said. "He is a delightful boy. I hope you were nice to him."

She looked at Mistral searchingly as she spoke.

"I think so, Aunt Emilie," Mistral answered.

She did not know why, but her Aunt's question made her feel guilty.

"Good!"

Emilie turned towards Jeanne.

"We shall need two of our best gowns tonight, Jeanne," she said. "Mademoiselle will wear the grey chiffon trimmed with lace. She has not been seen in that one as yet, and I will wear the gold brocade."

"I will see that they are ready, Madame," Jeanne said.

Emilie turned towards Mistral.

"Well, have you an invitation for tonight?"

"An invitation, Aunt Emilie?" Mistral enquired.

"Yes, did the Prince ask us to dinner or supper?"

"Neither, Aunt Emilie."

Emilie's expression seemed to darken.

"Strange! I should have thought that he would have suggested one or the other when he left you. Are you sure that you were nice to him?"

"I . . . I think so, Aunt Emilie."

"Well, don't think," Emilie said sharply. "Know one way or the other. I have told you, Mistral, what I want of you; and if you are deliberately disobeying me, you will be sorry for it."

"But, Aunt Emilie, I was nice to the Prince. I enjoyed the drive and I think he did too, and he said that he would be seeing me again very soon."

Emilie seemed to relax.

"That is better," she said. "Why didn't you say so at once, you stupid child?"

"It would be easier if I understood exactly what you wanted me to do or say," Mistral said tentatively. "You do see, Aunt Emilie, that I have had very little to do with men until now; in fact I have known very few of them."

"That is all the better," Emilie said. "You don't want to know a lot of men, Mistral. Most of them are brutes who disguise their bestiality with words spoken in lying tongues. Women are happiest without men in their lives, but the silly fools never know it until it is too late.

"Beware of men, shun them as you would shun the devil himself, for they bring you nothing but misery, heartache and unhappiness."

Emilie spoke passionately in a low, monotonous tone. It was almost as if she were talking to herself, and she only appeared to be aroused when Mistral said:

"But, Aunt Emilie, if men are so bad, why do you tell me to be nice to the Prince?"

"The Prince is of importance in your life, Mistral. Do not forget that. When you think of men, remember what I have said."

"I . . . I will try, Aunt Emilie," Mistral replied;

At the same time something within her cried out

125

that what her Aunt had said was not true. She was certain that all men were not brutes and beasts, not Sir Robert at any rate.

She could not imagine him being brutal or bestial in any way whatsoever. Perhaps Aunt Emilie had been unfortunate in the men she had met. Jeanne had hinted that her life had been difficult with Monsieur Bleuet.

Mistral suddenly felt very sorry for her Aunt. She was old and cross and at times her face was as hard as granite.

"She could not look like that and be happy," Mistral thought, and she felt a sense of pity well up inside her.

She was just about to say something affectionate to Aunt Emilie, she even contemplated slipping her hand into hers, when Emilie perceived a card lying on a table just inside the door of the sitting-room.

"Who left this?" she asked, walking towards it and picking it up.

"I have no idea," Mistral answered. "Jeanne did not say that anyone had called."

She looked round for Jeanne, but the maid had gone.

It was then that Emilie gave a cry and it seemed to Mistral to be a cry of horror. She was holding the card close to her eyes so that she could read it, and her face, drained of all colour, was strangely contorted.

"Henry Dulton!" she said in a high voice which suddenly cracked. "Henry Dulton!"

# 7

Emilie sat alone in the sitting-room waiting for Henry
Dulton. On his card, written in the thin spidery writing
which she knew so well, were inscribed the words:

*I will call on you at three o'clock tomorrow after-*
*noon.*

She read the sentence over and over again, striving
to find in it some meaning but the obvious one—that
he had recognized her and was coming to claim her
acquaintance.

All night she had tossed sleeplessly on her bed, trying to think how she could delude and circumvent him
or how she could keep him quiet for at least a few
more weeks.

To the last question she knew the answer. Money!
She could recall all too vividly Henry Dulton's greed
for money, the way he would undertake any commission, however squalid and unpleasant, if it was made
worth his while.

She could see him now coming to 5 *Rue de Roi* for
his commission on the clients he had introduced.

She had always hated him, hated the way he came
softly, almost silently, into a room, the way his eyes
were shifty behind the pale lashes which, matching his
almost colourless hair, gave him the appearance of a
sleek ferret.

Yet he had his uses. It would have been stupid to

dismiss him because of a mere personal prejudice, and she had accepted him, as she had accepted the other employees at No. 5, with a philosophical toleration.

Yet it was the most diabolical ill-fortune that Henry Dulton of all people should have turned up at Monte Carlo just at this particular moment.

She had never imagined him working anywhere except in Paris; and yet she should have known that where there was wealth and luxury and pickings to be obtained from those who were rich Henry Dulton would be around.

What could she say to him? With a sudden groan Emilie rose to her feet and walked across the sitting-room to the window. The brilliant sunshine, the sparkling blue of the sea and the soft movement of the palm trees were a hollow mockery to the dark tumult of her feelings.

"The little rat!" Emilie said aloud. "I always hated him!"

Even as her words were spat forth on to the soft air, she thought that she might have been speaking of almost any man she had ever met.

Yes, she had hated them all with a hatred bred in her from childhood by the ignoble position in which she had been born. That was her Father's fault. She had hated John Wytham, half for her own sake, and half because she was jealous of the undying love her Mother bore him.

And after her Father with his careless regard for the ties of parenthood she had hated Léon Bleuet, her husband.

Only for a very short while had Léon evoked in her any feeling but one of disgust and dislike. She could recall their first meeting as if it had happened yesterday.

She had travelled from Brittany to Paris, and how

vividly she could remember that journey! How strange she must have looked, severely dressed in her best Sunday black, her face grave and resolute as she set out on an almost desperate adventure!

Jacques Riguad, her grandfather, had died but two months after her Mother had passed away.

It had been suggested by the family that the younger of old Jacques' sons, although he already had a farm of his own, should help Emilie keep the family estate together.

She might continue to live in the farm-house, but would spend all the hours of daylight in the fields and tending the animals. She could see their heads nodding together as they agreed on this, their work-worn hands almost applauding their own generosity.

But Emilie had already made up her mind as to what she intended to do. She had indeed been making her plans for years; and while to her family they were astounding, to her they had already become common-place because she had considered them for so long.

First Mistral was to go to school, not to the kind of cheap establishment which lay within the limits of the Riguad purse, but to an Academy for Young Ladies or to one of the expensive Convents at Lucerne or near Paris.

On this Emilie was determined. She had decided a long while ago that Mistral must be properly educated, decided it when she was walking the motherless baby up and down the kitchen floor. Hidden in a secret place were the pearls which Alice had given into Emilie's keeping the night before she died.

"These are for my child," Alice said. "They are the only things I brought away with me. If the necessity arises, you must sell them. They are very valuable."

Her eyes had closed wearily when she had finished

speaking; she had already been in labour for some hours. Emilie had stared stupidly at the beautiful translucent necklace which Alice placed in her hands.

She had never seen any pearls like them before and she was sure that Alice spoke the truth when she said they were very valuable.

How had Alice kept them hidden from her all these months? she wondered. And she hated with a bitter, burning hatred the man who had changed the happy, talkative girl she had left at Monaco into a miserable, reserved woman.

Nothing she could do or say would make Alice talk about what had happened. Emilie had pleaded, commanded, entreated—all without effect.

"I do not wish to talk about it," Alice would repeat over and over again.

And only when Emilie, goaded beyond endurance, had threatened to write to the Grand Duke did she vary the sentence with:

"You have promised on the Bible; you cannot break your vow! There is nothing you can do."

No, there was nothing Emilie could do but watch Alice with frustrated, angry eyes.

When Alice died, Emilie had hidden the pearls away and had spoken of them to no-one; but from the very first she was determined not to sell them. They became another part of the weapon that she was creating—a weapon which would ultimately revenge both Alice and herself.

The pearls had gone with her to Paris. When she told the Riguad family that she was leaving for the Capital, they were even more astonished than at her decision to give up the farm.

"Paris!" they exclaimed. "But what will you do? And how will you live? Paris is very expensive."

"I shall work," Emilie said.

"But what at?" they asked. "You have only worked here on the farm. There are no farms in Paris."

"I shall find something to do," Emilie said confidently.

Her confidence was justified, although she did not feel as self-assured as she looked when she set off on the long train journey.

Yet hidden in the bottom of her black bag was the pearl necklace and she knew that, if all else failed, she could sell it. Not only for herself but for Mistral's schooling.

The fees for the first term at the Convent had already been paid out of the small sum Emilie had realized in selling her share of the farm to her uncles.

But despite her lofty airs with the family, the expenses had shocked Emilie. There were so many extras. In addition to the Convent's fees Mistral had required new clothes and finally there had been the journey to Lucerne.

Was she fond of the child? Emilie asked herself the question as Mistral clung to her at the final moment of parting, afraid of leaving all that was familiar, afraid of the unknown. She was not sure of the answer.

Her love for Alice had been an overwhelming, devouring emotion. She could never recover from the shock of Alice's deception, her reticence and secrecy and finally her death. Mistral was Alice's child; she was also a constant reminder of Alice's betrayal.

At times Emilie would hate not Mistral herself, but the fact that she was alive while Alice was dead.

But Mistral must be educated, Mistral must be brought up expensively and luxuriously because Emilie's plan for the future depended on her having all the social adjuncts to a personal success.

Even while Emilie reassured her own fear of failure and thought of the pearl necklace as security against

131

utter destitution, she resolved with an almost fanatical determination that she would not part with it, however hard it might be to resist the temptation to do so. It was essential to her scheme.

Emilie had reached Paris at six o'clock in the evening. It was growing dusk—the blue, dusky twilight which makes Paris seem very mysterious and exciting, a place of adventure, a place of love, of soft music and of happiness.

But Emilie saw none of these things. As she stepped out of the train, she felt cold, dirty and frightened. She had reached Paris, it was true, but she was alone in a strange city in which she had not even one friend.

She stood forlornly in the station, her face white and drawn against the black crêpe of her unfashionable bonnet.

It was then that Léon spoke to her. She started and looked round to see an elderly man with a little pointed beard that was turning grey and dark eyes which seemed to Emilie to be comfortingly friendly.

"Can I be of assistance, Mademoiselle?"

"No, thank you, Monsieur."

"The friends who were meeting you have perhaps been delayed?"

"I am not being met."

"No? Then Mademoiselle is well conversant with Paris?"

"No."

"But . . . but . . . it is dangerous for a young woman to arrive so late. You will perhaps permit me to direct you to where you are staying."

"I have no idea where that is."

Léon's sympathetic ejaculation was pleasant to hear.

Emilie did not know then, but she learned later that it was part of his business routine for him to speak to unattached young women on railway stations, and that in the dim light he had been deceived into thinking her far younger than she was.

But, having begun the conversation, he continued it. She told him the truth, that she had come from Brittany in search of work.

"Can you cook?" he asked.

"By farm standards well," she replied. "By Paris standards doubtless excruciatingly."

He had liked the dry note of humour in her voice.

"By a stroke of extraordinary good fortune I can offer you employment," he said, "for I myself am looking for a housekeeper."

Afterwards Emilie had realized that it said much for Léon's personality and the confidence that he invariably evoked in his victims that she had no qualms at all about leaving the station with him and driving to his house.

It was a fortnight before she discovered that her duties as housekeeper involved a more personal relationship with her employer, and it was a long time after that before she discovered how exceptional indeed was the interest Léon took in her.

Frenchmen seldom mix business and pleasure, and as Léon's business concerned only women and the possibilities of their attractions, he was to all intents and purposes inoculated against the wiles of feminine charm.

But, as Emilie was to learn slowly and painfully in the years ahead, a man's physical temperament is often a tortuous thing with unexpected twists and turns where one least expects them.

Léon Bleuet, whose sole interest was in catering for the amusement and pleasure of other men, was seldom pleased or amused himself. He had a strong feminine streak in him, in strange contrast to his appearance of bluff geniality which was accentuated by his being stout.

He enjoyed being bullied and ordered about by a woman; the sharp edge of her tongue was more enticing to him than honeyed words. To him a woman was most captivating when her eyes were dark and flashing with anger, her voice raised, her whole body tense with antagonism.

Emilie could hardly believe the truth when she first discovered that Léon was attracted to her by her very brusqueness and by the aloof disdain with which she treated him almost from the moment she first entered his employment.

Her gratitude towards him at having offered her both shelter and employment on the night she arrived in Paris lasted for but a very short period—indeed only until she discovered how inefficiently his house had been kept and how uncomfortable a succession of ill-chosen servants had made him.

The place was dirty to begin with; and if there was one thing that Marie Riguad had taught her daughter almost from the moment she could toddle, it was to keep a house clean.

Emilie scrubbed and polished, washed and brushed until the place shone and the atmosphere was impregnated with the fresh fragrance of soap and beeswax.

While she worked, Emilie found her respect for her employer vanishing with the dirt she threw away. He might look prosperous, she thought, but he could not be much of a business man to let his home get into this state.

Used to speaking her mind, she said what she thought when Léon Bleuet returned for his mid-day meal, and soon she found herself giving him what she called a "talking to" every time he was at home.

Surprisingly he made no attempt to stop her; in fact he seemed to enjoy her caustic comments, to delight in her barely concealed dislike, and he sought her society more and more.

When she first arrived, he was invariably out for dinner; but soon he began to dine at home, having his meal at an early hour because he said it was essential for him to be at his place of business not later than seven o'clock.

Emilie was not particularly curious as to what he did. So long as he paid her, she was not interested as to where the money came from or how it had been earned. When he told her the truth, she accepted the information with a shrug of her shoulders. It neither astounded her nor horrified her.

While there were men in the world their tastes must be catered for, she supposed, although it did nothing to enhance her already very low opinion of the male sex.

Léon's proposals which concerned herself came into a very different category.

"It is no use your talking to me like that," she said. "I have got no use for men. I hate them! My Father was an English nobleman and a lot of good he did my Mother. I have never met a man I would give a snap of my fingers for, and I have been brought up to be respectable.

"I don't intend to be anything else, and if that's what you want, then I had better be looking for other employment."

To her astonishment Léon Bleuet asked her to marry him. She was too astonished to blurt out an instantaneous refusal; and while she hesitated, he told her something which made her hesitate still further before giving him a definite answer. What he revealed in that moment was what he was worth.

She had not thought of him until then as a rich man; but even though he was by no means wealthy by some standards, to Emilie the value he placed on the various establishments he owned and the considerable sum of his credit at the bank seemed astronomical.

His income for a week exceeded the sum they had managed to live on for a year at the farm in Brittany.

Emilie hesitated and was lost.

She married Léon Bleuet—married him because he could pay Mistral's school fees. Marriage she reckoned would enable her to live in comfort until the girl was grown-up and would make it possible for her to save at the same time. Léon was not a young man. When he died, she would be a widow with a considerable fortune.

But there he had lied to her. The first part of the contract was fulfilled to the letter. Mistral's school fees were paid and Emilie lived in comfort; but when Léon Bleuet died, she discovered that the bulk of his money had been left to his nephew, a young man for whom he had a deep affection, while she had been left only their house in Paris and the property at 5 *Rue de Roi*.

Emilie could never decide whether the latter legacy had been a joke on the part of Léon or whether he intended it to make up for his deficiencies in other ways. He had considered it the best and most paying of the houses he owned, and it was of all his interests his favourite.

Nevertheless he knew what she thought of the place, he knew, too, that she had never crossed the threshold nor taken the slightest interest in it save from the point of view of how much it contributed to their income.

To leave it to her, to make it his only provision for her after five years of married life, was to all intents and purposes an insult.

Emilie did not at first realize exactly what a difference Léon Bleuet's death was to make to her. When she visited his lawyer three days after the funeral she was

136

already aware of the contents of Léon's will so that she was steeled to endure a certain loss of comfort.

After the lawyer had spoken to her of the value of the house in which they had lived, pointing out that, as it was in an unfashionable part of Paris, it would be difficult to effect an advantageous sale, she had spoken of 5 *Rue de Roi*.

"I shall sell it," she said. "Have you any idea what it will fetch?"

The lawyer put his glasses on his nose and shuffled amongst the papers on his desk.

"I anticipated that would be your decision, Madame, and I have therefore made a few tentative enquiries. I think you would do well to obtain ten thousand francs for this property, as a going concern, of course."

"Ten thousand francs!" Emilie's voice rose almost to a scream. "Is that all?"

"It is, and if I may say so, Madame, quite a reasonable price. I am informed by people who know about such things that the place in the last few years was not doing so well as previously. Monsieur Bleuet did not give it so much personal attention as he had done in the past.

"The clientele, which was always of a particularly select class, has deteriorated a little, maybe the fashion has changed. These places rise and fall, you know, and no-one knows quite what makes a rendezvous which has proved extremely popular suddenly become démodé."

"Ten thousand francs!" Emilie muttered. "How am I to live on it? If that is all I am to have . . ."

Mistral was eleven. She saw another seven years of waiting ahead until she could put her plan into operation, the plan which was always in her thoughts by day and of which she dreamed at night.

137

Seven years—seven vital years in which Mistral must have special instruction, special grooming, special lessons so that she could be well-versed in the part she had to play!

Money, money, money! She had to have money, it was essential; but where and how could she obtain it?

Emilie's fingers drummed for a moment on the lawyer's desk; then suddenly her head went up and her lips tightened.

"I shall not sell the property," she said sharply.

"Madame! But what will you do with it?" the lawyer expostulated.

"I shall run it myself," Emilie replied.

She was never to forget the moment when she crossed the threshold of the big stone house standing in a discreet side street conveniently near the fashionable quarter of the city.

It impressed Emilie as she had not expected to be impressed. The grey walls picked out in gilt were in good taste, the staircase with its soft carpet, the mirrors which reflected and re-reflected the well-proportioned salon were restrained and not without charm.

There was nothing wrong with the house itself; it was the personnel who, Emilie knew immediately with an unwavering instinct, were at fault.

The Madame in charge, a silly, over-dressed middle-aged woman with frizzed hair and an irritating giggle, was far more embarrassed by Emilie than she was by her. The girls, too, were not as well dressed as they might have been, and their hair was untidy, their make-up badly applied.

There was a laxness and a lack of discipline about their behaviour. Emilie knew that she could put her finger on the weak spots.

She applied herself to turning out, cleaning and polishing 5 *Rue de Roi* as she had applied herself to Léon's own home five years earlier.

Within a month of her taking the reins of management into her own hands the receipts were doubled, in six months they were trebled, and in a year the house was spoken of as the smartest and most expensive place of entertainment in the whole of Paris.

The results gratified Emilie in two ways. First in knowing that her efficiency was conducive to making her into a wealthy woman in her own right, and secondly in lowering still further her opinion of men.

In the past she had hated those she had known; now she despised them all for being fools, hood-winked, deceived and besotted by the shrewdness of women.

Emilie gained a great knowledge of men during the next seven years, and the value of that knowledge was proved by the very substantial sum she obtained when she sold 5 *Rue de Roi*.

As she thought of the place, a succession of men passed before her eyes—Léon Bleuet, with his perverted pleasure in her hatred of him; the men with whom she had to pretend to be friendly because they were good clients of the house; old men, young men, tall men, short men, fat men, thin men, men of all nationalities, men with only one object, only one interest at the moment when Emilie met them.

"You are a real friend, Madame!" they would say when Emilie did them some particular service.

But while she smiled her thanks, they had no idea of the loathing with which she regarded them, of the scorn with which she took their money.

Men, always men, and little to choose between those who were rich and ready to purchase an hour's forgetfulness from the cares and troubles of their everyday world and hangers-on like Henry Dulton who was ready to extort every possible penny by exploiting the weaknesses of the human race.

Henry Dulton! Emilie's thoughts brought her in a circle back to where she had started. It was then, as she looked out of the window, staring at the blue sea with unseeing eyes, that she heard a knock on the door.

She had sent Mistral and Jeanne out together with instructions not to return until four-thirty, and so, as she was alone, she must cross to the door and open it herself, open it to the ill-fortune which she knew was awaiting her outside.

Henry Dulton came into the room. He set his hat down on a chair and looked at Emilie in his usual sidelong manner, his eyes half veiled by their flickering, colourless lashes.

"You wish to see me, Monsieur?"

Emilie's voice was cool and impersonal. Henry Dulton looked to see if the door was shut behind him and his lips twisted themselves into the travesty of a smile.

"Your servant, Madame Bleuet."

"I think you have made a mistake. I thought that was what had happened when I received your card. I am not Madame Bleuet and I have no knowledge of having met you before."

Henry Dulton's smile was a little more pronounced. He advanced further into the room and, taking a silk handkerchief from his pocket, wiped his moustache.

"I was not born yesterday, Madame."

"I beg your pardon."

The words were icy. Henry Dulton put away his handkerchief, glanced round the room and seated himself in the most comfortable chair.

"Let us dispense with the preliminaries, Madame," he said. "I recognized you; it was impossible for me not to do so after all the years we have known each other. I know who you are and you know that I know it, therefore let us be frank with one another and talk business."

Emilie drew a deep breath. She was defeated by the man's very assurance, but she made one last desperate stand.

"You have made a mistake, Monsieur," she said, "and I must ask you to leave the room. I am not Madame Bleuet and I defy you to prove I am."

"That would not be difficult," Henry Dulton said quietly, looking not at Emilie but at a diamond ring he wore on his little finger. "I have but to tell some of the people who are making so many enquiries regarding the identity of *Madame Secret* and her beautiful niece, *Mademoiselle Fantôme,* and if their interest is sufficiently aroused, my assertion can always be verified by the Police."

"By the Police!" Emilie echoed in an uncertain manner.

"Why not, Madame, if you have nothing to hide?" Henry Dulton asked. "And I assure you that the curiosity regarding you in Monte Carlo is so intense that there are quite a number of people who would be prepared to pay for the information."

Emilie dropped her pretence.

"How much do you want?" she asked, and her voice was harsh.

Henry Dulton stroked his chin.

"Now we are talking sense," he said. "I thought it would not be long before we became friendly—as we always have been, Madame. But first will you permit me to congratulate you on the admirable way in which you have taken Monte Carlo by storm? It is a masterpiece, a work of art for which any artiste would be proud to take credit."

141

"I asked you how much," Emilie said.

"And I will answer you," Henry Dulton said. "One hundred thousand francs."

"A hundred thousand! You must be insane."

"On the contrary, Madame, extremely sane and quite sure of receiving the money."

"And where do you think I can get such a sum?" Emilie asked.

"I know from where you have already got it," Henry Dulton replied. "You see, dear Madame Bleuet, the new proprietor of 5 *Rue de Roi* is a friend of mine."

Emilie sat down suddenly in the chair opposite him.

"But why do you imagine that I would give you all that money?"

"You would give it to me to keep silent," Henry Dulton said. "I have no idea what your scheme is, Madame; I have not yet guessed the whole secret of *Madame Secret;* but whatever it is, it is of importance to you, of great importance; and unless this scheme, whatever it may be, is to fail, it is essential that I do not speak of what I know."

Emilie seemed to slump suddenly in her chair. The regal bearing which had been the admiration of many women in Monte Carlo vanished and instead she looked an old and tired woman. But her eyes were dark with anger and hatred.

"It is too much," she said. "It is impossible."

Henry Dulton shrugged his shoulders.

"Then I shall speak of what I know," he said. "There are several people already who have approached me with a view to finding out who you are and of course, what is of more moment, who is *Mademoiselle Fantôme."

"You cannot tell them that," Emilie said. "You have no idea who she is."

"Does it matter?" Henry Dulton asked. "Any pretty

142

girl in the company of the notorious Madame Bleuet requires but one name. There were Lulu, Fifi, Ninon and Desirée. They had no other name! Did it matter? Who cared?"

Emilie jumped to her feet.

"Do you dare to speak of my niece in the same breath as those low creatures?"

"So she really is your niece," Henry Dulton said. "I am surprised. I had no idea you had one."

"Will you be quiet, you sewer rat, you parasite living on the fat of other people's bodies?"

Emilie's voice shook with emotion and her face was white with rage. But Henry Dulton only smiled his twisted smile and remarked:

"Hard words make little impression on me, Madame. It is only money that counts, only money."

"Yes, my money, money I have worked for, money I have slaved for, if it comes to that, and now you would take it from me, beggar me at the moment of my triumph."

"I have left you some," Henry Dulton replied softly.

"That is kind of you," Emilie said sarcastically.

Then, even as she spoke, his eyelashes flickered and she knew as surely as if he had said it aloud that, even if she paid him this time, he would come for more and yet more.

He would rob her of everything she possessed, break her in fact, and even then she could not be certain that he would keep his word and not reveal what he knew.

He was utterly untrustworthy, as treacherous as a shifting sand, as dangerous as an adder.

She raised her hands for a moment to her temples, pressing hard in an effort to make her brain think clearly, to find a solution to this almost unsolvable problem.

143

Henry Dulton's voice interrupted her.

"I would not wish to hurry you, Madame, but I have an appointment at three-thirty. It does not concern you or your beautiful niece, but the gentleman who wishes to see me would undoubtedly be extremely interested in any information I might give him concerning the identity of the most talked-of women in Monte Carlo."

"I will give you the money," Emilie said hoarsely.

"I thought you would," Henry Dulton smiled.

"Wait here," Emilie said. "I have it locked away in my bedroom."

She went from the room, shutting the communicating door behind her. For a moment, when she was alone, she could only stand still, conscious that her breath was coming quickly, her heart beating with sheer unbridled rage.

Then with something suspiciously like a sob she unlocked the drawer of her wardrobe and took from the bottom of it the big jewel case which had been in Jeanne's keeping on their journey.

Emilie set it down on the bed and drawing a key from the bosom of her gown she slipped the long chain on which it was threaded over her head and unlocked the jewel box.

Inside were all her worldly possessions—the Deeds of the house in Paris, the Bank Statement ending with the withdrawal of everything she had deposited there, and finally a great pile of notes of very large denominations.

She had withdrawn everything before she left Paris, determined that all traces of Madame Bleuet should cease and that, when she opened a new banking account, it should be in another name.

As she looked at the money lying there in the box, the money which it had seemed to her she had earned so hardly, almost giving her life-blood in her toil for it, she felt a sob break in her throat.

A hundred thousand francs! It was over half of everything she possessed in the whole world.

She picked up the notes, one by one and, as she did so, she was suddenly aware of something which lay beneath them, something she had taken from Léon's desk the last day before they left Paris.

She was not even certain why she had brought it with her except perhaps because of the memory of her last journey to Monaco and the tales of travellers being held up by robbers which had terrified Alice and herself as they bumped over the road from Nice.

Slowly, her face working strangely but her hand steady, Emilie drew it from its hiding-place beneath the money. It was a pistol, and Léon, who had always been desperately afraid of burglars, had on more than one occasion shown her how to use it.

There was always money in the house in Paris, for he banked but once a week, and the safe in which he kept the nightly receipts from 5 *Rue de Roi* and his other places of business stood behind a Chinese screen in their sitting-room.

"If you are alarmed by anything you hear, fire at once," Léon had instructed her. "Bullets are more effective than words."

Emilie could almost hear his voice beside her. Mechanically her fingers loaded the pistol. Then she looked down at it. There was the same look in her face as had been there twelve years ago when she had set out alone for Paris.

"Bullets are more effective than words!"

She took up a handful of notes. She did not bother to count them, for she knew now what she must do; then she glanced round the room as if in search of something.

Jeanne had left her dolman trimmed with jet lying over the chair in case she wished to go out during the afternoon. Beside it was her hat, gloves and a little muff of black fur.

Emilie walked across the room and picked up the muff. Her hand holding the pistol slipped into it. It was a most effective place of concealment.

Next she set both her muff and the notes she held down on the dressing-table. It took her but a moment to place her hat on her head, to pin it securely with its two jet hatpins, to put on the dolman over her dress of silk.

Henry Dulton would not be surprised at her re-entering the room with her muff in her hand. She would tell him that she was going out.

Now she was ready. She glanced at herself in the mirror. For a moment she wondered if the stranger who faced her was herself. She had no idea that her face could look so strange or her eyes could shine so venomously.

"Bullets are more effective than words!" Yes, she could hear Léon's voice distinctly. He had known the value of money.

She moved across the room, held the muff under her arm for one second as she opened the door, then slipped her hand into it again and entered the sitting-room.

Henry Dulton was sitting where she had left him, his legs stretched out comfortably, a cigar between his lips. He made no attempt to rise at her entrance.

Fiercely she resented the gross familiarity of his ill-manners.

"Got the money?" he asked. "Good for you! I'll say that for you, Madame—you always deliver the goods."

"Yes, I have always managed to do that so far," Emilie said, and her voice was quiet and very steady.

"Count it, will you? I have no wish to give you too much."

"Not much fear of that," Henry Dulton said jovially. "If I know you, it's more likely to be too little. Give it to me."

His hands reached up for the money greedily. He took the thick wad of francs from Emilie's hand, balanced them on his knee, and licking the first finger of his right hand, he started to flick through them with a practised air.

"You have missed one there," Emilie said, coming nearer so that she could bend down and touch the notes with her left hand.

"I bet you I didn't," he replied; but he went back to the beginning, concentrating intently on counting them.

"Five thousand . . . ten . . . fifteen . . . twenty . . . twenty-five. . . ."

It was then that Emilie shot him through the temple. The report of the pistol was deadened by her muff, but nevertheless it sounded to her own ears unnaturally loud.

For a moment, after he had toppled forward and then fallen slowly with a dull thud to the floor, she did not look at him, but listened only for the noise of footsteps outside, for the sound of voices of people asking questions, demanding what had happened.

But there was no sound of any sort. Emilie knew exactly what she had to do next. Everything fell into place in her mind as clearly as if she had planned it for a long time.

She must gather up the notes, drag Henry Dulton's body into her bedroom and hide him in the closet. Later, when it was dark, she and Jeanne would get him out of the hotel.

On every floor of the Hotel there was a wheel-chair

left for the use of guests who came to Monte Carlo, not only for the pleasure of visiting the Casino but also for their health.

There were special baths to be had under the hotel, and those who were crippled by rheumatism or other complaints could go downstairs in the comfort of a wheel-chair, descending in the luggage lift at the far end of the corridor.

There was a man in attendance on the lift who pulled the rope to make it rise and descend. He was old, inclined to be deaf. He would take little notice of an invalid, wrapped in rugs and perhaps a shawl, accompanied by two elderly women.

Besides the lift was unlit and only as they passed the gas brackets on each floor would whoever sat in the wheel-chair be illuminated. They could slip out of the hotel by a side door. The gardens of the Casino were but a stone's throw away.

No-one would be interested in three elderly people taking an evening walk.

They would lay Henry Dulton amongst the flowering shrubs and it was more than likely that his body would not be discovered until the morrow. She would leave the pistol beside him.

Suicides in Monte Carlo were invariably hushed up by the Police and the authorities. There were too many people in the world already decrying the vice of gambling for them to invite further comment by the newspapers.

Henry Dulton was of no importance except to himself.

Emilie drew a deep breath, then she bent down and took up the notes as they lay sprawled over the hearth-rug. The ugly wound in Henry Dulton's temple was bleeding and without flinching she wiped away the blood which would have dripped on to the carpet.

148

Slowly and with the utmost composure she went into her bedroom, put the notes away in her jewel case, and took off her hat and dolman. She laid her muff down on the chair exactly where Jeanne had left it; then having opened the door of the closet, she went back into the sitting-room.

As she did so, she heard a clock strike the half hour. Henry Dulton would be unable to keep his appointment.

# 8

Mistral was worried and unhappy.

She was not quite certain why except that she sensed that something was wrong though she could not find a reasonable explanation for the feeling.

When she and Jeanne returned from their walk that afternoon, Aunt Emilie had met them at the door of the sitting-room and said sharply:

"You will go to your bedroom, Mistral, and stay there until either Jeanne or I fetch you. Is that understood? You are not to leave it until you are told to do so."

"Yes, Aunt Emilie," Mistral had replied. "But . . . is anything the matter?"

"Kindly do as you are told without argument or idiotic questions," Emilie answered, and abashed Mistral had gone to her room and closed the door.

For some time she sat wondering what she could have done to incur her Aunt's anger; yet ponder as she might over her movements of the morning, there was nothing that she could find which might be construed in any way to be upsetting or annoying.

At length, having removed her mantle and bonnet and put them away in the wardrobe, she wandered round the hotel bedroom looking at the curtains, the elaborate bedspread and the French furniture, wondering why, when everything in itself was so charming, the whole effect seemed somehow bare and unwelcoming. Then the explanation came to her.

It was, of course, because unlike most people she had no possessions of her own to leave about—no photographs to arrange on the chest-of-drawers, no ornaments, boxes or little nicknacks with which most women surround themselves.

The dressing-table contained only the plain wooden brush she had used at the Convent, a comb and a jar of hand ointment which Jeanne had given her.

It was, she told Mistral, a grease she made every winter because Aunt Emilie often suffered from chapped hands.

But one pot of hand balm could hardly be counted an ornament and Mistral, contrasting her own room with Jeanne's, knew that the latter was far more homely.

Photographs of Jeanne's great-nieces and nephews stood on the mantelpiece, a shell box held her hairpins, a china tidy with a motto written on it for her combings.

The table by her bed contained besides her Missal a statue of St. Anthony, her best Rosary of ivory and silver beads, which she only used on Saints' Days, and an embroidered spectacle case, which had been a Christmas present over twenty years ago.

There were pieces of Normandy pottery, a pincushion fashioned into a glass slipper, a lucky elephant from India, and a needlework picture of the Holy Family, which went with her everywhere. There was no doubt

150

about it, Jeanne's bedroom, wherever it might be, would always be individual.

What was wrong with hers, Mistral thought, was that she had nothing personal with which to surround herself.

Even as she thought of it, the memory came to her of those long years at school when she had longed so often and so passionately for someone to love her, someone to care for her individually.

The Nuns had been kind and they had taken an unceasing interest in all their pupils; but it was impossible not to realize that their hearts were given to God, that first and foremost in their affections, in their loyalty, and indeed in everything they did came He to whom they had vowed their service.

Mistral was deeply religious, but she also wanted human love, human understanding and the knowledge that she belonged.

She felt the loss of this most in the holidays when all the other girls, excited and chattering of their plans, had gone to their homes and she had been left at the Convent with only two other pupils to keep her company.

One was a child whose Mother and Father were in Africa, and the other had no Mother, but her Father was Governor of Devil's Island, where she visited him only once every three years.

But deprived as the other two girls were of holidays at home, they had at least relations who wrote to them, parents who gave them presents on their birthdays, at Christmas and Easter; Grandparents, Aunts, Uncles and cousins to whom they could pour out their hearts in long letters and who sent them loving messages in reply.

Mistral wrote dutifully to Aunt Emilie every week; but sometimes three or four months would pass before she would get a letter in return.

151

Then it was brief, telling her no news of any kind or description. In fact, the letters were almost identical in that they invariably commanded her to work hard, to apply herself more fervently to her lessons and to do exactly what the Nuns told her.

As Mistral did all these things automatically, she found her Aunt's letters bitterly disappointing, although invariably she experienced a sudden thrill when she saw a letter addressed to herself set out on the table where the girls received their post.

If Aunt Emilie's letters were few and far between, her visits were even more so. Perhaps once a year she would journey to the Convent, talk with the Mother Superior and later walk in the garden alone with Mistral. Aunt Emilie's visits were almost as disappointing as her letters.

Every sentence she spoke seemed to Mistral to begin with:

"The Reverend Mother tells me that you could do better in . . ."

"The Reverend Mother suggests that you should learn . . ."

"The Reverend Mother and I think that you are now old enough to begin . . ."

It was lessons, lessons, lessons all the time!

Mistral, who looked forward to her Aunt's visits with an almost over-excited eagerness, would find herself shrinking back into her shell of reserve, that same reserve which enabled her to conceal her feelings of utter loneliness from the other girls.

Sometimes at night ,when she was alone in her little narrow bed in the Dormitory, she used to pretend that her Mother's arms were round her, that she was telling her all the things she thought and felt and that her Mother was listening, understanding and sympathizing.

Once, hearing sobs from the bed next to hers, Mistral had got out to comfort the miserable girl.

"What is the matter, Yvonne?" she asked in a whisper, for they were not supposed to talk after lights were out.

"I want my Mother!" Yvonne had wept. "I want my Mother!"

Mistral had soothed her as best she could and tucked her up; then she had crept back, cold and shivering, into her own bed. For the rest of the night she could not sleep.

, She, too, wanted her Mother! She could understand what Yvonne was feeling only too well; but Yvonne's Mother was not far away, a real tangible person, living in a home to which Yvonne would return in three months' time, and which in a few years time, unless she wished to get married, she need never leave again.

It was a very empty thing, Mistral thought in the darkness, to have neither home nor parents, no place that one could call one's own, no-one who cared whether one was ill or well, happy or unhappy, joyful or sad.

It was not often that she let herself dwell on her own loneliness, she was too sensible for that and was also happy by nature. But now she thought it had been an undercurrent to her whole childhood.

Always she had felt a little apart from other girls. They had so many experiences to exchange, treats to which they had been taken during the holidays, the excitements of riding, bathing, ski-ing or travelling.

More than this, they had an indissoluble link in common—they were all part of a family. They could talk of their Mothers and Fathers, their sisters and brothers. They could complain as they often did, of paternal authority:

153

"My Mother won't let me go to dances, she says I'm too young!"

"My Father is terribly strict. . . ."

They could also boast of their families' possessions or exploits—and this was an endless diversion. The size of their houses, their Father's wealth, their Mother's jewels, their sister's beaux, their brother's success with girls were all subjects for which they could take personal credit.

Mistral would listen to them, then creep away by herself. There was nothing she could contribute to the conversation. For her the whole world was bounded by the tall grey walls of the Convent.

Fortunately she was able to read. At times she thought that if it had not been for the books lent to her by Father Vincent her restlessness might have got beyond control. But Father Vincent was wise.

He was her Confessor and he realized the seething undercurrents which were apparent sometimes behind the clear frankness of Mistral's eyes.

Perhaps, too, he appreciated that her brain was exceptionally clear and active and perceived not only that she easily surpassed girls of her own age, but also that it was becoming quite a problem to find qualified teachers for her.

Father Vincent was an extremely well-educated man. He was an aristocrat who had chosen to enter the Church rather than follow the family tradition and go into politics. He had acquired a vast library of books to which he added year after year.

They were not perhaps the reading that the Mother Superior would have chosen for a young girl; but Father Vincent had assured her that he considered it essential to Mistral's development and well-being that she should have freedom of choice in this if in nothing else.

"You can ride a young horse on the bridle for too long," he said, and the Mother Superior had understood.

"Mistral is a sweet child," she said. "I half hoped that she would have a vocation, for I understand she has no home and I worry as to what will happen when she leaves here."

"Do not try to persuade her to take the veil," Father Vincent said authoritatively. "She is one of those who need the lessons which only life in the outer world can teach. We can but give her the right standards and ideals by which later she will be able to judge the gold from the dross."

And so Mistral was given the freedom of Father Vincent's library. She read a strange and varied assortment of books.

There were books on religion, travel, philosophy, and books which, while being romances, were also some of the greatest achievements in French literature. As she grew more proficient at languages, Father Vincent gave her German books to read, and later Italian.

But perhaps among all the volumes gathered together in Father Vincent's library and reaching from floor to ceiling she liked the English ones best.

Samuel Johnson and Thackeray she found entrancing, Shakespeare was an acquired taste which grew on her after she had read and re-read *A Midsummer Night's Dream*.

The more modern authors like Sir Walter Scott, Jane Austin and Dickens were read over and over again, while the poets held her spellbound. The Mother Superior would have fainted if she had known that Mistral had read Lord Byron's books and found them fascinating.

There were dozens of others which at first she liked

because they were English, but which later became, as books should, real friends and often closer than the real people in her life.

But even books could not compensate Mistral for her lack of parents and a home life, and when she learnt that she was to leave the Convent and go to Aunt Emilie, it had been a moment of sheer exaltation.

At last she would be like other girls, at last she would be able to love someone and be loved in return.

She knew now that nothing had happened in the way she had anticipated. The first night in Paris, when she had arrived at her Aunt's house unannounced, she had gone to sleep confidently assured that this was to be her future home.

But in the morning she had learned differently, and now it seemed she had only exchanged the confines of the Convent walls and the gentle affection of the Nuns for the impersonality of a hotel bedroom and the uncertain temper of Aunt Emilie.

Aunt Emilie did not love her, Mistral was sure of that. She was not even certain if she liked her.

At times it seemed as if there was a dark hostility in Emilie's eyes, a hostility which seemed to take a delight in finding fault, in discovering some trival misdemeanour for which she could utter a most stringent rebuke.

Mistral crossed her bedroom and opened a drawer in the dressing-table. In the blue leather box lined with velvet lay the pearls which had belonged to her Mother. She took them out and held them in her hands. She stroked them a little and felt that they were warm beneath her touch.

They had been her Mother's! Mistral pressed them against her cheek. If only they could talk, if only they could tell her what her Mother had been like and if she would have loved her had she lived. Aunt Emilie

156

would say so little and what she did say was often terribly disconcerting.

Why, for instance, had her Mother christened her "Mistral", and why had she been here at Monte Carlo shortly before her own birth?

They were questions which continually presented themselves, but to which Mistral could find no answer, and Aunt Emilie would give none. She had always found that following in their train was the question— who was her Father?

Long, long ago, soon after she had first gone to the Convent, Mistral had realized that she used her Mother's name while other girls used their Father's. She had said nothing, but when Emilie next visited her she had asked her about it.

"Is my Father dead?" she asked.

"No!"

Emilie's voice was abrupt and harsh.

"Does he not want to see me—ever?" Mistral enquired a little wistfully.

"No!"

"He does not like me then?"

"The question does not arise," Emilie said. "Your Father has no part in your life. Forget him! You are your Mother's child. It is her name you bear."

"But why am I different?" Mistral had insisted. "Other girls use their Father's name."

"Your Mother wished you to use hers," Emilie said. "It is a good name, the name of a fine English family. Is that not sufficient for you?"

There was something so hostile in the question that frightened and intimidated, Mistral had agreed that it was, and probed no further.

She was so anxious to do as Aunt Emilie wished that she tried not to think about her Father, yet inevitably a consciousness of him remained. He existed and

157

she was part of him, whatever Aunt Emilie might say, however much she might try to prevent every possible reference to him.

He was somewhere in the world, but did he know that she was grown up and that sometimes she longed for him with an overwhelming longing?

Home! That word had never meant anything to Mistral. The long hours, as she sat alone in her bedroom thinking of things which in the Convent had been forbidden subjects, depressed her and made her suddenly sad. Things were not improved when Jeanne finally came into the room.

"I have come to put out your dress for the evening," she announced. "Your Aunt wishes you to wear the grey satin."

At the sound of Jeanne's voice Mistral turned eagerly from the window where she had been watching the stars coming out in the sky one by one now that darkness had fallen.

With difficulty she checked the exclamation which rose to her lips. Jeanne was looking ghastly, her face was as white as that of a corpse, and her lips were bloodless.

Her hands were shaking too as she turned the gas jet a little higher and opened the door of the wardrobe.

"Jeanne, what is the matter?" Mistral asked. "You look as if you might swoon. Sit down and rest. I will find my own dress."

"No, I will do it," Jeanne said gruffly; then, as she went to the wardrobe, Mistral heard her mutter: *"From all sin, Jesus, deliver us!"*

"What did you say?" she asked, half believing that her ears had deceived her.

"Nothing, I said nothing," Jeanne replied; but Mistral heard her add beneath her breath: *"From the snares of the devil, Jesus, deliver us."*

What was the matter? What had happened? Why was Jeanne repeating a Penitential Litany? What had upset her? What had made her seem to age twenty years since they had come in from their walk in the gardens?

Impulsively she crossed the room and put her arms round the old woman.

"You are tired, Jeanne, or ill. Go and lie down on your bed. I can dress myself and Aunt Emilie tonight."

"No, Mademoiselle." Jeanne's voice was shrill. "Madame does not wish to be disturbed, not until dinner time. You are not to go near her."

"Very well," Mistral said. "But sit down, Jeanne, please sit down."

To her surprise the maid shook herself free of the embracing arms.

"Don't touch me," she said, "and let me go about my business, Mademoiselle. I have things to do. . . . *O Lamb of God who takest away the sins of the world spare us . . .*"

She laid out the dress that Mistral was to wear that night and went from the room, still praying, a terrified look in her eyes.

Mistral had not understood it and it was a relief to find that Aunt Emilie seemed unperturbed when they met in the sitting-room before dinner. Indeed, if anything, Emilie looked more regal and imperious than usual in a dress of sapphire blue brocade with an overskirt of draped net.

If Mistral had been afraid that her Aunt would be affected in the same strange way as Jeanne, she was mistaken. Emilie's head was held high and there was a faint smile on her lips. It even seemed to Mistral that her eyes were unusually bright and that her voice had a ring of triumph in it.

Whatever had shattered Jeanne had apparently had the reverse effect on her Aunt.

"Tidy the sitting-room, Jeanne," Emilie said, "and leave me some wine to drink when I return. Remember to mend the tear in the dress I wore this afternoon. It must have been caught by a bramble or a prickly bush. It is only a small mark near the hem, but it should be attended to at once."

It appeared to Mistral that Jeanne almost crumpled up and she trembled all over. But she only muttered:

"Yes, Madame . . . I will do it at once, Madame."

But when her voice had lied away, her lips continued to move and Mistral knew that she was still praying.

Aunt Emilie led the way downstairs to dinner and they made their usual late and impressive entrance into the dining-room. People stopped eating and talking to look up at them.

Mistral wished, as she did every night, that the earth would open and swallow her up rather than that she should encounter the scrutiny of hundreds of curious eyes and be humiliated by the knowledge that her every movement was being criticized and commented upon.

At school the Mistress who taught deportment had always impressed on her pupils that self-consciousness was both vulgar and conceited.

"Do not think of yourself at all on such occasions," she commanded.

Every evening at dinner time Mistral tried to obey her. She forced herself to think of other things, to repeat some lines of poetry as she threaded her way in Aunt Emilie's wake between the tables of the crowded dining-room.

Tonight some lines of Lord Byron's came to her mind:

She walks in beauty, like the night
Of cloudless climes and starry skies;
And all that's best of dark and light
Meet in her aspect and her eyes.

"How lovely to be like that," Mistral thought, and had no idea that the lines might have been written of her.

They reached the sanctuary of their table. Mistral, seating herself, thankful that the nightly ordeal she dreaded was over, was aware that she was hungry and agreed almost eagerly to the dishes that the waiter suggested for their delectation.

Unfortunately it seemed that Emilie could eat little. She took only a spoonful of soup, a mere mouthful of fish, and then she sent away the other dishes untouched.

But she talked vivaciously, commenting on the people around them so unfavourably and in such a loud voice that Mistral was afraid her venom would be overheard.

She was thankful when the meal was finished and they could go to the Casino. Tonight it seemed that Emilie was in an extravagant mood. She changed four large bank-notes for gold pieces, then had difficulty in carrying so much money. Mistral helped her.

"You are going to play higher than usual, Aunt Emilie?" she asked.

Having spoken, she was half afraid her Aunt would resent her remark, but Emilie only smiled and replied:

"I can afford it! Yes, I can afford it—tonight."

As usual Mistral stood behind her Aunt's chair and watched her play. At first she had found both the game and the playing interesting and often amusing, but lately she had grown weary of her role of spectator.

The piles of money placed on the numbers, the

161

croupiers' level, expressionless voices, the claw-like hands of those who had won going out to grasp the gold, were now all too familiar and monotonous to hold Mistral's attention for long and tonight her eyes wandered round the room not once but continually— watching the newcomers as they entered and the crowds moving from table to table.

She pretended to herself for a time that she was not looking for anyone special, but she knew in her heart that she was waiting for the moment when she would see Sir Robert again.

He had not dined at the *Hôtel de Paris* tonight, and she had a sudden terrible fear that he might have gone away, that his holiday had come to an end.

Suppose that was the truth? Suppose she never saw him again? As she asked herself the question Mistral felt a loneliness and a sense of desolation such as she had never experienced before.

The glittering scene vanished from before her eyes and she thought she was alone in a vast and dreadful darkness without a friend or companion.

She did not understand her own fear, she only knew she was afraid.

Then with a feeling of relief so violent, so overwhelming that she felt as if her very knees were too weak to hold her, she saw Sir Robert enter the room. He was with Lady Violet, and it seemed to Mistral that they both looked cross as if they had been quarrelling.

Sir Robert went straight to the nearest table and started to play. Mistral watched him. She half hoped he would look up and see her and then, as often happened, there would be a flicker of recognition in his eyes and a faint smile on his lips.

But tonight he was concentrating too intensely on his gaming, she thought, to think of anything else. Yet she minded nothing save that he was there, that she could watch him from under her eyelashes.

"Mistral, what are you thinking about" Emilie's voice recalled her wandering thoughts. "I have spoken to you twice and you have not answered."

"I am sorry, Aunt Emilie," Mistral said quickly.

"Take my cloak and put it in the Cloakroom. It is too hot in here."

"Yes, Aunt Emilie."

*"Numéro Quinze. Rouge et impair,"* the croupier called.

"There, I have won again," Emilie remarked with satisfaction. "I always win in the end. Do you realize that, Mistral? I always win in the end."

Emilie gave a little chuckle. It was a strange sound; and because she so seldom laughed, Mistral felt as if there was something almost sinister about the sound coming from between her lips.

Hastily she took her Aunt's cloak. The Ladies' Cloakroom was at the far end of the passage from the Main Entrance and to reach it she passed several other rooms. As she hurried along past the Card Room, a man came out.

She drew a little to one side to let him pass, but found him barring the way.

"Mademoiselle Fantôme!" he exclaimed. "This is indeed fortunate for I wish to speak with you."

Mistral recognized the Rajah of Jehangar. She knew him by sight and she had noticed during dinner that he was continually looking in their direction. Aunt Emilie had noticed it too.

"That is the Rajah of Jehangar staring at us so impertinently," she snorted. "A poisonous little man but fantastically rich. He spends seven months of the year in Europe, then goes back to India to collect more money to squander."

163

"I think the lady with him is very pretty," Mistral said.

"Lady!" Aunt Emilie had ejaculated in a scornful, sarcastic manner.

Mistral had not understood either her remark or the tone in which it was made, but she had not liked to ask Aunt Emilie for an explanation.

Now, looking at the Rajah's dark secretive face in which his teeth seemed strangely white, she thought her Aunt's description of him might well be justified. Hastily she moved as if to pass him, saying:

"You will excuse me, Your Highness, but I have been sent on an errand for my Aunt."

"It can wait for a few moments," the Rajah answered. "What I have to say to you is of vast importance to you personally."

"To me?" Mistral said in surprise. "What is it?"

"Come with me," the Rajah said authoritatively. "We cannot talk here."

He led the way into the deserted Concert Room. The high windows were open on to the terrace and the Rajah followed by Mistral passed through one of them so that they stood outside, the light from the moon illuminating the stone balustrade and the great stone urns planted with cascading geraniums and blue heliotrope.

"My Aunt will be waiting for my return," Mistral said nervously, holding Aunt Emilie's velvet and fur-trimmed cloak in front of her as if it were a shield.

There was something about the Rajah which revolted her. She had often wondered why the pretty, fair-haired woman who invariably accompanied him to the Casino could not find a more attractive escort.

"I will not keep you many minutes," the Rajah said.

"What do you wish to speak to me about?" Mistral enquired.

"You are very direct; you come straight to the point," the Rajah answered.

Mistral thought that she disliked his face more when he smiled than when he was serious.

"I cannot linger here, Your Highness, or my Aunt will be displeased with me."

"And no-one must ever be displeased with anyone as lovely as you, Mademoiselle," the Rajah replied.

Mistral's chin went up as if she resented his compliment and he added quickly:

"But I must speak bluntly in European fashion. In my country we are not so crude. Very well, I would talk to you about your pearls."

"My pearls!"

"Yes, I see you wear them again tonight. They are very beautiful, but perhaps too sombre, a little dull for someone so young and gay like yourself. If you will permit me, I will exchange them for diamonds or for any other precious stones that you admire."

"Exchange them?"

For a moment Mistral was completely bewildered as she echoed his words, then an explanation of what he was saying came to her.

"You mean that you wish to own my pearls, to buy them from me?"

"Exactly! How lucky that we can express ourselves in so friendly a fashion! Yes, Mademoiselle, I would buy your pearls from you for any sum that you wish to name, any reasonable sum, of course; or, as I have said, if you prefer it, I will replace them with a necklace of diamonds, sapphires or rubies. Most women seem to prefer diamonds."

Mistral drew herself up proudly.

"I am afraid Your Highness must have been misinformed. The pearls that I wear are not for sale or for exchange."

"Now, Mademoiselle, do not make such a hasty decision."

The Rajah took a step forward.

"Your pearls, as I have already said, fine though they are, are not entirely a suitable ornament for anyone so young and so beautiful as you. But however rich one is, money is always useful.

"You may never have another offer like this in the whole of your life. I have set my heart on obtaining the pearls, therefore you can blackmail me a trifle. Does the idea not amuse you?"

"I am sorry, Your Highness, but I would never consent to part with my pearls. And now if you will excuse me. . . ."

Mistral turned towards the window, but the Rajah was in front of her. Now he was standing on the step so that she must look up at him.

"How can I convince you that I always get what I want?" he asked. "It would be much wiser of you, Mademoiselle, to agree to let me have the pearls now and at your own price."

There was no mistaking the threat in his tones. Mistral was suddenly angry at his impertinence.

"Kindly stand aside," she said frigidly. "Your Highness has no right to keep me here. I have answered your question and refused your offer. There is no more to be said."

"On the contrary, I have a great deal more to say," the Rajah replied. "You are very young, Mademoiselle, and the young are usually both impetuous and intolerant. I shall obtain the pearls, but it would have been so much more pleasant if we could do it amicably—you and I."

Mistral was suddenly aware that his voice had taken on an almost hypnotic quality. His eyes were looking down deep, deep into hers, and she felt as if some dark mist were rising within her.

Even as she sensed this, she saw that the Rajah's hand had gone out towards her neck and she knew that he meant to touch the pearls.

With an exclamation which was almost a cry she forced her eyes away from his, and with a sudden unexpected movement pushed her way past him and into the lighted Concert Room. She was so quick that, the Rajah, reaching out to step her, was too late.

She was free, and before he could do anything was running as quickly as she could down the corridor and through the door which led to the Ladies' Cloakroom.

There was another passage between the outer and inner doors of the Cloakroom, and as Mistral reached the second door, still running blindly and with a terror which lent wings to her feet, she collided with another woman who was coming out.

"Lor . . . I'm sorry!" the woman exclaimed in English.

Mistral looked up to see that it was the pretty, fair-haired woman whom she had often noticed in company with the Rajah.

For a moment she could only stare at Stella, her breath coming unevenly from between her parted lips; then she realized that in the collision the tulle which trimmed the bodice of her grey satin dress had become entangled in one of the jewelled butterflies with which Stella's dress was ornamented.

They were joined together, and after a second's stupefaction from the force of the impact Mistral reached up to try to disengage the butterfly.

"I am sorry," she said. "It was my fault for entering so quickly."

"That's all right," Stella replied. "You did seem to

be in a bit of a hustle. Thought you must be off to catch a train or something."

Mistral tried to smile.

"No, it was not a train which made me run."

Stella looked at her.

"You're awfully pale," she said sympathetically. "Something must have upset you. Never mind about that stupid butterfly, give it a good tug. Let me try."

"No, pray do not move," Mistral begged.

With skilful fingers she disentangled the tulle from the tiny metal claws framing each of the colourful pieces of glass of which the butterfly was constructed.

"Thanks," Stella said when she was free.

"Unfortunately the butterfly is hanging by only a thread," Mistral replied.

"I expect the attendant can mend it," Stella remarked; but she did not move, and Mistral realized that she was waiting for her to lead the way.

With a shy little smile she went into the Cloakroom and handed Aunt Emilie's cloak to the woman in charge. Then she turned to see Stella had come in behind her and was looking down at her sleeve.

Her dress was astonishing now that Mistral could see it in the gaslight. Of bright green satin, it was covered all over with butterflies embroidered with tiny jewels. They glittered and sparkled as she walked so that while in some ways it was pretty and attractive it was also incredibly gaudy.

Her hair, too, dressed in a profusion of curls, was ornamented with a wreath of butterflies, while her cheeks were vivid with rouge and her lips as crimson as the bouquet she carried of tiny roses.

But Mistral saw, too, the friendliness of her wide smile, the pleasant gentleness of the expression in her blue eyes.

Stella looked at her reflection in the mirror then put

up her hand and gave the butterfly a little pull. The last thread broke and it came away in her hands.

"There, it's come right off," she exclaimed.

"It must be sewn on again," Mistral said, "because I am afraid the satin is torn a little underneath. I do apologize most sincerely for my clumsiness."

"You needn't do that," Stella smiled. "It doesn't matter to me, I promise you. To tell the truth I don't like this dress much, but it was so expensive that Crissie . . . I mean my sister . . . thought I'd better have it."

It seemed to Mistral such an extraordinary reason for buying a dress that she could think of nothing to say. After a moment Stella remarked in a low voice:

"You ought to be going, you know; you mustn't stay here talking to me."

For a moment Mistral did not understand, and then slowly in sheer embarrassment the blood came into her cheeks. She had not thought of the pretty woman who was always with the Rajah as being a bad woman, but now she understood what Stella was trying to explain to her.

Even as she understood, she knew, too, that this English girl could not speak French. One of the reasons why she had not asked the woman to sew on the butterfly was because she had no idea how to give the order.

Mistral's smile was very sweet.

"Thank you," she said, "but first of all I must repair the damage that I have done to your gown. Will you allow me to ask the cloakroom attendant to mend it?"

Stella looked relieved.

"I'd be glad if you would," she said. "I can't speak their jargon. I have enough trouble getting my cloak every night."

Mistral turned to the attendant.

"Please bring a needle and thread," she said in

169

French. "Mademoiselle has damaged her dress and needs it repaired."

"*Certainement, Mademoiselle, je viens tout de suite,*" the woman replied.

"That's awfully kind of you," Stella said.

"It is very little to do after half ruining your gown," Mistral replied.

The attendant crossed the floor with a needle and thread. Stella paid little attention to her.

She was looking at Mistral and it seemed from the expression on her face that she was struggling in her mind whether she should say something or not. At length the words almost burst from her.

"Look here, let me give you a tip," she said. "If anyone wants to buy those pearls of yours, you say no."

Mistral stared at Stella in astonishment; then it came to mind that it must be for her that the Rajah wished to purchase the pearls.

"They are not for sale," she said quietly, "for they belonged to my Mother."

"I thought it would be something like that when I was looking at you just now," Stella said; "but just remember what I've said. If anyone asks you to part with them—tell them there's nothing doing."

"Thank you for the advice," Mistral said slowly. "It was very kind of you to give it to me."

"Kind?" Stella made the word a question; then she laughed. "It is kind of you to be talking here to the likes of me. If anyone sees us, you'll get into trouble, you know."

"People often have very silly ideas," Mistral said: "I can see nothing wrong in my talking to you."

The way she spoke was gentle and friendly and so was the smile on her lips. Stella gave a little sigh.

"Lots of people would be only too ready to tell you how wrong it is," she said. "That's the trouble with this world, you're never certain if what you're doing is right or wrong; at least I'm not."

"You sound as if you were troubled about something," Mistral replied, instinctively sympathetic.

"It's funny you should say that," Stella exclaimed, "and it's just about the truth, for I am. Funnily enough, what's troubling me is a real mixture of right and wrong."

"Perhaps someone could help you," Mistral said. "When I have been in doubt over things that really matter, I have always found it comforting to go to someone who knows the answers."

She did not like to suggest outright that a Priest would solve the problem. She was on the verge of doing so when she remembered that the majority of people in England were not Catholics.

Stella seemed to be cogitating over her words. The woman had finished sewing on the glittering butterfly and with a muttered word of thanks Stella gave her a franc.

*"Merci, Mademoiselle, merci,"* the woman said, returning to her chair by the cloaks.

Mistral knew she should go back to Aunt Emilie. It would be difficult to explain why she should have taken so long to do a simple errand, yet something made her stay. She felt instinctively that Stella wanted to confide in her. Her expression was worried, her eyes with their heavily mascara-ed eyelashes were almost piteous in their appeal for help. Mistral knew that she must stay a little longer whatever the personal consequences.

At last it seemed that Stella had made up her mind to speak.

"Look here," she said, "there's something about you which makes me feel that you could solve my problem for me. It's this. Supposing you had the chance of giving up something that was wrong and doing some-

171

thing that was right, but in doing it you would hurt someone very much. Really hurt them, I mean—someone you were fond of and who was fond of you. Would you think that right or wrong?"

Mistral drew a deep breath. Somehow she knew that events of the greatest importance hung on her reply.

"That is not really a difficult question," she said in her clear, sweet voice. "To give up something that is wrong is always the right thing to do, however hard it may seem, however many difficulties there may be in the way.

"One must always try not to hurt other people; one must always give them the greatest possible consideration and kindness; but there is something more important than their feelings, however dear they are to us.

"In doing what is right we are doing the will of God, and that comes first. We must do what is right, however great the cost to ourselves or—to other people."

Stella threw back her head and it seemed to Mistral as if she threw a great burden from off her shoulders; then she said quietly:

"Thank you! I knew you could help me—you are good!"

# 9

Violet Featherstone moved restlessly about her sitting-room.

It was a very attractive room with windows opening out onto a balcony from which there was a magnificent view of the sea.

Wistaria hung over the balustrade in long purple tendrils, and from two ancient stone urns, which Violet had discovered broken and forgotten in some peasant's garden, pink geraniums cascaded in luxuriant profusion.

The Villa was furnished with period pieces brought from England and there was none of the gaudy, ornate pomp which so many residents in the South of France thought desirable. Violet had always loved beautiful things; she had an inborn instinct for what was good, and Eric's considerable fortune had enabled her to indulge her taste.

But today Violet had no eyes for her own possessions. She moved from the Sheraton bureau to the Knole settee, from an Adam console table to the window and back again without seeing any of them.

She was thinking of one person and one person only —Robert Stanford! It was the middle of the afternoon and still he had not called on her.

She guessed that in all likelihood he was out riding and alone, nevertheless it was a departure from their usual routine and with a sudden fear she began to recollect the times recently when Robert had seemed less eager for her company and to add them up to a formidable total.

When he had first come to Monte Carlo but a few days after her own arrival, it had seemed that he could never see too much of her and that the days were too short for all the things they had to say to each other.

But slowly, so that she had not realized it until now, he had changed. She could not explain even to herself how it had happened. It had been so gradual; and intent on hiding the depth of her own feelings from him, she had not noticed the change in his.

Now, twisting her hands together as she walked up and down on the valuable Persian rugs with which the room was carpeted, Violet knew there was a barrier

173

between them, a barrier of reserve and unspoken secrets.

What was it and how had it come to be erected? She could not answer the question even to herself. She only knew that Robert was different; Robert, whose tempestuous, exciting love-making had swept her off her feet, was now quieter, his impetuosity gone. Why had she been so blind?

She should have been alert, perceptive enough to notice the very first severance in the links which bound them together. She should have been on her guard, knowing that her power over him was never as strong as she would have herself believe.

She caught a sudden glimpse of her own reflection in an ancient gold-framed mirror which hung on one wall. She looked old, with a frown between her eyes, her lips drooping.

She threw back her head defiantly—this was no way to captivate a man or to keep him enraptured. But her eyes were still frightened and uneasy.

Always, all through her grown-up life since she had discovered her power over men, Violet had been the one to tire first. Men had found her irrestible.

It was she who exhausted their talents and their charm to the point where each became just another familiar face and one which inevitably began to bore her.

Never had she had to fight and scheme to keep a man in love when once his heart had been laid at her feet. It had all been so easy. She had merely to smile and he was enraptured, she had merely to beckon and he followed her eagerly—too eagerly at times to make the effort worth while.

But Robert Stanford was different. She had known that from the first moment when they were introduced at a Ball. He asked her for a Dance, then said quietly:

"Why have we not met before?"

She looked up into his face and knew only too well what he was feeling, what a tumult of excitement the quiet, conventional question covered.

She, too, was wondering how life had continued for so long without him, how anything could have seemed amusing or gay when he was not there. She had known then, as the music started and he held out his arms, that she was surrendering herself to far more than an invitation to a waltz.

And she had determined that night, when they had danced tirelessly until the dawn, that she would marry him.

She had not thought of anything save her own desire for Robert and of his for her. She had not known at first how rich and important he was. She had known nothing of his family, of the famous house that he owned or of his vast circle of friends.

She had heard of Cheveron, of course, for it was as much a part of England as Windsor Castle; but she had not realized or else had forgotten to whom it belonged, and she had not for a moment visualized what an important part it was to play in her life.

Often when she and Robert were together and she was striving to bewitch him and make him utterly and completely her captive, she had thought it was only Cheveron which stood between her and her goal. Robert talked of his home so often that she knew full well that it was not only the background of his life but a very part of it.

It was Cheveron which fought her, Cheveron which stood for all the things she could never give him— respectability, local prestige, the respect of his own class, the admiration of his employees, and more than that, much more than that—children.

She had known almost from the first that the task

she had set herself would not be an easy one; but Violet had always had courage, the type of moral courage which laughs at chattering tongues and the narrow, confining codes of social convention.

But it was only as she grew to know Robert better that she realized how deeply rooted he stood in his traditional environment. She had rebelled against the smug pomposity that was an unescapable part of her father's ducal home in Lincolnshire.

But Robert had no wish to rebel or to escape from anything that was Cheveron.

It all came back to her so vividly, for she had been born and bred in just that very same atmosphere which she knew existed at Cheveron.

There were the tenants who had served the Great House generation after generation, the employees who for centuries had relied on the same family for their livelihood, their jobs passing from father to son as part of their natural heritage.

There was the Church built in the Park, its Living in the gift of the Lord of the Manor, its huge carved pew set apart for him.

There was the Home Farm from which employees in the Estate obtained free milk, the gardens which meant free vegetables to the same number of families, the laundry where many of the girls first started their domestic service, the Stables, the Carpenter's shops, the Estate Office—all creating a world within a world, a state within a state, with one interest, one ambition— service to the Great House.

Little things, trivial things, but all meaning so much when they were added together.

The Great House was an institution, too, for many others. For the neighbours who would drive over for dinner parties, come to tea on Sundays and attend the big annual garden party when all the County would be invited.

They had almost a language of their own, too, in their knowledge of local gossip and local customs. The conversation was invariably the same, Violet used to think.

There would be trouble between the M.F.H. and a farmer who was incensed because the foxes had eaten some of his hens; there would be arguments about the shooting prospects and the right way to rear pheasants; gloomy predictions about the crops; optimistic hopes of a new hunter or a litter of puppies; and a general agreement that the country as a whole was "going to the dogs."

How well Violet knew it all! How much she had hated that life, and how glad she had been to escape from it! Yet Robert loved it. She knew he did from the warmth of his tone when he spoke of his home. She could hear the added depth in his voice, see the affection in his eyes.

Yes, Cheveron was her rival and it was perhaps a more dangerous one than any woman could have been. Cheveron demanded of Robert his whole future.

Could she be strong enough to hold him? Until this moment Violet had never doubted her power or her ultimate triumph. Now she was not sure.

Three o'clock and still Robert had not come! What could have kept him? She thought of the mornings when he had called her from the garden before she was properly awake. She found it difficult to get up early.

She was usually tired after their late nights and she liked to sleep until nearly luncheon time. Robert had teased her for being "a lazy bones", and in her complete confidence in herself she had not been afraid that he would think that her sloth was due to her years.

177

That was the truth, of course, for as she grew older she did find things more tiring. At Robert's age she had been able to dance all night and be riding in the Row at ten o'clock; but now she could hardly bear the sunlight on her face before midday. Why should he know that?

She had made every effort to do exactly what he wished, always remembering to tease him a little by her unexpectedness, by an elusiveness which would promise a thing one moment and refuse it the next.

Invariably they had lunched together, although it had never been spoken of as a definite rule, for Violet was too clever to allow anything between them to degenerate into a monotonous custom. As luncheon-time approached Robert would say:

"If you have not a better invitation, I hope you will honour me."

And she would smile at him and answer:

"Just for once I will cancel my other appointments."

Those luncheons had been such fun. Meals eaten together at the little Cafés down by the harbour, meals at the big prosperous hotels at Nice, picnics when they went high up the mountains and ate with a wonderful vista of the Côte d'Azure lying far below them.

They had laughed and had been happy—happy, Violet thought, until just recently when there had been a tiny cloud on the horizon, a shadow between themselves and the sun of their happiness.

Robert had been more grave, his laughter had come less spontaneously from between his lips. But Violet had thought that perhaps this new solemnity was a good thing.

She imagined that he was considering asking her the question she longed to hear from his lips; and because it would be unlike him to make a proposal of marriage

178

lightly, he was therefore in anticipation more serious and less light-hearted.

Now she knew that her judgment was at fault.

Yet he had seemed so devoted, so desperately in love that she had believed not only what he had told her but what she wanted to believe with her whole heart.

Suddenly Violet heard a bell tinkle. Robert at last! She glanced towards the mirror and saw that already the frightened look had vanished from her face. How silly she was to imagine things!

There was doubtless some very reasonable explanation as to why he could not come earlier, but now that he was here all would be well. She must be gay and bright and amusing. Men had no use for dismal women who complained.

She patted her hair into place and gave a last look at her face in the mirror, then slipped across the room to stand in the open window looking on to the balcony. He must not think that she had been anxiously awaiting his arrival.

She must appear at ease and indifferent, as if not for a second had she been perturbed or worried by his failure to arrive earlier.

She heard the door of the room open, but she did not turn her head. She heard it close and still she went on looking out to sea, knowing that she made an attractive picture in her leaf-green dress, the sun bringing out the chestnut lights in her well-arranged hair. There was a little cough.

"Hello, Violet!" a voice said.

She swung round, the astonishment of her expression almost ludicrous.

"Eric! What in the world are you doing here?"

The words burst from her lips, she was so surprised. Her husband smiled deprecatingly.

179

"Sorry if I startled you, old girl; I came over from Nice."

"Nice! Really, Eric, I could not be more astonished if a balloon had dropped down the chimney."

"So it appears," Eric Featherstone smiled, "but I wanted to have a talk with you."

Violet realized they were both standing with half the width of the room between them.

"Come and sit down," she said, moving towards the sofa.

As she watched him seat himself, she thought he was looking well. Eric Featherstone had no pretentions to good looks, but he would never be mistaken for anything but what he was—an English gentleman.

Six feet two in height, slightly stiff in his bearing, there was something quietly authoritative and reliable about him which made both strangers and animals trust him instinctively.

He was nearly fifty and there was hardly a grey hair on his head. He had, too, the healthy weather-beaten complexion of a man who spends most of his life out of doors.

"What can you be doing at Nice?" Violet asked when finally they were both seated on the sofa. "I thought you hated the South of France."

"It isn't much in my line, as you know," Eric replied, "but Uncle Harold is dead. He died about three weeks ago."

"Not really?" Violet exclaimed. "I must have missed it in *The Times*. I never can remember to read the Deaths column. Fancy his being dead at last. We always thought he would live to be a hundred."

"He died two days after his ninety-first birthday," Eric said. "I couldn't be particularly sorry, for the old man had had a good innings."

"Sorry!" Violet exclaimed. "He was so disagreeable,

180

so mean, that I don't think anyone could be hypocritical enough to pretend to be sorry. But what has that got to do with your coming to the South of France?"

"Well, as a matter of fact he has made me his heir," Eric Featherstone said apologetically.

"His heir!" Violet exclaimed. "Oh, Eric, I am glad."

"Had to come down and see about the sale of some property he had in Nice," Eric explained. "I have no desire to keep it, too tricky having to deal with foreign lawyers and all that sort of thing."

"Eric, this means you have come into Medway Park!"

"That's right! I was always fond of the place, but I never thought it would be mine."

"Oh, but I'm simply delighted," Violet said. "You used to enjoy going there despite the fact that your Uncle Harold was the most disagreeable host it was possible to imagine. And the place was like an ice-house even in summer. For goodness sake, Eric, put in central heating and some more bathrooms."

"I'm seeing to all that," Eric said. "Ought to have a good season there next year too."

"Season?" Violet queried for a moment, then remembered. "Oh, partridges! Yes, of course. There will be splendid duck shooting, too, won't there? How you will enjoy being a Country Squire! You will get fat and pompous for a certainty."

"Not fat," Eric retorted. "There is too much to do on the Estate. The old man neglected it rather badly, wouldn't spend any money on fences or keepers. There is a lot to be done."

"And you will adore doing it," Violet laughed.

She thought of the big rambling mansion in Norfolk with its five thousand acres of shooting and knew that, if anyone had attained his dream of heaven upon earth, Eric had.

He loathed London and the five-storeyed house in

Park Lane which she had loved. He had hated the Balls, Concerts and Theatres which she had thought an inseparable part of their existence.

He lived only for the time when he could get away to shoot, fish or hunt.

He had no conversation except on those three subjects, and any attempt to make him talk of other things was doomed to dismal failure. Yes, Eric would be happy in Norfolk. The house was nice, Violet thought, or could be provided one spent money on it.

The Drawing-room would have to be re-furnished. New curtains and carpets everywhere would make a great deal of difference, and there must be some very valuable pictures mixed up with a lot of junk. Of course she would have to . . .

Violet drew her thoughts up with a jerk. How ridiculous she was, planning what she would do, when there was no possibility of her ever going there! She had left Eric for good, as she had told him when she walked out of the house in London.

But any woman would find it irresistible not to play with the idea of renovating and redecorating a house like Medway Park.

"I am so glad of this for *your* sake," Violet said firmly, accentuating the "your".

"There is another thing I wanted to tell you," Eric said, shuffling his feet and looking a little sheepish.

There was something in the expression on his face which made Violet draw in her breath. "He wants to marry again," she thought and was surprised that the idea was extremely distasteful to her.

But there was no reason why Eric should not re-marry, she told herself. She had told him firmly enough that, if ever he wanted his freedom, she would make no objection and would leave it to him to make all the arrangements that might set them legally free.

"There is no point in creating a scandal until we have to," she said just before she left Park Lane. "There is no-one I want to marry at the moment and, until I do, I suggest we remain as we are. People will talk, but why should we worry what they say?"

Eric had agreed with her, as he invariably did; but when she considered having a divorce, it had always been because she wanted it and not he. Now it seemed that the boot was to be on the other foot.

"What is it?" Violet asked, and surprised herself by the hardness in her voice.

"It's about Alwyn," Eric said.

"Alwyn—your brother?" Violet asked.

"Yes, Alwyn," Eric replied. "He has gone off big-game shooting in Africa and says he is never coming back. It's all the fault of that damned wife of his. You remember Vera? She was always the wrong sort of girl for him."

"Yes, of course I remember Vera," Violet answered. "I always thought her stupid and rather common. What has she done to upset Alwyn?"

"She has run away with an actor," Eric explained. "A ghastly chap with long hair who spouts Shakespeare, a complete outsider, of course. Vera would not listen to reason, so Alwyn is divorcing her."

"I should think it is the best thing he could do, if you ask me," Violet remarked.

"I thought you would say that," Eric answered. "But unfortunately there are the children to be considered."

"I had forgotten them," Violet remarked. "There are three, aren't there?"

"Two," Eric corrected. "A boy of seven and a girl of five. I am taking them."

"You are what?" Violet ejaculated, feeling she could not have heard aright.

"I am taking them," Eric said again. "They will live

with me. Alwyn has made me their legal guardian and all that sort of thing."

"Eric, what on earth will you do with two children?" Violet cried.

"Like to have them as a matter of fact," Eric answered in an off-hand manner which hid his embarrassment. "I'm going to teach the boy to ride; he's a plucky little chap. Shouldn't wonder if he doesn't turn out to have a really good seat. Later I'll teach him to shoot. The girl is pretty, too, just like the pictures of my Mother. She may be a beauty one day."

He spoke proudly and Violet stared at him in amazement.

Suddenly she rose from the sofa and walked to the open window, to stand with her back towards him. This was what Eric had always wanted and had missed in the years they had lived together—a home with children.

He had never reproached her, never once voiced his disappointment because she had not given him a child and the Doctors had finally said that it was impossible that she would ever have one.

Violet had taken the verdict lightly. She was not particularly keen on children, but now she knew what this must have meant to Eric and she was sensitive enough to know how bitterly she had failed him.

"I thought I ought to tell you this myself," Eric remarked from the sofa. "Didn't want anyone else to come carrying tales. That is why I came over from Nice. I had better be going now."

He got to his feet and Violet, turning to look at him, thought how he dwarfed the room, making everything in it seem small and gimcrack.

"I am glad you have taken the children," Violet said quietly.

Eric looked relieved.

"Pleased to hear you say that," he said. "I thought you might be angry."

"Angry! But of course not!" Violet said. "Besides, if I were, it wouldn't matter very much, would it?"

Eric looked away from her.

"I wouldn't want to do anything that you really disliked," he said. "I know you don't care for the country and all that, but if you wanted to come to Medway . . . well, it's there."

"Eric, what are you trying to say?" Violet asked, putting out her hand and touching his arm. "Why, you ridiculous man, are you suggesting that you would take me back after all this time?"

Eric squared his shoulders.

"No question of taking you back," he said. "You're my wife, aren't you?"

"Eric!" Violet was perilously near to tears. "You shouldn't be like this. Someone might take advantage of you."

Eric hesitated for a moment and then suddenly he took her hand in his.

"I've never been any good at expressing myself, Violet, as you well know," he said, "but I'm fond of you and always have been. You were too young to get married, I see that now. I ought to have let you have your head first, but you were so pretty and you seemed to like me a bit."

"I did . . . I did." Violet said a little wildly.

"Well, you're having your fling now instead of when you were eighteen," Eric said gravely. "That's how I look at it. If you ever get tired or bored with it all—well, your room is waiting for you at Medway Park. I shouldn't worry you much—got too many things to do there."

The tears were falling unchecked down Violet's cheeks now. Her fingers tightened on his.

"Eric, you old stupid," she said. "You are so absurdly kind, you have made me cry."

"Here, I say, I didn't want to do that," Eric said in consternation.

"I shall remember what you have said," Violet went on. "I shall think about it, Eric; and if one day I take you at your word, don't be surprised. I have a feeling that you might be an awfully nice person with whom to grow old."

She would have bitten back the words as soon as she said them, for she saw the sudden light in Eric's eyes.

"Do you mean that?" he asked, and there was an eagerness in his voice.

In answer Violet shook her head and taking her hand from his arm wiped her eyes.

"Don't think about it, Eric, please," she said. "I was only touched by your generosity and understanding. I must be frank with you. I am in love."

The light died from Eric's eyes. Suddenly he looked all his fifty years and more.

"Robert Stanford?" he asked.

Violet nodded.

"People are talking, of course," Eric said. "Decent chap, Robert, all the same. His Father was a friend of mine."

His words somehow dated both herself and Robert more effectively than if he had compared their ages.

"I love him!" Violet said a little defiantly.

"Has he asked you to marry him?"

Violet was startled at the question.

"Not exactly!" she said, "but he will."

"I should damned well hope so," Eric said truculently.

"Oh, Eric," Violet laughed a little weakly, but the sound was not far from tears. "You can't be angry with

186

Robert because he hasn't proposed marriage to your wife."

"Why can't I?" Eric said. "He has got you talked about, hasn't he? Coming down here after you, his Mother in tears, the flag at Cheveron practically at half-mast."

Violet laughed again.

"Stop, Eric, stop! You're being terribly sweet and frightfully funny all at the same time, but you mustn't mix yourself up in my love affairs . . . it's . . . it's indecent."

"Who says so?" Eric demanded. "Somebody has got to look after you, and hang it all, you are still my wife, aren't you?"

"I can't explain," Violet answered. "It is all too difficult. Go now, for Robert may be coming at any moment and I don't want you to meet him when you are like this."

"There are quite a lot of things I would like to say to him." Eric retorted.

"But you can't say them, you can't," Violet replied. "He mustn't be badgered into proposing to me. Besides, I wouldn't want him to if he were."

"What's that?" Eric asked. "Look here, Violet, you said you were in love with the fellow just now. Well, if you are, he'll damn well marry you or I'll know the reason why. If you're not, well it's a different story."

"I'm not certain! I haven't made up my mind," Violet said quickly, alarmed now by the anger on Eric's quiet face and the way his hands were clenched. "Go back to Nice, Eric, please go. I will write to you at Medway Park and later I may come and see you there."

"Is that a promise?" Eric enquired, only half appeased.

"Yes, a promise," Violet said. "Good-bye, Eric."

She raised her face to his and he kissed her on the cheek. She went with him to the front door of the Villa and watched him walk down the steps which led to the road. A carriage was waiting for him, and as it drove off he raised his hat and waved to her. She waved back.

When he had gone, she went up to her bedroom to repair her face; but having reached the dressing-table, she sat for a long time doing nothing, just staring at her own reflection in the mirror as if she had never seen herself before.

She must have sat there for nearly twenty minutes before she heard footsteps outside the window, and looking out she saw Robert coming up the garden. Instantly her heart gave a leap of excitement.

She forgot the thoughts that had been troubling her, the conflicting emotions that Eric had roused within her, the feeling of depression which had been upon her since she awoke that morning.

Robert was here, nothing else mattered. She ran from her bedroom down the stairs and opened the front door.

"Robert, what happened to you?" she gasped, forgetting all pretence at indifference.

"Sorry to be late, Violet," he said casually. "I rode over to Roquebrune, lunched there, and didn't get back until after two o'clock."

"I was half afraid you had had an accident," Violet said.

"I told you never to be nervous about me," Robert replied.

He entered the small, square hall, shutting the door behind him, and Violet led the way into the sitting-room.

He followed her, but to her surprise he did not put his arms round her as he did usually the moment they were alone together. Instead, he walked to the balcony and looked out at the sea.

She watched him, aware that while he had smiled in greeting his eyes were grave.

"Is anything the matter?" she asked at length.

He turned then, making a little gesture that was half a shrug of the shoulders.

"Not really."

"There is something nevertheless," Violet answered.

"Nothing to make a fuss about," Robert said a little testily. "I have had a letter from my Mother telling me that old Hathaway, the Keeper, has died. I have known him since I was a little boy. He has been at Cheveron for fifty years and naturally we shall miss him."

"Naturally!" Violet said a little faintly.

"He used to take me shooting," Robert went on. "I remember I used to think he was very fussy about the way I carried my gun, that I must make absolutely sure I had unloaded it before I crossed a fence or jumped a ditch; but as I grew older, I realized how wise and sensible he was."

Robert's voice died away and he continued to look out to sea.

"I am sorry, Robert," Violet said.

It seemed as if he did not hear her for a moment, and then he turned his head.

"What did you say?"

"I said I was sorry."

"Yes, of course. Cheveron will seem strange without Hathaway. I would like to have been at his funeral, but of course that is impossible. He would have been buried yesterday."

"Yes, of course," Violet said.

Cheveron, always Cheveron! She could feel it there, grasping out towards Robert, holding him firmly, tenaciously, drawing him away from her, entwining itself around him with tentacles that she could never break.

She must have given a little sob, for suddenly Robert turned from the windows and walked into the room.

"I am sorry," he said. "I must not let my feelings bore you. Would you like to go for a drive or visit the Casino?"

She thought that the politeness in his voice and the courtesy of his expression were harder to bear than if he had reproached her. Indeed she would rather he had cursed her for having enticed him to Monte Carlo when he might have been at Cheveron than that he should speak of her like this.

But she knew this was not the moment for a scene, not the moment for reproaches of any sort.

"Let us go to the Casino," she said. "I have a feeling that I might be lucky. I dreamt that I saw seven birds last night. They had long tails, they might have been pheasants."

Even as she said the words she wished them unsaid, for she knew that pheasants would remind Robert once again of Hathaway. Quickly she went on:

"Seven is always my lucky number anyway, and I shall back it to the limit. Are you feeling rich?"

"Rich enough for that," Robert answered again in that considerate, polite voice which she hated.

"I will go and get ready," Violet said. "I shall not be long. We might find someone amusing at the Casino and ask them to dine with us tonight. Have you seen Arthur today?"

Robert shook his head.

"No, I have seen no one," he said, "except little *Mademoiselle Fantôme*. I saw her walking by the shore with her maid. A stray dog had followed her and she was throwing sticks for him."

Violet realized that Robert was making an effort,

as she had done, to speak of other things than Cheveron.

"She is very lovely—the little ghost," Violet said. "Was she wearing grey?"

"Of course! Does she ever wear anything else?"

"I wonder if she is in mourning or if it is just a clever stunt to attract attention."

"If she was in mourning, surely her aunt would be in black?" Sir Robert said quickly, as if he had considered the matter before and knew the answer.

"Yes, I suppose so," Violet said.

"I don't trust that woman."

"Whom? The Aunt?"

"Yes, there is something sinister and unpleasant about her. Besides, she bullies her niece."

"How do you know?" Violet asked in surprise.

"I . . . I guessed," Sir Robert replied, but not convincingly, and Violet looked at him curiously.

"Have you ever spoken to the girl?" she asked.

She did not know why she asked the question. There was just something strange in the way Robert was speaking of her. There was a little pause before he replied, then he said quietly:

"No, I haven't spoken to her."

Surprisingly Violet felt relieved. It was so ridiculous that she could not for a moment acknowledge the feeling even to herself.

"If we are going to the Casino, we had better go," she said. "I won't be more than five minutes, I promise you."

She went from the room, shutting the door behind her. When she had gone, Sir Robert walked again to the window and stood looking out.

He wondered why he had lied about Mistral, then knew that it was his instinctive desire to protect their acquaintance from chattering tongues, even Violet's.

He had only to say that they had met for Violet to ask him a dozen questions, for everyone in Monte Carlo was avid with curiosity about Mistral and her Aunt.

What was the mystery? he wondered. There were all sorts of explanations, but none of them particularly plausible.

But one thing was obvious, that if *Madame Secret,* whoever she might be, had desired to arouse public curiosity and attention, she had more than succeeded. Mistral's beauty, her clothes, her pearls, the way she was allowed to speak to no-one save the Prince, were all the subject of continuous and unceasing comment.

Prince Nikolai said openly that, while he was honoured by their acquaintance, he knew as little as anyone else who the two women were or where they had come from.

But of one thing Sir Robert was quite sure. There was nothing scheming or crafty about Mistral. Sometimes he would meet her eyes across the Casino and think there was an appeal for help in them.

At those times he longed to comfort her, to take her away from those glittering rooms to the quietness of the garden where they could talk together. There was something wistful and lost about her.

She was only a child and he knew without being told that she was often unhappy and still more often afraid.

Yet what could he do? He was powerless, as was everyone else, in the face of *Madame Secret's* determination to speak to no-one save the Prince. Many people had tried to rub up an acquaintance at the gaming tables.

It was quite an easy thing to do as a rule; but any attempt at conversation was met with a stony silence on the part of *Madame Secret,* while anyone who spoke to Mistral in her presence was speedily and effectively vanquished.

He was perhaps the only person who had managed to talk with Mistral, and he had been careful to tell no-one that he had been successful where everybody else had failed. She liked him and trusted him, he knew that.

There had been undisguised pleasure both in her smile and in her greeting when he had drawn his horse up beside her on the sea shore that morning.

"Where did you find your new acquaintance?" he asked, referring to the dog which was bounding round her with yelps of delight.

"He found me," she replied, "and now he will not leave me."

"I'm not surprised at that," Sir Robert remarked.

"All the same, it will be difficult to convince him that I am not able to take him into the *Hôtel de Paris*. Can you see their faces of horror if he walked across their beautifully clean carpets with dirty feet?" Mistral gave a little sigh. "I have always wanted to have a dog of my own."

"I would like to give you one," Sir Robert said. "May I?"

Mistral glanced up at him with a startled expression.

"Of course not," she replied. "Aunt Emilie would never let me keep it."

Sir Robert had swung himself down from his horse to stand beside her. The maid had withdrawn, he noticed, to a discreet distance and was looking out to sea.

"Why are you so afraid of your Aunt?" he asked. "I don't believe she is as ferocious as you make out. Let me come and call on her and I will tell her that at Cheveron I have a litter of highly bred spaniels. They are black and white and very affectionate. You shall have the pick of them all."

"How wonderful that would be!" Mistral exclaimed. "I would love a spaniel, but it is quite, quite impossible. As to speaking to Aunt Emilie. I beg of you to do nothing of the sort. She would be very angry with me if she knew I was talking to you now—very angry indeed.

"And as it is, she seemed extremely strange yesterday and again this morning. I do not think she can be well. Everything I do is wrong; so, please, you must not make things worse for me."

There was a touch of real panic in the young voice which made Sir Robert say quickly:

"I would not do anything that you didn't want me to do, but I wish I understood a little more."

"So do I," Mistral answered miserably. "If you only knew how I long to understand what it is all about, but . . . no-one will tell me."

"But surely you have some other relations besides your Aunt?" Sir Robert suggested.

He saw an almost secretive look come over Mistral's face.

"No, there is no-one," she said, "and I cannot discuss it. Please, Sir Robert, continue your ride."

She looked round as if she would call Jeanne to her side. Sir Robert instinctively put out his hand to stop her. His fingers closed on her wrist, and her movement was arrested by the touch of his hand. She turned to look up into his eyes.

Something magnetic passed between them, something which left them both breathless and spellbound. For the passing of a few seconds the world was lost and everything forgotten save themselves.

Then there was a sudden yap of the dog, the murmur of the waves at their feet, the screech of a seagull as it whirled overhead. Mistral's eyes dropped before Sir Robert's and he took his hand from her arm.

"Do you ever come to the gardens early in the morning?" he asked, more because he felt obliged to speak and break this strange, poignant silence than because he expected an answer.

Mistral shook her head.

"No, I go to the Chapel," she said in a low voice.

Sir Robert swung himself into the saddle. He gathered up the reins from the horse's neck and looked down at Mistral. The sun was glinting on her golden hair. She raised her head suddenly and their eyes met once again.

Both were conscious at that moment of magnetism and of wonder; then without speaking Sir Robert raised his hat and rode away.

What had happened? Why had he felt like that? Even as Sir Robert asked himself the question, he heard Violet calling him. She was ready. They must go to the Casino. He felt a great yawn of weariness and boredom welling up inside him.

The sun was shining, it would be hot and stifling at the Casino. He had a sudden longing for the breeze blowing along the sea shore or, better still, the wind blowing across the parkland at Cheveron.

"Robert! Robert! I am ready!"

Violet was waiting. He turned from the window and crossed the room.

As he did so, he thought that the grey of Mistral's dress was just the colour of the mist which hung over the lake at Cheveron in the early morning.

# 10

Crissie opened her eyes and could not for a moment remember where she was.

Then the softness of her bed, the silk spread which covered her and the sunshine coming through the Venetian blinds, which cast variegated patterns on the walls, told her clearly that she was still in Monte Carlo.

She had been dreaming that she was back in London, and for a moment after waking she still seemed to hear the shrill voices of dirty children playing outside in the street and smell the inevitable stink of stale cabbage and bad drains which seemed to impregnate the atmosphere of every lodging house.

No, she was still in Monte Carlo. She lay still, sensuously enjoying the unaccustomed luxury and comfort of her surroundings. Then her sensation of satisfaction was supplanted almost immediately by one of irritation. She remembered why she had come to lie down in the middle of the day.

It was Stella's fault—Stella, whose stupidity and foolishness had made her so angry that it had brought on one of the agonizing headaches with which she was periodically attacked, especially after her feelings had burst the bounds of self-control.

Yes, Stella was to blame for her headache. It had been a bad one and only when she was almost blind and practically speechless did Crissie give in and go to bed at what she called "the wrong time of day".

She had slept and the headache was gone, but the

cause of her irritation still remained. At times Crissie would say and believe that Stella's idiocy would drive her insane if she did not break a blood vessel in the meantime through sheer unbridled rage.

But Stella would only smile and say she was sorry, and what, Crissie asked in disgust, could anybody do with a person like that?

The row at luncheon time had started because Stella let slip the information that the Rajah had given her some money to gamble with at the Casino the evening before; and having lost part of it, she had given him back what was left.

"How much?" Crissie had snapped across the table. Stella looked uncomfortable.

"Not much," she replied.

"How much?" Crissie insisted.

"I can't remember," Stella answered.

"You're lying," Crissie accused her. "You must have a pretty good idea. Was it fifty francs, a hundred, or more?"

Stella shook her head and went on eating the ice cream made in three different colours and flavours which had been served with fresh *fraises des bois* and whipped cream.

"Answer me!" Crissie ordered.

"I really don't know how much it was," Stella prevaricated. "I had lost a great deal of what he gave me."

"And how much was that?"

"A thousand francs."

Crissie gave an exclamation that was half a choke and brought her clenched fist down on the table, making the glasses ring.

"You stupid, brainless fool!" she cried. "A thousand francs and you actually gambled with it? Why didn't you put it in your pocket and tell the Rajah you had lost it?"

"It wouldn't have been true for one thing," Stella answered mildly. "Besides, he would have seen I was not playing."

"You could have put on a few francs," Crissie conceded. "But it makes me see red to think that, having been so stupid as to gamble and to lose, you returned him what was left. Can't you get into your thick head that we've got to save, that every franc we put aside will seem worth its weight in gold when we return to London?"

"I'm sorry, Crissie," Stella said quietly.

"Sorry! That's all you ever say," Crissie shouted. "What's the point of being sorry if you don't try and do better next time? You had better get double out of the Rajah tonight to make up for it."

Stella put down her spoon and pushed her plate away from her.

"I can't ask him for anything more. He was ever so kind about the pearls."

"And when are you going to get them?" Crissie enquired.

"Well, if it comes to that, I don't want them," Stella answered. "I spoke to the girl that owns them last night—'the Ghost' as they call her, and she was sweet. She talked to me, Crissie, as if I was a friend, someone of her own world. I wouldn't want to take her pearls from her—they belonged to her Mother."

It was then that Crissie screamed and, screaming, rose from the table to stamp about the room raging and cursing until the native servant who had been waiting on them peeped round the doorway, uncertain of what was occurring.

It was some time before Stella was allowed to speak; but when she could hear her own voice, it was only to murmur that she was sorry and didn't mean to upset Crissie so much.

198

But Crissie was not to be appeased and raged on and on until finally physical pain brought her voice to a standstill.

Stella was in tears by that time. It took a lot to make Stella cry, but Crissie had accused her of ingratitude and cruelty, of deception and lying and even of stealing by her stupidity about the money which might have brought them security from starvation.

"Oh, don't go on so, Crissie dear," Stella begged at length. "I'm sorry, and I've said I'm sorry. If I hadn't been so stupid I wouldn't have told you that I'd spoken to *Mademoiselle Fantôme* or said anything about giving the money back to the Rajah."

"Tell me! Of course you'd tell me!" Crissie said. "The day that you can keep anything to yourself I shall fall down dead with surprise. If I wasn't here to look after you, you'd starve within a week—if someone didn't shut you up in a lunatic asylum first. What success you've had has been due to me and me only, and don't you forget it."

"I never do, Crissie," Stella said miserably. "Please don't be so cross with me."

But Crissie could not be placated and when finally the agony of her aching head sent her to her bedroom, her shrill voice was still upbraiding Stella as she went upstairs.

She sighed now and nuzzled her cheek a little deeper against the soft pillow. Thank goodness her headache was gone. She had felt as if it would split her brain in half.

She wondered how long she had been asleep, and found that without moving she could read the hands of the clock which stood on the mantelpiece.

It was nearly five o'clock. She must have slept for over two and a half hours. Well, she felt better for it, strong enough to instil some sense into Stella before the evening, when she would see the Rajah. The idiocy of the girl was unbelievable.

All that money hers for the asking and she couldn't even frame the words! She had always been the same, Crissie thought angrily. She had never been able to exploit her good looks and the opportunities they had brought her.

She remembered the fuss there had been over Stella's first admirer—the first man who had ever offered her his protection. Stella—the silly little fool—had made a terrible to-do.

There was no doubt that the gentleman was elderly and inclined to drink too much, but what did that matter when he was so rich? Crissie recalled the scenes she had had with Stella before she could get her to do what she wanted.

She was only seventeen at the time, outstandingly pretty with a dewy, youthful freshness which she was to lose very quickly. But her head had been packed full of fantastic notions about falling in love and rubbish of that sort.

Crissie had made her see sense, hammered it into her as it were. What a job it had been! She could hear Stella crying now:

"I can't! I can't! He's so old and horrid!"

"What's that got to do with it?" Crissie enquired harshly.

Finally she had won and Stella had given in. For nearly a year they had lived in comfort in a smart little house off Regent's Park. There was a hired carriage to take Stella to the Theatre, a maid to wait on them.

Then like all the other men who were to follow him Stella's protector grew bored.

"Why can't you be amusing?" Crissie demanded. "Make him laugh! Talk to him!"

"There's nothing to talk about," Stella complained.

"We don't like the same things and his stories always make me yawn."

Crissie could remember hitting Stella after that. It was not the first time by any means, nor the last. There was little satisfaction in it, for Stella only cried and said she was sorry.

Tears made her look so unattractive that Crissie was afraid to evoke them too often in case she lost her job at the Theatre.

The whole thing was heart-breaking, Crissie thought now. If only she could have had Stella's opportunities, if only she could have had Stella's face and Stella's figure.

At the thought she turned her face for a moment deeper into the pillow, her thin fingers clutching and crumpling the silk bedspread.

It wasn't fair that some women should have so much and others nothing. She remembered once overhearing two chorus girls talking about Stella and herself. They had been standing in a dark corner at the back of the stage awaiting their call at a rehearsal and had not noticed her lurking near them in the shadows.

"You have to hand it to Stella, she's a good sport," one said.

"Yes, when she gets the chance, but that sister of hers is as mean-fisted as hell," the other replied.

"Oh, her! Don't speak to me of that monkey-faced lump of misery! She fair gives me the creeps!"

Crissie had bitten her lips until they bled to prevent herself saying what she thought of them.

At the same time, as always when she overheard some insulting reference to her appearance, she felt sick with a heart-burning resentment which would rankle for days. She couldn't help what she looked like, could she? She didn't make herself!

She hated those who affronted her with a rabid

201

savagery which made her more unpleasant than usual to the pretty, thoughtless creatures with whom Stella shared a dressing-room.

They were not deliberately unkind to Crissie, and had she been good-tempered and friendly, they would soon have accepted her as one of themselves.

But she was always on the defensive, ready to take offence long before anyone had slighted or provoked her, and the ordinarily happy-go-lucky men and women of the theatre sensed her enmity and instinctively disliked her.

She was like an ill-treated dog who has learnt to snarl at everyone, both friend and foe.

Sometimes Stella would argue with her when they were alone together.

"Why are you so nasty about everyone, Crissie?"

"Why shouldn't I be? They're nasty enough about me when they get the chance."

"How do you know?" Stella asked. "You frighten people when you snap their heads off, and it makes them snap back. They would be nice, if you'd let them."

"I don't want their niceness," Crissie cried savagely. "I want to be left alone."

But it wasn't true! Like everyone else she wanted friends. She wanted to be liked and—loved. Yes, loved, fêted and courted by men as Stella was!

At times she hated Stella with a primitive, burning hatred because men desired her. Crissie would watch their eyes as they rested on Stella's warm, glowing prettiness. She would see the smouldering passion, the rising flame of desire and she would know a sudden frightening response within herself.

Then they would catch sight of her watching them, or perhaps the very ferment of her emotions would draw their attention. Crissie would wait for their expressions to alter. Disgust would replace desire, they would be both repelled and revolted.

Only occasionally was there pity in their regard, and that, Crissie felt, was harder to bear than anything else.

Was it any wonder after such incidents that Stella found her irritability and asperity hard to bear? Was it surprising that at night Crissie often wished to die so that her body might rot unseen in the darkness of the earth?

She had, however, the bitter, perverted satisfaction of knowing that Stella's beauty would have brought her nothing without her own brain to exploit it.

There was a satisfaction, if a vicarious one, in forcing Stella to do as she wanted, in controlling her as one might a puppet, in using her mercilessly in the pursuit of money.

Money! Crissie had decided long ago that was the only thing worth having in life. Money could buy comfort, luxury, security and the envy of less fortunate persons. Money, she told herself, was infinitely more desirable than love or friendship. Money was a salve and a balm for everything, even for the torments of a frustrated, stunted womanhood.

Every penny Stella brought her was to Crissie the elixir of life. It was also her revenge on Stella for being pretty and desirable. If she suffered to obtain it, all the better.

Why should things be easy because she had a pretty face and a well-formed body?

A face out of the past confronted Crissie with a leer. She remembered Lord Wrotham whom Stella had hated. He was a notorious blackguard, but rich and powerful. Stella tried to avoid him for he was a by-word in the theatrical world.

One evening he sent her a bouquet of orchids and an

invitation asking her to have supper with him after the show. Stella shuddered and thrust the flowers away from her.

"I've not sunk so low that I have to take a meal off him," she said firmly. "Send a message, Crissie, and say I'm otherwise engaged."

Crissie made no reply; but when the next Act started, she wrote Lord Wrotham a note of acceptance and signed it with Stella's name.

Stella was hopeless, though, Crissie sighed. One could never teach her common sense. She had to be instructed on every point as if she were a child or an imbecile. Her behaviour with the Rajah was a case in point.

Crissie felt her gall rising again at the thought of the thousand francs Stella had wasted last night. A thousand francs! In England it would keep them for a month or two.

She heard the handle of the door turn softly and raised her head.

"Who's there?" she asked.

The door opened wider and Stella came into the room.

"Are you awake, Crissie?"

"You can see I am," Crissie replied sullenly.

"I wanted to speak with you for a moment."

"Then draw the blinds," Crissie commanded. "It's time I got up anyway."

Obediently Stella crossed to the window and after several fumblings drew up the Venetian blinds.

The windows of Crissie's bedroom looked over the garden at the side of the Villa, and from her bed Crissie could see the soft green branches of the olive and palm trees and beyond them the sharp sides of the mountain climbing skywards.

Stella stood for a moment looking out, then she turned towards her sister.

She was wearing a dress of green tarlatan trimmed with a vivid green and red plaid which was matched by the quills in her hat of chipstraw. Crissie thought she had never seen her look more elegant or for that matter prettier.

There were no longer any traces of tears on her face, her eyes were shining and her lips were smiling. But as the eyes of the two women met, the radiance vanished from Stella's face and her expression became serious.

"Are you going out?" Crissie asked.

"Yes," Stella replied. "That's what I came to tell you."

"Well, try and be a bit more sensible than you were last night," Crissie remarked. "Get the Rajah to take you to the shops."

"I'm not going with the Rajah," Stella said, her voice very low.

"If you expect me to go with you now, you're mistaken," Crissie said. "You've upset me enough for today. I'm going to have a cup of tea if I have to go down to the kitchen myself and make it."

"I wasn't going to ask you to come with me," Stella said. "I . . . I'm going with someone else."

Something in her voice and bearing suddenly struck Crissie as peculiar. She sat up in bed.

"What's all this about?" she asked suspiciously. "What are you trying to tell me?"

Stella took a deep breath.

"I'm leaving, Crissie! I am going away from here."

"Away?" Crissie said the word slowly; then quickly like a shot from a gun she followed it with other questions: "Where are you going? Who with? What's all this?"

Stella's face was very white, but her voice was steady.

"I'm going to be married, Crissie. At once, as soon as it can possibly be arranged. I'm sorry, but he won't let you come with me."

"Married? To whom? Who are you talking about?"

"It . . . it's François."

"François!"

Crissie only whispered the word. For a moment she was almost speechless.

"Yes, François," Stella said, and now suddenly her voice was light. "He loves me, and I love him. It's the most wonderful thing that has ever happened. He told me so two days ago and asked me to marry him; but I wouldn't give him an answer. Then after lunch today he found me crying and made me promise I'd marry him right away. Oh, Crissie, I am so happy, so terribly happy."

"How dare you say that to me!"

Crissie's face was as grey as ashes.

"I was afraid you'd be angry, Crissie; but you must try and forgive me. It's hard, I know, that I can't ask you to my wedding or to my new home; but François won't have it. He's been saving for a long time so that he could buy a restaurant.

"He has one in mind and he hopes that within a few months we shall be settled there. Crissie, he wants me by myself. It's difficult to say this to you, but I must tell you the truth—he doesn't think that you have a good influence on me. It's absurd, of course, and I've told him so, but he won't listen.

"He says that I've got to choose between you and him. And oh, Crissie, horrid though it is of me, I love him so much that I can't give him up."

"You're mad!" Crissie ejaculated at last, the words coming in a stifled fashion from between her pale lips.

"You've told me that so often that I'd begun to

206

believe it; but François says I'm not mad. He says it's just that I'm not suited to the type of life I've been leading. He's right, too, Crissie, for I always hated it . . . you know I have.

"I want a home of my own. I shan't be lazy when I have that. I'll work for François, work to keep his house nice and help him in his restaurant. There's nothing I wouldn't do for him . . . nothing in the whole world."

"Obviously, if you are so besotted as to think you can throw up the Rajah and all his money for one of his servants—this common cook of whom you know nothing."

"I know that François wants to marry me," Stella said with a strangely effective dignity. "You mustn't say unkind things about him, Crissie, for he wants to do what he can for you. I know that you'll be angry at my leaving you, but François has promised that he'll send you some money every month.

"I have forgotten how much he said, but it is about two pounds a week in English money. You can manage on that, Crissie, even if you don't get any work. We've had less than that for both of us many a time; and besides, I want you to have all the jewellery the Rajah has given me and all the money you've saved.

"He'll think I've taken it with me, so he's not likely to ask for it back. You keep it, Crissie; it'll take you back to London, and if you send me your address, François will post you the money every month. He's promised me that."

"You've got everything arranged, haven't you?" Crissie snarled. "Well, you're not going! Make no mistake about that, my girl; you're not going."

"Yes, Crissie, I am," Stella said quietly.

She put a piece of paper down on the dressing-table. "There is the address of François' home. It is in the old town of Monaco and I'm going there now. I think we'll be married early tomorrow morning. Afterwards he's taking me somewhere where we can be alone. We're going on a honeymoon, Crissie, before François looks for another job."

Her eyes were shining again; then she crossed the room a little nearer the bed.

"Please, Crissie, wish me happiness and don't let us part in anger. I know I've got a lot to thank you for . . . and I'm grateful, really I am, for all you've done for me, but I've got to live my own life now. I've always dreamt that I should find someone somewhere, some day, whom I could love and who'd love me. And I've found him, so don't grudge me my happiness."

"You're not going, I tell you," Crissie said stubbornly.

"I've got to go! François is waiting for me, I've packed all my things and the boxes are already downstairs. The jewellery is in the drawer of my dressing-table. Good-bye, Crissie."

Her words of farewell seemed to galvanize Crissie into action. The numbed horror with which she had heard Stella's announcement left her. She sprang from the bed to stand in front of the door, her lank hair falling round her wizened face.

With her lips curved back from her yellow teeth she defied Stella furiously. For a moment the two women faced each other, then Stella said quietly:

"If you don't let me pass, Crissie, I shall send for the Rajah and tell him I'm leaving this house. I've left him a letter; but if, instead, I have to give him the news myself, I shall also return to him all the presents he has given me, including the jewellery which at the moment I'm leaving for you."

Stella's voice was firm and her eyes were steady. Crissie had never known her speak like this before.

There was something resolute about her, a strength in her bearing which had never been hers before.

For the first time in her life Stella was fighting for something which really mattered.

Crissie drew a deep breath. She was defeated and she knew it. In answer she moved from the door and flung herself face downwards on the bed, her hands clenched, the nails digging into the palms, her humped back ugly and monstrous as she lay there.

For a moment Stella hesitated. Her eyes were soft with pity, and then she glanced away from Crissie towards the door.

She was free to go, free to join the man she loved, to live decently for the first time in her life. And yet she must take her happiness at someone else's expense, she must leave Crissie defeated and unhappy.

There was something terrifying in that she had managed to silence the voice that had nagged her for so many years.

Armoured by her love, within a few seconds she had destroyed the power that her elder sister had always had over her. But she had not wanted to wound Crissie, and for a moment Stella contemplated going to her, putting her arms round her and telling her to forget it all.

They would get along together somehow and she would do what Crissie wanted, as she had always done in the past. After all, they were flesh and blood. Wasn't that what counted more than anything else?

Then she thought of François. He was so kind, so understanding. There was nothing she could not tell him, nothing that he would not understand. He loved her really and sincerely. She had seen enough of men in her life to know the truth when she met it. François loved her, and she loved him.

She felt her heart throb at the thought; and then

her eyes rested once more on Crissie, on the piteously deformed back, at the prematurely aged and wrinkled neck, at the legs that were too short, at the arms which were too long. Poor, poor Crissie, how could she leave her?

How could she believe François when he said Crissie was a bad influence? He was wrong, he did not understand how stupid and tiresome she had always been, how lazy and incompetent. She could not go! She must not!

And then, as she wavered, it seemed to Stella that she saw Mistral, saw her wide eyes, honest and truthful, looking into hers and her voice, clear and sweet, saying:

"In doing what is right we are doing the work of God, and that comes first. We must do what is right, however great the cost to ourselves or to other people."

It was right to marry François, Stella was certain of that as she had never been certain of anything in her life before. She walked slowly towards the door.

Crissie had neither moved nor made a sound, but Stella knew that she was waiting, waiting for her to capitulate, to surrender both her will and her new-found freedom.

"I'm sorry, Crissie," she said softly. "Good-bye!"

Crissie did not move nor cry out. She had lost the last battle, and she knew it. Stella had gone and she would never return. How long she lay on the bed she did not know; but when at length she raised her head, it was to look at the clock. The Rajah might by this time have read Stella's note.

When he had done so, there was a chance that he might come to the Villa Mimosa; but before he came, there was something Crissie must do.

Quickly, as if impelled by a sudden fear, she went to

Stella's room. All her things had gone; the dressing-table was bare, cupboard doors stood open to reveal their emptiness. It was a room impersonal and without individuality, as it had been on the day of their arrival; a vacant room, Crissie thought suddenly, waiting for the next occupant.

She wrenched open the drawer of the dressing-table. The jewellery was there as Stella had said it would be.

There was the diamond necklace in its velvet-lined case and the other articles of jewellery, each shining and glittering as Crissie opened their boxes to look at them.

For a moment she only stared at the gems, then suddenly she hugged them against her narrow breast.

They were hers—hers to convert into money, to hoard or to spend as she wished. She chuckled to herself and the sound was eerie in the empty silence of the room.

As Crissie had anticipated, the Rajah was at that moment reading Stella's note in the Villa Shalimar.

He had come in late, having been delayed by a man who wished to sell him some polo ponies. He had done a big deal and driven a shrewd bargain, and he was feeling exceedingly pleased with himself.

As he drove up to the Villa, he had pictured himself telling Stella how clever he had been. The Rajah invariably wished to spread his tail like a peacock and it was not often that he had such a clever stroke of business to boast about.

As he thought that Stella would appreciate how intelligent he had been, he decided that she should also have the chance to appreciate yet another example of his generosity. He would give her the sapphire ring. After the way *Mademoiselle Fantôme* had behaved to him last night he might have some difficulty in obtaining the pearls, despite his assertion to Stella that nothing could prevent him from getting them.

The ring would keep things sweet between them and give him breathing space in which to make his plans.

Perhaps it would be wiser to tackle the old lady next. She might be more amenable. But the girl had been pretty, very pretty. He had always admired fairhaired women. Unlike Stella's colour her hair was natural, he was sure of that.

Her beauty was delicate and exquisite where Stella's was flamboyant. But that was how he liked his women, the Rajah decided almost defiantly. There was little fun to be got out of them when they looked at you with cool disdain.

That was how the girl with the pearls had looked at him last night, and there was something about her which made him feel small and insignificant.

It was ridiculous, of course, besides being insulting. Was he not rich and powerful? Was he not absolute ruler over a State fifty thousand times as big as this tiny Principality?

Yet he, the Rajah of Jehangar, could be rebuffed by a girl and made to feel inferior by the look in her eyes, by the way some magic, which he had not expected her to possess, had defeated his own dark powers.

Why did he keep thinking about her, he asked himself angrily, and why compare her with Stella? Stella was pretty enough in all conscience, and she should have the ring. He would give it to her tonight when they went out to dinner.

She would thank him with a little cry of pleasure and he would slip it on her finger. When he came to think of it, he had not given her nearly so much jewellery as he had given some of his other favourites.

She was not greedy and not always asking for things like other women he had known.

Lola, the Spanish dancer, for instance, had cost him half a million francs in furs and clothes alone, and even now it annoyed him to think of the diamonds he had given her. He had been young in those days, but he had grown more cautious as he grew older.

Yes, Stella deserved the sapphire ring and she should have it. If it came to that, he had very nearly saved the price of it over the polo ponies.

The Rajah had been smiling as he entered the Villa Shalimar. The servants in the hall bowed low as they always did at his appearance, but something in the expression on their faces, in their grovelling obeisance made him suspicious that something was wrong.

Invariably his oriental instinct made him scent trouble almost before it was upon him. Sharply he glanced at one of his Aides-de-Camp who had come hurrying from a sitting-room at the sound of his arrival.

"Anything wrong?" he asked.

The Aide-de-Camp looked surprised. He was new to the job and had not yet gained the confidence of the Rajah's servants who had been with him for many years.

"No, Your Highness, nothing. Why do you ask?"

The Rajah made no reply. It was then that another servant approached with a note on a silver tray. The Rajah glanced down at it, but did not recognize the writing.

"From Miss Style, Your Highness."

The Rajah took the note in his hand. Impatiently he tore open the envelope. Stella's large, untidy, almost illiterate writing covered two sheets of paper. The Rajah read it through with some difficulty for the spelling was erratic; then without saying a word he walked into the sitting-room, followed by his Aide-de-Camp.

As the door closed behind them, the servants exchanged glances. They were well aware that Stella's and François' action in leaving the villa together would mean trouble for them. When the Rajah was angry, he could be very unpleasant.

The Rajah walked across to the writing-desk and laid Stella's letter down. He turned to his Aide-de-Camp.

"When did she leave?" he asked.

"Who, Your Highness?"

"Miss Style!"

"Leave? But I did not know that she had left," the Aide-de-Camp replied uncomfortably.

"You are a fool!" the Rajah said rudely.

"If Your Highness says so."

"I do say so, and you are dismissed. It is part of your job to know what is going on in this household, and if it does not meet with my approval, to prevent it."

"But, Your Highness——" the young man began.

"Go, I tell you, and at once!"

Humiliated and crestfallen, his dark eyes filling with tears, the Aide-de-Camp walked towards the door. As he reached it, the Rajah said:

"Send Khusru to me!"

Khusru, who had been expecting this very summons, was waiting in the hall. He was a big, bearded Sikh who, since the Rajah's birth, had been his personal attendant. In a few minutes the Rajah was in possession of all the facts.

Khusru knew the workings of the Rajah's mind better than anybody else, and he was well aware that a scapegoat must be found. Humiliation and "loss-of-face" could not be endured by a despot, and the Rajah was that among his own people.

Khusru let the Rajah rage uncontrollably and with the petulant fury of a spoilt child against Stella until the worst of his anger gave place to an ugly and dangerous self-pity. This was Khusru's moment.

"If I may presume to express an opinion, Your Highness, I do not think it was entirely the lady's fault," he said softly. "François is a very persuasive man. The French are like that, eloquent, full of soft words and sweet sayings, but François would never have succeeded in his seduction had the lady been happy. . . ."

"What do you mean?" the Rajah asked sharply.

"Your Highness knows full well that I do not mean she was unhappy when she was with Your Highness. Then she was in a paradise of delight, as are all those on whom Your Highness is gracious enough to smile. But when she was not in the sunlight of Your Highness's company, it was a very different matter."

"Explain yourself," the Rajah commanded.

"It was the sister of the lady, the ugly cripple, who caused her much unhappiness. Often I heard her voice raised in anger, often I heard her say cruel, hurtful things to the lady that Your Highness honoured. It was not right, I thought; but who am I, a humble servant, to carry tales?"

"You should have told me," the Rajah said.

"Yes, yes, Your Highness—I am guilty of great stupidity. Your unfortunate servant sees that now, but at the time I thought it of no consequence. Now it is obvious that the lady has been forced to escape the cruelty of the hunchback, from which even Your Highness's kindness and generosity could not save her."

The suggestion salved the Rajah's pride, his eyes were less sullen.

"I see what you mean, Khusru," he said. "The hunchback has not gone with her?"

"No, no, Your Highness. She is alone in the Villa Mimosa."

"Turn her out at once," the Rajah said sharply. "I will not have her there."

"Tonight, Your Highness?"

"You heard me! I said at once! I always disliked her! She has brought bad luck on the place."

"Your Highness has great wisdom! Your Highness's instinct could never be at fault."

"Turn her out then."

"And if she has no money with which to return to her own country—to England?"

"Is that my concern?" the Rajah asked. "Let her starve! Why should I care!"

"Let it be as Your Highness commands."

Khusru bowed himself to the door. As he reached it, another servant entered the room. He carried a card on a silver salver which he handed to the Rajah. The Rajah looked at the card.

"*Monsieur Gutier, Chef de la Sûreté!* What does he want?"

"To see Your Highness. Monsieur regrets if it is an inopportune moment, but he will not keep Your Highness more than a few minutes."

"Very well, show him in," the Rajah said.

As he waited, he frowned. What could the Police want with him? He could think of nothing in which he might have contravened the laws of the Principality.

The door opened again and Monsieur Gutier came into the room. He was a dapper little man, who looked his best in the spectacular blue and white uniform of the Monte Carlo Police.

"You wish to see me?" the Rajah asked.

"I must apologize if I am disturbing Your Highness," he answered. "But there is a small matter on which I should be grateful for your help."

He drew from his breast-pocket a leather wallet.

"I have here," he said, his voice solemn and slightly

216

pompous, "the personal effects of a man who, most unfortunately, he was found dead in the Casino Gardens the night before last."

"Murder or suicide?" the Rajah asked with a faint sneer.

He was well aware how much the authorities disliked either occurring in the precincts of Monte Carlo.

"We assume it to have been suicide," Monsieur Gutier replied.

"I suppose, as usual, he had lost all his money at the tables?" the Rajah asked.

"I should hardly imagine the gentleman in question had much money to lose." There was a reproach in the Detective's voice, as if he resented the Rajah's instantaneous assumption that the Casino was to blame. "At the same time, Your Highness may be able to tell us more about the deceased."

"I?" the Rajah ejaculated. "Who was he?"

"A man named Henry Dulton."

"I have never heard of him!"

"Indeed!"

Monsieur Gutier's tone was slightly sceptical.

"Why should you think that I had?" the Rajah enquired.

"There was a letter in this wallet addressed to Your Highness; perhaps you would like to read it."

He held out a sheet of paper and the Rajah took it. The spidery, tiny writing was easier to read than Stella's had been and he read quickly:

*To His Highness, The Rajah of Jehangar.*
*Your Highness,*

*I understand you are interested in the identity of the lady staying at the Hôtel de Paris and registered as Mademoiselle Fantôme. I can give you the information you require. Should you be sufficiently interested*

217

*to persuade me to divulge it, I will call at your convenience.*

*I beg to remain,*
*Your Highness's most obedient servant,*
*Henry Dulton.*

The Rajah handed the note back to the Chief.

"I personally have no knowledge of the man," he said, "but I think one of my Aides-de-Camp may have got in touch with him. He spoke to me of someone who could obtain information regarding the lady in question. You would wish to see him?"

"I would be grateful if Your Highness would allow me to do so."

"I will have you shown to his sitting-room," the Rajah said, then paused before ringing the bell. "It is a pity the man died before he could give me the information I required."

"A great pity, Your Highness. I regret that we cannot help you in this matter. *Mademoiselle Fantôme* and the lady with her, *Madame Secret,* are not known to us. Several people have already made discreet enquiries, for the two ladies have aroused much curiosity in Monte Carlo."

"It is unfortunate that Mr. Dulton—or whoever he might be—died quite so quickly," the Rajah said. "You are sure that it was suicide?"

"Quite sure, Your Highness. The pistol with which he killed himself lay beside him, and the bullet in his head had obviously been fired by that very weapon."

"Convincing evidence, of course. There was nothing else of interest in his possession?"

The Rajah shrugged his shoulders.

"Very few things, Your Highness. Only this wallet and I am afraid there is nothing here which might help us. Just some of his own visiting cards and a few others advertising places of amusement in Paris."

Monsieur Gutier opened the wallet as he spoke and, pulling out some of its contents, laid them on the writing-table.

"We gather that Mr. Dulton was what one might call a tout," he said primly. "For instance, there are a number of cards here from 5 *Rue de Roi*. Your Highness has doubtless heard of the establishment; its reputation is well-known. Henry Dulton would have received a commission on the introduction of clients. We shall make enquiries in Paris, but I doubt if they can be of any assistance with regard to his death."

The Rajah picked up one of the cards which the Chief indicated.

It was a plain piece of pasteboard with the words "5 *Rue de Roi*" written across it and at the top left-hand corner a single sentence: *"La Maison plus chic de tout Paris."*

In the bottom right-hand corner in very small type were the words "Madame Bleuet".

The Rajah gave an exclamation:

"Madame Bleuet!" he said excitedly. "Madame Bleuet! I never forget a face, never!"

# 11

The *Restaurant des Fleurs* was having a Gala evening and all the most distinguished visitors to Monte Carlo were seated in its big dining-room, the windows of which overlooked the sea.

There were flowers everywhere, flowers artistically arranged on every table, flowers decorating the walls and hanging in twisted garlands from the ceiling.

Every woman had been given a bouquet on arrival, a small, beautifully arranged posy of scented flowers set in a holder of white perforated paper, and each male guest had received a buttonhole.

These, combined with the variegated colours of the ladies' dresses and jewels, their sequin-sprinkled fans and shimmering head-dresses, produced a scintillating effect of colour and of gaiety.

On one side of the Restaurant there was a garden where the guests could wander and cool themselves after dancing.

This, too, had been turned into a fairyland of enchantment. Coloured Chinese lanterns hung from every tree, flickering candlelights in coloured glass containers decorated the edges of the paths.

It was all very seductive, and at the end of a melodious waltz many couples disappeared from the crowded Restaurant out into the soft shadows of the garden.

Mistral, sitting alone with Aunt Emilie, wished she had someone to dance with, someone who would take her into the garden so that she could see closer the wonderland of lanterns and fairylights and not have only to guess at their beauty from a table inside the Restaurant.

Everyone she knew by sight in Monte Carlo was present tonight, and the habitués of the Casino as well as those staying at the Hotel seemed to have moved over in a body.

Even the old Countess Kisselev whom Mistral had helped to her carriage that first night in the Casino and who had distressed her so unnecessarily by her tears was with a party of young people.

Sir Robert was also in the Restaurant, but his table was a long way from Mistral's and only occasionally could she catch a glimpse of his profile. He was with Lady Violet, of course, who was wearing a striking gown of mauve crepeline trimmed with sprays of ivy.

Prince Nikolai was entertaining a dozen friends at the most important table in the room, and not far from him was the Rajah of Jehangar.

The Rajah was with two of his own countrymen and Mistral wondered why he was not accompanied by the pretty lady to whom she had spoken in the Cloakroom of the Casino the night before.

She had looked forward to seeing Stella again, and at the same time had been extremely apprehensive as to what Aunt Emilie would say when she bowed and smiled, as she had every intention of doing.

She had been ready to defend her reasons for acknowledging an acquaintance she had made in so unconventional a manner, and was strangely disappointed that the necessity did not arise.

Everyone seemed to be gay and happy tonight; and Mistral, watching them, thought wistfully that it would be amusing to be with someone of her own age. But having formed the thought, she instantly rebuked herself for being ungrateful.

She was exceptionally fortunate to be in Monte Carlo at all, she told herself; and it was kind of Aunt Emilie, however irritable she might be at times, to have brought her here, to have given her so many expensive clothes, and to afford her the privilege of watching many of the most distinguished people in Europe.

Impulsively she turned to her Aunt.

"I feel I have not thanked you sufficiently, Aunt Emilie, for all you have done for me," she said sweetly. "Why, I might at this moment be still at the Convent. I should be in bed by now in the darkness, for we

221

were not allowed to read after nine o'clock. But instead, I am here—listening to this wonderful music, watching all these exciting people! I am grateful—really I am. Thank you so very, very much."

Emilie glanced at her in what seemed to Mistral a curiously speculative manner, then she said sourly:

"Unfortunately your gratitude does not succeed in enabling you to obey my instructions."

Mistral's eyes widened.

"What instructions, Aunt Emilie? I try always to do what you tell me. Have I forgotten something?"

"No, you have not forgotten what I have told you," Emilie said. "You are merely inept—perhaps stupid is the right word—at carrying out my commands."

Her tone was scornful and Mistral felt the blood rising in her cheeks.

"I am sorry, Aunt Emilie, if I have failed to do something you required of me. Will you not explain what it is?"

"You know the answer quite well," Emilie snapped. "You have two eyes and they are not blind. You can see the Prince over there. He is entertaining a party of friends. There are women in the party, but are you among them? No! Why has he not invited you?"

There was a long pause while Emilie waited for an answer, her eyes dark, her lips pursed together.

"I . . . I suppose because he did not want . . . me," Mistral faltered at last.

"Why not?" Emilie inquired. "I left you alone together this afternoon while we were watching the yacht-racing. I thought that you could not fail to entice him into offering us hospitality either for tonight or tomorrow. What did you talk about?"

Mistral looked down and crumbled a roll of bread between her fingers. She remembered how embarrassed she had been by her Aunt's deliberate and all too

222

obvious manoeuvring to attract the attention of the Prince.

There had been a great many people watching the yacht-racing and the Prince, whose own yacht was one of the competitors, was obviously far too interested in the races to take even a perfunctory notice of the many beautifully-dressed women crowding the terrace.

Other men behaved very differently. They turned their backs on the sea and even went as far as to focus their binoculars on a pretty woman's face or a well-turned ankle.

The Prince was concentrating on the races, and Mistral thought that only Aunt Emilie would have been brave—or should she say brazen?—enough deliberately to force him to acknowledge their presence.

She had moved down the terrace, pushing her way through the crowd until finally she reached the Prince's side. As he stared through his glasses, oblivious of everything save the little white yachts racing across the blue sea, she said in her most ingratiating tone:

"Good afternoon, Your Serene Highness. Would you be kind enough to explain to us the intricacies of this race? My niece is extremely interested in yachts."

There was nothing the Prince could do but put down his binoculars, kiss Aunt Emilie's hand and smile at Mistral.

"Are you really so inquisitive?" he asked, and she saw the amusement in his eyes.

She had felt the colour rise in her cheeks and even while she lied, knowing that she dared not speak the truth in front of Aunt Emilie, she had despised herself for being a coward.

"Yes . . . I . . . I am most interested," she stammered.

She knew that he did not believe her, and yet with that strange new gentleness which was quite unlike his original attitude towards her he made way for her to stand beside him and said quietly:

"Let me explain what is happening."

Emilie immediately moved away, leaving them alone; and while Mistral knew that such an unconventional action would cause a great deal of chatter and comment among the fashionable throng who were watching every movement, she was thankful when her Aunt was out of earshot.

Hastily in a low voice she said:

"Please do not trouble about me, Your Serene Highness. I know you want to watch the race through your glasses."

The Prince gave her a smile of friendly understanding.

"I don't believe the dragon knows the difference between a yacht and a rowing boat, so she won't be able to cross-examine you afterwards."

Mistral laughed. She could not help it. It might be disloyal to Aunt Emilie, but the Prince had such an amusing way of putting things and she was also certain that he was right where Aunt Emilie was concerned.

After that she had ceased to be embarrassed and had, under the Prince's instruction, even begun to understand a little of what was happening out to sea.

The Prince's yacht won and he cheered in his excitement, boyishly waving his cap above his head.

A great many other people cheered, too, because he was young and popular and because they liked his unsophisticated enthusiasm. But as soon as the cheers had died away, he said to Mistral:

"I must go down to the harbour and reward the crew. Good-bye for the moment, and don't let the dragon gobble you up before I see you again."

Mistral dimpled at him.

"I am so glad your yacht won," she said.

"So am I!" the Prince exclaimed. "And it was a splendid effort, for it is manned entirely by local fishing lads."

He hurried away and Mistral knew that he had not given her another thought. A little self-consciously she rejoined Aunt Emilie, who at the time said nothing as to what she had expected from the interview, but who now was making no effort to disguise her disappointment as she watched the Prince's party.

Mistral sighed. How difficult it was to do the right thing in Aunt Emilie's eyes!

"The Prince did not mention that he was coming here this evening," she faltered at length.

"And you had not the sense to question him, I presume," Emilie snorted. "Well, I shall have to do my best to rectify your inefficacy. You will ask him to come here to speak to you and, when he comes, you must see to it that he invites you to dance."

"But Aunt Emilie, I could never do that," Mistral said in a horrified voice.

"You will do as you are told," Emilie said. "I hoped that he would be attracted by your innocence, but perhaps he is too young himself to appreciate those schoolgirl airs you give yourself. You must try other methods, my dear, and the sooner the better."

"But, Aunt Emilie, why must I do this? Why is it so important for me to attract the Prince?" Mistral asked.

"I have told you before, Mistral, not to ask questions, but to do as I tell you," Emilie replied. "It is imperative that you should captivate the Prince, but there is no need for you to know the reason. All you have to do is to carry out my instructions."

Emilie paused suddenly and her eyes narrowed.

"He was attracted to you at the beginning," she said. "You can not deceive me. I knew it by the look in his

225

eyes and by the way he spoke to you. But he has gone no further. What have you done, what have you said?"

"Nothing . . . nothing at all," Mistral answered hastily. "The Prince is always very kind, always charming . . . but I do not know what else . . . you want him to be."

"I want him to be in love with you," Emilie replied. "There, is that clear enough?"

". . . I am sure he does not . . . think of me . . . like that!" Mistral stammered.

"Then make him!" Emilie retorted.

She beckoned the waiter to their table, and demanded a piece of paper and a pencil. He gave her the small block on which he wrote down the orders. Emilie handed it to Mistral, then passed her a pencil.

"Write to him!" she commanded.

"How can I?" Mistral cried. "Please, please, spare me this, Aunt Emilie, it is too humiliating."

"Stuff and nonsense," Emilie replied. "Men are always pleased when they think a pretty woman is running after them."

"But I have no wish to run after the Prince," Mistral said with a pathetic effort at defiance. "It makes me embarrassed, Aunt Emilie, when you throw us together so obviously. People must talk because they know that he is the only man to whom I may speak. They must be laughing at me."

"I want people to talk," Emilie said. "If they laugh —it is of no consequence. Stop making absurd excuses, Mistral, and do as you are told. Write to him."

Mistral knew then that any appeal that she might make to her Aunt was hopeless even before she formulated the words. Her face was very pale as she picked up the pencil.

"What am I to say?" she asked.

"Must I even tell you that?" Aunt Emilie questioned

savagely. "You seem to have no ideas of your own. Very well then, I will tell you what to say. Write this:

*'I have something of import to tell Your Serene Highness. Could you most graciously spare a moment to come to our table?*

*Mistral.'* "

Mistral wrote down the words as they were dictated, then she raised her eyes to her Aunt's face.

"But I have nothing to say to him."

"Then you had best think of something," Emilie remarked grimly.

"But what is there to tell him about?" Mistral asked wildly as she watched Emilie fold the note and hand it to the waiter with instructions to take it to the Prince's table.

"You would do well to decide that and quickly," Emilie replied and her voice was like steel.

It was as if she were caught in a trap from which there was no escape, Mistral thought, and was ashamed of her own weakness in obeying Aunt Emilie.

She was frightened, it was true, but nothing could be worse than knowing instinctively that she had betrayed her own code of decency in writing to the Prince, in coercing him to her side by making a false appeal to his chivalry.

Inexperienced though she was in the ways of the world, she was sure that ladies did not do such things. They did not deliberately seek a man out and force their company upon him, especially when he was of such social importance as Prince Nikolai.

As if it were a nightmare Mistral watched the waiter take her note to the table at the other end of the room. She saw him pause at Prince Nikolai's side, saw the

227

Prince's hand go out to take the piece of paper from the tray.

Then she could look no more, but bent her head and, clenching her trembling fingers together in her lap, wondered wildly what she could say. He would come to the table, she was certain of that, because he had good manners and also he had told her that if ever she was in any need of his help she was to ask him for it.

But when he came, he would know her appeal was but a pretence and a subterfuge, and he would despise her. With a rising sense of panic Mistral heard Emilie say in a tone of satisfaction:

"He is coming!"

Wishing the ground would open and swallow her up, Mistral waited in misery as the Prince came walking quickly across the room, pausing every now and then to speak to people who hailed him from adjacent tables or to those who were dancing and who touched him on the shoulder as he passed them by. Still Mistral could not raise her eyes, not even when she heard her Aunt purr:

"Good evening, Your Serene Highness. How nice to see you, and how delightful it is here this evening, so gay and amusing."

"The Gala would be incomplete without your presence, Madame," the Prince said with almost an exaggerated courtesy. "Good evening, Mademoiselle."

He bowed to Mistral and at last she was forced to raise her eyes to his. He saw the appeal in them and he smiled at her reassuringly. Then he bowed again to Emilie.

"Is it permitted, Madame, that I invite Mademoiselle to waltz?"

"Certainly, Your Serene Highness."

Emilie's permission was given in just the right tone

of graciousness and condescension, but Mistral, rising to her feet, felt only miserable and ashamed.

Then, as she preceded the Prince on to the floor, she caught a glimpse of a dark face looking towards her, of dark eyes watching her every movement. In that moment she knew that her pride was saved.

She had something to tell the Prince! A story of an incident which might have perturbed her more had she not almost forgotten it in worrying over Aunt Emilie's strange and varied moods.

She would tell the Prince about the Rajah, tell him how he not only had attempted to buy her pearls but had tried for one second to hypnotize her. There was no need to exaggerate the story, it was horrible enough in all conscience.

At her relief at not having to abase herself and tell the truth as to why she had sent him a note, the colour came back into Mistral's cheeks and her eyes shone.

She looked exquisite as she stood for a moment on the dance floor waiting for the Prince to put his arm round her, her wide skirts of rouched net billowing out around her, her neck and shoulders white as ivory above the closely swathed bodice.

The light from every gas jet in the room seemed to shimmer in her hair, its pale gold framing the exquisite outline of her face, in vivid contrast to the mystery of her dark-fringed eyes.

The Prince looked down at her and laughed a little as he swung her round, their feet moving in perfect unison to the strains of "The Blue Danube".

"She is very lovely," Lady Violet said, and there was no need for Sir Robert to ask whom she meant.

He had been watching Mistral from the moment she rose from her table and now, as he watched her dance across the room, her head thrown back a little for she was speaking to the Prince, he thought that her grace was comparable only to that of the swans which moved over the silver waters of the lake at Cheveron.

"Yes, she is very lovely," he heard his own voice say and was surprised at the depth in it.

"We are not the only people who think so," Lady Violet said. "Look at the Rajah."

Sir Robert turned his head in the direction in which she was looking. The Rajah was bending forward, his elbows on the table, his head resting on his hands. He, too, was watching Mistral, and the expression on his face made Sir Robert suddenly angry with a white fury that he had never experienced before.

How dare the fellow look at Mistral like that! He had a sudden wild desire to rise from the table, to stop Mistral from dancing with the Prince and take her away from the Restaurant, from Monte Carlo, from everywhere where she might be besmirched by coming in contact with such men as the Rajah. She was too sweet, too good, for this sort of thing, Sir Robert thought, and he wondered what would happen if he walked across to the Rajah's table and punched him hard in the face.

He was suddenly aware that Lady Violet was staring at him in surprise.

"What is the matter, Robert?" she asked.

Slowly his hands unclenched themselves.

"Matter? Why, nothing!"

The veneer of civilization had fallen upon him again. He felt rather foolish as if in actual fact he had made a scene in public.

"You were looking so angry," Lady Violet said. "I thought something must have upset you. Or is it just my imagination?"

"I am tired," Sir Robert said abruptly. "How soon can we leave?"

"Oh, not yet," Lady Violet protested. "It is very early. Besides, I am enjoying myself."

Mistral and the Prince stopped dancing, but they did not go back to the table where Emilie sat alone. Instead they went through the open doors into the garden. Sir Robert watched them go.

That child was getting herself talked about with the Prince, he thought, and enough was being said about her without that. Prince Nikolai was quite a pleasant young man from all accounts, but nevertheless out to enjoy life.

He would doubtless flirt with Mistral and make love to her. She would not understand, she was too young.

Sir Robert felt his anger rising once again. He had not realized until this moment that he disliked the Prince as much as he disliked most of the foreigners he met in Monte Carlo. He thought of Mistral walking beside the Prince in the garden.

It would be cool and dark out there. But there would be just enough light for the Prince to perceive the loveliness of her little face, the velvet texture of her white skin, the curved sweetness of her lips.

Perhaps he would lose his head out there in the darkness. Perhaps he would attempt to touch Mistral, to hold her in his arms, to force a kiss from her. She would be frightened and shocked. There would be no-one to help her, no-one to whom she could turn for aid.

With an almost superhuman effort Sir Robert forced himself to stay in his chair.

"The Rajah is leaving," Lady Violet remarked casually.

Sir Robert saw the Rajah rise from his table. He was whispering to one of the men with him and there was an unpleasant smile on his face which showed all his white teeth.

"I wonder why he is so pleased with himself," Sir

231

Robert thought, but his mind went back to the Prince, wondering if all women would find him irresistibly good-looking.

Outside in the garden Mistral told the Prince about the Rajah.

"He said that he meant to have the pearls and it would be wiser for me to give them to him willingly," she said. "I am not really afraid, but there is something horrible about him, something uncanny."

"Have you told your Aunt about this?" the Prince asked.

Mistral shook her head.

"She would have been angry with me for listening to the Rajah in the first place," she replied; "but somehow it was difficult not to do as he asked without being rude."

"Don't worry about it," the Prince said. "I will speak to Monsieur Gutier, the *Chef de la Sûreté,* who is an old friend of mine. If the Rajah dares to be tiresome to you or to anyone else, he will be told to leave the Principality and not to come back. Monsieur Gutier will drop him a hint in the meantime.

"They have very clever ways of dealing with people of the Rajah's type here. In consequence we have but few scandals."

"Thank you," Mistral said. "It is kind of Your Serene Highness to take so much trouble."

"It is no trouble and I am very glad you have told me of this," the Prince replied. "You are not to worry any more about it. Promise me?"

"I promise."

They smiled at each other and the Prince said:

"When are you leaving, and where are you going when you do leave here?"

Mistral hesitated.

"I cannot answer either of these questions, not because I do not want to, but because I do not know the answers."

The Prince's face was suddenly serious.

"I wish I could help you," he said. "I would like to, but I don't understand . . ." He broke off suddenly. "We are not going to discuss it now, at any rate. There is no time, for I must go back to my party; but we will meet tomorrow. We will go driving if the dragon will let you, then we can talk it over."

"I would like that," Mistral said simply.

"Then I will call for you at three o'clock," the Prince said. "Come alone. The *beau monde* will chatter, but they have nothing else to do!"

He put his hand under Mistral's arm and guided her back down the narrow twisting paths of the garden towards the Restaurant. Mistral was silent as they moved. She longed to stay where she was in the enchanting, lantern-lit garden with the star-strewn sky above.

She did not want to go back to the crowded Restaurant, to know that hundreds of curious eyes were watching her, that Aunt Emilie was waiting at their table like a hungry spider spinning some sinister web in which both she and the Prince were entwined. But there was nothing she could do but obey the pressure of the Prince's hand.

A few seconds later they had reached the table, the Prince had bowed and gone back to his guests.

"Well?"

There was no mistaking the question in Emilie's voice.

"His Serene Highness has asked me to drive with him tomorrow afternoon," Mistral replied.

"Good!"

There was warm approval in Emilie's tones. She

233

picked up the bouquet with which she had been presented on arrival.

"We will go back to the Hotel now," she said.

Mistral was relieved at her Aunt's decision. She also was ready to leave, for she had experienced too many conflicting emotions this evening for it to have been in any way a happy one.

Emilie had already paid the bill and now she led the way across the room, choosing a moment when the band was not playing and the floor was clear of dancers.

Their exit was dramatic and well-timed, with everyone's eyes directed on them. Mistral tried to move slowly and with dignity across the empty polished boards, striving as usual to think of other things, to forget both herself and the people watching her.

She could not, however, forbear to give one quick glance towards Sir Robert's table. He was not looking at her, instead he was paying the bill which a waiter was presenting to him.

Lady Violet appeared to be irritated, drumming her fingers on the table, her mouth drooping sulkily, and Mistral quickly looking away again wondered how she could be anything but happy when she was with Sir Robert.

Emilie and Mistral reached the entrance hall of the Restaurant, where attendants ran in search of their cloaks and the linkman outside was instructed to call a carriage.

They waited for a few moments and then were informed that the carriage was outside. Emilie swept out on to the steps. A carriage was drawing up and an attendant hurried ahead to open the door.

Several other people came crowding out behind them, and Mistral noticed one of the dark-skinned men who had dined with the Rajah. She met his eyes and looked away hastily. There was something in his expression which made her feel uncomfortable.

Emilie moved forward to step into the carriage. As she did so, the man who had been with the Rajah pushed past Mistral and put his hand on Emilie's arm. He whispered something in her ear, but Mistral could not hear what it was.

She only saw her Aunt start violently and heard the man say ominously:

"You must hear me, Madame."

Emilie turned her head and saw Mistral listening.

"Get into the carriage," she commanded.

Mistral did as she was told, though surprised at the order. She wondered what the Rajah's friend could possibly have to say to Aunt Emilie.

It was dark inside the carriage, and she seated herself at the far side leaving the seat nearest to the open door for Aunt Emilie. Suddenly the door was closed and almost instantly the horses started off, moving at first slowly and then quicker and quicker. Mistral gave a little cry.

"Wait!" she called. "There is someone else to come! A lady has been left behind!"

But even as she shouted, she knew that her voice would not be heard. The carriage was heavily padded and both the windows were closed. Agitatedly she jumped up and tried to open the one nearest to her, but she could not move it. She tried the other with the same result.

Breathless she sat down again and thought perhaps that it did not matter. It was a very short way to the *Hôtel de Paris,* and Aunt Emilie would easily get another carriage. It was annoying and an added expense, but that was all.

Mistral relaxed and wondered again what the Rajah's

friend could possibly have had to say to Aunt Emilie. Her Aunt's expression had been startled by what he had whispered. What a lot of mysteries there were about everything! Mistral sighed.

She wished everyone would be honest and straightforward, especially Aunt Emilie. It was so irritating to be surrounded by so much intrigue and to have no idea what it was all about.

She looked out of the window. They should be at the hotel by now. It was then that she realized that the horses were climbing uphill, climbing steadily and quickly up the wide road which led away from the Casino through the new town and towards Mont Agel.

There was obviously some terrible mistake, Mistral thought.

Once again she tried both windows, finding it easier to exert her full strength now that the horses were trotting quite slowly; but nothing she could do would move them. She decided that the only thing to do was to try the door, but to her astonishment she found it had no handle inside the carriage.

She did not believe this at first, but groped for some time first on one side and then at the other, feeling sure she was mistaken. But at length she was convinced there were no handles and the doors were as securely closed as the windows. She began to get a little frightened. She shouted again:

"Stop! Open the door!"

But there was no reply. The horses went on climbing uphill and there was no sound save the jingle of their harness and the rumble of wheels over the hard ground.

What could have happened? Had she taken someone's private coach by mistake? Was she being driven to one of the grand Villas on the higher roads of the town? That, she thought, must be the explanation, in fact it was the only possible one.

Aunt Emilie would be angry when she found she was not at the *Hôtel de Paris*. But she could hardly be blamed for something which was not in the least her fault.

On and on the horses went and now at last Mistral, peering through the windows, could see that they were drawing up in front of a Villa. It was very large and white and there was a garden in front of it. Wide marble steps led down to wrought-iron gates.

People of importance must live here, Mistral thought, and they, too, would be angry at being left behind at the Restaurant while she drove away in their carriage. Nervously she rehearsed an explanation of what had occurred.

The carriage stopped, the door was flung open by a native servant in a red coat over voluminous Eastern trousers which were of white lawn like his turban. Several other servants dressed in the same manner came hurrying down the steps. Mistral got out of the coach.

"There has been a mistake," she said clearly. "I was brought here from the *Restaurant des Fleurs,* but I wish to go back to the *Hôtel de Paris*. I would be grateful if the carriage could take me back."

Another servant with a beard, who seemed older and more distinguished than the others, stepped forward. He bowed very low, said something in a language which Mistral did not understand, then pointed to the open door of the Villa a few yards away.

"Is there anyone here who can speak French or English?" Mistral asked.

The servant shook his head and again, speaking in a strange tongue, he pointed to the door.

"Perhaps someone inside will understand," Mistral said.

Feeling there was nothing else that she could do, she

walked up the steps and went in through the big double doors of the Villa.

She found herself in a large pillared hall of black and white marble. The servants followed her. The one with the beard led the way up a flight of stairs, which were closely covered with a thick, soft-piled carpet so that his feet made no noise, and the whole house seemed curiously silent.

Mistral suddenly felt terribly afraid. Where was she going? What did this mean? Somehow she must get back to the *Hôtel de Paris* even if she had to walk.

They had reached a wide landing when Mistral made her one last desperate effort to make herself understood.

"I wish to speak to the mistress of the house," she said. "Oh, isn't there anyone here who can understand French, or English, or German?"

The man muttered something and opened the door. Mistral saw a huge room dimly lit by flickering golden lamps. There was the exotic perfume of sandalwood and everywhere the glitter of gold—gold-spangled curtains, gilt furniture and low tables of beaten brass laden with gold ornaments. Mistral stared about her in bewilderment.

Then someone came from the shadows at the far end of the room and walked slowly towards her. Mistral saw a flash of white teeth against dark skin, the glitter of sparkling jewels on a pale turban, and recognized the Rajah.

She gave a little gasp of horror. As she did so, she heard the door close softly behind her.

*"Mademoiselle Fantôme!* It gives me great pleasure to welcome you to my house," the Rajah said softly.

"I have been brought here by mistake," Mistral replied quickly. "My Aunt ordered a carriage to take us to the *Hôtel de Paris*. I got into it first, but the coachman drove off without waiting for my Aunt and without apparently waiting for proper instructions. I would be grateful if Your Highness would have me sent at once to the *Hôtel de Paris*."

"Do you really imagine it was chance that brought you here?" the Rajah asked.

"Then it was not a mistake?" Mistral asked.

"I seldom make mistakes," the Rajah replied.

"But this is intolerable! Your Highness will kindly order me a carriage or if not, I will walk."

Mistral turned impulsively towards the door. As the Rajah did not move she turned the handle of the door herself, but it did not open. She knew then that the door was locked. The Rajah laughed.

It was a horrible, mocking sound which frightened Mistral more than anything else she had heard in the whole of her life.

Her face was very white, but she held her head high as she turned to face him.

"What does this mean?" she asked. "How dare you keep me here?"

"Why not, when I so greatly desire your presence?"

"Do you imagine my absence will not be noticed?" Mistral asked scornfully. "Do you imagine my Aunt will not be worried? This very moment she will have sent for the Police."

"You are mistaken! Your Aunt will not send for the Police, my dear."

"She will, I am sure of it," Mistral retorted. "I must beg of Your Highness to let me go immediately. This indiscretion will do you no good and nothing will be gained by it."

The Rajah laughed again.

"You are very lovely when you are cross," he said.

239

"I have always liked pretty women when they are defiant. But let us face facts. Nothing you say will deceive me—for the game is up. It was a clever one, but then your Aunt is a very clever woman. Yes, the game is up and I am the winner."

"I have no idea what you are talking about," Mistral replied. "All I know is that you have brought me here against my will and I command you to open this door."

"Very prettily said," the Rajah remarked. "You are an excellent actress. Your Aunt, as you call her, must have spent a great deal of time in teaching you to be so proficient; but now let us dispense with all this nonsense and get to know each other—you and I."

He drew nearer to Mistral as he spoke and put out his hand as if to touch her. Mistral gave a little cry and moved away from him.

"Don't you dare to touch me."

"How fond you are of that word 'dare'," the Rajah smiled. "I shall dare many things before the night is out, dear little *Mademoiselle Fantôme*. But first of all you must tell me what is your real name? There is no need now for such rigid formality. We are alone! May I offer you some champagne?"

He walked across the room to a table set in the window. On it were many bottles and several glasses. There was something in his calm assurance, in the smile on his face, which made Mistral more afraid than anything he had said or done until this moment.

She put up her hand to her neck and touched her pearls. Her fingers were very cold and she could feel them tremble. . . .

"If it is my pearls you want," she said breathlessly, "I will give them to you . . . if you will let me go now, and . . . at once."

The Rajah turned, a glass of champagne in his hand; and his eyes were amused.

"I am no longer interested in your pearls. You shall keep them with the other presents that I will give you. It is you I am interested in."

Mistral felt as if her knees gave way beneath her. In an uncontrollable panic she ran to the door and turned the handle once again. The Rajah watched her.

"It is locked," he said softly, "and the only way out of this room leads into my own apartment. You can go there if you wish, but I think you will find yourself more comfortable here."

He made a gesture as he spoke towards the end of the room and Mistral's eyes followed his. There, a little out of the golden light shed by the lanterns, she could see the outline of a great circular divan covered with silk cushions and curtained with transparent net.

For a moment she stood very still. Then she felt as if she were paralysed with a terror such as she had never known before. She longed to scream, but she knew no one would come to her rescue. The servants in the house would have had their instructions.

Desperately she clutched at her pride, feeling that only by keeping control of herself could she hold the bestial desires of the Rajah at bay.

He was watching the expressions on her face as if he could read her thoughts and realized the effort she was making not to scream.

"I knew that you would be sensible once you realized you were defeated," he said at length. "I know, too, that your most clever and experienced Aunt will not have left you ignorant, for you had thought to catch Prince Nikolai. I commend you both for an extremely clever idea, but I am the Rajah of Jehangar and far

241

more wealthy than the Prince. You have lost one fish but caught another."

As he spoke he moved nearer to her; and when he had finished speaking, Mistral realized that he was very near. She looked up at him, her eyes wide with horror.

"Do not touch me or I swear I will kill you."

The Rajah threw back his head and laughed.

"You are extremely entertaining," he said. "I see that I shall be very amused by you. And now I will give you ten minutes in which to prepare yourself for me. By the divan you will find some diaphanous garments—such as our dancing girls wear. It delights me to see white women in our traditional garb. You will put them on. Do not be perturbed if they are more revealing than the cumbersome clothes with which you disguise your natural charms."

He paused and looked down at her, and Mistral saw the lust in his eyes.

"Change quickly, and, as we say in my country, await your Lord and Master."

He moved silently across the room towards a sliding panel in the wall, which led to his own apartment. He touched the spring, then he looked back at Mistral.

"You will have ten minutes in which to prepare yourself, most beautiful *Mademoiselle Fantôme*," he said clearly. "If you are not ready by then, you will find me a most experienced lady's maid."

# 12

Mistral put her hands to her eyes. For a moment she thought she must faint, but with a sense of desperation she knew that, if she did, she would be lost for ever.

Ten minutes, the Rajah had said, and already a minute of it must have gone.

She felt panic rising within her again; she wanted to scream, to beat with her fists on the door; yet common sense told her that it would do no good.

She was conscious of a strange thudding sound and realized that it was her own heart beating as if it would burst from the fragile confines of her body.

She must do something and quickly. She thought of the windows and ran to the one nearest to her, pulling aside the heavily embroidered curtains. She opened the window and looked out and knew immediately why the Rajah had not feared she might escape that way.

Most windows in the South of France opened on to a balcony, but those in this room were the exception. Outside there was a narrow ledge and then a sheer drop into the garden below. Mistral could just see the road.

For a moment she contemplated screaming in case someone might be passing. But even as she parted her lips, she realized how hopeless it would be.

Everything was quiet and still and there appeared to be no-one about. But even if there were and she screamed, long before anyone could come to her assistance the Rajah would be able to pull her back into

the room and to explain away any enquiries which
might be made downstairs.

She was helpless, the prisoner of a virulent, over-
powering evil. She felt her heart begin to palpitate, but
with a tremendous effort she forced herself to think
not of what lay ahead but of some means of escape.
Should she jump from the window?

She would have to risk a broken leg, if not worse,
in the garden below. Then as she thought of it, she
looked further along the outside wall of the Villa. There
were three windows to the room in which she stood
and the last one was almost at the corner of the house.

Mistral looked and saw something beyond it which
gave her a sudden hope. Running, because time was so
infinitely precious, she rushed from the first window to
the one at the far end of the room near the great
circular divan. Opening it quickly, she looked out.

As she had thought, this window was perhaps four
feet from the corner of the house, and the narrow ledge
of white stone which ran in front of the windows ended
at the corner.

Covering the other wall, which faced north towards
the mountain, was a trellis of green lattice built to
support the roses and creepers which were growing all
along that side of the Villa.

It was difficult to see every detail in the darkness, but
there was enough light to distinguish the strips of
wood clearly silhouetted against the white walls and
to know that they were about an inch in thickness.

It was not a stalwart means of support, but Mistral
thought it might hold her, for she weighed very little.
If it did not, well, she must just fall and risk being
badly injured. The difficulty would be to reach the
corner of the house without slipping off the narrow
ledge.

Looking up above her, Mistral was relieved to see

that an elaborate design had been carved in the stones with which the Villa had been built, and it would afford her some fingerhold.

The Villa was very large, and beyond the wall covered with the lattice there was another wing jutting out again and yet again as it followed some grandiose plan of the Architect's to give an impression of opulence and splendour.

There were many windows at an angle which would give those who chanced to look out of them a good view of Mistral should she attempt to escape in this way, but she knew she must risk it.

It was either that or she must wait in the golden room until the Rajah returned, and she told herself that even death was preferable to that alternative.

For one moment she stood still at the open window, the night air on her face, and murmured a prayer. Then she climbed on to the window-sill and out on to the ledge beyond. The first steps were easy, for she could hold on to the frame of the open window and edge herself along with her face to the wall and her back to the abyss below her.

But now the moment came when she must leave the window behind and must find support only in the stone-work. Somehow she managed it.

Moving very slowly, pressed so closely against the wall of the Villa that her breasts touched it, she edged herself forward inch by inch until her left hand could reach out and grasp the trellis.

She was relieved to find it was firm and fixed securely to the wall. She had anticipated that it would be, guessing that the Villa, like all the others in Monte Carlo, was new and that the wood would not have had time to rot nor the nails which held it to rust and loosen.

Very, very carefully she put her foot from the stone

ledge on to a bar of the trellis. Her wide, voluminous skirts were hampering her, but somehow she managed to control them.

The difficulty was that only the very tips of her toes, like the tips of her fingers, could find a place on which to hold, and her body had to be almost perfectly balanced with every step she took or she would have fallen backwards into the darkness.

The first few feet she climbed downwards were not as difficult as she had anticipated. Then she came to the roses and creepers and they made everything far more difficult. It seemed almost as if they defied her to find a foothold amongst them.

They caught at the delicate gauze of her dress, ripping and tearing it as she tried to move, scratched her bare neck and arms, and more than once her foot slipped on a leafy shoot and she thought she must fall.

She had almost reached the ground when she heard a sound above her. It was a voice raised first in astonishment, then in anger. It grew louder and it seemed to her to have the frustrated snarl of a savage animal deprived of its prey. She knew it was the Rajah who shouted and guessed that he was summoning his servants to go in search of her.

Desperately, knowing that even now she might lose her chance of freedom, Mistral tried no longer for a foothold, but jumped.

She did not fall far, but she struck the ground with a sickening thud, heard a frill of her dress tear with a sound something like a scream as it caught on the thorns of a rose. She wrenched herself free.

Then without waiting to wonder if she were hurt she jumped to her feet and started to run. She made for the wall which surrounded the Villa, feeling through the thin soles of her evening slippers first the soft soil of the flower-beds then the hardness of the paved path.

As she ran, she heard behind her the sound of many chattering voices and the Rajah shouting a command. She reached the wall and, as she did so, a carriage came dashing up the hill, the horses managing to travel at a good pace even against the steep incline.

The carriage drew up at the gate of the Villa and before the horses were even at a standstill, a man flung open the door and jumped out. Mistral, scrambling over the wall, could see him very clearly. It was the Prince.

With her last remaining breath she managed to scream, to attract his attention.

"Help, Your Serene Highness! Help!"

He heard her and turned back in the very act of opening the iron gates.

"Mistral!"

He called out her name in astonishment and then came running towards her. She ran too and, as they met, she threw herself at him, clutching the lapels of his coat and raising a white, terrified face to his.

"Take me away! Quickly, quickly! Please take me away!"

The Prince took a quick look at her and swept her up into his arms. He carried her to the carriage, lifted her inside and gave an order to the coachman. Then he jumped in himself and slammed the door.

As they drove away, Mistral saw that the door of the Villa was open and that the light was streaming out. Servants were running into the garden, spreading out down the labyrinth of paths, peering among the bushes and flowering shrubs. But it was too late! She had escaped!

She gave a gasp of utter relief and would have put her hands up to her face; but as she moved them, she became aware that the first finger of her left hand was bleeding. She must have caught it on a nail.

The interior of the carriage was lit by a candle

lantern and by its light the Prince could see the red blood running down the palm of Mistral's hand and on to the front of her torn grey dress.

"You have hurt yourself," he exclaimed and drew a handkerchief from his pocket.

"It . . . does not . . . matter," Mistral replied, catching her breath and conscious of a strange constriction in her throat. "You have saved me . . . you have taken me . . . away. They would . . . have caught me . . . otherwise."

"You should have let me deal with that swine," the Prince said angrily.

"No! No!" Mistral said quickly in terror lest he might go back. "Only take me . . . away. Nothing matters now. . . . If you had not come . . ."

She could not complete the sentence. All too clearly she was aware of what would have happened if the Prince had not arrived at that very moment.

The Prince had wrapped her hand in his handkerchief, but already the blood was seeping through the white lawn.

"I am afraid you have hurt yourself badly," he said. "You must not go on bleeding like this. My own Villa is not a hundred yards away. Would you mind if we stopped there and bandaged your hand properly?"

He spoke anxiously, for Mistral's face was so white and it seemed as if she had already gone through so much that it would be dangerous for her to lose much blood.

"Perhaps that would be best . . . if it is no . . . trouble," Mistral said, a little alarmed herself at the way the crimson patch on the handkerchief was growing larger every second.

The Prince rose, opened a small shutter near the roof of the carriage and shouted an order through it.

He spoke in Russian and the coachman replied in the same language. Then he sat down again.

"It won't take us more than a few seconds," he said, "and then I will take you back to the Hotel. What happened?"

"It was the . . . Rajah," Mistral murmured faintly.

"I knew that," the Prince said. "I came out to the steps of the *Restaurant des Fleurs* with one of my guests. She wished to leave early and I had ordered my carriage for her. As we came through the door, I heard your Aunt say angrily,

'Do you think I will allow him to abduct my niece?'

"I saw a carriage driving away and I saw, too, who stood beside your Aunt—one of the Rajah's Aides-de-Camp. The man said something.

"I don't know what, for I didn't wait to hear. I ran down the steps, jumped into the carriage which was just coming up for my guest. I didn't even offer her an explanation or make my apologies but just drove away to try to find you.

"I would have been at the villa sooner, only my fool of a coachman did not know where the Rajah lived. We had to stop and ask someone. Thank God, I arrived in time."

"Yes, thank God!" Mistral answered fervently.

As she spoke, the horses were drawn to a standstill.

"Here is my Villa," the Prince said. "Be careful how you move that hand."

"Strangely enough it does not hurt me," Mistral said.

"All the same it must be seen to," the Prince replied.

Very gently he helped her out of the carriage and led her through a small, well laid out garden and in through a door painted scarlet to match the shutters.

The Prince's Villa was very different from that of the Rajah.

There was nothing pompous or ornate about the

small, perfectly proportioned hall which they crossed into a big sitting-room. Here there were comfortable chairs and sofas covered in brown velvet, and the furniture, while being both attractive and valuable, contrived also to appear exclusively masculine.

There were sporting prints on the walls and the tables and mantelpiece were decorated with silver trophies which the Prince had won himself at various sports or which had been gained for him by his yachts and race-horses.

But Mistral had little time to take in the details of her surroundings. She only knew that the atmosphere was peaceful and unfrightening and she could relax in the arm-chair to which the Prince escorted her. At his command a servant knelt to set light to the fire already laid in the fireplace.

"You will feel cold," the Prince said. "One always does when one has lost blood. And before we do anything else, we must wash that hand. If there is dirt in it, it may go septic."

Mistral managed to smile at the seriousness of his voice.

"How do you know all these things?" she asked.

"Mostly because I have hurt myself so often," the Prince replied. "I have had at least a dozen accidents while ski-ing and I would hate to count how many times I have come to grief out hunting. But before we talk I would like you to drink a glass of wine."

Mistral shook her head.

"I would much rather not," she said. "I have no liking for it and at the moment I feel that, if I ate or drank anything, it would choke me."

"It shall be as you wish, of course," the Prince replied, "but it would do you good."

"I want nothing," Mistral said in a low voice. "I

250

want only to be assured that I need never see the Rajah again."

"You need not be afraid of that," the Prince said. "I shall tell my Father tomorrow exactly what happened and he will speak to the Police. He has a great influence in the Principality, having always lived here, and I assure you that the authorities will not stand for behaviour of that sort."

"He was so extraordinary," Mistral said. "He seemed to think that I had been . . . trying to deceive him . . . or that my Aunt had. I think he must be mad. He was unpleasant the other night when he spoke to me at the Casino . . . but tonight it was worse . . . far worse. He was different in some way I cannot explain. . . ."

"Don't think about him," the Prince said firmly. "Here is Potoc with some warm water and cotton-wool and bandages."

The Russian servant with the strange face whom the Prince had called his keeper came into the room carrying a sliver basin which contained warm water scented with the fresh fragrance of lemons.

Very gently, while Potoc held the basin, the Prince unwound his blood-soaked handkerchief from Mistral's hand. It was the first time he or Mistral had been able to see the wound in a proper light and now they both gave a sigh of relief.

It was a long jagged cut, ingrained with the soil of the flower-bed into which Mistral had fallen, but it was not deep or dangerous. In fact it was only a flesh wound and would heal without stitches. Mistral winced when the Prince put her hand into the basin of water, but after a moment the water was soothing and she was glad to see the dirt come away.

The Prince took a little time to get the finger absolutely clean, but the bleeding stopped and when at last he had bandaged it expertly with a clean linen bandage, Mistral was able to say:

"You have done it so well, Your Serene Highness, that there will be no need for me to visit a Doctor."

"Not tonight, perhaps," the Prince answered, "but you should see one tomorrow. There is no use in taking risks. Besides, you should get him to examine you properly. You may have hurt yourself in other ways although you are not aware of it at this moment."

He glanced at the scratches on her arms as he spoke and for the first time since she had escaped from the Rajah's Villa Mistral became conscious of her appearance. Until this moment she had been so concerned at knowing that she was free and so numb with the shock she had experienced, combined with her fall, that she had not had time to think of anything else.

Now, looking down at her torn dress, she gave a rueful laugh.

"It will need more than a Doctor to mend my gown," she said. "But otherwise I am sure there is nothing wrong with me."

The firelight shone on her hair as she spoke and, shy at being so dishevelled, she had not the least idea how lovely she looked. Her hair had become loosened in her descent down the wall of the Villa and now it fell in great golden coils over her white shoulders.

Its waves made her face seem very small and delicate and gave her, too, the appearance of being little more than a child. Indeed, with her eyes downcast and her lips a little tremulous, she looked like a child who had got into trouble through no fault of her own.

But it would have been impossible for any man to have looked at her and not remembered that she was a woman. The colour had come back into her cheeks and she looked inexpressively desirable as she sat there, framed against the dark velvet of the Prince's chair.

Potoc had withdrawn and they were alone. The Prince suddenly moved restlessly from Mistral's side across the room and back again.

"I want you to tell me something . . ." he said quietly as if he suddenly made up his mind to question her.

But before he could say more, the door of the sitting-room was flung open abruptly.

Both Mistral and the Prince turned their heads, then Mistral gave an exclamation of astonishment. Sir Robert stood there, looking peculiarly tall, stern and avenging, his eyes ablaze with anger.

"So this is where you have been brought!" he said.

He slammed the door behind him and advanced into the room. As he did so, Mistral stood up. With one glance Sir Robert seemed to take in her torn dress and loosened hair.

His lips tightened ominously and he advanced quickly and purposefully towards the Prince. As he reached him, he put up his hand and slashed him across the face with the pair of gloves he carried.

"You are a cad!" he said harshly.

Mistral gave a little cry.

"But, Sir Robert," she said. "Please . . ."

"One minute," Sir Robert replied. "I have not yet finished telling this so-called gentleman what I think of him."

"Do you think I would hear any more from you?" the Prince asked furiously. "I will have satisfaction, sir, here and now. No man can insult me with impunity."

"Nor can I allow you to insult an English lady and my countrywoman," Sir Robert answered. "The choice of weapons is yours."

If Sir Robert was angry, his emotion was equalled and surpassed by the Prince's rage. He could hardly keep his temper within control and his face was white

253

save where the mark of Sir Robert's gloves burned crimson.

He gave a quick glance round. Over the mantelpiece were two duelling swords, the *épées de combat* much favoured by the French. In a matter of seconds the Prince had taken them down and handed one to Sir Robert.

"I can kill you with this as well as with anything else," the Prince said through his teeth.

"On the contrary," Sir Robert replied. "It is you who will receive a lesson at my hands, young man, and one which will be richly deserved."

Mistral looked from one to the other in utter bewilderment. She was not certain what all this was about, but from Sir Robert's remark about his countrywoman she felt that it concerned herself, though why and for what reason she could not guess.

"Your Serene Highness! Sir Robert!" she began. "Please . . ."

But they paid no attention to her. The Prince thrust a chair to one side, kicked a footstool out of the way. The centre of the room was empty and the two men took up their positions.

Almost before Mistral could realize what was happening their swords had met, there was the clink of steel against steel, and they were fighting in desperate, grim-faced silence which was far more frightening than if they had shouted abuse at one another.

Feeling utterly powerless, Mistral could only stand and watch them—watch them feint, parry and riposte —think for a moment that Sir Robert had the Prince at his mercy, only to realize that the Prince had extricated himself with a display of brilliant swordsmanship. Now Sir Robert was on the defensive.

However much Mistral wanted to stop the fight it

was too late, there was nothing she could do. From sheer weakness and astonishment she could only watch with horrified yet fascinated eyes.

An expert would have told her that the two combatants were well matched. Sir Robert was slightly the more experienced of the two, but he was also heavier on his feet, while the Prince had an agility and quickness which not only saved him when he was in a tight corner but was also a definite danger to his opponent.

After some minutes the ferocity of the fight began to tell on both men.

Their breath came quickly and, though neither seemed in the least tired, an expression of strain could be observed in the tightness of their mouths and the wariness in their eyes. Still they fought on.

There came a moment when it seemed as if the Prince would be the winner. He had driven Sir Robert up against a bookcase and the flickering blade like the evil tongue of a serpent was within an inch of his throat.

At that moment Mistral knew who she wanted to win. She felt a sudden terror possess her that Sir Robert might be killed. The thought was almost a physical agony in the intensity of her fear.

She wanted to rush to Sir Robert's side, to receive the blow in her own breast rather than that he should be wounded. But she could not move, her very feet seemed rooted to the ground. She could not utter a sound although her lips moved.

Sir Robert was bending backwards and his face was livid. There was no hope, Mistral thought wildly, and she would see him killed before her very eyes. She knew then that if he were dead she would want to die beside him.

She loved him! She had loved him from that very first moment when they met before the dawn. She loved him with an overwhelming emotion which seemed so utterly a part of her that she had not recognized it until this moment.

She could not think how she had ever lived or ever imagined she could find happiness without him. She loved him and she could do nothing to save him. She could only stand there, tense and terrified, every nerve in her body strained to breaking point.

Then, as it seemed to her that her very brain must give way under such emotional stress.

Sir Robert extricated himself from his position and with a sudden lunge took the Prince unawares. The sword passed through the Prince's shoulder. He gave a cry which was little more than a groan and his sword clattered from his right hand on to the floor.

He clapped his left hand to the wound and as he did so, Mistral fell. She felt as if the floor came up to hit her.

She was conscious only of an overwhelming darkness which carried her down, down into a merciful oblivion from which she felt there could never be an awakening. . . .

When she opened her eyes, it seemed to her that centuries must have passed. For a moment she could not remember what had happened, feeling only that she had been a long way away and that she was still travelling.

Then she became aware that there were wheels moving beneath her, that something strange lay beneath her cheek. She moved and was instantly aware that there was an arm which held her close and that her head rested against someone's shoulder.

In that moment of wakening she knew whose it was.

An ecstasy of joy and wonder seemed to run

through her brain like fire as she realized whose arm held her.

"Are you all right now?"

Sir Robert's voice was low and tender and his face was very close to hers. She could see him very clearly in the light from the lantern. They were in a carriage together and for a moment she could think of nothing save his closeness and that his arm encircled her.

Then something moved and she realized that it was her own hand. She caught sight of the bandage and instantly everything came flooding back to her memory.

"The Prince?" she asked wildly. "The Prince?"

"He is not dead," Sir Robert said grimly. "Which is a pity, for I meant to kill him."

Mistral gave a little sob.

"But what has he . . . done?" she asked. "He rescued me from . . . the Rajah! It was the Rajah who . . . took me . . . away."

"The Rajah!"

There was no mistaking the astonishment in Sir Robert's voice.

"Yes, the Prince . . . saved me," Mistral repeated. "I tried to tell you . . . I tried . . . but you would not let . . . me."

Sir Robert stared down at her as if he sought the truth in her eyes raised to his and from her lips which were only a few inches away.

"Tell me what happened," he said at length.

"I was leaving the *Restaurant des Fleurs* with my Aunt," Mistral said, speaking at first weakly then gathering strength as her story proceeded. "Just as we were stepping into the carriage, one of the men who had dined with the Rajah earlier in the evening came forward and spoke to my Aunt.

"She told me to get into the carriage; but as soon as

257

I did so, the door was slammed and the carriage started off apparently without the driver having received any instructions.

"At first I thought it was a stupid mistake, that I had got into the wrong carriage and that the coachman had mistaken my identity. But after I had tried the windows and the doors and found them all securely fastened, I began to feel alarmed.

"The carriage drew up at a Villa and I got out, trying to explain that there had been an unfortunate mistake and asking that I should be sent back to the *Hôtel de Paris*.

"The servants, however, spoke only a foreign language, so I entered the Villa, hoping I would find someone to whom I could make myself understood.

"I suppose I should have been immediately suspicious because the servants were natives, but it did not strike me as peculiar because many people here have dark-skinned attendants, and it was only when the Rajah appeared that I realized that I was trapped.

"He told me that he had abducted me deliberately. He said some very strange things and behaved in a very strange manner. I cannot tell you what he said . . . I could never repeat it to anyone. But he left me alone for ten minutes. . . ."

Mistral drew a deep breath as if the very memory of those moments were unsupportable. Then she continued bravely:

"I managed to escape through a window and climb down the lattice which was nailed to the side of the house. Before I reached the ground, the Rajah discovered that I had gone and he would have caught me again.

"I heard him calling for his servants and sending them in search of me. But even as they came from the house, the Prince arrived.

"He had heard my Aunt say that I had been abducted and had rushed from the Restaurant to try and find me. He took me away in his carriage. My finger was bleeding so badly that we stopped at his Villa to bind it up.

"He had just finished bandaging it when . . . you . . . arrived."

Mistral's voice, low and hesitant, died away. She felt Sir Robert's arm tighten about her; then with his free hand he took her bandaged fingers in his and raised them to his lips.

"I will deal with the Rajah later," he said grimly. "I suppose I owe the Prince an abject apology."

"You thought that he had kidnapped me?" Mistral asked.

Sir Robert nodded.

"My mistake was perhaps understandable," he said. "I was leaving the Restaurant with Lady Violet just after I had noticed you depart. I came out on to the doorstep.

"I saw your Aunt swooning and one of the Rajah's Aides trying to revive her. He was supporting her with one arm and shouting to a waiter to bring a glass of wine. There was another woman standing on the steps. I have an idea that I had seen her in the Prince's party. I turned to her and said:

"Is anything the matter?" "An elderly lady over there seems to think that her niece has been abducted," she said, "and my escort has also rushed off in a great hurry. It all seems to me very peculiar."

"She spok disdainfully, but looking up the road I saw the Prince's carriage vanishing into the distance. I recognized the brilliant uniform of his servants and I sprang to the conclusion, and not an unnatural one, that he had carried you off.

"I had seen you dancing together and the way he

259

looked at you and the possessive attitude he adopted had annoyed me considerably.

"Without stopping to make enquiries or to question my own impulse I got into the nearest carriage and told them to follow the Prince. I was too late, of course, for the Prince's horses, which must have been his own, were much faster than the hired beasts which seemed to take a lifetime to climb the hill."

"And . . . and Lady Violet?" Mistral asked.

Sir Robert gave an exclamation.

"It is a terrible thing to confess," he said after a moment's pause, "but I had forgotten all about her until this minute. I must have left her standing on the steps."

"She will think you very rude," Mistral said.

"Does it matter?" Sir Robert asked. "Does anything matter except that you are safe?"

His voice was very low and deep. His eyes looked down into hers and suddenly Mistral felt herself begin to tremble. She did not know why, for she was not afraid.

Indeed the most wonderful feeling she had ever known was creeping over her, burning through her like a flame, making her breath come quickly from between her lips.

She could no longer meet Sir Robert's eyes and her lashes were dark against her cheeks as she heard him say:

"You are so lovely, so perfect!"

She felt as if she could no longer bear the intensity of her own feelings. With a little inarticulate murmur she turned her face and hid it against his shoulder. He drew her closer and she could feel his heart beating quickly and strongly beneath her cheek.

She knew then with a happiness she had not believed

possible that he loved her even as she loved him. They were both silent for there was no need for words.

They were close, joined by a glory which seemed to vibrate in their veins like music.

The horses drew up and the carriage came to a standstill. Mistral raised her head. She was aware without looking out of the window that they were back at the *Hôtel de Paris*.

She wanted to cry out that this moment must not end, that they must drive on, that she could not leave Sir Robert; but even as the night porter came hurrying from the hotel, he said quickly:

"I will see you tomorrow. There are many things I want to say to you, my darling, but I am not free to say them yet. You must trust me a few more hours."

She could not answer him. There were no words in which she could reply. She could only look into his eyes for a long breathless moment.

She knew then that they belonged to each other for all time. That strange magnetism which she had known first when they had met by the sea-shore joined them once again. She felt as if he drew her irresistibly and possessively into his keeping.

She surrendered herself to his will, knew herself captured and conquered and gloried in the ecstasy of it.

The door of the carriage was opened. Mistral felt as if she were rudely dragged back to earth from a radiant sunlit Paradise. Her shyness returned and her eyes were veiled. Sir Robert got out and handed her out of the carriage.

She did not look at him as they walked up the steps to the door of the hotel; then she felt his lips, warm and insistent, against her fingers.

"Until tomorrow, my beloved, he said softly and was gone.

# 13

Sir Robert watched the first pale flush of the dawn light the sky and then spread, growing golden and yet more golden every moment, until the whole vista of sea, sky and land was ablaze with brilliant colour.

As he watched, he thought, as he had done often before, that it all had a sense of unreality about it. It was both as beautiful and as ephemeral as a dream.

That, he thought suddenly, was the right way to look at Monte Carlo. It was a dream world one could enter for a little while and accept as lightly and as unselfconsciously as one accepted the dreams which pass in the night.

It was a place made for enjoyment, for excitement and often for happiness, but it was never meant to be lived in or to be a foundation on which one could build a real life or the future.

It had a loveliness almost beyond description, he thought, as he watched the sea turn to vivid blue with streaks of emerald and then pale where it met the horizon to amethyst tinged with silver.

But he knew that for him personally, while he could acknowledge the beauty of Monte Carlo, his heart would always find perfection not on the Côte d'Azure, but at Cheveron.

There was a sudden flight of pigeons winging their way over the white roofs below him, and vividly they conjured before his eyes the pigeons coming home to roost in the woods with which Cheveron was surrounded.

The trees would be in bud, the snowdrops and crocuses would be out on the lawns, and everywhere there would be that freshness, that breathless sense of wonder which each year heralded the miracle of spring.

Soon the lilac bushes would be heavy with purple and white blossom, and the apple trees would be scattering clouds of pink and white petals, while the water lilies would be golden against the shining waters of the lake.

Cheveron was calling him, and unconsciously Robert made an impulsive movement as if he could not wait another moment but must leave immediately for the home he loved so dearly. Yet he must curb his impatience, for he knew that when he went he would not go alone.

He had not slept last night, but had walked for a long time by the sea-shore, and when at length he had gone to his own room it had been to sit on the balcony, looking out into the darkness until the dawn came.

He had been thinking of Mistral, of her head against his shoulder, her face raised to his. How lovely she had been in even the flickering, uncertain light of the carriage lantern! How hard it had been not to kiss her, and how very nearly he had done so!

Her lips had been so near to his and he had known by the soft trembling of her body and by the expression in her eyes that she would not have refused him.

But some deep-rooted sense of honour within himself had held him back. He had forced himself to wait, to shut the door on the past before he opened the one which led to the future.

He had done the right thing, he was sure of that,

but every nerve in his body ached all night at the thought of Mistral's loveliness and her nearness of which he had not taken advantage.

When he left her at the *Hôtel de Paris,* he had told the carriage to drive immediately to the Villa des Roses. Mistral's innocent question had recalled Violet to his mind and he realized now how unbearably rude he had been to leave her without explanation or apology standing alone outside the *Restaurant des Fleurs.*

But all thought of her had vanished completely from his mind when he imagined that Mistral was being abducted by the Prince. His only thought has been to rescue Mistral, and a blind, insensate rage had made him oblivious of everything and everybody.

Now he must apologize to Violet; but worse still, he must tell her the truth.

It would not be easy to explain not only that he was in love with Mistral, but that he intended, when morning came, to ask her to be his wife.

He knew now that he had never been in love before, never even had begun to realize what it might mean in his life or to plumb the depths of which his emotions were capable.

Violet had attracted him, it was true. He had desired her almost from the first moment of their meeting; but it was she who had made their relationship a deeper and more intimate one.

It was she who had led him further and further into a maze of his own passions and emotions until, when it was nearly too late, he had found the way of escape that was almost closed against him.

He had not meant it to be like that.

He had intended nothing serious that first night at the Devonshire House Ball when impulsively he had written his name against every dance on Violet's programme and flirted with her with the experienced sophistication of a man of the world.

It was later, much later, that he had begun to guess that Violet was falling in love with him, and it was only when his Mother's reproaches and expostulations began to irritate him that in a kind of obstinate defiance he thought of asking Violet to be his wife.

By that time he had been infected with some of her contempt and indifference towards the conventional.

Until he met Violet, he had always done exactly what was expected of him and behaved with a correctness and a formality which would have done credit to an older man.

But after some weeks in Violet's company he felt rebellion stir within him, a rebellion against the slanderous tongues of their friends who, anticipating evil, invariably forecast that it was an inevitable conclusion.

If that was what was wanted, he would give them something to talk about, he decided.

But deep in his heart Sir Robert had known that Violet fell very far short of the ideal he had held secretly all his life of the woman who would be his wife.

It had to be someone who would love Cheveron and who would be happy there, someone whom Cheveron would both love and accept. He had known, even while he defied his Mother and those who whispered about Violet, that they were right.

He could not take to Cheveron a woman who had been divorced, he could not enthrone her there as an example to those on the estate who trusted and respected him.

And yet he had played with fire, wanting, as so many men had wanted before him, to have both Cheveron and Violet, salving his conscience by assuring himself over and over again that Violet was not really serious, that her love for him was as light and transitory a thing as his for her.

But as the horses neared the Villa des Roses after having left Mistral at the Hotel, Robert was afraid.

He let himself in with a latch-key. It was a relief to see that the lights were lit in the drawing-room and that Violet had not yet gone to her bedroom. She was sitting at her bureau writing as he entered the room.

As she rose, he saw that she had changed from the formal gown she had worn earlier in the evening into a négligé of some soft flowing material. Her only decoration was a bunch of artificial roses which she wore at her breast. Her face was pale as she said quietly:

"I thought you would come."

"Naturally! I owe you an apology."

His voice was grave and steady and, as he looked at her and looked away again, she saw an expression in his eyes which she had never seen before. And it seemed to Violet that for a moment she could not get her breath.

The fears and the anxiety which had been accumulating this past hour or so appeared to unite and in their combination to fashion some terrible weapon which stabbed her now to her very heart.

She knew the truth, knew it without words, without explanation. And she wished only that she might die before she heard it from Robert's own lips.

But Violet had generations of blue blood in her veins, and this enabled her to say easily and without a tremor in her tones:

"Won't you have a drink, Robert? You must have had a trying time since I last saw you."

"Thank you!"

There was almost a note of gratitude in his voice as Robert crossed to the wine table and poured himself out a whisky and soda. He was grateful for even a moment's respite, grateful that Violet seemed calm and unemotional.

He had no idea that, as she watched him cross the room, noting the breadth of his shoulders, the proud carriage of his head and the clear-cut handsome features, Violet wanted nothing so much as to be able to cry out her love, to rush towards him with outstretched, clinging arms.

Some primitive savagery within her told her to do just this very thing, to entwine herself about him, to impel him to realize how much she loved him and to arouse his passions by revealing her own. She had made him desire her once; why could she not do so again?

But even as the thought came to her, she turned away from it in disgust.

Then, as if the Devil himself tempted her, Violet knew there was another way that she could keep Robert—she had only to appeal to his honour, his chivalry. She had but to tell him clearly in no uncertain terms that he had compromised her and that he could only reinstate her in the eyes of the world if he made her his wife.

If she spoke of such things, she knew clearly and unmistakably that he would marry her. Robert was a great gentleman; he would not fail her.

But unfortunately, she thought wearily, she was a lady. If Robert would not behave like a blackguard, neither could she. If Robert was honourable, then she, too, had a sense of honour.

He turned from the wine table with the drink in his hand and walked across to the fireplace where she was standing. She knew he was nervous. And there was something infinitely pathetic in the knowledge that Sir Robert Stanford of Cheveron was nervous of her.

She had known him in many moods, she had watched

him experience many emotions; but never before had she known him afraid, nervous or embarrassed, and she knew that now he was all these things and perhaps more.

For the first time since they had met, Violet felt her age. Robert was so intensely masculine that always she had thought him as being so immeasurably older in the things that mattered. He had commanded and she had obeyed.

He had always been the stronger of the two, both physically and mentally, but now in this moment of crisis Violet realized that he was in some ways very young where women were concerned. His ideals had never been shattered.

To him a woman was a very wonderful and very lovely creature, lovely both in mind and body.

At that moment Violet felt a jealousy so violent in its intensity that it almost tore her in pieces—a jealousy of the woman whom Robert would love and who would be his wife.

He would lay all these great gifts of his at her feet, and what was more, he could offer her what was to all intents and purposes an untouched heart.

He was sensitive, he had imagination; he would be able to give to the woman he loved so much more than anyone else, including herself, had up till now been able to take from him.

Violet's jealousy burned within her like a fire. As suddenly as it had flared up, it died away, leaving her curiously depleted and for a moment emotionally detached.

Robert put his hardly touched glass of whisky down on the table. It seemed as if he were not thirsty although his lips were dry. He took a deep breath.

"I have something to say to you," he began.

It was then that Violet knew what she must do, knew

that to save him from humiliation and self-reproach she must sacrifice herself and the last remnants of her pride. She had lost him, lost him completely and absolutely, she knew that. She had failed in what she had set out to do and had destroyed herself in the effort.

She loved Robert as she had never loved a man before and never would again; but because she loved him, and loved him utterly and unselfishly, there was one last thing she could do for him.

She put out her hand as if she would lay it on his arm, then checked herself and let it fall to her side. She dare not touch him . . . she dare not.

"One moment, Robert," she said coolly. "Before you talk to me about what has happened tonight, I have something I wish to say to you. Eric came here today."

"Eric!"

"Yes, Eric," Violet repeated. "He drove over from Nice. He brought me news from England. His Uncle, Sir Harold Featherstone, is dead, and he has made Eric his heir."

"Indeed! That is an excellent thing, I suppose, for Eric," Robert said.

It was obvious that he thought the story was of little consequence, but politely he let her continue without interruption.

"Eric also told me," Violet went on quickly, "that his brother Alwyn was divorcing his wife. She has run away with another man and left her two children behind. Eric is more or less adopting them. He is taking them to Medway Park, the house his Uncle has left him in Norfolk."

She paused, then after a second she continued:

"There is one other thing Eric told me—that my room at Medway Park is waiting should I wish to occupy it. He is ready to take me back, Robert; indeed he feels that I have never really left him, that I have always been his wife in name if not in fact."

She could not look at Robert now. She could not bear to see what she knew would be there, the relief in his eyes. She had saved him from humiliating himself and he would never know it.

"I don't want you to think hardly of me, Robert," Violet went on. "I don't want to hurt you in any way, but I feel I cannot leave Eric alone to bring up two children, to manage a big house and estate without a wife to help him. When you came in, I was writing to him to tell him that I am going to join him in England."

"When?"

The monosyllable seemed to come abruptly from Robert's lips.

"Tomorrow or the next day," Violet replied airily. "As soon as I can close the Villa and pay off the servants."

She felt there was almost a note of hysteria in her voice, but it seemed as if Robert noticed nothing. He walked towards the window with his back towards her.

"You must do what you think best," he said at length. "If Eric really wants you . . ."

"He does," Violet interrupted. "He loves me, has always loved me in his own way."

"Then . . ."

Robert turned. Her eyes searched his face, taking in every detail, striving to remember the clear outline of his square jaw, the curve of his lips.

"Then I suppose that we . . ." he began, and stopped.

Violet made a sudden gesture with her hands.

"Don't let's talk about it! I hate good-byes! There is nothing worse than mooning over a love affair that is finished, or having a post-mortem on a passion that has died."

"Are you sure you mean that?" Robert asked.

"Yes, of course I mean it."

Violet turned towards the mantelpiece and moved a china ornament from one place to another.

"My dear Robert, everything comes to an end in time, even happiness. Don't let us say good-bye conventionally, with all the frills and conventional expressions of gratitude. Let us remember things as they were and forget that there is no tomorrow. It is so much better that way."

"It is of course exactly as you wish," Robert said, and this time she heard the relief in his voice.

She felt for a moment that she could not go on, that she must tell him the truth. But once again her love triumphed over her weakness. She gave a little sigh.

"Dear Robert," she said. "What fun it has been! I don't think I have ever enjoyed the South of France as much as I have this year. I shall miss the sunshine in Norfolk, for I always think it is a particularly grey county. . . ."

Even as she spoke the adjective she felt a pang shoot through her. The word was inseparably connected with one person!

She knew now that she could stand no more, that she must bring the curtain down on her act before her audience discovered how inadequate an actress she was.

She put her hand to her forehead.

"Robert, you must go," she said. "I am tired and I have a headache. If you can help me in any way tomorrow, I will send a note to your Hotel asking you to come here. If you do not hear from me, it will be because I am too busy. I must finish this letter to Eric and then I shall literally fall into bed. I am exhausted at making so many decisions in one day."

As she spoke, she moved across the room to the bureau, seated herself and took up a pen.

"Good night, Robert," she said over her shoulder.

He was nonplussed and bewildered by her behaviour; but he was, as she had known he would be, utterly convinced of the sincerity of her acting. He moved slowly towards the door. As he reached it, he looked back.

She could not help but look at him. There was consideration and a strange gallantry in his face.

"You are quite . . . sure, Violet?" he asked.

"Sure?" she questioned. "That I am going back to Eric? But of course I am sure. Can you imagine Eric bringing up two children without my being there to see to everything?"

She turned to her letter. She heard the door of the sitting-room close. She heard Robert's feet crossing the hall, heard him shut the front door and walk down the garden steps.

She sat very still, listening for a long time after there was no sound save the slow methodical ticking of the clock on the mantelpiece. Then slowly, very slowly she lowered her head on to her arms.

The tears did not come for a long time; but when they did, they shook her from head to foot, a tempest of utter misery such as she had never experienced in the whole of her life before.

And she knew then that she was weeping not only for Robert but her lost youth.

Robert walked away into the warm night with what seemed a paean of thankfulness in his heart.

It was only now in the utter relief that Violet's decision had brought him that he realized how terribly afraid he had been of telling her that their love affair was at an end.

He had known, though he had not dared voice it to himself, that if she appealed to him to save her good name, if she asked him to behave honourably towards her, he must do so, whatever the cost to himself.

But now he was safe! Safe and free to return to Cheveron. He felt as if he had come through some desperate battle by a hair's breadth. Even now he was not certain how near he had been to defeat or annihilation.

He was free, that was all that mattered; free, he thought as he watched the flowers turning their faces towards the morning sun, to ask Mistral to marry him.

He sat so long in the window that when he glanced at the clock he started hastily to his feet and was forced to bathe and change his clothes in almost record time. Even so, when he arrived at the Chapel of Ste. Dévote, the Service was nearly finished.

He had meant to get there earlier, but he had sat watching the dawn for too long. He guessed that today of all days, even though she might be feeling the ill effects of what had happened last night, Mistral would go to Early Mass.

He pushed open the baize-covered door of the Chapel. It was dim and cool inside, the only lights coming from the candles illuminating the Chancel. There were not many people there and most of them were elderly women in black.

He could see Mistral kneeling near the front. She was not wearing a hat, but her head was covered with a soft scarf of grey lace which matched her dress.

Robert hesitated, not certain what to do, a little wary of this strange service in a foreign church. Suddenly a bell tinkled, and the Priest at the Altar raised his hands. Robert did not know what was happening.

He only knew that he wanted to kneel, he wanted to make an act of worship. He found himself on his knees in the back pew, his head bent, his hands clasped

273

together in front of him. He did not understand Latin in which the service was being conducted, but somehow it was unimportant.

He only knew there was a Presence here in this small, dimly-lit Chapel which brought him a sense of self-revelation such as he had never known before.

He saw now how bitterly he had failed his Mother and the high ideals she had taught him from boyhood. He saw how he had failed Cheveron, tarnishing a little its pride and its glory, of which he had been so proud to be responsible.

He thought of all the people who worked there, of their loyalty to him and how their trust and respect meant more than anything else in the whole world.

And suddenly he was no longer the important, rich Sir Robert Stanford but a humble and penitent little boy who had done a great many things that were wrong.

The bell at the Altar rang again and Robert began to repeat a prayer that he had said every night of his life at his Mother's knee until he went away to a boarding school.

"Please God, bless Papa and Mama, my dogs and pony, and everyone at Cheveron and make me a good boy. A-men."

He prayed then as he had never thought it possible to pray, the words unimportant, the intensity behind them coming from the very depths of his soul in absolute and complete sincerity. And when he had finished, he felt as if he waited in a strange, frightening silence for a verdict on himself.

Then it seemed to him that a Hand was laid on his head and he knew he was forgiven. His repentence had been accepted, he was absolved, he was free once more to do better in the future.

With a feeling of sudden lightness and elasticity he opened his eyes. The Service was over and he had not known it. The Chapel was almost empty and the lights were extinguished in the Chancel. The Priest had gone. He saw Mistral rise and come down the aisle towards him.

Her face was alight with happiness, her eyes mystical as if she had kept company with the angels and had not yet completely returned to earth.

She was almost level with his pew before she saw him, still on his knees, watching her. She stopped, her hand going to her breast in an exquisitely graceful gesture. He rose then and taking her other hand in his he raised her fingers to his lips. He could not speak.

"I knew you would come," she said simply, and his fingers tightened on hers.

They stood looking at each other for a breathless moment and he thought that he had never known that any woman's beauty could be divine until this moment.

"I want to talk to you," he managed to say at length a little unsteadily.

"I am alone," Mistral replied. "Jeanne was not well this morning, so I came here by myself."

"Then I can say what I have to say now, and at once," Robert answered and drew her closer to his side.

As if in answer to an unspoken command Mistral sat down in the pew and after a moment Robert seated himself beside her. There were shafts of sunshine coming through the coloured glass window over the West Door and one of them just touched the top of Mistral's golden head.

"Is it wrong for me to talk to you here?" Robert asked, his voice very low.

"No, of course not," Mistral smiled. "We bring our sorrows to God, why shouldn't we bring Him our happiness too?"

"You are happy then?"

She nodded as if her heart were too full for words,

275

but he saw that she was trembling and felt her fingers quiver beneath his.

"You know what I want to say to you," he said. "I want to ask you to marry me, to honour me by becoming my wife. I love you, my darling, I love you more than I believed it possible for a man to love any woman. I will protect and care for you for the whole of your life, if you will trust yourself to me."

He knew her answer without waiting to hear her speak the words. He saw it in the radiance in her eyes, in the glorious, glowing happiness which seemed to light her whole face. But he waited—waited until very softly he heard her whisper.

"I love you, too!"

He put his arms round her and drew her close. He felt her quiver and then—he found her lips. Together they knew an ecstasy and a wonder that was not of this world.

For a long, long moment they were joined together —one and undivided—then it seemed as if human nature broke beneath the strain and Mistral hid her face against his shoulder.

"I love you," Robert said. "Oh, my sweet, my little darling, I love you so."

She raised her face, then she looked not at him but towards the Altar.

"I always knew," she said very slowly, "that love would be like this."

"Like what?" he asked.

"Holy," she answered. "Sacred, a part of our love for God."

The purity and wonder in her voice made Robert feel he was very near to tears. He bent his head and kissed her fingers with a prayer in his heart that he would never fail her.

Mistral drew a deep breath.

"We must go back," she said.

They left the Church together hand in hand. Outside the sun seemed almost blinding and they stood for a moment at the top of the steps.

"Did you bring a carriage?" Mistral asked at length, "or are we going to walk?"

"I was late so I drove here," Robert replied. "I told the coachman I should want him again and I expect he is just round the corner. I will go and call him if you will wait here."

"I won't run away," Mistral answered and laughed from sheer happiness.

Robert went down the steps. As he had anticipated, the coachman was half asleep in the shade of some olive trees further down the road. Robert hailed him and he awoke with a start. He gathered up the reins and reached for a whip.

Robert turned to go back to Mistral; but as he did so, he noticed for the first time that a man was approaching on horseback. He recognized him instantly and quickly walked back up the steps of the Church to Mistral's side. He took her hand in his.

"I have just seen the Rajah," he said. "I am warning you because I don't wish you to feel frightened when you see him again. I am with you now and nothing will happen, but I promise that I will deal with him later in the day."

He saw Mistral's face whiten, saw the sudden fear in her eyes, but there was not time to say more. The Rajah was in sight and with a quick glance he saw them standing hand in hand.

Robert expected him to pass without salutation or acknowledgement of their presence, but to his surprise the Rajah reined in his horse at the foot of the steps.

"Sir Robert!" he called.

Robert looked down at him with an expression of disdain and did not reply.

"I have something of great importance to say to you," the Rajah said. "Will you come to me or must I come to you?"

Robert felt Mistral give a sudden shudder. For her sake he went forward, descending the steps to the Rajah's side.

"What is it?" he asked harshly as he reached him. "I intend to call on you later in the day, for nothing that I have to say to you can be said now in front of a lady."

The Rajah gave an unpleasant laugh.

"What I wish to tell you, Sir Robert, concerns a certain lady and is, in fact, an expression of my good-will towards you."

"If you have anything to tell me, say it," Robert said abruptly, "and then go before I make you."

The Rajah's lips curled.

"St. George himself," he sneered, "eager for the defence of an innocent damsel. My dear Sir Robert, don't be deceived as I so nearly was. Young women don't remain innocent for long when they are in the company of the notorious Madame Bleuet."

"What are you talking about?" Robert asked angrily.

"I am speaking of Madame Bleuet, or if you prefer it, Madame Secret," the Rajah replied. "You have heard of her of course. Her establishment in the *Rue de Roi* is quite the smartest and best known *Maison de passe* in the whole of France. I feel sure you must have been there, my dear Sir Robert; but if your memory is at fault and you are not entirely convinced, I can give you proof any time you wish for it. Do not hesitate to call on me, I am always at your service."

The Rajah bowed and trotted away. Robert stood

as if he were turned to stone. For a moment he could not quite believe what he had heard, what the Rajah had said.

Then slowly and insidiously a face came before his eyes, a woman with brightly dyed hair and painted lips. She was smiling ingratiatingly.

He had hardly noticed her and yet it was an unusual face, a face one did not forget easily. Madame Secret was older, her hair was grey, undyed, and yet . . . and yet . . .

But it was impossible! He must be imagining things or going mad. He had only been to 5 *Rue de Roi* once after a party for men given at the Travellers' Club. They had gone round Paris in search of amusement and ended up in the *Rue de Roi*.

He had stayed only a few moments, for he was too fastidious to seek his pleasures in establishments of that sort. And yet he could remember that woman's face.

Slowly Robert walked up the steps to where Mistral was waiting. The lace had fallen back from her head and the sunshine was shining on her hair, making it seem almost like a halo.

Of course the whole thing was impossible! It was a vile lie of the Rajah's to revenge himself.

"What did he want?" Mistral asked. "Please have nothing to do with him, for he is evil. I know it."

"He is trying to make trouble," Robert answered, "but I am sure that he was really talking nonsense. He spoke of a Madame Bleuet and . . ."

He stopped abruptly. He had seen the sudden widening of Mistral's eyes, a flicker of recognition at the word.

"You have heard of her?" he asked incredulously.

"I . . . have . . ." Mistral began, but stopped as Robert's hand closed on her wrist like a vice.

"Listen to me," he said. "Go down on your knees,

279

here and now, and swear before all that you hold sacred that the woman whom you call your Aunt is not Madame Bleuet. Swear it!"

"But . . . I think that she . . ." Mistral stammered.

"Then she is!"

The words seemed to burst from Robert's lips, and the expression on his face made Mistral's hesitating voice die away into silence.

"She is!" he repeated. "Then the Rajah was right and I, too, have nearly been deceived by you! I believed in you. I thought that you were all that you pretended to be. I even asked you to marry me, God help me. But don't deceive yourself, I am not caught as yet.

"It was a trick, a very clever one, but it has failed. I have been saved just in time, and saved by a man I thought was my enemy.

"Go back to your so-called Aunt and tell her that she has made a mistake, tell her that I have unmasked you for what you are—a dirty, lying little trickster. I loathe you and all your kind. I hope I never set eyes on you again."

He turned away without looking at Mistral.

She stood very still as if turned to stone, the blood slowly receding from her cheeks until she was paler than death, her eyes dark pools of pain.

The carriage was drawn up at the foot of the steps. Robert jumped into it. He gave an order to the coachman in a loud, sharp voice and the horses started off.

He did not look back, did not see Mistral put out a quivering, trembling hand towards him as if she would beg him to stop.

She could not speak, her voice had died in her throat.

She could only stand staring piteously after the carriage, which grew smaller and smaller until the distance swallowed it up.

# 14

Mistral stood very still on the steps of the Chapel for a long time; then at last slowly, as if someone had hit her across the face, she raised her hand to her cheek.

Her brain would not function properly, she could neither sort out nor stem the flood of chaotic questions which repeated themselves again and again in her mind.

There were no tears in her eyes, she was just numb, stunned and shocked as a person might be who has been involved in a terrible accident or who has received a violent blow.

Over and over she turned the problem of what had happened to alter Robert so completely and instantaneously. What could the Rajah have said to him? What knowledge could he have imparted which could change his love to hatred?

She could hardly believe it had happened, that the man who had looked at her with reverence and adoration should be transformed in a few seconds into one who regarded her with dislike and disgust.

At length she was aware that her knees were weak, that her legs felt as if they could hold her up no longer.

Slowly she took her eyes from the end of the road along which the carriage carrying Robert had long since disappeared.

She turned and re-entered the Church. Instinctively she moved towards the last pew and sat down in the very spot where Robert had taken her into his arms and they had exchanged their first kiss—a kiss which to her had been in the nature of a solemn vow.

It was here, she thought, that she had first known real happiness, a happiness which was to last but a few minutes and be lost almost before she could realize it was hers.

What had happened? Why did he hate her? What had the Rajah said? The questions hammered themselves against her brain, but she could find no answers for them.

Now at last the numb feeling was passing and the pain of her anguish swept over her like a bitter wind. She had lost him, lost the man she loved, lost the one thing in life which seemed decent and worthwhile.

All too clearly now she could see beneath the tinsel and glitter of Monte Carlo and know it for what it was.

Many things which had appeared glamorous and even beautiful in these past weeks were now revealed to Mistral in the piteous, clear light of truth as being indecent and horrible. She saw the flashing teeth of the Rajah against his dark face, saw again the great circular divan in the scented room of his Villa, and shuddered.

She saw Stella's puzzled eyes strangely at variance with the painted flamboyance of her face and the gaudiness of her gown.

She saw the avarice and greedy expressions on the faces of the men and women playing at the gambling tables, their fingers bent like the claws on a bird of prey as they reached out to clutch their winnings; she saw Jeanne with trembling hands muttering the Penitential Litany; and lastly Aunt Emilie's air of triumph and defiance seemed in retrospect somehow infinitely sinister.

There indeed was the clue to everything—Aunt Emilie!

She knew the answers to all the questions; could, if she cared to do so, explain what had happened in the past few days, from the action of the Rajah in abducting her from the *Restaurant des Fleurs* to Robert's grim and bitter expression as he turned away to leave her on the Church steps.

Yes, Aunt Emilie knew the answers, but how could she ask her for them?

Last night, when she had arrived back at the Hotel, her dress dishevelled and torn, her arms scratched, her hair falling over her shoulders but her eyes alight with a happiness which seemed to radiate from her, Aunt Emilie had been in the sitting-room.

Mistral was too excited, too thrilled by the echo of Robert's voice still in her ears, to wonder then why Aunt Emilie had not sent the Police in search of her or at least had seemed perturbed and anxious about her absence.

Instead, Emilie was sitting slumped in a chair in an attitude that was almost one of collapse. She looked up as Mistral entered and it seemed as if for a moment she could hardly believe that her presence was real.

Then slowly she sat forward in her chair. Her face was white and drawn and there were dark shadows under her eyes. At length she said in a low voice which had somehow a note of defeat in it:

"So you have come back!"

"Yes, I have come back, Aunt Emilie," Mistral replied.

"And the Rajah?" Emilie asked, still in that strange listless tone.

"It was the Rajah who kidnapped me," Mistral an-

swered. "The carriage took me to his Villa. There he
. . . Oh, I cannot repeat what happened or what he
said, but I managed to escape. I climbed out of the
window and down the side of the Villa, and when at
the last moment the Rajah would have sent his servants
to bring me back, the Prince rescued me."

"The Prince!"

Emilie sat bolt upright, her voice regaining its
elasticity.

"Yes, the Prince!" Mistral repeated. "He guessed
that it was the Rajah's carriage in which I had been
driven away from the Restaurant. He arrived at the
gates of the Villa just as the right moment. If he had
not come . . . I do not know what might have . . .
happened."

She shuddered. The events of the night had been so
strange and so complicated, following swiftly one upon
another, that not until this moment had she begun to
think clearly of the fate which would have awaited her
had not the Prince arrived in the very nick of time.

Emilie jumped to her feet.

"The Prince!" she exclaimed. "The Prince! This is
splendid, splendid! Nothing could be better!"

Mistral opened her lips to continue her story, to tell
her Aunt how the Prince had taken her to his Villa
and bound up her hand, how Sir Robert had found
her there and had jumped to entirely the wrong conclusion, how he had duelled with the Prince and had
carried her off unconscious.

Yet even as she was ready to begin her tale, she
realized how many new difficulties the telling of it
would present.

She would have to explain her friendship with Sir
Robert, would have to admit that she had deceived her
Aunt not once but many times when they had met and
talked together.

She would have to relate how Sir Robert, having fought the Prince, had left him wounded and she would have to confess, too, that Sir Robert was no longer her friend but something much deeper and dearer.

Swiftly Mistral made up her mind that she would leave the remainder of her story until tomorrow; she would wait until Sir Robert called to see her, as she knew he would, and then he would help her to face Aunt Emilie with the truth.

She would never be afraid of anything again with him beside her; but now after the tumultuous events of the night it would be too much to endure Aunt Emilie's anger. It was not difficult to keep silent, for Emilie had no idea there was any sequel to what she had already heard.

"So the Prince rescued you!" she said again in tones of the utmost satisfaction. "I could not have hoped for anything better. Did he say anything special to you?"

"He was very kind," Mistral replied, "and bound up my finger."

"You had hurt it?" Emilie asked without sounding particularly concerned.

"I think I caught it on a nail in the wall," Mistral replied. "It was bleeding rather badly."

"You can have it seen to tomorrow if it is not better by then. Now you had best go to bed, for you look exceedingly dishevelled."

"I am afraid I have ruined my gown," Mistral said apologetically, "and I know this was one of my most expensive ones."

"It is of little consequence," Emilie said surprisingly. "You have plenty of others. Wear your most attractive day-dress tomorrow, for the Prince will be calling, you can be sure of that."

Mistral was just about to say that she thought it unlikely as the Prince was wounded, but she closed her lips. She would wait until the next day when Sir Robert would explain everything.

"Good night, Aunt Emilie," she said quietly.

But Emilie did not hear her. She was walking up and down the room, a light in her eyes, a faint smile on her hard lips. Mistral knew the expression well.

It meant that her Aunt was planning something, was invigorated by her secret thoughts, which seemed always to give her an almost inexhaustible strength and vitality which was often out of all proportion to her age and appearance.

Mistral hurried to her own room, glad not to be questioned further. But it was some time before she undressed. Instead she looked out into the darkness of the night and whispered Sir Robert's name over and over again. She loved him, loved him with every beat of her heart, every throbbing vein in her body.

She knew now what she had wanted all her life, what she had longed for in her loneliness at the Convent. It was love! It was to find someone who would love her and whom she could love in return, someone who would protect her and keep her, who would give her the security of knowing that she belonged and was wanted.

She clasped her hands together and whispered a prayer of thankfulness and gratitude. How could she have ever doubted that there was a Divine reason for everything?

These past weeks, when she had been worried by Aunt Emilie's strangeness, she had somehow felt that God had forsaken her.

She had wondered if she had done the wrong thing in leaving the Convent and coming out into the world; but now she could see that everything had led up to this moment when she could be certain of Sir Robert's love.

Unknowingly she had worked for this, studied to educate herself, developed her talents and pored over the books in Father Vincent's library because the knowledge she gained from them would be helpful to her in the future. And yet, much as she had learned already, how much more was there to learn!

She felt an excitement rising within her at the thought of going to England, of seeing the country that was her Mother's native land and which would be her future home when she married.

At the word the blood flew to her cheeks and she felt herself blushing. There was nothing to embarrass her. She knew as clearly as if he had already asked her that Sir Robert intended to make her his wife.

He would come to her tomorrow as he had promised, and then after that she need never be afraid of anything again.

Mistral had been unable to sleep. She had undressed and got into bed, but her happiness seemed to fill the room with the radiance of the warm sun long before the dawn broke.

Then at length the first golden rays began to percolate through the curtains and she rose to stand on the balcony watching the dawn and remembering her first morning in Monte Carlo—that fateful morning when she met Sir Robert for the first time.

Long before it was time to leave for Church she was dressed and ready; but when she peered into Jeanne's room, it was to find the old woman in bed with a leaden face, saying her Rosary.

"Are you coming to Mass this morning?" Mistral asked.

"I will get up right away," Jeanne replied, but Mistral saw the pain cross her face as she tried to move and said quickly:

"Not if you are unwell! You look tired!"

"I have been in pain the whole night," Jeanne answered, "but the suffering of the body is nothing to the suffering of the mind."

Her voice quivered on the last words and Mistral saw there were unshed tears in her eyes. Impulsively she said:

"What is the matter, Jeanne? Something is worrying you. I can see that. Will you not confide in me and trust me? Perhaps I can help."

Jeanne shook her head violently.

"No, no, Mademoiselle, it is no concern of yours. Ask no questions. Besides . . . nothing is wrong."

It was so palpably a lie that Mistral looked hurt.

"I wish you would trust me," she said.

Jeanne looked up into her face and put out her hand to take Mistral's fingers in hers.

"You are young and lovely, Mademoiselle. You are good, too, I know that. I have watched you when we have gone to Church together, you and I. You are a child of God. Let me beg of you to keep clear of evil. There are bad, wicked people in the world, Mademoiselle, and only by avoiding them, by not even coming into contact with them, can we keep ourselves pure and holy as *le bon Dieu* intended."

Jeanne spoke passionately and Mistral realized that this in some way concerned herself, but how she had no idea.

She could only smile down at Jeanne and wish that by some magical means she could erase the suffering and unhappiness from her old lined face.

"Pray do not worry about me, Jeanne," she said at length. "Something wonderful is going to happen to me, in fact it is already happening; I cannot talk about it yet. But you shall be the first to know, I promise you that."

She was rewarded by seeing Jeanne's face light up.

Her happiness was reflected in the older woman's eyes, and then Jeanne's smile faded and there was a trembling note in her voice as she asked:

"Is it the Prince, *ma chère?*"

"No, no," Mistral answered hastily. "It is not the Prince, but do not tell Auntie Emilie, I beg of you."

Jeanne's face was alight again.

"Thanks be to God if that is the truth."

"It is the truth," Mistral answered. "But . . . do you not like the Prince, Jeanne?"

She was rather surprised at the old woman's concern.

"There is nothing wrong with His Serene Highness as far as I know," Jeanne replied, "but he is not for you, Mademoiselle."

"Indeed he is not," Mistral answered. "That is why it has been so embarrassing when Aunt Emilie has so insistently thrown us at each other's heads."

She laughed a little, remembering how embarrassed and mortified she had been last night when Aunt Emilie forced her to write to the Prince and ask him to come to their table at the Restaurant.

And yet, as it turned out, how fortunate that action had been! If she had not told the Prince about the Rajah, he would not have suspected where she had been taken when he heard that she had been kidnapped.

He would not have come to her rescue and at this moment she might not have been standing in Jeanne's room.

How lucky she had been, how grateful she should be to her Guardian Angel for preserving her from all harm!

Leaving Jeanne in bed, Mistral took the road which led from the hotel down to the Chapel of Ste. Dévote.

She felt that the sunshine matched her mood. She wanted to sing and dance in her very light-heartedness.

Soon, very soon, she would see Sir Robert again. How often she had thought of him as she walked down this very road to Church!

Yet never until now had she been able to feel his arms holding her close, to hear the sound of his voice saying "My darling".

Now, as she crouched low in the pew, everything, Mistral thought, was dark with her utter misery. How long she knelt she did not know; after a time she could not pray, but could only suffer. It was astounding that her body could endure such agony and not be torn in pieces.

And there was some subtle horror in not understanding what was wrong, which made everything infinitely worse.

It was all because of Aunt Emilie, she knew that, but what she had done or how it could possibly be bad enough to make Robert behave as he had was beyond her comprehension.

At last, stiff and cold, Mistral rose from her knees. She must go back or Aunt Emilie might be angry not only with her, but with Jeanne for having let her go to Church alone.

Feeling tired and dispirited, aware for the first time that her body was aching from her fall the night before, Mistral left the Chapel and began the long walk uphill to the Hotel.

It was a glorious day, the sun was as golden as the mimosa flowering in every garden. The sea was azure blue, the waves sparkling as they splashed against the yellow sand; but Mistral could see only the look in Robert's face as he had turned from her in disgust, could hear only the bitter loathing in his voice as he told her that he never wanted to see her again.

She had not cried, her eyes were dry, for it seemed

to her that she was past tears, past everything but an utter and overwhelming despair which was beyond even her worst imaginings of purgatory.

When she reached the Hotel and heard the clock strike eleven, she realized in surprise that three hours had passed since she had first entered the Chapel for Early Mass.

Three hours in which she had seemed to live a lifetime of emotion, in which she had been elevated into Heaven and then cast down again into a bitter hell.

Three hours! Aunt Emilie would be very angry!

Hurriedly Mistral crossed the hall and ran up the broad stairway. As she reached the landing where their rooms were situated, she paused for a moment to get her breath; then summoning up her courage, she opened the door of the sitting-room.

To her surprise a man was standing at the open window looking out. He turned as she entered and she saw that it was the Prince. His arm was in a sling and she perceived with a feeling of quick concern that he was very pale.

"Your Serene Highness!" Mistral exclaimed and added: "You are better? I've been so worried about you! But you are not too ill to be here?"

Her voice sounded incoherent to herself, but the Prince seemed to understand. Smiling, though his eyes were serious, he crossed the room to her side.

"Yes, I am well enough to come here, although the Doctor tried to prevent me. I had to come, for it was of the utmost importance, you understand."

"Is it? I mean . . . I do not understand," Mistral answered, her eyes wide. "Please explain. But before you do so, sit down. I have not yet been able to thank you for coming to . . . my rescue last night."

"There is no need to thank me," the Prince said quietly.

"But of course I must thank you," Mistral expostulated. "I would not have you think that I would have gone away and left you . . . . had I not been . . . unconscious."

"I understood," the Prince said. "I saw what happened, and Sir Robert's assumption was, under the circumstances, quite justifiable. It was about that that I came to see you this morning."

"Oh!"

Mistral could think of nothing she could say. The mere mention of Robert was enough to bring all her misery back to her again.

"I have been thinking about last night," the Prince said, "and I realize that it was both unconventional and indiscreet to take you to my Villa. At the time I was so perturbed about your finger that I forgot the construction other people might put upon the fact that you were alone and unchaperoned in my house."

"But nobody saw us." Mistral said quickly.

"Sir Robert did for one," the Prince replied.

"But Sir Robert would not . . ." Mistral began, and then let her voice die away in silence.

She had been about to say that Sir Robert would not speak of it, but she wondered if she could give such an assurance. What did she know about what Sir Robert would do or not do? She had thought that she had understood many things about him, only to find herself completely and utterly mistaken.

He was the one person in the world whose actions or reactions she could not possibly anticipate at this moment.

"Sir Robert is a gentleman," the Prince said as if he had not heard Mistral's interruption. "But there are also the servants, and one cannot rely upon them. In Monte Carlo the very air carries secrets, the walls have ears. No, Mademoiselle, we did a very foolish thing last night and I cannot allow you to suffer for something which was entirely due to my stupidity. I have therefore come here this morning to ask if you will honour me by becoming my wife."

Not for one moment had Mistral expected him to say anything of the sort. At his words she stared at him incredulously, far too astonished to reply. As he waited, his eyes on her face, the door which led into Emilie's bedroom opened and she came into the room.

The way in which she entered and the expression on her face told Mistral that she had been listening. The door had been ajar and she must have been standing there waiting for some time.

She swept into the centre of the room dramatically. The Prince rose to his feet and so did Mistral.

"Your Serene Highness," Emilie said, making him a small curtsey. "You must forgive me for not being here to receive you the moment you arrived, but doubtless you have not regretted my absence. Will you forgive me if I tell you that I overhead your last words as I entered the room?"

The Prince gave Emilie a speculative look which told Mistral even as if he had said the words that he knew she had been listening. But his voice was courteous as he replied:

"In that case there is no need for me to repeat myself, Madame."

"None at all," Emilie said; "and now we will all of us go at once to the Chateau d'Horizon."

"To my Father?" the Prince asked in surprise.

"To the Grand Duke," Emilie said firmly, and Mistral could hear the rising excitement in her voice.

She clutched at her scattered senses and took a step forward.

"One minute, Aunt Emilie," she said. "I have not yet answered the Prince."

Her Aunt turned on her with an expression of such ferocity that Mistral quailed before her.

"You will say nothing, Mistral," she said. "There is no need. We will, as I have already said, leave at once and seek audience with the Grand Duke."

"But I do not understand, Madame," the Prince said. "If you wish to see my Father, there is, of course, nothing to prevent your doing so; but he is in ignorance of my intention in coming here, and I would wish to break the news to him myself and in my own way."

"You will tell him now," Emilie said, "and you will repeat in front of him the proposal that you have just made to my niece."

The Prince looked for a moment as if he would defy her; then with a shrug of his shoulders which expressed most eloquently his opinion of her, he gave in.

"If that is what you wish, Madame, I have no objection."

"But, Aunt Emilie . . ." Mistral began.

"You will be silent," Emilie snapped at her, and Mistral felt it was quite hopeless to try to intervene.

She only wanted to say that she had no desire to marry the Prince. She understood only too clearly that he was asking her out of gallantry and that it would be impossible for her, even if she loved him, to take advantage of such an action. Besides, she did not love him.

Whatever Robert might feel about her, even if she were never to see him again in the whole of her life, she would love him always.

She knew that as clearly and as decisively as if she could foresee into the future. There would never be another man in her life, there would never be anyone else whom she could love so completely and so whole-heartedly.

In fact her heart was no longer hers. She had given it to Robert that moment in the Church when his lips met hers, and she had surrendered herself utterly into his keeping. He might not want her; but she was his and nothing that anyone else could say or do would alter that indisputable fact.

Yet it was impossible to fight with Aunt Emilie or even to argue with her.

Mistral felt as if she moved in a dream as in silence all three of them went downstairs. Outside the Hotel the Prince's carriage was waiting. Still without speaking they got into it, Emilie and Mistral sitting side by side on the back seat, the Prince facing them.

This could not be happening, Mistral thought, as the carriage drove off. And yet there was the Prince sitting opposite her, his pallor making him perhaps more handsome than usual, although his brows were drawn together as if in pain. And there beside her was Aunt Emilie.

There was something terrifying in her very bearing, in the strange, hard glitter of her eyes and in the triumph of her expression.

"This is what she has been working for," Mistral thought suddenly. "It is for this that she has been scheming and plotting! Yet what happens now? What does it all mean? Why are we going to the Grand Duke?"

They drove on in utter silence. Mistral longed to speak, but she knew that directly she uttered a word she would again be commanded to be silent.

The Prince stared out of the window. She wished she could tell him not to worry, that whatever Aunt Emilie said or did she could not force her to marry against her will.

She might bully or subdue her, but marriage was a

295

Sacrament of the Church and in that at least she must be allowed the expression of her own free will.

But it was no use trying to tell the Prince that in Aunt Emilie's presence and Mistral could only suffer in silence, at times feeling so weak that she felt she must faint. It was lack of food, she knew, remembering that she had had no breakfast.

It was with relief that she realized that they were nearing the Chateau d'Horizon.

It was a huge mansion surrounded by spacious gardens. As the horses turned in at the great wrought-iron gates, fountains were playing and there was a riot of colour everywhere, from the deepest shade of crimson to the palest blush rose, from azure blue to purple, from pale yellow to bronze.

And besides the flowers the almond blossom was in bloom on hundreds of trees, its shell-pink blossoms silhouetted against the blue sky.

Mistral thought it unbelievably beautiful. But at the same time she could hardly take in anything but the ominous excitement in Aunt Emilie's bearing as she stepped from the carriage and climbed the marble stairway to the great glass and gilt doors of the Villa.

"Where is His Imperial Highness?" the Prince asked, and a grey-haired butler led them through several big lofty-ceilinged rooms.

The Chateau had a space and a magnificence beyond anything Mistral had ever known in the whole of her life.

Worried and perturbed though she was, she could not help noticing as she passed them the splendour of the tapestries, the exquisite pieces of furniture, the magnificent collection of portraits hanging on the walls.

In most of them she detected a resemblance to the Prince; then chid herself for taking an interest in anything save the Prince himself as he followed behind Aunt Emilie.

They were ushered finally into an even more beautiful room than the ones through which they had passed. It had three windows overlooking the sea, and the sun was shining through them, but despite the warmth a huge log fire was burning in an open fireplace.

Beside it in a high-backed armchair which gave the appearance of a throne was sitting an elderly man.

He glanced up as the butler announced them, then rose to his feet, and Mistral's first thought was that he was the best-looking man she had ever seem in her life, her second that she could trust him absolutely.

He was very tall, his hair was turning grey, and it was easy to see from whom the Prince got his good looks. But if anything the Grand Duke was more handsome than his son.

His features were classic, clear cut and the very zenith of refinement and good breeding.

He looked what he was, an aristocrat and a man who had both lived his life fully and suffered in the experience. There was something very charming in his smile, something, too, of the philosopher and thinker in the gravity of his eyes as they rested first on his son and then on Emilie.

"Good morning, Nikolai," the Grand Duke said. "This is a surprise visit."

"I must apologize, Father, for not warning you that it was my intention to call on you this morning," Prince Nikolai replied, "but I did not know it myself until a few moments ago. May I present *Madame Secret?*"

He indicated Emilie with a little gesture of his hand, but she made no movement to curtsey.

"And *Mademoiselle Fantôme,* this lady's niece."

Mistral curtsied, then as she raised her eyes to the Duke's face, he put out his hand and took hers.

*"Mademoiselle Fantôme?"* he said. "I think I have heard of you."

"I have spoken of her, Father," the Prince said.

"Perhaps now you will repeat to your Father the proposal that you made to my niece a short time ago in the *Hôtel de Paris,"* Emilie snapped, and her voice was harsh and somehow discordant.

The Prince gave her a glance of dislike, but his voice was calm as he replied:

"Certainly, Madame, I was just about to do so. Father, I have asked *Mademoiselle Fantôme* to honour me by becoming my wife."

"Indeed!" the Grand Duke said.

He was still holding Mistral's hand and now, as he released it, he said quietly:

"Will you tell me your name, Mademoiselle?"

"It is Mistral, Sir."

"And your other name?" the Duke asked.

Mistral hesitated, then Emilie's voice interposed:

"Yes, tell him, tell him the truth, the real truth. I want him to hear it."

There was something so horrible in the way she spoke that Mistral felt herself tremble; then she looked up into the Grand Duke's face and felt curiously reassured. He was looking down with calm, friendly eyes. He had not turned his head nor taken any notice of Emilie's outburst.

"My name is Mistral Wytham," she answered in a low tone.

"What is your age?" the Grand Duke asked.

"I am eighteen," Mistral replied.

"Tell him when you were born," Emilie said harshly.

The Duke seemed to straighten his shoulders. He looked across at Emilie.

"Why was I not told of this before?" he asked.

Emilie laughed. It was an ugly, discordant sound.

"You may well ask that question. It was because Alice did not want you to know. It was because she made me promise on her deathbed that I would never tell you.

"I have not told you now, you have discovered it for yourself, discovered it because your son—yes, your only son, of whom you are so fond—wants to marry the daughter of the woman you treated so vilely that she fled back to me for protection.

"A pretty tangle, isn't it? And how are you going to solve it, I wonder? Your son is in love, and who is he in love with?

"With Mistral, the daughter of Alice Wytham, whom you brought here nineteen years ago and whom you bespoiled and betrayed for your own vile pleasure."

There was so much bitterness and spite in Emilie's passionate declamation that instinctively Mistral turned towards the Prince as if for protection and found him beside her. He took her hand in his and held it tightly.

She clung to him, thankful for his strength. She knew that he was as astonished as she was at what was occurring. Yet neither of them could say anything.

They could only cling together, two children lost in a wood of terror and bewilderment.

Only the Grand Duke seemed calm and utterly unperturbed. He looked at Emilie and his voice was stern as he said very quietly:

"I made enquiries as to what had happened to your sister and I was told that she was dead."

"Yes, she died," Emilie replied, "and you were instrumental in her death. You made enquiries, you say? Yes, you made them eight months after she left you! I took good care that you should not learn then of the child that Alice had left behind, for she left her to me and not to you.

"The thought of a child might have pleased you, but it

299

was too late then to regret that you had shamefully betrayed an innocent and decent girl."

"You are very fond of that word 'betrayed'," the Duke said quietly. "I think we must be talking at cross purposes. I did not betray your sister. Of her own free will she consented to marry me."

"She married you?"

Emilie's question was almost a scream.

"Yes, she married me," the Duke replied. "Did you not know that? We were married here in my Private Chapel both by a Priest of my religion and one of Alice's. The records are there should you wish to inspect them."

"Married! I didn't know! I didn't guess!"

Emilie's hand went up to her throat as if she felt something was choking her. The Grand Duke looked at her and his eyes were stern.

"You should have known your sister better than that," he said, "but from what I heard of you and from what I have learned now I am afraid that you know no one save yourself. It was you who ruined our marriage, Emilie Riguad. I believe Alice loved me as I loved her, but her love was not greater than her fear of you.

"You frightened her, and she was too frightened after she married me to write and tell you that we were man and wife. When I suggested it, she grew quite hysterical, telling me that you would be angry, that no one must know, not even your cousins down at the quay.

"And so we kept it a secret; but gradually I found that the poison you had instilled into my wife had gone too deep for me to save her from her own fear and her own misery.

"You had poisoned her by instilling in her a hatred of men such as you yourself had for every man with whom you came in contact, and she had grown to believe what you had taught her, that all men are evil and bestial.

"Nothing I could say, nothing I could do, would change her. She shrank from me. Her love for me turned to hatred—a hatred that you had taught her from her very childhood.

"That was what you had done and that was why she left me, turning away from love and happiness, flying back to you and your hate, which was stronger than anything I could offer her.

"It was you who smashed our marriage, Emilie Riguad, and it was you who killed your sister, not I."

Emilie gave a strange cry.

"It isn't true," she shouted. "You lie! You are saying this to justify yourself, to escape the revenge I planned for you. I have planned it all these years and I have succeeded in what I have set out to do.

"I wanted to ruin your life and the life of your son, and that is what I have managed to do now. You won't forget this moment, you won't be able to escape from it.

"You ruined Alice, you killed her, and her daughter —your child and hers—has been brought up and educated by the money obtained from a . . ."

"Be silent!"

The Duke's voice, clear and authoritative, broke across the ugly word.

Even as he spoke something strange happened to Emilie. She seemed to choke; a terrible expression crossed her features, torturing and twisting her face.

She put out her hands as if she would grasp something for support, and then, before anyone could reach her, she pitched forward on the floor.

# 15

Emilie lived for three days, but she never regained consciousness.

Jeanne nursed her devotedly and Mistral was at her bedside practically the whole time, but there was nothing either of them could do.

She had been put to bed in the Château d'Horizon and the Grand Duke sent for his own Doctor, but from the very moment he set eyes on Emilie his verdict was decisive and without hope.

"This lady has had a severe stroke," he said, "and it is practically impossible for her to live for more than a few days. If by some miracle she does survive, she will be partially paralysed for the rest of her life."

Mistral, watching Emilie sink deeper and deeper into unconsciousness, felt that this was the most merciful and kindest thing that could happen.

Her face was horribly distorted and it was even difficult to recognize Emilie's undoubted good looks when one looked at the poor twisted features of the woman who lay oblivious in the bed.

For long hours at a time Mistral sat beside her Aunt; and, sitting there, it seemed to her that she herself thought little and felt nothing.

It was as if time stood still and she was in a No-man's Land between the past and the future, a kind of vacuum in which she moved and had her being, but in a dazed, bewildered manner which left everything indecisive.

She did not understand that she was suffering from shock and that, because she had been through so much, nothing had the power to hurt her further, that her nerves were sealed off, as it were, from the outer world.

Then on the third day Emilie died. Mistral had left the darkened bedroom and gone into the sitting-room next door because she had been told that the Grand Duke wished to speak to her. The room was bright with sunshine and yet Mistral felt as if she saw it through a grey fog.

The Grand Duke was standing by the fireplace and she had just reached his side and her eyes, dark-rimmed with sleeplessness, were raised to his, when suddenly the door was pushed violently open and Jeanne came into the room.

She was crying, the tears running down her withered cheeks.

"She is dead!" she said. "Madame is dead!"

Jeanne looked as if she were about to collapse and Mistral moved swiftly to her side. But the old woman drew herself away, putting out her hands as if to ward her off.

"Don't touch me, Mademoiselle," she commanded. "There is something I must say and I must say it now."

She looked at the Grand Duke as she spoke and he said quietly:

"Sit down! You have been through a great deal!"

Jeanne shook her head.

"I will stand, Your Imperial Highness," she said obstinately.

Then she began her story. It was as if everything had been bottled up in her for years and now at last it was released, to spurt out in a flood-tide of verbosity, being shocking, horrifying, disgusting and infinitely pathetic all at the same time.

She held both the Grand Duke and Mistral spell-

303

bound, for they could neither stop her nor do anything else but listen to the tale she unfolded.

She told them how she had served Emilie for nineteen years, but she had known her before that when as children they had gone to school together in Brittany. She spoke of Emilie's strange nature, of the burning hatred she had of her father and the fierce possessive love she bore her half-sister, Alice.

She told of Mistral's birth, the revenge Emilie had planned, which she had nurtured and fed until it became the greatest and most important thing in her whole life.

She told them how Emilie had set off for Paris, determined to make enough money to pay Mistral's school fees, how she had married Monsieur Bleuet and sent to Brittany for Jeanne to come and keep his house with her.

And as the tale of those years was unfolded in Jeanne's weak, tearful voice, Mistral began to see how Emilie's desire for revenge and retribution had gradually replaced all that was kindly and decent in her nature.

It was a definite, positive evil which had poisoned her soul as some deadly poison might have destroyed her body.

She had kept on Monsieur Bleuet's notorious establishment because it brought her money and it was money she needed for her vengeance. She had worked fanatically hard for the same reason, never taking a holiday, never indulging herself in any way—saving, scraping, cheeseparing for the day of her reckoning with the Grand Duke.

At last Jeanne came to the moment when Emilie's plans had been threatened by Henry Dulton and rather than submit to being blackmailed she had murdered him in the *Hôtel de Paris*.

Only then, as the full horror of what had been done came to her, did Mistral feel a sudden agony within herself as if a vast hand squeezed her heart.

For the first time since her happiness in the Chapel of Ste. Dévote had been snatched from her, to leave her alone in an utter darkness, the tears came slowly and painfully into her eyes and began to trickle down her cheeks.

And while Jeanne was still speaking, the full horror of her Aunt's history burst over her.

At last she understood why the Rajah had insulted her, why Robert's love had turned to hatred and loathing.

She saw it all too clearly, and because the abyss of evil through which she had walked unscathed appeared so horrifying in retrospect, she could only cry like a frightened child who still weeps after the real danger is past.

It was all muddled and distorted in her mind. She was crying for herself, for Robert, for Jeanne and for Emilie. Yes, for Emilie too, who must have known the darkest unhappiness of all, that of having deliberately forsaken God.

Blinded and shaken by the tempest of tears, Mistral would have sunk down on the ground, but instead she found herself caught up in strong arms and carried away to her own bedroom.

There somebody administered to her, speaking soothing words which still had not the power to stop her crying. The Doctor came and she strove to do what he said, but she was past even obeying the dictates of her own commonsense.

She remembered drinking something, feeling the liquid smooth and rather bitter sink down her throat.

Then at last she was at peace. She slept, woke, ate, and slept again. She had no idea how long a time

305

elapsed between her sleeping and her waking. She was aware of only one thing.

She was no longer frightened and Jeanne was at her side whenever she woke. Perhaps her only coherent thought was a desire to sleep.

There was an aching want within herself to return to that dreamless, inexhaustible oblivion.

When Mistral finally awoke, it was with a feeling of happiness and a consciousness of being ready to take up the threads of life again. Someone had already drawn the blinds in her room. The sunshine was flooding in.

Through the big open windows she could see a vast expanse of blue sky and against it the delicate branches of mimosa, golden as the sun itself.

Mistral lay for a long time looking at them, letting the events of the past steep back slowly into her memory. Then at length she raised her head and was aware that she was hungry.

She was wondering whether to ring the bell when the door opened softly and a maid came into the room. She was young and pretty, a white cap framing her dark hair, and she had a smiling, sunburnt face. She advanced to the bed and curtsied.

"Would Your Serene Highness like some breakfast?" she enquired.

Mistral was startled by the title, and it was some seconds before she asked:

"Who are you?"

"I am Yvette, Your Serene Highness, and if it pleases you I am to be your maid and look after you."

Mistral smiled.

"That sounds very pleasant! I would like some breakfast, please."

"I have already ordered it," Yvette replied. "The Doctor said that Your Serene Highness would awake this morning feeling well; and if one is feeling well, one is also hungry."

There was something gay and joyous in the girl's voice and Mistral felt her spirits rise. She sat up in bed while Yvette brought more pillows which she placed behind her and draped a warm wrap over her shoulders.

A knock on the door announced the approach of breakfast and Yvette brought it to Mistral's side.

She found that she was indeed hungry and the fresh rolls, yellow butter and the perfectly made coffee were undeniably tempting. Yvette slipped from the room while Mistral ate; and as soon as she had finished, the maid returned again to remove the tray.

"How long have I been in bed?" Mistral asked, half surprised at herself for asking the question, for she felt it must have been but yesterday since Emilie had died.

To her astonishment Yvette answered:

"Six days, Your Serene Highness."

"Six days!"

Mistral stared at her as if she could hardly believe her ears.

"Yes, indeed," Yvette replied. "But the Doctor assured us that we were not to worry. He said you needed sleep and that, if you could sleep, both your megrim and your unhappiness would pass. He promised that Your Serene Highness would awake refreshed, and see, he has spoken the truth."

"He has indeed," Mistral replied.

She threw back the bedclothes.

"I want to look at the garden," she said.

She stepped out of bed and instantly Yvette hurried to drape over her shoulders an exquisite négligé of white velvet trimmed with ermine. Mistral stared down at it in astonishment.

"Where did this come from?" she asked. "It is not mine."

"But indeed it is, Your Serene Highness. Look!"

Yvette ran across the room and pulled open the doors of a big wardrobe which covered the whole of one wall. With a dramatic little gesture of her hands she indicated the contents, and Mistral gasped.

Never had she seen such an array of lovely clothes. There were gowns of every colour and description, and their hues rivalled the very colours of the flowers in the garden. There were dresses of blue, pink, green, rose and yellow. Mistral stared at them with wide eyes.

"For me?" she asked in astonishment.

"Yes, indeed," Yvette said. "His Imperial Highness ordered them from Nice. There are others to come from Paris. These arrived last night and I crept into your room with them while you were still asleep, as I wanted them to be a surprise when Your Serene Highness awoke."

"They are certainly that," Mistral said.

She was woman enough to feel excited and thrilled that these wonderful garments were hers. The one thing she had noticed immediately was that there was nothing grey amongst them. There was not even a pair of shoes of that colour.

That, too, had been relegated into the past; and yet there were some things which had happened that could never be forgotten and which Mistral knew would haunt her for ever.

But now was not the time to think of such things. Because she was afraid of her own thoughts, Mistral said hastily:

"Where is Jeanne?"

"She is packing, Your Serene Highness. She leaves this morning."

"She leaves?" Mistral echoed quickly. "But where is she going and why? Ask her to come to me at once."

Yvette hurried from the room and Mistral was suddenly aware that her legs felt weak. She sat down in an armchair by the window.

Now she could see the garden, and her eyes rested on the almond blossom and mimosa tresses and beneath them beds filled with the radiant beauty of spring flowers. From the window she could see one of the fountains.

Its crystal water sparkling in the sunshine created a rainbow, vivid and beautiful, against the sculptured grey stones. It had a fairylike loveliness, and Mistral had a sudden longing to share such beauty with someone she loved.

Yet even as she formulated the thought she tried to prevent herself from thinking it, knowing that for the moment she dared' not remember Robert too vividly.

She was thankful when the door opened and Jeanne came in. She was wearing her quiet black travelling clothes, but her face was calm, her eyes at peace.

At her entrance Mistral rose to her feet and crossed the room quickly towards her as a child runs to a beloved nurse.

"Jeanne, I have been told you are going away," she said.

"It is true, Mademoiselle."

"But why? How can you leave me?" Mistral asked.

Jeanne smiled.

"You will not be forgotten, my chère. You have a family now who are longing to look after you, to spoil you, to love you. You have come home, and I too am going home. I am going back to Brittany."

"You are glad of that?" Mistral asked.

"Glad indeed," Jeanne answered. "His Imperial

309

Highness had been kindness itself. He has given me enough money to buy a cottage and to live there for the rest of my life without working. I shall be able to entertain my great-nephews and great-nieces in my own house; and when I am gone, they will inherit all that I have to leave. Yes, I am glad to be going back, Mademoiselle. I never thought that such good fortune would come my way."

"Then I am glad too!" Mistral said. "Dear Jeanne, you have been so kind to me!"

At the words the tears came to Jeanne's eyes, but they were tears of happiness and very different from the last ones Mistral had seen running down her unhappy face.

"I shall miss you, Mademoiselle," she said, "and I shall never forget you. But it is best that I go away. His Imperial Highness wishes you to forget the past. He is right! The future lies ahead. You are young and lovely. Don't think of what has happened; there are so many more and better things to come."

"I will try to forget," Mistral said solemnly, knowing that Jeanne spoke of Emilie.

"It is not always easy," Jeanne said quietly, "but when one forgives even as *le bon Dieu* forgives us, then forgetfulness follows."

Mistral hesitated for a moment; then in utter sincerity she said simply:

"I have forgiven Aunt Emilie."

As she said the words, she knew them for the truth even though it involved forgiving her Aunt for the part she had played in driving Robert away and changing his love to disgust. Mistral knew the wound he had inflicted on her then was still unhealed, still raw and tender.

Yet it would be unfair to blame Emilie for something

310

that had occurred unbeknown to herself, and for an incident in which she had played no active part.

Mistral knew now that she might be unhappy, she might be utterly bereft without Robert; but none the less because Emilie was dead, because she had gone defeated and unrepentant to the grave, she could bear her no grudge. Jeanne smiled, and Mistral thought that perhaps instinctively she guessed a little of the conflicting feelings in her heart. Jeanne's words confirmed the impression.

"We must pray for Madame," she said quietly.

"You went to her funeral?" Mistral asked.

Jeanne nodded.

"She was buried very quietly at dawn. There was no one there save myself, the Priest, and the pall-bearers. His Imperial Highness wished there to be no talk."

"I understand," Mistral said. "I will never forget to pray for her."

"Nor I for you, Mademoiselle," Jeanne answered. "Sometimes when you have a moment perhaps you will write to me and tell me how you are and if you are happy."

"Of course I will do that," Mistral replied, and impulsively she lifted her face and kissed the older woman on the cheek. "Good-bye, Jeanne, and thank you once again. I shall never forget you."

Jeanne bent and kissed her hand and then, blinded a little by her tears, went from the room.

Mistral sighed. It was like losing a friend to see Jeanne go. It was also the breaking of yet another link with the past.

Yvette came hurrying into the room. Soon she had helped Mistral to bathe. Then laughing a little because in some ways it was so exciting, the two girls inspected the dresses in the big wardrobe.

311

They chose a gown of pale green muslin trimmed with rose-pink ribbons. Mistral looked in the glass when she was dressed and hardly recognized herself.

She was so used to her own ghost-like appearance in the grey garments which Aunt Emilie had given her that now she could hardly believe that this radiant, colourful creature who looked back at her from the mirror was really herself.

Very slowly, feeling overwhelmingly shy, she went from her bedroom in search of her newly found family.

She was not sure which way to go. But a wide arched corridor brought her to the big room overlooking the garden where she had first seen the Grand Duke.

It was empty, the high-backed velvet chair in which he had sat unoccupied. Mistral stared about her, looking curiously at the tapestries on the walls, at the fine Persian carpets covering the floor, at the valuable inlaid French furniture and the ornaments of almost priceless antiquity.

She had just crossed the room to look at a Grecian vase when she heard a voice behind her and started as two hands gripped her shoulders and swung her round.

"My goodness, what a pretty sister I have got!"

It was the Prince, and Mistral blushed as he bent forward and kissed her cheek.

"So you are awake at last!" he teased. "I began to think that you were Mrs. Rip Van Winkle and would sleep for at least a hundred years."

"You are making me feel I ought to apologize," Mistral said.

"You need not do that," the Prince reassured her. "Besides, I could not help forgiving anyone as pretty as you, whatever you did. You look different now."

He stood back as if considering her appearance, then he gave an exclamation.

"I've got it. I know what was puzzling me. You are no longer a ghost!"

"All my grey gowns have disappeared," Mistral answered.

"And a good thing too," the Prince said. "That is Father's doing, of course."

"He has bought me instead this dress and dozens of other perfectly lovely ones," Mistral said.

"I thought he would do something like that," the Prince smiled. "By the way, I think I am a little jealous of you. I have never seen my Father so pleased about anything as at the fact that you are here."

Mistral's expression was suddenly serious.

"I am glad of that," she said. "I have been afraid that you might not want me."

"I personally am a little doubtful," the Prince said solemnly, but his eyes were twinkling. "You may be one of those interfering, bossy sort of sisters who will tell me what I should do and what I should not do."

"As though I would dare," Mistral replied half indignantly, then she met his eyes and began to laugh.

It was so ridiculous somehow that this good-looking, handsome young man should be her brother. And yet it was wonderful to think that she had one. Here at last was someone to whom she belonged.

"May I share the joke?" a voice asked.

They looked round to see the Grand Duke standing in the french window which led to the garden.

Mistral crossed the room swiftly to his side. She looked up into his handsome, aristocratic face and said softly:

"Thank you! Thank you so very much."

"For what in particular?" the Grand Duke enquired.

"For my lovely clothes . . . for having me here," Mistral said incoherently.

The Grand Duke put out his hand and she laid hers in it.

"We have got a lot to say to each other, you and I," he said quietly.

"Yes, Your Imperial Highness."

His fingers tightened on hers.

"Must we be so formal?" he asked. "I have a very urgent desire to hear you address me in another way. Can you guess what it is?"

"Yes . . . Father," Mistral faltered.

He smiled down at her and bent to kiss her cheek. Impulsively she put her arms round his neck. The Grand Duke's eyes were very gentle and his voice strangely moved as he said quietly:

"Thank you, my daughter."

He led the way to two comfortable chairs set out on the balcony overlooking the garden. There was a canopy overhead to shade them from the sun, and the song of the birds flitting amongst the trees was like distant music.

The Prince had disappeared and Mistral realized that he knew that his Father wanted to be alone with her.

The Grand Duke settled himself comfortably in the chair, then he said:

"I do not intend after this to speak to you again of Emilie Riguad. She is dead and we can only hope that her troubled soul will find peace in another world, for it had none in this.

"There is nothing we can do for her now but try to erase from our memories the troubles and difficulties she made for many people, yourself amongst them. I have given instructions to the *Hôtel de Paris* that they are to answer no questions concerning the two ladies who stayed there under the names of *Madame Secret* and *Mademoiselle Fantôme*.

"To all enquiries they will merely reply that the ladies have left for an unknown destination.

"In a few weeks I will let it be known that my daughter has arrived in Monte Carlo to live with me. You will be presented to my friends, you will visit the Palace, and there is no reason at all why anyone should connect you with the girl of doubtful antecedents who stayed for a short while at the *Hôtel de Paris*.

"The winter season is nearly over and most of the visitors who have been staying here at Monte Carlo these past weeks will be returning to their own countries.

"If they come again next year—and incidentally the Rajah of Jehangar will not be amongst them—they will not recognize you or connect you in any way with the notorious *Mademoiselle Fantôme*.

"You will agree with me, I am sure, that it is the best way to arrange things."

"Yes . . . I am sure it is, Father," Mistral said; but somehow her tone lacked conviction. The Grand Duke went on.

"There are many things that you and I will wish to discuss together in the future, but there are just a few things that I must explain as regards the past. One of these concerns your Mother.

"I do not want you to imagine that I did not love her and that the reason I let her go away from me was not that I did not sincerely desire her happiness. I loved her passionately, as I have loved only one other woman in the whole of my life—my first wife, Nikolai's Mother.

"Perhaps I was too impetuous, too ready to believe that her inexperienced emotions matched my own much more experienced ones. I did not know, when we were first married, that she had been badly treated as a child and that her whole outlook and character were

315

distorted by fear—fear of people and especially a fear of men.

"Her half-sister, Emilie Riguad, had brought her up to believe that all men were brutes; and after we were married, her love for me was not strong enough to counter-balance the horror she felt at my natural love and desire for her.

"When she left me after a stormy scene in which she told me she hated me and was determined never to live with me again, I thought I was being clever in letting her have her own way.

"I knew that she was really frightened of her half-sister, Emilie, and I knew that she disliked the sordidness of the farm in Brittany.

"I believed in my vanity that, if I left her alone, she would before very long return to me of her own free will.

"But I was mistaken, as you know; and when at length I could be proud no longer and my need for her was so great that I was ready to beg her to return on any terms she desired, it was too late. I was told that she was dead. I had not the slightest idea, of course, that she had borne me a child."

The Duke's voice was raw with pain. Mistral put out her hand and laid it on his arm.

"Do not tell me this if it makes you unhappy," she said softly.

"I want you to understand," he replied. "And there is something else I would tell you. I have taken away from you the pearls that belonged to your Mother.

"I had always hoped that Alice had sold them and bought with the money some comfort and luxury for herself. I had no idea, of course, that Emilie Riguad would set them aside as a weapon to be used in her diabolical revenge.

"She was sharp enough to know that they were unique

316

and to anticipate that, if you came to Monte Carlo wearing them, I would be certain to hear of them and make enquiries as to how they had come into your possession.

"As it happened, Nikolai did speak of them when he told me of the two strange women who had come to the *Hôtel de Paris,* one of whom claimed my acquaintance. But that part of Emilie's plot misfired.

"I did not connect the pearls which *Mademoiselle Fantôme* was wearing with the ones which had been a part of the fabulous collection of my great-grandfather—the Czar. I thought Nikolai was talking nonsense, and so I did not, as Emilie had anticipated, make the enquiries which would have speeded up the hour of her triumph."

"It was a strange revenge to choose," Mistral said reflectively.

"But a clever one," the Grand Duke replied. "She knew, you see, that the one person I really adored was my only son. She had doubtless heard that Nikolai was very gay and very easily attracted by a pretty woman.

"She thought that, if she could inveigle him into being in love with you, she would in common parlance kill two birds with one stone. I would be forced to enquire as to your identity and Nikolai's heart would be broken and his life ruined by the knowledge that he was in love with his own sister.

"A clever plot, but as I say, not an entirely successful one. I think I am right in saying that Nikolai is not in love with you or you with him."

"No, he is not in love with me," Mistral repeated, "nor I with him."

For a moment she hesitated, uncertain whether to tell her Father of Sir Robert.

Then she felt that she could not speak of it to anyone, could not confess her humiliation and misery that

317

he had not believed in her, that he had not been certain of her innocence.

Murmuring some excuse, she rose from the chair beside the Grand Duke and walked down the stone steps into the garden.

He watched her go and made no effort to prevent her. His eyes were wise and understanding. He knew that it was too soon as yet to force her confidence.

The rest of the day passed happily. Mistral explored the garden. The Grand Duke took her to his greenhouses, where he had the most celebrated collection of orchids in the whole of France.

Later he took her round the Chateau and showed her some of the treasures he had brought there from Russia. Mistral was awe-struck when she learned the distinction and importance of many of her relatives.

It was strange to think that only a few days ago she had been nobody, a girl who at school had not even been entitled to use her Father's name, and now she was a Princess in her own right, related to the monarchs of many European countries and a direct descendant of the Czar of all the Russians.

She thought then that she would never get used to being addressed by her title; but when she murmured these apprehensions to the Grand Duke, he laughed at her.

"The strangeness will soon wear off," he said. "Besides, you will find it all comes natural to you, for you are a true aristocrat, my dear. Your English blood is noble and of great antiquity. One day we will go to England, you and I, and make the acquaintance of your relatives there. Incidentally, your second cousin has recently been made Secretary-of-State for Foreign Affairs."

"It is quite frightening to have so many relations," Mistral said half ruefully, "after having had none."

"That is life," the Grand Duke replied. "Either one has everything or nothing. Often there appears to be no half measures."

And yet, Mistral thought as she went to her room to change for dinner, in the midst of plenty she was still like someone dying of thirst for a drink of water.

The one thing she really wanted, the one thing of great moment in her life, was not hers.

In the privacy of her own room, when she could relax, it was impossible to keep the thoughts of Robert from pouring over her, excluding all else and filling her with a dull, incessant pain which she felt would never be assuaged until she could see him again.

That was of course impossible. But now he would doubtless have gone from Monte Carlo and forgotten her. Even if he had wanted to find her, he would not be able to do so. Mistral covered her face with her hands.

She wanted him so desperately that it seemed to her that nothing in the whole world mattered beside her love for him, the aching need of her whole body.

She was trembling a little with the intensity of her emotions when there came a knock on the door. It was a moment before Mistral could compose herself enough to say:

"Come in!"

The door opened.

"I am sorry if I interrupt, Your Serene Highness," Yvette said, "but there is a woman downstairs who is very anxious to speak with you."

"Someone for me?" Mistral said in surprise. "But who is it?"

"It is a Madame Boulanger," Yvette said. "She said you would not know her by that name, but she explained that once she had a dress with butterflies embroidered on it, and it is of the utmost urgency that she should speak with you for a moment."

Stella's pretty face sprung into Mistral's mind.

"Of course I know who she is! Bring her here, Yvette."

"Very good, Your Serene Highness."

Mistral crossed the room to pick up a paper which had fallen from the writing-desk. As she did so, she saw that Yvette had laid out a gown for the evening. It was of white lace trimmed with tiny posies of roses.

It was a very different dress from the one she had worn that night when the Rajah had first threatened her and she had become entangled with Stella in the cloakroom at the Casino.

Why had this woman come to see her now? She half regretted her impulse in sending for her without first informing the Grand Duke. But it was too late to change her mind.

A knock on the door told her that Madame Boulanger already stood outside. Yvette announced her and Stella came into the bedroom. For a moment Mistral hardly recognized her.

She was dressed very simply with no hat and over her shoulders was a woollen shawl which she had obviously flung back from her head. Her face was not painted, her eyelashes undarkened, and yet she looked prettier and younger than when, dressed in an expensive gown and gorgeously bejewelled, she had accompanied the Rajah to the Casino.

For a moment the two women looked at each other, then Stella curtsied respectfully.

"It is kind of Your Serene Highness to see me."

"How did you know I was here?" Mistral enquired. "It is supposed to be a secret."

"Yes, I know that," Stella replied. "But my husband's cousin is Butler to His Imperial Highness. He

320

told us of the lovely young lady who had arrived at the Chateau. He described you and it was not hard to put two and two together after we heard that *Mademoiselle Fantôme* had unexpectedly and without warning left the *Hôtel de Paris*."

"You will not speak of it to anyone?" Mistral asked.

"But of course not," Stella replied. "I didn't even tell my husband's cousin who you were. I came here not to make mischief, Mademoiselle, but to tell you something I think you would wish to know."

"What is it?" Mistral asked.

"It's about Sir Robert Stanford," Stella replied.

Mistral started violently; then with an eagerness she did not attempt to hide she asked quickly:

"What about him? Is he still in Monte Carlo? Is he in trouble?"

"Yes, Mademoiselle, he is in trouble," Stella replied.

"Oh!"

The monosyllable seemed to be drawn from the very depths of Mistral's heart, then she added quickly:

'What is it? Please tell me!"

"He had been hurt," Stella replied. "Wounded!"

Then realizing that the blood had left Mistral's face she went on:

"Do not perturb yourself. He is much better! In fact I believe he leaves tomorrow for England."

"But how was he hurt?" Mistral enquired.

Stella glanced over her shoulder to make sure the door was shut.

"You will not make trouble, Mademoiselle, if I tell you the truth? You were kind to me and therefore I wish only to do you a service."

"I promise you I will not make trouble for you or for anyone else," Mistral said.

"It was Potoc," Stella said.

"The Prince's servant?" Mistral enquired.

321

"Yes," Stella repeated. "He stabbed Sir Robert in the back as he walked through the Casino Gardens."

"Stabbed him!" Mistral gasped. "But why and for what reason?"

Even as she asked the question she knew the answer herself. He was revenging himself for the wound Robert had inflicted on the Prince.

He would never forgive anyone who harmed his beloved master and he had taken his revenge swiftly and secretly. Mistral clasped her hands together as if to steady her self-control.

"Sir Robert's life is not in danger?" she asked.

"Not now!" Stella replied. "Luckily he was found very shortly after it happened. He was taken back to the *Hôtel Hermitage* and the Doctor stopped the bleeding and sewed up the wound. Tomorrow, as I have said, Sir Robert leaves for England."

Mistral put her hands up to her eyes.

"What can I do?" she asked.

"I'm telling you this, Mademoiselle, because you were kind to me," Stella said. "You made a decision for me which has altered my whole life, which has brought me unbelievable happiness. I know, because my husband is working as Chef at the *Hotel Hermitage,* that Sir Robert loves you.

"Servants talk, especially French ones, Mademoiselle, and when he was delirious the first night, Sir Robert called your name over and over again.

"You may think I am presumptuous in coming to you on such a slender pretext, but one day when you were standing on the shore talking to Sir Robert I passed by in a carriage. I think you did not see me because you were oblivious to all save each other.

"I thought then that you loved Sir Robert; and when he called for you all through the night, I knew that

322

he loved you. If I have been impertinent and indiscreet in coming here, you will perhaps forgive me."

At the humility in Stella's last words Mistral put out her hand impulsively and laid it on the older girl's arm.

"No, you were right to come. I am more grateful than I can possibly say. It means everything to me to know that he loves me. You were right in thinking that I love him."

Stella smiled happily.

"Thank you! You have set my mind at rest. Now I will return to the Hotel and to my husband."

"You have been married recently?" Mistral asked.

"Yes," Stella replied. "It was entirely due to you, Mademoiselle, and I can never thank you enough."

The hands of the two women met in a warm hand-shake of friendship, and then Stella had gone leaving Mistral alone again.

Now there was no indecision about her, she knew what she must do and that it must be done quickly. She rang for Yvette and changed into the evening gown of white lace. Then she ran down the corridor into the drawing-room where the Grand Duke would be waiting before dinner.

He looked up as she entered. Then, as he saw her face, he rose to his feet.

"Father, something has happened! Please listen to me! I want to tell you all about it," Mistral said breathlessly.

Looking down at her, the Grand Duke knew that from this moment there would no longer be any secrets between them.

It was nearly two hours later that Sir Robert, sitting in an arm-chair by the window of the sitting-room in the *Hotel Hermitage,* heard a knock on the door. The windows were open and he was looking out on to the dusky night. A new moon was rising over the sea, the evening stars were coming out one after another.

He did not turn his head at the interruption, thinking it was a servant coming to replenish the fire or to bring him a drink.

He went on looking out into the darkness. He heard someone enter and the door close. Then there was silence.

Still he did not move until some sixth sense told him that he was being watched, that someone was standing looking at him. Impatiently he turned but the words he was about to say died on his lips, for it was Mistral who stood there.

For a moment he thought that she must be a figment of his own imagination. The light from the chandelier illuminated her very clearly and never, he thought, had he seen her look more lovely.

Her dress was white and somehow it made her seem younger and more appealing; and yet it may have been the expression on her face, her eyes very wide and dark against the pale gold of her shining hair.

As he stared, unable for a moment to move or speak, Mistral with a swift movement slipped down on her knees beside him, her little hands clasped together on the arms of his chair.

"I have come to say something to you," she said and her voice was very low and sweet. "You asked me to swear to you on my knees, by all that I held holy, that I did not know that my Aunt was Madame Bleuet.

"I did know that she had been called Madame Bleuet, but . . . until she died I did not know who she was or how . . . notorious she had become under that name. I had no idea of anything . . . she did or of . . . the . . . the wickedness with which she was connected. This I swear to you now . . . before God and by . . . all His Holy Saints."

As Mistral's voice faltered into silence, Robert, as if he awoke at last from a dream, bent forward and clasped her in his arms.

"Mistral!" he exclaimed. "I have wanted you so much. I have asked for you, prayed for you, but they told me you had gone away. Do you think I don't know you were innocent? That I could trust you?

"Oh, my darling, I must have been mad and crazy to have thought for one moment that you were anything but what you appeared. You are pure and holy—the most perfect woman in all the world. Forgive me, only forgive me, and say that you still love me."

His words tumbled over one another, his lips were very near to hers, his arms were drawing her closer and closer into his embrace. Mistral's head fell back against his shoulder.

"Forgive me," Robert whispered, and now at last she could answer him in three words.

"I . . . Oh . . . I . . . love you!"

He heard her voice break on the words, and then his lips were against hers.

She felt in that moment all the rapture and wonder that had been theirs that moment in the Chapel when they had pledged their troth before the altar; and she knew that this time no evil could ever separate them and take them one from the other.

They were one, man and woman joined together in the sight of God, one for all eternity.

"Oh, my darling, my precious one."

Robert was murmuring his endearments against her cheek and she looked up to see that there were tears in his eyes. As she drew a deep breath, as she stirred for a moment within the encircling confines of his arms, he said:

"No, no, I cannot let you go. You are mine. I am afraid that you may vanish, and I want you, Mistral. I should never have rested until I found you, but I had no idea where to begin! But you have come back to me and I love you too much ever to let you go again."

Once more he was kissing her, and this time his kisses were more human, more possessive, more demanding, and she felt a flame of desire rise within herself in response to his.

Then the world stood still and they were lost in a heaven in which time ceased to count.

Robert took his mouth from hers and looked down at her.

"You are so beautiful," he said, his voice low and hoarse with emotion. "Tomorrow I am going back to England and I shall take you with me. I am going to take you to Cheveron, to my home. We will be married there, or here before we leave if you prefer it."

"I am afraid on this question you will have to ask my permission," a voice said from the doorway.

Robert looked up. And as Mistral blushingly extricated herself from his arms, he rose slowly to his feet.

"Your Imperial Highness!" he exclaimed in astonishment.

The Grand Duke came further into the room.

"I am sorry to interrupt you," he said; "but before you make too many plans, I must beg you to accord me the formality of asking for my daughter's hand in marriage."

"Your daughter?"

There was no disguising Robert's surprise, and Mistral gave a little laugh of sheer happiness.

"Yes," she said, "The Grand Duke is my father. It is so wonderful to have a family of my own at last."

"Yet if my eyes do not deceive me and my ears

326

have heard aright," the Grand Duke said, "you are all eagerness to leave me."

Mistral lookd up at him with a worried expression.

"Please understand, Father," she pleaded.

The Grand Duke smiled reassuringly.

"I think I do," he said. "Robert, your Father was an old friend of mine. You and I have met on several occasions. My daughter tells me that she has fallen in love with you and you with her. I gather there has been some misunderstanding between you, but from what I saw on entering the room I imagine that is now rectified."

"It is forgotten, Sir," Robert said.

"I am glad of that," the Grand Duke replied. "There are many things that are best left in the past and ignored completely in our plans for the future."

"May I, Sir, then beg your permission to marry Mistral?" Sir Robert asked.

"You have that," the Grand Duke replied, "on one condition. Yes, a condition," he repeated, as he saw both Mistral and Robert look at him a little apprehensively.

"Which is?" Robert asked.

"That you do not take my daughter away from me too quickly," the Grand Duke replied. "No, do not look too disappointed, I am being wise for both of you. You have the whole of your lives ahead of you. You will live together and, please God, be happy one with another; but I wish you to start on in the right way, without scandal, without shadows attached to you from the past.

"You, Robert, came out here for a very different reason. That reason has ceased to exist, but people have long memories and longer tongues. I want you to go back to England tomorrow, to return to Cheveron and take up life where you left it.

327

"You doubtless have many things requiring your attention on your Estate; you have your peace to make with your Mother. In three months' time Mistral and I will come to England."

"In three months!"

The dismay on Mistral's voice was very evident.

"Yes, my dear," the Grand Duke said firmly. "In three months. It seems a long time now; but remember, you have another fifty years ahead of you to spend in Robert's company. You can spare me three months, and June in England is very pleasant, I remember.

"I would like to introduce you to London, for I have many friends there; and when you have made your curtsey to the Queen at Windsor, we will perhaps journey to Cheveron and stay with the son of my old friend—Sir Robert Stanford."

"Oh, Father!"

Mistral clasped her hands together, her eyes very bright.

"If you were to get engaged when you meet at Cheveron," the Grand Duke went on, "it would be quite a natural and charming thing to happen. Do you understand?"

He looked directly into Robert's eyes.

"I understand, Sir," Robert said, "and thank you for being so much wiser than I am."

"I do not say I am wiser," the Grand Duke replied, "but perhaps I am more experienced in the ways of the world."

He held out his hand.

"Good-bye, my boy. We shall meet at Cheveron in June."

The two men clasped hands and the Grand Duke took his watch from his pocket.

"I will wait for you in the carriage, Mistral," he

328

said. "The horses will get restless if you are not down in five minutes."

"Thank you, Father," she said in a low voice.

The Grand Duke went from the room and the door closed behind him.

For a moment Mistral and Robert stood looking at each other, then he held out his arms and she flew into them with a little cry of happiness.

"Your Father is right, my darling," he said. "We must wait. But you won't forget me? Promise that you will think of me every moment of the day and of the night until we meet again?"

"I promise," Mistral answered.

"I shall go to get my home ready for you. I shall dream of you there, as I have dreamt before of seeing the two most perfect things in my life joined together —you and Cheveron."

He held her closer to him, his lips against her hair. He knew then that this was what he had searched for all his life, that his search was at an end, his goal in sight.

With a sense of urgency at the passing of time he sought her lips.

"I love you," he whispered against her mouth and knew there was no need for words as she surrendered herself to the passion behind his kiss.